# Gretchen

# Gretchen

## SHANNON KIRK

Text copyright © 2019 by Shannon Kirk

Published by Thomas & Mercer, Seattle

www.apub.com

Amazon, the Amazon logo, and Thomas & Mercer are trademarks of Amazon.com, Inc., or its affiliates.

ISBN-13: 9781542041348
ISBN-10: 1542041341

Cover design by Laywan Kwan

Printed in the United States of America

*Max, thank you for listening to the
early outline of* Gretchen.
*You have no idea how much your interest
motivated me.
This story, like all my stories, is for you.
Love, Mom*

This is the worst part,
Reckoning with what I've become
A half being
The unsaid one
Unmentionable
Unintentional secret

This is the worst part
I am the worst part
Halved here,
Half of the life
You will not live

—*SCK, 10/18/18 (excerpt from "The Worst Part," poem)*

# PART I

# CHAPTER ONE
## LUCY

Mom and I are living in our tenth state. Some middle state in the Midwest, and I don't even care to remember the name of the specific one we're in right now. I feel the pattern calling. I just know we'll be running toward our eleventh state soon.

I never know when it will set in, what triggers the drop in my stomach, the sudden glaze of black that envelops my guts. Heavy curtains falling in my brain. But when dread comes calling, it's like a predictable pattern, some wheel Mom and I are stuck on. Us two, a couple of spokes.

Someday, I hope we can break this pattern and stay in one state. But I'm fifteen, living in our tenth state, in my third high school already, and I felt it this morning. I felt the dread calling again, the click gaining closer to reset the pattern. Again. Again, again. Again. Around the loops and voids of our lives.

When the click happens in our pattern, it's a variation of the same theme: Mom or I think someone recognizes her or me, or goddess forbid, both of us. A woman pumping gas lets it overfill because she's staring too long at Mom, seemingly trying to place her. Or the cashier in a pizza place says, while handing a large pepperoni over the counter, "You remind me of . . . hmm . . . someone." Or I'm grocery shopping and run into a bunch of kids from some new school, and one says to another as I pass, "The new girl looks like . . . who's she look like? An actress? That actress? I know I saw something . . . a picture, a movie? Right?"—a throwaway line to anyone else, but to us, a red flag. We are rarely together in public, so one always reports these red flags to the other. It's how we've been able to stay on the run for thirteen years.

Because I don't look like anyone in any school I've ever attended, and I don't know of any actresses who do either. Also, Mom makes me wear colored contacts to hide my violet eyes.

I felt the pattern *turn turn turn* this morning. All I was doing was the regular, a collection of meaningless morning actions: making toast—from bread I baked homemade—and steeping French-press coffee. Standing by the open window of our latest rental cottage, the bright morning sun heralded heat for the day. The sill was warm, so I set my hand there as I waited on the toast to pop. Something about my hot palm, the morning sun's brightness, the scent of baking bread, the cozy closeness of the pantry's galley counters . . . maybe all of it together conjured a buried memory. Whatever clicked the dread to descend, I felt the distinctive drop in my stomach, an acknowledgment that led to my heart racing. I saw the whole day roll out before me and held my breath—and this sickening anticipation always makes me want to hurl.

I bent in the pantry, placing my hands on each of the facing counters, such that I was a diving bird with wings spread. I closed my eyes and counted to thirty. Imagining the course of the day, I saw Mom and me running back to the cottage. I went through the motions in my mind of the fevered packing, the beat of my legs in panic to get to the car while it was dark and shadows could hide us and neighbors wouldn't see us, stop us, ask questions. I heard in future memory my mother calling the landlord with our preset emergency excuse. Something about a rare jackdaw in the wrong climate of some vague state—some genius bird Mom must document for her book of birds. That's the latest planned excuse, because that's the current lie we're living. And there's always some truth to the lie, easier to remember.

The smoke alarm screamed from my burning toast. I waved a tea towel for the smoke to clear. And once the screaming alarm stopped, I scratched Allen's fat-cat tummy and gave him a treat I'd concocted from leftover salmon. Then I ran out to Mom, who was waiting in our crappy, brown, used Volvo to take me to my third high school. I'm a freshman, soon to be sophomore. Two years ago, she stopped home-schooling me, although with tons of restrictions. My last two finals are tomorrow to end the school year.

As I got in the car this morning, I didn't tell Mom I felt the pattern coming into play. I'm hoping I'm wrong. I'm hoping we can stay longer. I like it here. I mean, it's not paradise, but it's comfortable enough. And a legit Jenny's in my class. I like Jenny.

I flipped Mom a fake morning smile as I got into the Volvo's passenger bucket seat, and I wondered whether I was right to feel the dread at all, all the flashes of anticipation and anxiety I'd suffered in the short time I took to burn toast. I wondered if we ran tonight, if anyone would clear the charred bread from the toaster and dump the perfect brew of Costa Rican beans I'd left to waste in the pantry.

Mom dropped me at school; I closed the door on the brown Volvo from a sketchy dealer—one we hit up when we took the train two towns over five months ago. We paid in cash. We always pay in cash.

As I walked to the school's front doors, I plucked my silver jellyfish pendant, the floaters solid and wild S shapes. With my other hand, I placed my palm on the head of the jellyfish on my T-shirt, my favorite T-shirt, my favorite sea life. It calmed me to concentrate on holding an image of a jelly, a tough survivalist, surviving literal millennia on this planet, all alone and practically invisible, and yet solid, indestructible— like I'm supposed to be.

The school day droned on, the fluorescent lights zapped brain cells, the cleaning solution in the girls' bathroom stabbed up my nose with a relentless, toxic lemon, and the day grew brighter and brighter and blinding outside, so either the atmosphere sedated me into being a student zombie or the dread inside me waned. I even found myself comfortable enough to talk nonsense with Jenny. We ate our lunches outside because it's been such a long winter and the teachers said we all needed a good dose of vitamin D.

Jenny and I grabbed our cheeseburgers and headed to a green bench under a willow. She has this beautiful face with millions of teeny freckles and the deepest cockeyed dimples. The dimple on her left cheek is higher than the one on her right. Her blonde hair hangs in one fat braid. She might be a milkmaid in another land and another century.

"Hey," Jenny said, in a cautious tone and sneaking me a closer look, which nobody does. Nobody gets too close. She's the only girl I've held snippets of conversations with at this school, the only one I'll sit with in silence during lunch and outside during recess. Basically, our relationship is sitting together, not talking very much, and reading books.

"So I was wondering if you wanted to hang at my house this weekend?" Jenny said as we took our seats on the green bench.

"Maybe," I said, unwrapping my lunch-lady cheeseburger. "Sounds good. Let me talk to my mom."

I didn't look straight on at Jenny. Too personal. She might get too close. She might detect my blue eyes are phony fakes. But I did note her hiding a relief of a smile at my answer.

I convincingly pulled off acting excited when Jenny suggested I stay at her house this weekend, because there's always some truth to the lies. I said I'd get back to her tomorrow, and when I said this blatant lie, I tamped down the dead black dread trying to rise in me again.

Kids here in my tenth state are used to me now. They don't gawk and probe anymore. The mystique has worn off, the glamour too. The boys learned long ago that no matter how many times they asked me out, the answer would always be no. And the girls who might be jealous of my shiny black hair and my long legs and my fake blue eyes, or who might want to be my BFF, all keep their distance out of respect. After all, they're cautious, given my backstory—that I watched my father die a gruesome death in a foreign country (devoid of details and any specific location and can't be rebutted by a search on Google), and I'm "grieving" and "need space."

False. Most all of it false. I can't confirm the whereabouts of my birth father or whether he's alive. The only kernel of truth here is he's in a foreign country, we think, I think, because that's what Mom says.

I'd love to go to Jenny's house and let her single-parent mom make us homemade cheesesteak sandwiches out of prime-cut, thin-sliced, perfectly marinated beef, with aged cheddar from Vermont, and on fresh-baked rolls. To watch a classic like *The Princess Bride* while sipping icy Cokes and reenacting the albino priest who says "Mawaige." I hold many granular and specific imaginary-friend scenarios in my mind. Jenny's like other Jennys, other Emmas, other Sophias, along the way: naturally pretty, but she doesn't hawk her looks; quiet in public, but riotous underneath; troubled in some domestic way, but rising above, in her own way. She reads a lot and alone at recess, like me. She wields her own created strength—she doesn't need your strength to bolster her—and she does this without broadcasting her personal fight so as to pile on accolades for herself. She doesn't need them. Every school has about one Jenny/Emma/Sophia. Gems. But I can't have gems as friends for real. I wish I could. I wish I were worthy to gain strength by osmosis in being close to them.

This particular Jenny is the crème de la crème. The best one I've encountered yet. I wish I could pack her up and take her everywhere I know we'll have to go.

I wish I didn't have to lie to her on the green bench today.

Now, here I am, and school is done. Here's Mom in the brown Volvo, waiting in the pickup line. I walk to the car. The windows are down. Here now, right now, as I approach, the roller coaster begins. *Click, the dreadful click, of the pattern is coming.* Setting my palm on the jelly on my belly does nothing to calm me. My jelly pendant wards nothing off.

"Lucy, love you, Bug," Mom says, calling out to me by leaning over the passenger seat and talking through the open window.

"Hey, Mom," I say as I set my backpack in the back seat and pop myself into the front passenger's.

"Hungry? Want to get an ice cream? Go down to the lake? Enjoy the sun?"

"Sure. Sounds good. But I got my Spanish and biology finals tomorrow, so need to get home sort of soon."

I don't want ice cream. I'm feeling like I could hurl. I know, I just know. It's coming. The run. But Mom's in a good mood, and I don't want to shake her mood. I can't shake her mood, that's part of the deal. Plus, she rarely allows us out in public together, and I'm finding of late, I want to push the boundaries of our restrictions. I'm not sure why.

"Such a good girl, Lucy. Okay. A quick ice cream by the lake."

She's humming along to the tinny original version of "Turn! Turn! Turn!" by the Byrds, and I watch the sun shadows and flickering light dancing between the spaces of lime and leafy trees. I prefer the updated, acoustic version of "Turn! Turn! Turn!" performed by Sara Niemietz, but we play Mom's songs when we're together.

As I always do as soon as I'm out of school, I pop out my blue-tinted contact lenses and throw them in the saline case in my pocket.

"Wear your sunglasses at the park, then," Mom says. Meaning, *don't let anyone see the real color of your eyes.* She will keep her own colored lenses and sunglasses glued on her face, as she always does in public.

We get our cones, walk across a village street to a park on the lake, and sit on a bench. A group of mallards squats in the grass next to us, pecking at a pile of cracked corn. It's sunny and we have ice cream and Mom is smiling, but I have a dissonance of dread inside, so my skin is electric with tension. I fight my hands from shaking and my stomach from flipping. We look happy on the outside, and I'm playing my part for her, but my smile is false. This sunlight is fake. Nobody knows how you really feel in the very center of yourself.

"Got to use the bathroom," Mom says, rising from the bench. "Be right back." She heads behind us and across the street to the ice-cream shop. I remain on the bench, staring at the lake.

My cookie-dough ice-cream cone has lots of dough chunks, so I'm basically chewing my ice cream. I try to concentrate on the chunks of dough and literally nothing else. I tell myself this morning's dread premonition was not real, was just me allowing worry. I tell my brain to turn it off. *Turn it off. Turn off the worry. No worry.* I flip my sunglasses to the top of my head because a tree shades me and obscures the true colors of the water and the boats on the lake.

A red Frisbee whizzes overhead and is sailing fast, seems it might land in the water. A man's voice shouts behind me, "Get it, get it, get it. Hurry!" And now a boy, actually a teen, maybe my age, is running toward the high-flying Frisbee. He's jumping, but he's too late and the Frisbee is too high. After a precipitous descent, a drastic wind pushes the Frisbee to earth, and the Frisbee lands in the water but, thankfully for the teen, close to shore. The man who shouted for the teen to "get it" is beside my bench, bending at the waist and inhaling deep buckets of air to catch his breath. He's disrupting the sitting ducks, who are quacking and scuttling away and scattering their kernels of corn.

The man stands, hands on hips, as he watches Teen Boy fish out their Frisbee. This man has icy-blue eyes, blondish-brown hair, and a clean-trimmed beard. He looks to be a little older than Mom, so he's forty something or other, and handsome. He's fit, long, and lean, like a marathoner. And I'm so into how he wears pressed shorts with cool flip-flops and his toenails aren't gross like on most men.

He turns to my bench and smiles at me. I smile back but return quick to watching the lake. We do not hold strangers' eye contact long. And, in a tragic mistake I'm just now realizing, my contacts are in their case, and my sunglasses are on my head.

9

I stall in sliding my sunglasses back over my eyes. I'm not sure why. *I'm not sure why.* I turn back to hold a stare with the ice-blue-eyed man. His blues to my violets. *I'm not sure why. I've never done this before. Why? Look away. Put on your sunglasses.* If Mom is walking back from the bathroom, I'm sure she's frozen on the street and afraid to move a muscle. I don't look to see if she's there, can't add ammunition to this powder keg. I look away and to the water.

"Hey," he says. From the corner of my eye, I see his face is directed to me. He's not talking ahead to Teen Boy. This Teen Boy doesn't go to my school; I'd remember his face, which is very much like this man's face, minus the beard. I wonder if these two are out-of-towners. We're in a vacation town, and we like to stay in vacation towns because there's a lot of people coming and going and new faces, so we're not weird to townies. Easier to blend.

"Um . . . wow . . . ," the bearded, blue-eyed man says. I slightly turn my face, and he's pointing at me. "Gosh, you resemble . . . so much like . . . where . . . who was . . . ?" He's snapping his fingers and closing his eyes as a way to squeeze the name of whoever I remind him of from his brain. "Damn. What's the name?" His eyes are open now, and he's staring at me, scrunching his brow and thinking real hard. "So distinctive. Hey, Thomas, come here. Who was . . ."

And thus the card clicks, and so shall begin our pattern. Our dreadful, predictable pattern. I knew it. I fucking knew it. Shit.

"Babe," Mom yells from way behind the bench and up nearer the street. When I turn, she's gone and mixed herself with a crowd forming around the ice-cream shop. I know enough to know I need to pop and trot fast to meet her at the Volvo.

I drop my face to my chest, stand, and hurry to the trash can to toss my cone. I reset my sunglasses. I'll be blamed for this one.

When we're back in the car, it's no *Love you, Bug* from Mom. It's, "Dammit, Lucy. You know better. Now we have to leave tonight. You should have kept those sunglasses on. And why would you look at him? Why engage?"

I have no answers.

"I should never have stopped homeschooling you. Never stopped keeping up my guard. These trickles of us out in public together are too risky. No more."

"Mom, I'm sorry."

So here we go. Here we go to pack and run at night and leave messages full of lies for the people in our tenth state, as we head for our eleventh. Jenny will go back to her solitude in reading at recess, without me somewhere near on the lawns or a bench doing the same—a broken team of solitary and separate beings. I wonder if she'll wonder later in life whatever happened to the new girl who disappeared one day from school. I wonder if she'll even care to remember my name next week or ever.

My heart feels heavy in thinking on how much I already miss Jenny and how she was strong enough to let being silent companions be enough for her. She never questioned me, never probed me. She accepted me for whatever I am, and she didn't change one single thing about herself to make sure I accepted her. No competition, no challenges between us. We came together in an organic way. I'll hold Allen, my only non-Mom friend in the world, on my lap in the back seat of the brown Volvo and hide my crying from Mom as we drive all night.

I knew this morning. I knew the sun was too kind too early. The law is this: life is never bright for me and Mom for too long. It is never wise to trust the sun.

# CHAPTER TWO

Early dawn. I wake up for a second to see we're in the parking lot of some rest stop. I go back to sleep. A couple of hours later, I wake up for good and move to the front passenger seat.

The Volvo's analog clock reads ten in the morning. Bright-blue early June morning as we cross the border out of Massachusetts to be welcomed by a big green sign with the word **BIENVENUE** and the state's motto, **LIVE FREE OR DIE**. Our eleventh state is New Hampshire.

*Live free or die. Are we free? Am I free? Running like this all the time. Worrying always about when the pattern will begin again.*

"Welcome," Mom says, catching me mouthing the words. "*Bienvenue* is French for 'welcome.'"

"Kind of figured from the context, Mom," I say, and shoot her a corner-of-my-lip smile. I'm not being smug. I'm trying to show I accept, and am willing to agree, that all is normal and regular as usual—so much so, we can do a happy-times teasing banter. I turn to check on Allen in his cat cage, where he's chilling on the catnip I overfed him to calm his car nerves.

Mom rolls her eyes. "Whatever, smarty-pants." She shoots me a thoughtful smile, taking quick glances ahead as she steers straight on this endless highway. The fact she's smiling and going along with the teasing banter means she's not going to raise, this morning, how I'm to blame for this latest run. Relieved we're not fighting this minute, I loosen the tension in my shoulders. But I must be cautious, can't be the one to raise the topic, even if I want to apologize. My apologizing would only lead to a fight. Mom's lesson: never return to the scene of a crime.

The sides of the road are in high green, all sorts of thick shades, from lime to deep forest green, in the birch saplings, tall pines, leafy oaks, and fat maples. The world outside this brown Volvo is green and happy and blue and full.

"Baby, this life . . . just till you're eighteen, okay? When I know for sure they can't take you again. Another country away from me. God, no. Your father's family, they'd never let you leave, and the way they treat women, they have no rights. None. Women are trash. I can't . . ."

"Mom, I know. I know. We've been over it a literal million times." I decide to take a chance. "Sorry for not wearing my sunglasses. Sorry for engaging that man."

She stares at the road ahead, brings a hand to her lips, which she sucks in, I'm guessing as a way to stem her own words—caustic or loving, I'm not sure. Her forehead accordions in a crinkle as she side-sweeps another look at me, checking that I am looking back, and I am. She's got her serious face on. "Lucy, I'm sorry about this life." She winces and soon looks to the road again. I've noticed how ever since I started my period a few months ago, and since my body and face have been changing more and more, she winces more and more. Sometimes, and maybe this is all in my mind, but lately it feels like the sight of me hurts her, so she looks at me less and less. Or so it seems.

"Mom, really. I get it." Because it's true, I get it. My father is a powerful man with centuries-old connections to royalty in some other country (Mom won't say which one because she doesn't want me googling and freaking myself out). She won't say his last name, because his last name, she says, would quickly identify his country, his very specific nationality. He's from a place in which she says mothers have zero legal right to take back their own babies. He'd already tried to abscond with me once before, but Mom had a plan, and Mom had her own connections. I was two years old when she stole me back and we ran. And now this life with two new names and constantly new states. We always use the same IDs and variations of the formal names on those IDs, since I need to be able to cleanly transfer into new schools, and frankly, Mom says, the first fake IDs were hard enough to get.

All this cash we live on. I'm not clear on where Mom got all the stacks of cash we keep in a series of places around the country, which we call the "base money," to be used when our "steady stream money" is low. The "steady stream money" comes in various increments and in random bursts by way of direct payments to Mom's business, Birds Flash & Snap, for the sale of her online digital photos of birds. She's a birder. And also, her online editing services for client authors who never meet her.

Mom bounces her head, indicating she's still thinking on the topic of my father—or someone he hired—kidnapping me at age two. But I don't want to rehash the terrors of international snatching of kids by parents and the difficulties with getting a snatched kid back to the States. Don't want to talk about being on the run or the fact that New Hampshire will be our eleventh state. I follow the passing pines along the freeway and clutch the door handle. I'll pull and jump if she goes there again.

"So . . . ," she sings, a lightening of mood in her tone. I wait for the punch line. "I know you've been wanting a place in biking distance to restaurants and cafés, so maybe you can get your first job. And I did some research, and I found a rental in a village called Milberg. About an hour and a half from Boston. Sounds like everything you want, baby."

*She's going to let me work? Only two years ago she allowed me to stop homeschooling and go to public. I need permission for everything.*

"What about the rental?" I ask, not wanting to expose my excitement over the prospect of getting a job. She works so hard to protect me; I need to play my part.

"Here," she says, digging in her open shoulder-sling tote in the space between our bucket seats. She fishes around for her iPad, which is pinned beneath her birding binoculars. When she yanks on the iPad with a jerk, out tumbles an avalanche: a few balled dollar bills, a tissue, the folded page from an old magazine listing the "Hidden Vacation Gems of America," some random receipts—why she keeps them I have no clue, because she won't be filing taxes. A tiny yellow hairbrush that clings to everything. All of her detritus falls upon the middle space around the nightstick parking brake.

"You are such a disaster, oh my God," I say, stuffing her things back in her bag.

She playfully hits me as I pinch a used tissue and dangle it in her face. I drop it on her lap. "Nasty," I say.

"Please, Lucy, as if you keep your bedroom spick-and-span."

"A cyclone. A total dump purse," I go on, teasing. "Gross. And this yellow hairbrush is, I mean . . . who uses something like this?"

"Not everyone has thick, perfect hair. Need a rake to comb through your mane."

I'm scanning the open tabs on her iPad. "So, what town?"

"Milberg, New Hampshire."

"One of the 'gems' from the magazine article?"

"Sure is, baby."

"What's the tab for the rental?"

"Don't close any. I left the tabs open after using Wi-Fi at the last rest stop. The one you want says, 'Milberg Ranch, two bedroom, two bath.' See it?"

"I get my own bathroom?"

"And you can clean all your hair clogs all on your own." She scrunches her nose while rubbing a strand of my black hair. "God, silk. Thick, thick silk. You're a goddess." But when she takes her eyes off the road and sees her hand on my hair, she pulls back fast and winces again. The snap of her hand off my hair and her expression to one of horror are as if I'm a column of flames. When she returns to gripping the wheel, she smiles in profile to me—a closed-mouth smile.

*It's all in my mind. I'm tired from driving all night. What's wrong with me? Nothing's wrong with me. I'm tired. Tired. Imagining things.*

I scroll down the page through the pictures of the furnished rental. This thing is furnished so completely, it even comes with new linens. Perfect. And the way it's decorated, I place myself inside reading a book, in its cozy-colorful-artiness. I hope this works out.

"Cool," I say. And because I need a break from worrying I'll anger or scare her or say something wrong or that something's wrong with me, I snap my Beats over my ears and turn up "DNA" by Kendrick Lamar on my five-dollar, yard-sale iPod Nano, the kind without internet. We drive a full hour more.

Here we are, pulling off a windy country road onto a dirt road, and I'm so scared the online pictures won't live up to reality. So nervous the landlord won't agree, as they often don't agree, to take cash. So scared Mom will sense the landlord senses something off about us, and we won't get to stay in this place. The setting is rural, or perhaps I should say, forested. I can't wait to see the inside of the rental and match living colors to the pictures.

I pull out my contact lens case and pop my blues on my violet pupils.

We're rolling on a narrow, packed-dirt road that weaves between patches of the tallest pines on both sides. The pines' lower limbs appear to have been sheared off, making the trunks a forest of telephone poles with the darkest green tops, like bristles on a bottlebrush. I think of this patch at the entrance as Bottle Brush Forest. The gravel crunches and skitters as we continue a slow roll over a tiny bridge above a shallow creek.

Rising up the dirt road, we move past Bottle Brush Forest, and as we do, the trees on my side, the right side, start to thin, but the trees on Mom's side start to thicken, the limbs of the pines not sheared now. Other trees mix between the messy pines: oak, maple, birch. The floor of the forest on Mom's side is a thick carpet of rust-red pine needles and brown leaves from what appears to be centuries of falling.

"Milberg has always been a destination because of Great Katherine Lake on the outskirts. And I read that the downtown is, quote, 'quaint, charming, up-and-coming, and becoming a magnet for foodies,'" Mom says. I'm not a foodie, but I am obsessed with good ingredients, and I like to use the best ingredients to make common meals awesome. I think this means I want to be a chef someday, and Mom thinks I must think that too. But I also really like reading true books about octopus intelligence and jellyfish and sea things, and I love tubes of paint and colors, and I saw a documentary on women who dress as mermaids and swim in pools for parties, so I don't know. I hope it's okay to not know what I'm supposed to be. Maybe I'll be a librarian. Maybe a mermaid. Maybe a painter. Maybe an oceanographer. Maybe a chef. Maybe I'll drive around the country forever with no roots. Alone and with no Jennys in my life.

I place a palm on the wispy floaters of the jellyfish on my T-shirt's belly as we drive up the packed dirt road. I still haven't changed from yesterday, but at least I wet-napped my pits this morning at another highway rest stop and slapped on deodorant. Mom doesn't smell—she did the same. And she seems jacked on caffeine and fired to set up our new life. She didn't sleep at all last night. Mom can be relentless, tireless. Her endurance can be shocking. I'll have to be extra special even and happy today to fulfill my part in this scheme.

We drive through a patch of road that's especially darkened by the trees' shade, and that ever-sneaky anxiety over newness makes itself known in me again, making me queasy and fearful. I grasp the fabric of my T-shirt, squeeze the jellyfish in my hand, and do the same with my jelly pendant, as if I'm holding on for dear life. I'm making small movements in this, trying to hide this feeling from Mom. I'm only almost strong; a wedge of weakness slices into me, a wedge I can't seem to close. Feels like I could be a solid wheel, but I'm missing a slice of myself, and I don't know what the slice is or where it went off to or even how to define it. So I have no idea what to look for to make me whole—the missing item that would stop this sliver of sneaky panic that rises out of nowhere and chokes the stronger slices of me.

"Mom," I say, and this time I can't hide the crackle in my voice, which makes me feel worse, because now I've failed her. "Can we go to the Boston aquarium? I read they have jelly, and they let you see the octopus up close."

"Of course, baby. Yes, of course," she says, as she grabs my left biceps and squeezes, her way of telling me to toughen up. I hate the water in my eyes. This tremble in my lips. The crackle in my voice. This clouding in my mind. If I'm some simpering girl, then I'm a liability, and I can't jeopardize the team.

"It will be okay, Lucy." She changes her tone to serious and offers her constant mantra: "We are safe. We are present. It will be well. Be strong. We must do this. We have no choice."

I breathe in deep and nod. The wave of panic recedes as I look to her being solid, which is her forgiving me for being weak. We drive up and up.

We're driving up, as in really up; this is a hill and somewhat of a steep climb. The pines are super tall, and I sort of feel like what it must have felt for Hansel and Gretel in their deep, dark forest. It's midday, the start of June, and Mom somehow convinced (in a call during our drive) my most recent school to close out my grades for freshman year since all I'd missed was my biology and Spanish finals, and I'd maintained straight As anyway. So, it's summer for me, a new state, and indeed, the day is sunny and hot. And yet the thickening forest on Mom's side casts stagnant, unmovable shadows—not the dappling, lighter mood of light dancing through rippling leaves and mixing with moving shadows; the darkness on her side is a wall of cold dusk. I roll down the window and breathe in a crisp floral scent mixed with dirt on my side of the road.

Mom slows the Volvo, squinting to find a number on the side of a one-story ranch on our right. The ranch is a light-beige stucco, and on the back, which faces the road coming up the hill, are forest-green shutters flanking one picture window, which is divided into twenty panes. The window overlooks snarly blueberry and holly bushes that fill the hill down and away from the ranch. Coming closer to the side of the ranch, a driveway veers off the dirt road we're on, and the driveway leads to the front of the ranch. If we were to keep climbing the dirt road on the left side of the property, we'd hit a colossal brick house, maybe a mansion, which lords over another hillside of blueberry-holly snarls, a long shed opposite the ranch, the ranch itself, and the first blueberry-holly hill snarls below that.

Mom takes the driveway to the ranch, and we enter a mini compound of sorts.

"Hmm," she says. "Pretty close to the pictures, yeah?"

We park between the ranch and the low, long shed. Out ahead of us is a patch of cattails and tall, swamplike lime grasses, as if dancing green snakes are climbing rods to eat brown Twinkies speared on the tops. I can't see beyond the patch of cattails and lime snakes because the patch is thick, and I sense the land drops behind the patch. I think a pond or maybe a creek is directly below. In the far, far, lower distance, beyond the patch, is a grassy field surrounded by beautiful oaks and maples and birch and not gangly, messy pines, like behind us now and surrounding the giant brick house at the top of the hill. So to sum up, in front of us, out beyond the cattails and lime snake patch, is an inviting lightness, a dancing light and rippling leaves, the promise of a burdenless summer. A place for running. A place for picnics. But everywhere else is dark and still. It's like this whole hill and the area around is three-quarters a foreboding *Hansel and Gretel* forest with a quarter wedge of happy Magic Faraway Tree countryside.

I turn to the blue-painted door on the ranch to my right, and a man steps out. He's lightly rubbing and rolling his fingers in his palms, one hand and then the other, as if they are the most precious ten items on the planet. He wears pleated dad khakis, loafers, a dad polo, and square dad glasses, and he looks really, really boring. He squints at us as if he's confused, so this means Mom didn't call ahead.

She does this sometimes. Engineers a surprise appearance so it's harder for landlords to deny us a rental in person.

Mom steps out of our Volvo, and as I watch her do this, I look closer at the long, low shed opposite the ranch. The shell is made of gray metal, or a mismatch of metal and wood, I think. There are four roller doors on the front, in two pairs. The blue of the roller doors matches the ranch's front door, but it is weatherworn and chipped. On each of the roller panels is an orange sign with black block letters: KEEP OUT. Chains with padlocks loop through and around the roller door handles. I step out to join Mom at the hood of our Volvo.

"Hi, I'm Susan. My daughter and I saw your ad for the rental here. Is she still available? Or, oops, are you the new renter?"

"Ad?" the dad khaki man says. He takes care to hold one hand in a hammock he forms with the other. His tone is kind, his eyes still scrunched and confused.

"Yes, an ad for this ranch. It was placed on a community website, actually, and a bit buried. But I think it was posted just days ago? So I thought the place might still be available?"

"Hmm," he says, sucking in his lips and inspecting his own shoes, which are penny loafers, covered in a dusty dirt.

I look to Mom, and she looks to me, and we share confusion between us.

"I placed the ad," comes a high, shouting girl voice from the side of the low, gray shed. And indeed, a girl in an ivory cotton sundress with a repeated apple print appears; she looks about my age. She's shorter than I am, thinner and somewhat frailer than I am, strawberry blonde with blotches of birthmarks, and it seems her fair skin has patches of red that brighten and soften, like the pulsing colors on an octopus.

"Dad, it's time. We need to rent again. I placed the ad," she says, now standing only feet from us. The blotches of red on her white skin truly do pulsate up close, and I can't tell if this is from heat, temperature change, some condition, or emotion. I can't tell if this moving skin of hers is natural or healthy or what. She's sweating around her skinny neck and perspiring at the hairline, as if she ran down the hill from the big brick house to intercept us here, maybe, I'm guessing. So maybe her blotches of red are from exertion.

"Hi," she says in a burst toward me and Mom. I shudder from the sudden slap of her presence in our presence. Out of nowhere, this loud voice ripped the awkward scene, made itself known, and is directing this rental. And she must be my age. Just my age.

"Hi," she says again, giving a little wave to Mom. "I'm Gretchen," she says, extending her hand to Mom to shake, and then the same to me. I shake back. From the side of my sight, I can tell Mom's shaking hand falls limp and trembling, and she clutches it tight with her left. Something about this girl has frightened her. I'm not sure what.

Before we can say our own names to pulsing Gretchen, the father says, "Honey, I don't know about this." And turning to Mom, he says, "Excuse me. Pardon me, ma'am, I'm sorry. Let me have a word with my daughter."

Mom nods with eyes wide. She walks backward as if the world ahead holds an advancing category-five tornado—the moment of awe when you're stalled between fight or flight.

I follow Mom to the trunk of the Volvo.

"Lucy, this is all wrong. And her name is Gretchen. We need to leave."

"What? Because her name is Gretchen? No, Mom. Maybe because the dad dude doesn't want to rent to us, that would be a reason."

"Her name is Gretchen. It's a sign." The crackle of emotion has moved from my voice to Mom's, and now I'm obligated to be strong.

This is new. This level of paranoia from her is scary. Typically her paranoia is tied to actual humans who indicate in some objective way they might recognize us.

"Mom, it's just a name. What is it about Gretchen?"

I have never, ever heard any concern about the name Gretchen, and I have no clue what this is about. But she's shaking, so I'm not allowed to shake too. How would we fare in the world without one serving as a crutch for the other?

Over by the cattail patch, the dad and Gretchen are whispering and pointing at us and the rental. I'm trying to fix on what they're debating, but I'm way too thrown by Mom's weird paranoia, and also, a warm summer wind rustles through the lighter leaves in the forest in the far distance, and also behind us between the stalwart pines, making it sound like we're in the middle of a creek bed, water dancing over rocks and thus washing out words. I love this sound, one of my favorite sounds in the world.

I need Mom to snap out of being weird, because now I want to stay. I want to live here. I want to keep the window in my bedroom open so I can fall asleep to this sound. I love the picnic field in the out beyond. I could paint in the open. I could read by the willows. And if the inside of the ranch matches the pictures, I just have to live in those colors.

"Seriously, Mom. I want to stay. What are you talking about?"

Mom clenches her mouth, trying to hold inside whatever triggered her, and seems determined on this point about the name Gretchen. When she catches my eyes, she winces. And I know for sure, she did wince. This wincing of hers is not in my mind. *What is wrong with me?*

"Mom, what is going on? You can't seriously be afraid of a name."

She exhales, clicks her tongue, and looks away, as if realizing she's let something slip by her reaction. "Dammit. Never mind. We'll talk later. I'm not being crazy. There is a reason I'm frightened on hearing the name Gretchen. Don't worry. I have a good reason. It just startled me. You're right, Lucy. If he'll rent to us and agree to our terms, then we can stay. Assuming the inside is like the pictures and not a dump. We'll talk later."

"Okay. Are you okay, Mom?"

"You don't hear the name Gretchen often. I'm fine. We'll talk later. And you're right, you're right." She shakes her head at herself, standing straighter. "I'm being stupid. This is a great place. So far. Let's see what we can do. Gretchen's a rare name, right?"

I think and can't picture any girls named Gretchen in any of the schools I've gone to.

Gretchen and her father are walking toward the Volvo, so we meet them by the hood. I note, because I'm watching this time, the dad walks with a limp. He's still rolling his precious fingers in his hands in the lightest, most caressing way. I notice both father and daughter wear matching Apple Watches.

"Sorry," the dad says to Mom. He's a little older than Mom, must be in his midforties. "I'm Jerry, by the way. Jerry Sabin. Please forgive me for not shaking your hands," he says, looking at me and Mom, one by one in the eyes. "I know it's incredibly rude of me. It's, well, I'm a concert pianist with the Boston Symphony, and I'm recovering from a broken index finger. Nearly finished my career. So I'm a little—"

Mom cuts him off with a wave. "No explanations, Jerry. Understood."

"Anyway," he says. "So, thank you. Anyway. Anyway. Um, my daughter, Gretchen, here can be a little impulsive, or perhaps I should say headstrong." He pauses to give her a disciplinary kind of smile. "And she takes matters into her own hands when they should be left to the adult. Me." He smiles at my mother. "Teens," he says in an adult mocking tone about kids. Mom smiles back, mirroring his invitation to categorize all teens as impulsive and headstrong and in need of discipline. And she does this not because that's true of me—what a farce—but because she has to cement a connection with this Jerry guy so he'll rent to us. I get it.

I roll my eyes like a teenager would, and I note Gretchen doing the same. I think I nailed it. We both shoot each of our parents *that look*, and now Gretchen and I have a tiny bond too.

"Oh boy, do I know what you mean. Lucy here could run the world, according to her," Mom says, giving me a fake *mom* scowl. But then she gets serious. "In all seriousness, though, Lucy's a good girl. You wouldn't have any trouble from us."

"So here's the deal," Jerry says. "We had this renter for, oh, about ten years, and one day, about two months ago, he vanishes." I like the way Jerry looks to both me and Mom and straight in the eyes, talking to us on the same level and in an even, honest tone. I can tell he wants us to trust him. "He, again, no other word for it, vanished. After ten years of being our renter."

"Poof," Gretchen adds, blowing out her hands with the word.

"Yes, poof. Just gone. No note, no call, nothing. And I might have thought he left for some long trip somewhere—he was a loner—but the rent checks stopped coming, and when we finally went inside two months ago, all of his stuff was gone. Every last thing. Empty. He must have packed up one night and drove off. The pictures you saw, that was Gretchen. She's been staging the place and taking photos while I'm away at rehearsal in Boston. We'd agreed to talk before any ads went live. I wanted to wait for him a few more months. I had no clue until just now she made the ad live. Anyway, Gretchen here took matters into her own hands, and I suppose she's right. It is time for new renters."

"Well, then," Mom says, "if you're willing to rent, could you show us around? I'm Susan, Susan Smith, by the way. And this is Lucy. Did I say that already?"

Jerry nods and points at each person. "Lucy. Susan. Gretchen. Jerry." Next, he waves between me and Mom—"Smiths"—and between him and Gretchen—"Sabins. Come on in, I'll show you around."

Gretchen clasps her hands and bounces as if excited. "Ohhh, goodie. I hope you like inside, Lucy. It would be great to have a friend around here to hang out with. You fifteen?"

"Yeah," I say.

"Thought so."

"Oh."

It's an educated guess.

I cock my head and watch Gretchen smiling at us, at me. And while I do find it peculiar, and perhaps a bit forward, for her to assume we'll be friends and hang out, I sort of appreciate her taking command and having the authority to declare it so. Maybe this slight girl with octopus skin could be my friend. I'm pretty sure she's not a true Jenny; a Jenny wouldn't be so outwardly excitable. Wouldn't go out on a limb and try to rent a ranch all on her own, and thus invite strangers into her life without caution. But this Gretchen seems in need of a friend, and she wants me as a friend, so maybe that's good enough.

I scratch my head and continue to watch her smiling and bouncing.

Jerry and Gretchen go to open the ranch's front door.

"What about the shed?" Mom asks, pointing behind us and across the parking area.

"Oh, right. Right, right," Jerry says and shifts a microsecond of a glance to Gretchen, which I don't think Mom catches.

"That weirdo renter kept his creepy stuff in there," Gretchen offers.

Jerry throws his hands in the air and says, "Well, yeah, I suppose, yeah. He did."

"Creepy?" Mom asks.

"No, no," Jerry says, chuckling. "Gretchen's dramatizing. It's just a bunch of tools. He was a woodworker, metalworker, you know. So one of the other unsettling things he did, besides vanishing, was before he left, he locked the shed and put up all those Keep Out signs. I need to get a locksmith down here to pop the locks. Anyway, shed's not part of the rental. That okay?"

"Sure, we don't need storage or anything. But do you think he would come back and try to get inside? I wouldn't feel safe with some man showing up out of the blue. It's just me and my daughter. And Allen, actually. Allen, our cat." Mom nods toward the Volvo. "The ad said pets were fine?"

"I love cats!" Gretchen says, her smile even wider now.

"Oh, no worries on the old renter. I'm positive he's gone for good. And even if he were to show up, no worries. He's all of five foot two and skinny as a skeleton. Also about eighty. You won't have problems from Earl. That's his name. Earl," Jerry says.

"Okay, then. I guess," Mom says.

We follow behind Gretchen and Jerry into the ranch.

# CHAPTER THREE

Seems Gretchen was creative with the digital camera, taking shots for the rental ad from strategic angles, so as to give the illusion the interior is way bigger than it really is. So that's a downer. But it doesn't change how true the decor and colors truly are.

Right away we step into a galley kitchen with retro-style but modern turquoise and red appliances: a turquoise refrigerator, a red gas stove, a turquoise toaster, a red dishwasher. The counters are made of thick square tiles with a turquoise, blue, and red flower pattern.

"Wow," Mom says, running a finger along the tiles.

Next up, we spill out of the mouth of the galley kitchen into an open rectangular space, divided by a line of houseplants. On one side is a barn-board dining table with royal-blue velvet chairs. On the other side are two red love seats facing each other. Straight ahead is the back wall with the big picture window cut into twenty panes. The side walls are actually barn wood, as if we are inside a barn and not the interior of a stucco ranch; on them hang forty-by-forty acrylic paintings of green-green, like super green, big-leaf trees with smudges of blue sky as the backdrop. The paint of the trees is thick, the paint layered with a palette knife. Abstract splashes of red make for impressions of cardinals on branches.

There's a closed armoire, two cabinets in corners, and those seem modern but made to appear as if they are antiqued natural wood. The same is true of the coffee table and end tables. So to sum up, I'm guessing the functional aspects of the space are from some box store, but from the high-end section meant for wealthy hipsters who want an "authentic" look. Libraries and yard sales dump a lot of home-design magazines, and I always take any and all of them. Interesting lamps in shapes of purple grapes and yellow fish and figurines of blue bunnies, an orange fox, and red cardinals add pops of every other color in the rainbow. Down a hall off the left side of the dining area, I gasp when I see a purple print of an octopus and a jellyfish perusing books in an underwater library. I walk to it like a moth to a bulb.

"Oh, I think she likes it. The bedroom she's heading to would be hers," Gretchen is saying behind me. "The master is on the other side of the living room. I'll show Lucy her room."

I stop at the octopus-jelly-library print.

"Where did you get this?" I ask.

"You like it?"

"I love it."

"I made it."

"No way."

"Yes way. In art class. I think you'll like our school. The art teacher is super rad."

*Rad* is a word Mom says sometimes. A retro word from a generation before hers. But I let it pass.

"And weird, I see you like jellyfish. Spooky coincidence," Gretchen says, pointing to my T-shirt and pendant. "Woo, woo, boo," she giggles, making ghost sounds. I smile back. It is a cool coincidence. I don't know about spooky.

At the end of the hall is a small bathroom. I poke my head in to find the three essentials: sink, toilet, stall shower. All white, subway tiles, silver hardware. Clean on a clinical level. Fern-green towels are folded on a rack for a pop of color and match the one bath mat on the floor.

"Your bathroom," Gretchen says.

She makes lots of declarations. They're correct, but again, she assumes a lot. She's grinning so wide at me, I'm forced to grin back. She looks up to do so; I look down. I'm a tower in a city; she's a house in the country.

We enter what will be my room if Mom doesn't freak out or find some reason we need to flee or can't close the deal with Jerry. My hopeful room is a square with finished walls painted a light taupe. One wall holds two framed, monochromatic green pictures. The queen bed in the center is made up with a blue quilt with a pink coral print, and the curtains on the window match. Opposite the bed is a closed closet, and next to that, a built-in bookcase filled with books. The window is open to the glorious summer field in the out beyond. Wind rustles in the treetops, and I ache so hard to live in this world. Smells like real vanilla, not from extract, like a bottle of concentrated vanilla you buy from the gourmet cooking store.

"Do you like games?" Gretchen asks from behind, as I step toward the bookcase.

"Games? Xbox? Are you a gamer?"

"No, no. Not that kind. I mean like old-school games. Like Scrabble?"

"Oh yeah. I love Scrabble."

"Oh cool!" she says, her eyes wide and bright. "North American rules or British? Daddy and I play by tournament rules, of course, one on one."

*Daddy?*

"Um. My mom and I just play by whatever rules are on the box."

"Oh, ha. Right," she says, shaking her head at herself, indicating she knows she's being silly. She loses her smile and steps closer, as if she'd tested the waters and is now going deeper. A red patch on her collarbone pulses. "So, like, what about puzzles?" She scrunches her shoulders around her neck, seems she's bracing herself in case my answer whiplashes her. I'm looking into the top of her head; her blondish hair is thin. Her scalp is visible and has freckles.

"Puzzles? Like crossword? Sure. And I like Sudoku," I say, running my fingers along the books on a shelf. Some Stephen King, an old dictionary, a Debbie Macomber, a paperback Koontz, and several others I haven't heard of yet and am dying to pry open.

Gretchen leans back and shifts her eyes to the green pictures on the wall, which now I can tell are actually finished and shellacked puzzles. *Duh. She meant those kinds of puzzles.* I hadn't focused too much on the pictures, too distracted by the colors and the sound of the wind and the intoxicating vanilla and the fact I'll have a whole entire built-in bookcase with multiple shelves of books if we land this rental. I've been focusing on the forest and not the trees.

"Right, oh. You mean puzzle puzzles." I step to the wall with the framed puzzles. Looking closer, there is way more detail than two squares of green. What they each show are thick, layered leaves in a rich canopy. The layering of the leaves appears to be, and indeed is, the scales of mermaid tails; the barely perceptible limbs of the trees are the mermaids' limbs. The remainder of the mermaid bodies are found in the various ways the leaves cluster or are layered. And the individual puzzle pieces are themselves cut in the shapes of mermaids and leaves. Looks like a crazy, complicated puzzle.

"Yes, yes. Exactly. Jigsaw puzzles. I should have been more specific. Not crosswords," Gretchen is saying as I study the puzzle. When I'm done, I look to her, and she rolls her hands together while shifting her gaze to the floor. "But yeah, I do like Sudoku. I mean jigsaw puzzles, though. Do you like those?" She's pointing at the mermaid trees on the wall.

"Yeah. They're really cool."

"I made them. From scratch," she mumbles.

"Wow. Really?"

She shrugs and twitches. After a weird pause, she says, "Do you like to do puzzles?" She steps closer, not smiling. She's in my personal space, but then again, maybe I'm too sensitive. I typically do not like to be within five feet of people. I need to make myself try here. I need a friend. I like this home.

"Sure," I say. She leans in even closer, wanting more of an answer, and so I fish fast for more to say. "I mean. I don't hate them," I add. She seems to want me to be bananas about puzzles, but I can't lie. I can't start this friendship by being a total phony. "I can't remember the last time I did one. That's pretty incredible that you made these puzzles."

"Oh," she says. Her smile hasn't returned. "Yeah."

"They're super cool." I step away from her and to the farthest puzzle. "I'm sure I'd love doing puzzles with you." I suddenly don't want to let this pulsing girl down, and I wish she'd smile again, or at least that her wild skin would chill to an even coolness.

"Good!" she shouts, as if she's decided right this second to be happy again. "I have a lot. Like, a lot a lot of jigsaw puzzles. Like, not common die-cuts either. I have homemade, custom, antique, top-of-the-line Par, Stave . . ." She trails off when she realizes I'm giving her a confused look. I have no idea what she's talking about. "Never mind," she says, studying the floor, rolling again those nervous fingers of hers.

I begin to pace, circling the colorful queen bed, considering how, in comparing Gretchen to other girls in other schools, she must be somewhat of a nerdy outcast. She is surely no Jenny. I think she must be lonely, but unlike me in the sense I mostly don't mind being alone, and I usually find a Jenny to sit with in silence at lunch. Maybe Gretchen needs me more than I need a friend. *Is that even possible?* And with her living at the top of the hill, she's a built-in, convenient friend, and I wouldn't have to concoct all those lies to avoid get-togethers and weekend sleepovers with other potential friends. Because Mom doesn't allow sleepovers, and she never allowed playdates. Then she'd have to meet other parents, and she fears they'll connect the dots by seeing both of us together too much. I'm nervous, though, nervous this is exactly what Mom's thinking, out in the living room with Jerry, checking out the rest of the place. Surely she's feeding her paranoia, and any second she'll burst in here with an excuse for us to split.

"Ugh," Gretchen says, breaking into my awkward silence. She's standing in the doorway; I'm staring out the window to the big oaks in the picnic field of the out beyond. "I know. I know. I sound like such a nerd. I'm sorry. I don't have a lot of friends. I totally get it if you ditch me. You seem really cool. I'm totally out of your league."

Literally nobody is out of my league. I have no league.

"Gretchen," I say, turning from the window and facing her, "I have no fucking idea what you're talking about. I don't think you're a nerd." This is a lie, but a white lie—it's okay. "I'd love to play board games and do puzzles with you. Sounds like a different kind of fun I haven't had in a long time."

Gretchen giggles. "You're a swearer. I knew you were cool."

And the fact she categorizes teens who swear as swearers cements her as a definite loner nerd. Whatever. I'll take what I can get. It's not like I'm some grand-prize friend.

"Come on. Let's see if our parents made a deal."

We head to the living room and stop and stand at the end of the two super-cushiony red love seats facing each other. One parent on each middle cushion.

Whatever they were talking about, they stop. "Girls," Mom says.

"So, Susan," Jerry says, "what do you think?"

Mom's fake-ID name is Susannah Mary Smith, because the first two names can be contorted into a number of different variations and combos, and the last name is so completely ubiquitous—*ubiquitous*. I know complicated words. Maybe I can beat Gretchen at Scrabble under North American rules, box rules, or whatever rules, not with *ubiquitous*—that would be wicked hard to play—but something. Maybe all my reading gives me a vocab advantage. I could con her, convince her I'm a novice, and when I win, maybe impress her. She seems super into game play.

I nod to Mom, screaming at her in my brain how much I friggin' love this joint and, please, for the love of every jellyfish in the world, rent it. *Please.* Mom stretches all ten fingers straight, clenches them into fists, then straightens again. This is her way of landing on a decision.

"We love the place," Mom says to Jerry. She turns to Gretchen and adds, "Gretchen, you did a great job with the furnishing and decor. You must be very talented."

Gretchen smiles at Mom and scrunches her nose. "Thanks," she says in a shy way, which is so unlike her bounding, forceful voice when she first crashed on the scene. I'm unsure what's her true nature. Gretchen seems a puzzle herself.

"Gretchen ordered from Wayfair. The dressers, the tables, cabinets, beds, these sofas. Did everything by herself," Jerry says. "All while I'm away in Boston or when I'm practicing. I'm impressed." He winks at his daughter.

Gretchen holds herself, casting shy eyes to the corner of her father's love seat, and sways. "I really like puzzles," she says.

I'm confused, because I'm not sure why she'd continue on with the puzzles when we're talking about furniture. She catches whatever confused expression is on my face and nods with a head shake. "Oh. Sorry. Some of the stuff from Wayfair comes disassembled. You have to put everything together. Some come in a ton of parts. Like a puzzle."

"Ah," I say. "Cool." With a slight scrunch of my shoulders in Mom's direction, I toss her the conversation baton, because I don't know where to go from here.

"Now let's get down to it. Utilities are included?" Mom asks.

"Utilities, yep. All included," Jerry says.

"And you don't mind us paying in cash? I may be an extremist, sorry, about not trusting the US banking system. I'm a single mom, so perhaps I might be overprotective."

"Cash is actually better for us, if you know what I mean," Jerry says, and winks behind his giant dad glasses. This guy needs an update bad. Minus the pleats in his khakis, turn those rectangle rims into contemporary wayfarers, minus the god-awful loafers with no socks, and trim his receding hair into a Caesar cut, and he might, maybe, be handsome. Or at least not as boring as driving on straight highways through the Midwest for endless hours. Then again, he is a dad, and I don't have a dad, and it's probably better for dads to be boring, as long as they're present. I must be staring too long in thought at Jerry, because he pushes his lips in a kind smile my way, making his otherwise muscly cheeks puff out. I wonder about his wife, and if she's around, and if she's as nice as Jerry seems. Nobody has mentioned a wife or mom yet.

"Deal," Mom says. She extends her hand to Jerry, and the two adults shake.

As in every place we've rented, we've entered into a conspiracy to allow the landlord to hide rental income from the IRS. We like landlords like this.

Now I'm the one doing a happy bounce, and Gretchen is back to doing hers. I've never done a happy bounce before. I think Gretchen might be infectious. Inside my mind, I'm bouncing high, thinking of showing Allen all these rooms and snuggling with him tonight in our new, big, colorful bed, with the window open, listening to the symphony of wind rushing through leaves. I know Allen will purr, and I know he'll love it. He won't need catnip to chill tonight. And I won't cry myself to sleep.

Jerry interrupts my daydream.

"Why don't you two unpack, bring Allen in. I'm sure your cat needs to eat. Gretchen and I will go up and get the lease together. Nothing, a page for liability, is all. And then, oh, let's say around one-ish, we meet back here. We'll bring you some subs. We can then talk about some important boundaries you need to know about on the property. And I suppose we'll need to also talk about some rumors in town you might hear. Nothing big, just want to make sure you hear it from us first. Sound good? You like turkey clubs?"

Mom clenches and withdraws; she tolerates so little when it comes to where we live and who we associate with. So the mention of strict boundaries and "rumors in town" is throwing her, I know. But I steel my eyes into hers, forcing her to stay strong. I'm not letting the pattern begin again so soon.

"We love turkey clubs, Mr. Sabin, thank you," I say, before Mom can come up with some excuse to extricate us. "But could we have no mayo, please?"

"You got it, kiddo," Jerry says with a big-cheek dad smile.

# CHAPTER FOUR
## MOTHER

Whenever she thinks about the monster who took her daughter, strong, slicing shivers shake her whole body. The fear of it, the anger boiled into it, all for what? Why? She knows why, but she may never know the true *why*. The true answer that would explain how anyone could take a baby girl from the mother who loved her to a point of self-extinction.

Her baby girl was two when the monster clutched her to his (or her?) chest when her attention was distracted. Only a split second of comparing different baby-jar labels too long on a store shelf. *Gerber or Beech-Nut. Gerber or Beech-Nut.* And him or her, brazen and entitled and bold, caught on black-and-white video in his/her ball cap and mustache. The cops said the kidnapper could be a small man or a woman in disguise. Could be anyone, someone who knew her or someone who was hired by someone who knew her. Someone who knew the precise moment, the precise place, to strike, but to also make it appear to be an untraceable rando taking her baby in public.

She'd been tracked, they knew from spotting his or her unregistered Datsun on CCTV on the surrounding streets, following her into the Sunday-crazy-busy Bing's Superstore parking lot, following her down aisles, into the baby-girl clothes section, and then into the food section, all on the store's security cams. The perpetrator's face was obscured by a hat's rim and a mustache. And her own actions—she made the cops show her the store's video—her sauntering around all disgustingly, unforgivably unaware, humming songs in her daughter's face, blowing popping kisses on her perfect nose. Pushing the Bing's mega cart, fingering hanging shirtsleeves, running her palm over tempting white towels, reading sale prices on multicolored sneakers she didn't need, oblivious in her humming, kissing her baby's face when she giggled. And then the empty aisle with the damn baby jars. *Gerber or Beech-Nut, Gerber or Beech-Nut.* Her baby girl was two already and eating solids, but baby girl loved the taste of those jarred purees, so she'd mix them in her mix of meals. Whatever her baby girl loved, she loved.

She pulled her baby girl up out of the seat in the cart and let her stretch her chunky baby legs. She'd been walking since she was one, a whole year of practice. *Gerber or Beech-Nut.* Pulling her out of the cart was only to let her baby stretch while she decided between Gerber and Beech-Nut. *Gerber or Beech-Nut.*

What hypnotics were in those labels that so consumed her she didn't see her baby girl run down the entire length of the aisle in a second flat like she was Flo-Jo? What was it about the dietary nutritional facts in tiny font that blinded her when her baby girl turned the corner at the aisle's cap? The monster snatched her baby girl outright—fast as a cat to a moth. No shit, she'd been tracked. No shit, Sherlock.

Gerber and Beech-Nut can fuck off. They're the same damn thing to her now. She shouldn't have wasted a second on any consternation over any difference.

And now when she drives long miles between states, she questions her current motives. Why? Why this running? Will there ever be an end? Should this be the end? What if all this scouring and researching locations and looking over and around and under her shoulders at every nook and cranny everywhere could stop? When? No, she can't stop. It's her fault, all her fault, for bringing her baby girl into a dangerous world.

She has no right to settle down and stop. She's on an eternal mission to fix this and protect her.

Her sisters never understood. Well, maybe Carly understands. Carly, her big sis, the one who stepped in and acted like a mother when their parents died in a crash. She doesn't remember her parents because she was only two when they died, but Carly, thirteen at the time, she remembers. Living with their aunt and uncle was to Carly a fake existence, so, as Carly would explain, she had to act like their real mom and make the best of it for her littlest sis. Carly might understand, but she can't go be with her or her other three sisters now. Can't listen to their laments and their pleas and their judgments about what she's been doing for thirteen years. No.

Nobody understands this need. Thirteen years of driving. Thirteen years in a series of beast vehicles. Staring through the windshield at endless miles of tar. The overpasses, the grassy gullies dividing highways, the rest stops, the bathroom breaks, the dinners on a Coleman stove. Her sisters probably think she's still in that foreign country, fighting demons. They haven't had a proper conversation in thirteen years, just a one-minute call, no longer, on Christmas mornings to Carly, and one on Carly's birthday in June. A request in these calls for Carly to send her best to the other sisters. A couple of strategically mailed, no-return-address postcards sent throughout the year to keep the sisters from searching for her and getting in her way. But nothing and nobody and not even God's hand clawing through a cloud could wedge between her and her determination to protect her daughter. Nothing.

In her latest drive, she imagined herself driving a sleek, black Audi and herself in a lined, black suit on her way to collect a grant to run an open-air sanctuary in a tropical location. A wild, wild idea, totally random, which seemed to spring up in her out of nowhere. Yet the thought, she realized, calmed her and, she was surprised to feel, caused her to smile. Then the beast's engine rattled and knocked her conscience back to her vehicle's brown interior. Reality didn't give her the colors of a tropical sanctuary; reality gave her last winter's sleet stains on the floor mats, her recycled glass water bottle rolling around, an empty paper bag of popcorn, and a spinning blue-tree air freshener that offered its last molecule of fresh scent three months ago. She wanted to roll in her fingertips her daughter's silky black hair, each strand as thick as nylon fishing line, for the softness, the strength. She craved the rush of love such an act would smooth onto her skin and spread. A salve for all these years of driving.

She thought of pulling out her daughter's baby photos, pinned in an album in a box in the back. A tear rolled down her face. All these years on the road. And now her baby's fifteen.

Yesterday morning she woke up before everyone else in the world woke up. At a rest stop somewhere in some state—doesn't matter which one, because it has no ocean on any sides—she stepped out of her beast. *Just another middle state,* she thought. Stretching in the dawn light, she breathed in so deep, her chest rose and expanded, the tension against her ribs waking her more. She began her daily knee raises. A full five minutes of knee raises, which started slow and ended in a sweat-filled, high-lifting sprint in place. A janitor in a gray jumpsuit entered the rest stop's Burger King through a back door, waved at her, and mimicked her knee sprint with a thumbs-up. She gave him the thumbs-up back. The shadows of her movement cast long along the side of the beast and extended beyond to the tar, given the exceptional length of her limbs.

Next, she dropped to the side of the beast in a plank, holding firm for two minutes, and then she popped back up and repeated the five-minute knee-lift sprint. She checked her time and heart rate on her digital sports watch. The next interval was to drop to the ground and conduct one hundred full-body push-ups. Her hands were immune to the tiny pebbles in the tar. She thanked her years of archery and fly-casting and shooting clay pigeons and treetop adventure-birding course runs for the calluses. Next up, another five-minute interval of knee-raise sprints.

In moving to collect a weight from the back of the beast so as to place three pounds in the crook of her knee and do one hundred side thigh raises, she remembered her sister Carly. Remembered it was June. Remembered today was Carly's birthday. A day for a call. Pictured Carly's long face, her short pixie hair, the way they'd hold each other's hands during emotional parts of movies but never suffocate each other with drapey, needy snuggles. *The just-enough, the just-perfect kind of love between two independents.* She remembered being with Carly for a full eight weeks every summer at camp in Carmel, California: the Carmel Camp Calitoga, also known as the Triple C, "for Adventurous Girls."

"Carly," she whispered one night at the Triple C from her top bunk. She must have been seven. The air of the cabin smelled like fresh-cut cedar, and as the night was windy—no mosquitoes buzzed her ears. Big sis Carly happened to be the counselor of the grade-school cabin, and yes, Carly gave her little sis special dispensations over the other girls.

"Carly," she whispered again.

"Go to sleep, you little maggot."

"Carl, come on, get up."

"Oh my God, you are such a pain in my ass."

"Shh," cut in her bunk mate Laura, who was the real pain in the ass, a dry seven-year-old who was always everywhere—like a quiet, creeping fog.

"Zip it, Laura. Carly, you promised. Come on. Let's sneak out to the bales and shoot. I hate during the day when the other girls get turns. They suck. I want to do it by myself."

"I don't suck," Laura offered in her patented monotone.

Neither sister responded to Laura, because the comment was absurd as either wildly un-self-aware or a strategic joke. At the time, it was well known that Laura was the worst shot in the whole camp, to legendary proportions. The week prior, Laura had somehow shot the camp nurse in the ass with an arrow, the nurse standing behind the backs of the shooters, and behind a cabin. The shot was outrageous and impossible

40

and, actually, hysterical, once they knew the nurse would be fine as long as she slept sunny-side up. It was years later, when she formed a special secret with Laura, that she learned there was more to the story with this impossible shot, but at age seven, Laura was just a bumbling clod to her. Just another girl she had to wait in line behind for a turn on the archery course.

"It's windy. Your arrows will go all over," Carly said, ignoring Laura.

"That's totally not true and you know it. Come on. You promised."

"Put your shoes on, Maggot. Only fifteen minutes, though. I'm fucking tired."

At the highway rest stop yesterday, a navy Buick pulled up to a pay phone and broke her reminiscence on this camp night of long ago. She'd been eyeing the pay phone while doing her dawn exercises. The phone was so perfectly placed, only thirty feet from her beast and out in the clear, wide open. A slight-built, mustached man in a short-sleeve, collared shirt, tie, and polyester brown pants exited the Buick and nodded a hello. With the thigh weight in her hands, she scanned every half inch of his face. The cheekbones, the hairline, the thin mustache, the nose. She rewound his aging in the mental processing unit in her brain, overlaid it on the man-woman in the Bing's security video with the mustache and hat, the disguise that monster used, and—she almost said her verdict out loud—in her mind said, *Bzzzzzzz, fail. No match.*

"Morning," the man said.

She chin-upped toward him and turned her back, indicating this was not any kind of rest-stop solicitation, if in fact this dude was a druggie or pervert, here to score drugs or sex before trotting off to his depressing, fluorescent-lit work cubicle. Yes, she profiled him. She profiles everyone. She set the weight in her left bent knee, leaned on the beast with her right hand, and began a series of one hundred thigh-and-glute lifts.

The Buick man finished his call, reentered his car, and drove off. She checked everywhere all around, and all else was still sleeping. No other cars driving in. No rest-stop workers shuttling trash. It seemed safe to leave the beast for a moment. She walked up to the pay phone. The time was only 3:00 a.m. where she was calling, but she was just so anxious to hear her sister's voice.

Carly answered on the first ring.

"Maggot?"

"Hi, Carl. Happy birthday."

"Mag," Carly said, saying her actual nickname, drawing out the name in a tone of requited relief.

# CHAPTER FIVE

## LUCY

Mom is in a not-speaking mood. We pop the Volvo's trunk and grab our regular luggage, two boxes of special keepsakes, and Allen from the back seat, which takes all of a half hour, including me placing my clothes in built-in drawers in the closet in my room. I'm sensing Mom wants space on her side of the house, so I sit on the blue-with-pink-coral bed and flip through a Stephen King, a first-edition *Dolores Claiborne*. The book's theme of fractured mother-daughter relationships cuts a little too close to home, so I abandon *Dolores* and browse the other selections on the shelves.

Forty-five more minutes pass, and still Mom hasn't come to talk to me.

Given we now have about fifteen minutes until Jerry and Gretchen return with the lease and the subs and the story behind this mysterious allusion to boundaries and rumors, there's a rising tension in the rental. A coarse quiet with no talking and no music. Some of the time when quiet lingers between me and Mom, I don't notice, because the quiet is nothing, just the sound of comfortable calm, of settled domesticity. But other times, like right now, while we wait for Jerry and Gretchen, and with Mom's odd outburst over the name Gretchen hanging over us, this silence holds the weight of all the fights we've ever had, all the moments of mother-daughter tension balled together, girding the oxygen with brackets of steel.

I hate this feeling. This feeling of fighting with no words. That no matter what I say or ask, anything at all I do will cause one of us to blow the heavy-laden oxygen, and then we'll have to breathe in the particulates of tension until we clear and filter all the barbs out. All that takes work, and I'm tired. I crave the settled feeling, the calmness.

I need to be the one to blow this up and get the fight over with, because I insist on keeping my new blue-pink bedroom with the wind sounds. I want—no, I need—to live in the ranch's colorful spaces, while also having the potential of a friend who lives right here, built-in. Easy, convenient, like the shelves of books in my room.

After walking down my hall and past the dining area, a dividing line of plants, red love seats, and down another hall, I step to Mom's master bedroom. I note her bathroom is adjoined, but otherwise, our bedrooms are similar. Her bedspread is the same blue-with-pink-coral pattern as mine. The wall opposite her bed has a framed, shellacked puzzle, the same mermaids-in-layered-leaves image, but a different design and with a few additional details. Mom is concentrating on the contents of one of the special keepsake boxes she's set on her bed. Even though she must hear I've walked to her door, and I'm breathing a mattress width from her, she doesn't look up. The air is not only girded with steel but titanium, too, and the ceiling is lowering, crushing us in the thick tension.

She removes a metal box from within the cardboard keepsake box, lifts her eyes to me, and says, "You know to never open this unless I'm gone and there's an extreme emergency, right, Lucy?" The key for the metal box is on a long leather strap around her neck. The key itself is tucked behind her shirt. Only I know a key is at the end of the leather.

"God, Mom. Holy shit, how many times are you going to tell me not to open that box? Do you think I'm an idiot?" I've never opened this damn metal box, which holds, she says, a stack of emergency cash, intended to be used if we have to run without hitting any of our—her—other cash hiding places around the country.

"Lucy. Stop."

"No, wait. Why were you freaking out about the name Gretchen? Are you becoming unglued or something?"

"You're going to talk to your mother like that? Who do you think you are? And what the hell? You tell Jerry we're all hunky-dory with turkey clubs when he tells us there's rumors around town about this place? You know damn well we're not staying long. Please. This is way off. And you know it. Way off."

The air is all blown apart, and metal oxygen shrapnel is raining inside. We're both supposed to be filtering the air, but it feels like I'm the only one doing all the work, because I'm so super freaking mad and I'm on my tiptoes and my face is hot and I want to scream, but she's staying calm and not raising her shoulders or yelling, and this makes me even madder.

"We are staying," I scream.

"Watch your voice. They'll hear you."

"They live way up on the top of a hill, in a fortress of brick, and the wind between the properties is a sound moat. I will yell!"

"You know what? We're leaving. Get your things."

"No, we absolutely are not. What's with Gretchen? What's with the name Gretchen?"

I'm blocking the doorway, and because I hit puberty and have kept growing, I'm no longer the girl she could easily set aside. I'm tall, like really tall. I basically fill the doorframe in height. She doesn't even attempt to round the mattress to leave the room. She turns her back, the metal box clutched to her chest. As if I'd tackle her and take it. As if I'd break any of her steadfast rules. I never have and wouldn't. Underneath, I do love and respect her—she's given so much of her life to protecting me. But I also want to hate her in this moment and scream.

"Who is this Gretchen that has you so freaked out?"

She sighs, her back still to me.

She walks to a wicker armchair with a flowered cushion in a corner of the room. As she sits, I set my palms on each side of the doorjamb and hold solid. She folds her arms around the metal box. When she lifts her head, the lids on her eyes are low; she won't look at me.

"Lucy, some things I can't tell you yet. I don't want you searching around on the internet and getting yourself in trouble. They'll find you again. They'll take you. Don't go asking questions. I'm an idiot. I shouldn't have reacted like that. It's nothing. Nothing."

"I don't even have a computer here, Mom. Your work laptop is always locked, unless you're watching me download music on my crap Nano, which has no internet. Our phones are shitty burners. You keep the iPad and don't let me look up or watch anything without you monitoring—and we have to use other people's Wi-Fi. Do these people even have Wi-Fi? So, whatever. I'm not going to school this summer. How the hell am I supposed to search anything?"

There are several ways any basic fifteen-year-old girl, who's not a stupid dumb brain-dead moron, could get on the internet, and she knows I know it, so my feeble argument is met with her rolling her eyes.

The problem for us is my age. I'm asking questions now. I'm not a little girl who's satisfied with simple answers anymore. But our other problem is that when Mom digs in and wants something her way, she is impossible to beat. She fights dirty and won't hesitate to hurt my heart. I'm playing with fire taking on this fight right now, but I want to stay here that bad.

"What's with the name Gretchen?"

She shakes her head. "Lucy, we've always agreed, right, when you're eighteen, we won't run anymore. I'm sure the risk will be gone then. And you know, I've let up quite a lot in the last few years, because with every birthday, the less attractive you are to your father's family. We're not homeschooling anymore, right? You've been in schools a few years, right?"

"You are totally changing the subject. What's with the name Gretchen?"

She inhales long through both nostrils and swipes her head fast to the side. We're almost matched in how we argue; we know exactly the ways the other one of us tries to shift topics, shift blame. This is another one of our mother-daughter problems.

"Fine. Fine." She takes a moment to pause and look past me, not at me, and I know this lifeless face she's wearing now. *Shit.* She's actively removing herself from the cloud of emotion she's been in since hearing the name Gretchen. She's intellectualizing and calculating, and I know she's mad at herself for having the outburst of emotion in the first place. Her weakness. My mother finishes crosswords as an afterthought while cooking three-course meals. My mother writes whole books on birds in a month, edits novels for her clients overnight. One time she decided to write a symphony based on bird chatter she'd recorded in the forested Burton Peninsula on Vashon Island. Somewhere along the way, she mentioned she'd skipped two grades. Point is, I'm contending with a literal genius here, and now that she's stepping out of her emotion, this argument just got harder for me to win. I do well enough in school, straight As and all, but it's not like I could solve the theory of relativity or have whole conversations with ravens. And I suck at math.

"Lucy," Mom says, her tone not fighting me anymore, her tone settled. The metal parts in the air have lessened, but that also means I'll have to retreat. "Look," she says. "I'm sorry, okay? It was a huge mistake for me to react over a name. I shouldn't. I shouldn't have wound you up. I should let us stay here at least a little while longer, and I will. I shouldn't make you feel uneasy, I'm sorry. You should be enjoying life. You shouldn't be worrying about my strange reactions to things and thinking I'm losing my mind. You should be worrying about growing up and doing well in school. And you do do a great job."

"Mom. Can you please tell me what the deal is with Gretchen?" I've lowered my tone and indicate I'm resigned to the fact that she might not tell me, and she'll win, like she always wins fights about my past. With fights on this topic, she plays the card of her genius against me. I take my hands off the door sides and drop my shoulders.

She says nothing, stares past me, still not at me, and smiles—because she knows she's in control again.

I turn my back to leave. But as I'm stepping away, she says, "He tried to rename you Gretchen. On the passport they had for you, they used the name of one of his home-country ancestors, Gretchen Foulin. A native name. They didn't print that in the papers or anything, nobody knew that part. Because I snatched you back before your father and his sister could take off with you, and I took and burned that damn passport. They fled the country."

I turn around. Set my palms on my face. "He tried to name me Gretchen Foulin?"

"Yeah. He and his sister had you and were ready to fly out the next day. But I anticipated all this. I took you back. The passport, long gone."

"If none of this is in the papers, why are you worried about me doing an internet search?"

"Lucy, hello. I've never told you his last name before. Foulin. Foul, *I, N*." She stresses the pronunciation and spelling of his last name, as if she wants this name to sink in. But yet she doesn't want me doing research—I'm so confused.

I guess I'm shocked, because this is indeed the piece, his last name, I should have homed in on. In fact, this is the piece I *am* shocked about. His last name, my father's last name, has been the highest coveted secret kept from me all these years.

"Baby, please promise me you won't go search on the name Foulin? Please? Give us until you're eighteen, okay?" Her voice cracks when she says this, so the air is safe to breathe again, filtered and clean. I walk over to her in her wicker chair and give her a hug. She can't hug back because she's still clutching her locked metal box like I might rip her heart from her chest.

"Of course, Mom. Yes. I won't go searching him out." My heart is racing like a swarm of electric jellyfish. *My father's last name is Foulin.*

A rap on Mom's window startles us, and I'm reminded we're in a one-floor home. We turn our heads to see Gretchen peering into Mom's bedroom window with her bright face.

"We've been knocking! Lunchtime!" she sings.

Gretchen walks away from Mom's window and presumably toward the front door. Mom furrows her brow, and I have to admit in my own mind that that was intrusive.

"I think she's just a nerd, Mom. And she seems pretty lonely out here. Maybe she needs a good friend," I say. "She's obsessed with jigsaw puzzles, even makes them, so I think she's an artist, and that's good, right? She seems pretty creative."

Mom winces, a derisive scowl on her face. I'm imagining things, thinking things are wrong with me, but I note, she did not once look me eye to eye this entire fight.

*Should I call her out? Ask? Not now. The air is filtered. Let it go.*

"So I suppose we're going to learn about boundaries and rumors?" she says. "From some girl obsessed with puzzles and her father, who, by the way, is a fancy-pants Boston Symphony concert pianist. So that's the plan? Right? I guess this day is just going to get weirder and weirder." Her voice is resigned. She knitted together this litany of oddball facts the way she always knits oddball facts, to make some cynical point about the dark-comic surreality of life.

"Or maybe everything's fine, Mom. Let's give her, this place, a chance."

# CHAPTER SIX

Inside the rental, Gretchen opened the turquoise refrigerator to show it stocked with a six-pack of complimentary Coke and ten bottles of water. Three of us grabbed a drink, and all of us headed outside for a "stroll of the property," as Jerry said.

Jerry didn't grab a drink. Jerry doesn't hold a sub. Jerry says he needs to be careful with his hands.

We are walking toward the cattail and lime snake-grass patch that caps the parking area between our ranch and the low, long shed with the KEEP OUT signs. Three of us are eating turkey subs and drinking drinks as we walk. Gretchen explains how she wrapped each sandwich with wax paper so we could "walk and talk and eat." Jerry mentions how he ate buttered pastina with a rubber spoon while Gretchen made the sandwiches. This dude is obsessed with caring for his hands. Whatever. My mom is afraid of a name and won't look at her own daughter. So we're all fucked-up, all of us. Who cares?

Jerry and Gretchen are wearing binoculars around their necks. I note Mom doesn't mention she has her own top-of-the-line $2,500 Leica Noctivid birding binoculars in her purse. I note Mom is giving zero personal details.

"Turkey's shaved from Dyson's downtown. They roast five whole turkeys every single day and then sell sandwiches and meat the next day. Every day they sell out. People drive here from all over. So get there early."

This is the best turkey club I've ever had. The turkey is moist and just-right salty and seems somewhat marinated in a delicious gravy. The bacon is obviously organic and smoked, and the cheese, Jerry told us, is aged cheddar from an actual Vermont cheesemaker, some guy with a long white beard. The lettuce is crisp, local butter lettuce, not disgusting field weeds they try to pass off as "mixed greens." All these great ingredients are available at Dyson's. I'm thinking I need to get down to Dyson's to fill our fridge and maybe even get a job. I make a list in my mind of things to confirm permission for, a job being at the top.

"Sub roll is from the baker next to Dyson's, Scheppard's Bakery and Gourmet Coffee. If you like bread and coffee, honestly, can't find anything better. Not even in Boston's North End. Again, people drive from all over to our little town for our foods. And Scheppard's is packed all the time," Jerry says.

We're walking down a grassy, sloped trail on the right side of the cattails. On the right side of the trail is a sea of lime and airy ground ferns. I'm sure a whole magical world of fairies lives in the fronds.

Jerry stops, points his long index finger at me, and says, "Oh, and next to Scheppard's, you have to hit Ferry Farm and Fudge, young lady. They might be known for their fudge, but their secret weapons are their fresh-baked snickerdoodles. If you stand at their back door at four a.m., you can buy a dozen, a limit of a dozen, straight out of the oven. Got to pay in cash. Line around the corner in the summer at four a.m., yep."

"Oh my God, the snickerdoodles are re-dic-you-lous," Gretchen says, bugging her eyes on me. "We'll ride bikes downtown today. I will show you."

*I think the word is . . . yes, the word is presumptuous. Gretchen is presumptuous. And yet, I do want to ride bikes to town with her.*

I pretend my mouth is full and I'm chewing and do a little head nod. Riding bikes to town with Gretchen is now topic number one on my mind list to discuss with Mom; getting a job at Dyson's has moved to number two.

"Now," Jerry says, stopping. We're below the tall cattails, and having descended the winding trail off to the side of them, I can confirm there is a small pond here. Beyond the pond is that large summery, picnicky field in the out beyond and the beautiful trees with wind in their leaves. Jerry points to the field. "The field's fine to go to, run around, no problem. But—" And here he pauses, drops his head, shifts a look to Gretchen, and breathes in. "Here," he says, taking off his binoculars to hand to Mom. Gretchen does the same, handing me her binoculars. Three of us have to rewrap our subs and set them on the grassy trail to make the transfers.

Gretchen points with her Coke hand, and Jerry points with a finger to a darker wedge of pine forest that creeps up to the airy trees along the summer field. This darker wedge widens and forms the backdrop up the hill and behind Jerry and Gretchen's brick fortress house. Jerry is arcing his pointing finger from the wedge, up the hill, and all around their house.

"Okay, if you take up those binoculars, focus on the line of pine. See those signs?"

Mom and I take up our binoculars, and after a few seconds of dialing the image to focus and zooming in, sure enough, on almost every pine on the wedge that forms a boundary against the light, airy trees, and on all the ones heading up to Jerry and Gretchen's house, and even beyond the house, I'm guessing—can't really see from here—are orange signs.

**PRIVATE PROPERTY**
**NO HUNTING**
**NO TRESPASSING**
**WARNING: ALARMS AND TRAPS**
**ELECTRICAL FENCE**
**SECOND AMENDMENT IN EFFECT**

Practically every single tree has this all-caps, glowing-orange sign. Beneath the signs, starting at what I think is chest high on a man and down to the ground, are several lines of metal wire, strung tree to tree to tree, creating, I presume, the electrical fence mentioned in the signs. Mom and I lower our binoculars, pick up our subs and drinks, and wait on Jerry to explain.

"Probably I'll just say the shocking part first and you'll understand why we have to have boundaries," Jerry says. Gretchen looks up at her father, almost as if a supplicant, awaiting atonement or wise words from a high priest. She nods, waiting. Or I'm misinterpreting everything and her nod was simply that she's okay to hear whatever this shocking story is.

Mom is squeezing her turkey sub so tight I fear the thing will sever and the front half will plop to our grassy trail. Maybe the pond snake I see floating will slither out and snatch it as soon as it hits the ground.

Jerry's still paused and looking at Gretchen, and I'm waiting for him to deliver his shocking news. A grass blade moves in a ground wind and tickles my ankle.

"When Gretchen was four, her mother, my wife, was nine months pregnant with our baby son. She went for a walk in the woods behind our house, and a hunter shot her dead. An accident. Our boy had spontaneously birthed. He died soon after. Nobody was there to help. Hunter fled, never caught. Gretchen was there, but she was only four."

Mom drops her entire sub to the ground. But the pond snake has disappeared under the water, and I'm betting he's as shocked as we are to hear this news, so he's not slithering out of the pond to claim any bounty of food. I bet he, too, wants to disappear and hide and make all this sudden weirdness end. I bet he'd like the fairies in the fronds of the sea of ferns to swarm and spirit him away to the out beyond, like I do.

Feels like a clot of turkey is stuck in my throat.

My mouth is wide-open to hear such drastic candor, in front of a child, about that very child. Hell, Mom won't give me even the biographical details of my own childhood.

Gretchen winces. "I don't remember much. I kinda remember sitting next to my mom and holding the baby and screaming," she says. Her face is unreadable because she's so hunched over, submissive or hiding or scared, who knows. All I know is this—no wonder the girl is a little awkward, a loner, drives her mind into constant wordplay and puzzles. I do this with books and painting. Also like me, she has just one parent.

I imagine a four-year-old Gretchen, her white, moving skin pulsing in morphing blotches of red. I picture her holding her dead newborn brother in the woods next to her bloody mother. The newborn would still have an umbilical cord connected to his belly and to the placenta, and he would be covered in white, chalky birth goo—they showed us a live birth in sex ed this year. It would be normal for Gretchen to be screaming in this scenario. So although Jerry's story is awful, I'm comforted to know Gretchen had a normal emotional response. And I'm not quite sure why my brain needs comfort about Gretchen's emotional response right now.

"Anyway, look. It's terrible. I'm obviously skipping over all the emotions in all this. We've just met, I can't burden you with the grief. Just trying to give you the facts here, for your safety, is all. Believe me, the tragedy guts us. We've, yes, been to many therapy sessions. But look, the hunters around here are fierce. They want deer, they want black bear. Some hunt legally, some illegally. And I don't want any part of any of it. My land is prime for hunting. There's a bear den. Land's infested with deer. There's a beaver dam. Wild rabbits. Wild turkeys. Coyotes. Raccoons. All kinds of creatures in there. So I've put an electrical fence all around. From the wedge of pine"—he's pointing again—"to around the entire perimeter of my property, extending all the way to the highway. Five hundred acres of forest are surrounded by my electrical fence.

Except for the gorge, but that's a natural barrier. And alarms go off if any humans cross in or out around the perimeter of our house. And . . ."

Gretchen coughs, apparently indicating she wants to tell the next part. "And," she says, "Daddy designed a few traps, too, because when he started with the fence, hunters and teenagers kept coming in anyway, and he'd have to call the cops all the time. And a couple of people got zapped and tried to sue, but we're within New Hampshire law to have that fence. So Daddy also added spring traps, like those nets in movies, where if you step there, bam, you're flung up in the air in a net. Daddy had them put in all over."

"Look," Jerry says, "I know it's extreme. But it's for everyone's safety. Mine. Gretchen's. Theirs. We don't need any more hunting accidents. We don't need any bear maulings. And the gorge. Whoo. The gorge has two facing walls of granite cliff. If you don't know about the gorge, the way the trees clutter up to the edge, you can step right off and plummet a hundred and fifty feet."

Gretchen animates as her father talks. She uses her fingers to demonstrate a walking person falling off her palm and then blows all her fingers out straight, indicating the person's body flying apart in the fall. She looks at me and shakes her head, indicating how awful she thinks such a death would be.

"Ick," she mouths.

I cringe as my response, agreeing, obviously.

Jerry continues talking as if his sidekick daughter has done this demented shtick with him a hundred times. "Oh gosh, over the years, before I put up the boundary fence and house perimeter alarms, and, yes, net traps, ankle snatchers, electrical gates, too, air and rescue retrieved the bodies of three trespassers—a hiker, a hunter, and a woman who had posed on the edge for a self-taken picture. Found the woman's camera dangling in a tree halfway down. Lord knows how many people have gone off that ledge."

Gretchen's skin is a busy switchboard of blinking, pulsing red.

I can't look over at Mom, because we would give away an entire conversation by the looks we'd give. So I watch a blue jay swoop from a low branch nearby toward that out-beyond field I crave. I want Mr. Blue Jay to pick me up by my shoulders with his talons and drop me way down there, way far away. This is a moment when I need Mom to say the right thing, because my mouth is full of stinging jellyfish, and my brain is drained of all speakable words. To sum up, Gretchen found her mother and newborn brother shot up in the woods, and now they have deadly boundaries, including a murderous gorge, to keep them safe. I don't like horror movies.

Mom has been pacing a circle ever since she collected her consciousness and picked her sub off the ground. Her expression is flat, giving nothing away.

"I know it's shocking. I know I've told you in an abrupt manner. Apologies," Jerry says.

"Just, wow," Mom says, her face placid and her eyes raised. "Jerry, it *was* rather abrupt. I do appreciate you acknowledging that." Mom scratches her head with a free finger, gracefully and precisely, and so although she's also holding a bottle of water, not a drop spills. "And, Jerry, Gretchen, I am truly sorry for your loss. I can't imagine. It's just, and I don't want to start off on the wrong foot, but I kind of try to shield Lucy from gruesome news. So maybe next time . . ."

This is Mom, all right. Here's a guy telling us about the horrible death of his wife and child, and the horror of his four-year-old screaming in the woods with those dead bodies, and Mom is thinking about our little duo. She is always only laser focused on us, which, in the last year, I've recognized more and more, and in that recognition, I've come to appreciate her crazy level of protection, but also to detest it. Mom's obsession with protecting us is like a comforting, comfortable room sometimes, and others, a claustrophobic, windowless cell of steel air.

Jerry holds up his hand. "Gosh, you're right, Susan. Gretchen and I have grown too numb to the details. The counselors said she and I should talk openly about the whole event, but obviously they meant between us two. Apologies, Lucy," he says, looking in my eyes, as if I'm another adult.

"My mom is, like, being overprotective. I'm like fifteen, I can deal," I say. I roll my eyes at Mom, and I know she knows this is all an act for Gretchen and Jerry, so as to take away all this burdensome tension, because I know Mom knows I despise when people pepper unnecessary *likes* in their speech. "Gretchen," I say, "sorry about your mom." She bounces her head in thanks.

"Well, now, I am sorry, but there is one other important item we need to address, and this does concern Lucy. Do you mind walking up our driveway to the house? This concerns that rumor in town I mentioned."

"Any, you know, bad details, Jerry?" Mom asks, smiling, indicating she has removed her awkward warning about what Jerry can say in front of me.

"Oh, ha, no gore. Just rumors and imaginations. I'll explain. Probably better if you see what I'm referring to. Demystify what might look strange, so we have no curiosity later." Jerry looks at Mom and me. "You know, from rumors Lucy will probably hear in school, when school starts back up in the fall. Or maybe before. Right? Maybe she'll meet and hang with kids this summer, of course."

Gretchen shrinks herself and slows her pace, as if she wants to disappear. Her skin flares in pulses again. I'm guessing she's recoiling, or embarrassed, at the idea of hanging out with other kids in the summer. I'm guessing that doesn't happen for her.

"So on to rumors, then," Mom says, and I know she is being her best sarcastic self.

# CHAPTER SEVEN

We walk back up the grassy trail between the cattail patch and the fairies' fern garden in a single-file line: Jerry limping in the lead, short Gretchen in her apple-print dress behind him, then Mom, then towering me. As we ascend into the higher lime grass and the height of the cattails, we are surrounded on all sides by various shades of green. I pretend we're in a tropical jungle. Two hummingbirds and several yellow-and-black dragonflies skitter above and around us. When that lovely wind washes out the sound of our feet on the ground, I pause to breathe in a scent I'd call Country Clean. This is the magic I first sensed when we pulled in, and now I'm renewed in my wish to stay. I force myself to forget Jerry's horror story about the dark woods behind their house.

We're passing through the parking area, past our brown Volvo, and along the long, low **KEEP OUT** shed. At the far end, nearest the dirt road that leads up to their brick house, Gretchen points. "There's the ten-speed the old renter left. You can use that when we go to town for snickerdoodles."

I had forgotten about the snickerdoodles at Ferry Farm & Fudge. After what we're experiencing with Jerry and Gretchen, I know Mom and I will have to have a long talk before I go anywhere with Gretchen.

In a trash barrel at the far edge of our rental property, we throw away the remains of our subs and our empty drinks and set off to walking up the dirt road toward the brick house. The gnarly pine forest is on the left, and the mounds of holly and blueberry bushes are on the right, the berry hillside being the one behind the low, long shed on our property, which is below us. As we come out of a bend in the road, I note Gretchen and Jerry have a circular parking area. The far end of their house has an attached garage, the white garage doors solid and closed. And at our end, about twenty feet from this side of the house, there's a tall structure made of four wood poles, on top of which is a green aluminum roof, under which is a yellow Caterpillar construction thingie, the kind to dig deep holes with the long arm and scooping bucket with teeth. Jerry sees me eyeing it.

"Had a pool crew up here a couple years ago. Came and set up all their equipment. Marked all the spots behind the house. And the day they were going to start digging, feds shut down the pool company in a tax-fraud raid. Nobody's come to collect this mini hydraulic excavator. How weird is that?" Jerry says to my mom.

"Very weird, Jerry," Mom says.

"Anyway, no pool now. Lost a deposit of twenty-five grand. Can you believe it?"

"People are horrible, Jerry," Mom says. And this, this is her authentic self. She really does think most people are horrible. "Why not sell their scooper, then? Get some money back?"

"Yeah, I thought about it. Probably should," Jerry says. But I can tell in the way his voice trails, he does not intend to go through the trouble. So to sum up, for a couple of years, Jerry has kept this excavator—*not a "scooper," Mom, God*—on his property, and he's going to do nothing.

This time Mom does sneak in a screwed face to me, and I know she knows we're both thinking the same thing. The word *lame* comes to mind, but also so does *strange*.

We follow Gretchen and Jerry as they lead us behind their big brick house. Up closer, the structure is huge. A two-story rectangle, but each story is tall. I'm guessing inside the ceilings are at least fifteen feet high, each floor. The front door is solid and black. Eight tiny windows on the front, four up top, four below, seem more like squinting eyes than windows for seeing in or out; the placement and size of the windows are oddly minimal, almost like they're slits in those tall bunker monuments out of which soldiers shot muzzle-loaded guns during US wars. The windows aren't wider than those slits, truly, and given the yards and yards of bricks on the front face of this house, the scale of the windows is way off, way too small. Around the front door are three metal circles, one above the door and two on the knob side; they look to be armor shields bolted to the brick around the door as some weird military ornamentation or armory decor—I have no idea. Never seen anything like them.

When we pass the front of the house, I look down along the edge. Around the slit windows there appear to be newer bricks. Almost like correct-size windows were here at one point, but they were removed, and these slit windows put in. *Why?*

Jerry and Gretchen continue along the side of the house, and I crane my neck up and down to see if the side and back have bigger windows. Nope. Still the same slit windows with newer bricks around the casings. I'm wondering if Mom is noticing these construction or renovation—I don't know—details, but she's staring straight ahead, watching Jerry's every limping step. So I do too. Something has her attention in full, and she's set her eyes to analysis mode.

Behind the house, a sliver of grass divides the back side from a thick wall of tall pines, taller than the house. I think the sliver of dividing grass between house and forest is three feet wide, maybe four, no more. The trees grow straight, and since some trunks appear sheared here, too, like in the Bottle Brush Forest at the entrance, the closeness of trunks makes this forest of pines a solid wall. Some other varietals of evergreens grow lower, and their limbs are draped in boughs of dripping, possibly moldy, clumps of pine needles. Jerry grabs a white pair of cotton gloves off the thinnest picnic table I've ever seen and slips them on in a slow, aching sort of way. As he dons his gloves, I scan the back, trying to see how they exit the house to the backyard, but I can't find a door. *Are those newer bricks in a rectangle that used to be a doorway?*

"In case a limb is low, can't have a scratch," Jerry says, referring to his white gloves.

I'm behind Mom, so I look to the ground in case she's turning her head to raise her eyebrows. I remind myself, *We're all fucked-up.*

We step into the wall of darkness by way of a skinny trail, which is the only notch at which we can enter because the ground-to-chest wires of electrical fencing running tree to tree stop and start around this trail. It's possible another open notch for another trail is at the far end of the property, but I can't tell for sure from this vantage, with all the thick trees. Walking in farther, the air switches to a biting cold. Mosquitoes swarm me, so I swat everywhere.

"Our Mosquito Keeper has a range to only about here, like the alarms and motion floodlights. But those are off now, since we're showing you around." Jerry taps his Apple Watch when he says this; Gretchen mimics the action with her own watch. "Anyway, the bug zapper has a silent noise to repel the 'squiters from the perimeter around the house. But the second you walk into these woods, you're doomed. We won't be in here long, just a quick walk."

"Where you taking us, Jerry? We need to get back," Mom says, stopping in the trail. She stands erect, pushing me to stay behind her, keeping herself between me and Gretchen and Jerry. She doesn't lift a finger to hit any of the twelve mosquitoes on her cheeks and hands. I'm slapping my arms and legs and face all over. I'm under a full-on insect attack.

Gretchen points northwest, which follows roughly the snaking of the trail. "Use the binoculars," she says. So I do, and in following the direction of her finger, about two hundred or three hundred yards in, I make out a roof of some sort. A house roof. I think it's black, could be brown. Without the binoculars, it would have been camouflaged in this soup of brown we're in. The angle of the roof is not drooping or draping or clumped and uneven, like the rest of the forest, so with the binoculars, the shape is visible. I think spots of mold or moss bloom on the roof. This forest is a fungus obscuring itself and all within. I want out; the mosquitoes are devouring me. Gretchen, with her white pulsing skin, seems immune. Jerry too. I wonder if they sprayed themselves with deet before dragging us here. And yet, they didn't offer us any?

"What is that?" Mom asks, following Gretchen's pointing finger to the moldy roof deeper in the woods. "And what about ticks? Jerry, I think we should leave. You can tell us about whatever this is back out where there's no bugs."

Mom takes a step back, forcing me to take a step back.

"Oh, Susan, you're right. Ticks are merciless around here. You'll need to check yourselves. But that's everywhere. Even down at your place. New Hampshire is infested." He holds up his palms in a gesture that says *pause*. "Susan, Lucy, I know this is odd and awkward. But I'm sure Lucy will hear things in town from the teens, and I want to make sure there's no mystery here. And if she's asked about it, it would be great if she said she's seen it and it's nothing. Because if she doesn't, then I'm fearful the intrigue is ratcheted, and the teenagers will try to break in again—they haven't in a long time. I don't want anyone to get hurt. Like I said, the animals, the cliff, the electric fence, the spring nets, et cetera."

"Let's go fast. We're getting eaten alive. Just right there? To where Gretchen is pointing?"

"Yeah, just to that house. We'll be done and out in five minutes."

As Jerry and Gretchen move forward, I note how Mom checks the cell bars on the phone in her pocket and slickly sets it back inside. I do the same. No bars. I don't have Wi-Fi on this burner. Mom walks slow, and since I'm behind her, a good solid distance grows between us and Jerry and Gretchen.

We lose sight of the roof line we're trekking toward for a couple of seconds as the trail bends the other way, but then we're back on track and, indeed, a house in the middle of the forest is coming into focus. I think this is what they call a typical colonial. I read about different architectural designs in art class last year. We enter straight on dead center and stop a hundred yards away. Numerous pines in between obscure our view, so we cannot see the sides or the back. Given the placement of boarded-up windows, I have no idea what's inside.

This forest house is painted brown, same color as the trunks. So brown, brown, gross brown, everywhere. The paint is peeling off, and the exposed wood siding is warpy gray. The roof sags, the window casings sag, and although I can't see through the windows behind the boards, I can tell windowpanes are broken. I'm sure the interior is infested with mice and squirrels and birds and termites and mold *and demons and ghosts.* The front door is barred with boards too. Heavy soot and coal stains scar the exterior brick of the crumbling chimney.

"So here she is. A hermit, the brother of the man we bought this property from, built himself this place. No plumbing, no heating, other than the chimney and fireplace inside. He lived out here alone for fifty years. About ten years before I bought—and I bought, oh, twenty-some-odd years ago—hermit fell asleep, and a burning log rolled out of the fireplace. Set a whole room on fire, black soot and smoke filled every other room. Man wakes up and was lucky, at least in the short time, because he had a fire extinguisher. Gets the one room to stop burning. I think the fire didn't spread because every board was damp with forest moisture. And was good it was spring, not a dry August. The whole forest could have scorched. Anyway, man dies in the hospital of smoke inhalation a day later."

"So what are the rumors?" I ask as I take a step closer and head toward the house.

"No farther, Lucy," Gretchen says, grabbing my arm. I shoot her a death glare to let go. She does, and her skin starts flickering and pulsing. "Sorry. Sorry to startle you. I'm, oh. Sorry. Daddy says walking any closer is not safe."

Jerry looks quick to Gretchen and then looks away. Seems he winced in the same way Mom has been wincing at me. He takes a step to the side, away from Gretchen.

"Oh ho, can't go any closer, Lucy," he says. His voice seems unsure, almost like he didn't expect me to try to get closer. Like he's found himself in over his head, not sure how he got here in the woods in the first place. He scratches his cheek. I wait for an explanation.

"Here's the thing," he says.

Gretchen is shaking her head in micro moves as if she doesn't want him to keep talking.

"Daddy, maybe just tell them what the rumors are. I think they want to get out of here."

Jerry considers her and smiles. "Gosh, I'm sorry. It's just, every time I come out here and consider how cruel they can be, I get a little shaken. They're just kids. Anyway, kids in town have concocted some weird *Blair Witch* scenario that my wife and my son haunt this place. Obviously, they don't. But teens. Anyway, they sneak here and drink and do Ouija. Well, they used to. Used to. Took me a good year after my wife died to erect all the electrical fencing and whatnot. And during that year . . ."

Gretchen coughs, her face in a scowl.

"I broke my leg because of them," Jerry says in a super-fast rush, almost like he forced himself to take an unexpected chance and go on and take the tempting jump. "You see. It's just not safe. That's why I don't want anyone going beyond right here."

Jerry lifts his limp leg and rolls up the hem of his dad-man pleated khakis.

"Daddy, you don't need to show them," Gretchen says, annoyed.

He's pointing to a blue bruise pattern, the size of a baseball, on his calf. "Kids set up these rock traps in holes and hid them under piles of leaves. Couldn't see them. Gretchen says at school the kids say pyramids of rocks under leaves will catch ghosts. So I'm out here one day, and I step on one and, bam, compound fracture."

Gretchen exhales, clicks her jaw, raises her eyebrows at her father, and when she sees me watching these angry reactions, she swallows away all the furious signs and forms a slow smile. She sighs. "A compound fracture is when your bone snaps and breaks through your epidermis layers," she says directly to me. Swiveling fast to Jerry, she claps her hands and says, "Okay, can we go now? We get it, Daddy. No one will come out here, geesh," Gretchen says, and rolls her eyes at me.

*Why didn't Gretchen want her father to talk about the rock traps? Why did he show us his leg wound, which seems newer than years old? And what the what? Rock pyramids in holes to catch ghosts?*

Gretchen's arms are crossed. "This is so stupid. Come on, everyone. Let's get out of this mosquito pond."

Jerry is rolling down his pant leg as he continues, "So this here, this is the rumor and the danger. Please don't come back out here, Lucy, Susan. All around the house they hid those rock traps, and Lord knows what else. So you see, this is not haunted. It's just a hermit's burned house. There are no ghosts."

Gretchen sniggers. "Ghosts. Those kids are so dumb. Sorry Daddy scared you about the stupid rock pyramid stuff. All you needed to see was that this is not a haunted house."

"And what's that road?" Mom asks, pointing to what seems to be a narrow road covered in layers of fallen leaves.

"Just an old logging road," Jerry says.

Mom turns to walk up the trail, pushing me in the back to move along. "Thanks, Jerry, we've seen enough. Lucy and I won't come out here," she calls over her shoulder.

I smack all over my body to kill the bugs biting me. Several red splatters of blood dot my legs and arms.

*Holy freakville. They really do have demented* Hansel and Gretel *shit back here.* I practically sprint to exit this forest that is literally eating me.

We're walking between the side of Gretchen and Jerry's brick fortress and the CAT excavator, and finally, no more mosquitoes. Mom and I leave their binoculars on the skinny picnic table. I need a shower, stat. I'm sure a thousand ticks have burrowed into me too.

"Hey, hey, let's ride to Ferry Fudge. Snickerdoodles!" Gretchen says, showing she doesn't read body language—Mom's and my shoulders are stiff up around our necks—nor social cues; we practically ran from them in the forest and haven't said a word since Mom turned her back and said she'd had enough.

I don't answer Gretchen. I'm begging Mom in my mind to please extricate me.

"Lucy needs to help me unpack. Not today, sorry, Gretchen," she says, looking over her shoulder as we keep walking toward our rental.

When we're clear of their circular drive and far enough down the dirt road, Mom stops, turns, and places a smile on her face that I know is 100 percent phony bologna. We're back to playing parts, back to covering up the fact we're on the run and we're weird too. Again, Mom sets me behind her, and herself between Jerry and Gretchen.

"Jerry, sorry if I had to leave so abruptly, but those bugs. Wow. We won't be going back there. No trouble."

"Thank you, Susan. Thought it would be better to show you right off." He's out of his weird white gloves, which I guess he must have set back on the skinny picnic table. Again, he lightly cradles one hand in the hammock of the other.

"And Gretchen, sorry, honey, but Lucy and I drove all night, and we both need showers and to unpack and rest. Another day."

"But I leave early in the morning for camp for two weeks," Gretchen whines. "Puzzle camp." Something startles her, some thought, and she widens her eyes. "Oh, wait! Lucy, come with me! Daddy, can't we get her in? Lucy, you could drive with us to North Carolina! Puzzles for two whole weeks!"

Mom chuckles. "Oh, Gretchen, you are a sweet girl. But no, we are pretty exhausted. Two weeks will fly by, and before you blink, you'll be back, and then you and Lucy can get to know each other properly."

"Oh," Gretchen says, in the most heartbreakingly crushing way. Broken bird. And there goes her pulsing skin again. In a motion so slow and soft, as if Gretchen is wet tissue paper and he fears tearing her, Jerry places a hand on her back. He doesn't give Mom one of those parent-to-parent looks about how difficult teens are.

"Some other time, then," Jerry says, staring at me and with no smile.

"'Kay, gotta go. Gotta pee. Gretchen, have fun at camp. See you in two weeks," I say, and run down the hill. I'm fifteen, so my abrupt movements and leavings can be as abrupt and rude as Allen flinging in and out of rooms and whipping his tail in your face. I leave it to Mom to erase my teenagerness with a parent eye roll.

*What the ever-living hell have we gotten ourselves into?*

# CHAPTER EIGHT

I'm in the living room waiting on Mom. She walks in, sets her phone on the red-blue-turquoise tiled kitchen counter with a scraping slide. She walks to the mouth of the kitchen that meets upon the dining and living room, turns right, and keeps walking toward her master bedroom. She passes me; I'm standing and waiting for her verdict in the living room area. I graze the lamp shaped like a bunch of grapes with my hand. She says nothing. When she enters the hall toward her bedroom, she stops, crosses her arms, and turns to me. Her steel gaze is directed beyond me, not at me.

"I'm not going to fight with you. Only yesterday that bearded man in the park with the Frisbee, only yesterday he seemed to have recognized you. We've been here only hours, after driving all night, and it's weird and it's off and it's sudden, and yet you seem to insist on staying. As if you have roots here."

*What? When did I insist on staying? Didn't she just extricate me from going to puzzle camp? Puzzle camp? What? Doesn't she want to talk about how weird the house in the woods is? Is she creating a fight? Why?*

"Mom, why are you so mad? Are you saying you want to leave because they're a little weird?"

"A little weird? A little weird? Lucy, for cripes' sake, did you not go through what I just went through? Listening about a brutal hunting accident, a dead baby, a child witness, and then some creep-ass haunted place in a forest? Boundaries and traps and electrical fences? Hello? And what's up with showing us your broken leg skin, Jerry? A fungused, haunted house, Lucy."

"The house isn't haunted."

"That's not the point."

"So why are you mad at me? What are you saying?"

"I don't know what I'm saying. But don't you agree this doesn't feel right? Only yesterday. Yesterday. Yesterday that bearded man seemed to recognize you. And now we're in, what is this? What's next? A river of blood under the house? A portal to hell? This is weird. I think we should leave."

It is true. The whole incident with the bearded man was only yesterday.

"Mom, stop. Stop. We're both tired. Can't we make this decision in the morning or something? I'm sorry, I know they're weird. But I do want to stay. And twice sorry, but maybe I'd like to have a friend around for once."

I gasp at my own surprising words.

Mom cringes.

The air stiffens in metals once again.

I know saying I'd like a friend around "for once" is a strike that hurts. In fact, it's a strike I've never taken before, so I also cringe. Cringe at my own audacity to call out an elephant in the room, just like that. Bam, out of the bag, said faster than a second, without me taking a breath to think through the consequences. *Mom prefers it to be only us—she restricts my world to her.* As she steps backward, she doesn't try to hide her wide-eyed betrayal.

"Well, then," she says, "I guess you've made up your mind." She huffs, closing her eyes as if in disgust, and turns to walk toward her bedroom.

She stops in the middle of the hall.

"Oh and, Lucy, seems to me there was no space behind their house for a pool. Seems to me nothing had been marked for a pool ever. And no way anyone was anywhere near to starting to dig. Those trees have been growing for decades. Don't you think?"

I don't answer.

"Do you think?" she says, the question cutting and judgmental and rhetorical. She hurts my heart. And in a snap, the oxygen is only steel and titanium again. I believe she's striking back in retaliation for the crime of me saying I want a friend around *for once.*

I suck my lips into my teeth, hold my tongue.

"Well, I suppose you don't care about obvious lies and red flags. You dug in your heels and want to stay."

She walks to her room and shuts her door. Whenever she goes ice like this, her piercing words, her disconnection from me, the way she asserts her intelligence over mine, I feel sick inside. From the guilt for making her feel like this, from the guilt for not being appreciative enough of her protections, for the fear of how long this battle of wills will last, and from the anger at her and at myself for allowing emotions to get so raw.

It's been like this for as long as I can remember; although I think it's only been in the last year that I started to recognize that this dance we do might not be normal or healthy. So many times we've done this dance. One time when she went cold on me, asserting her intelligence over mine, was on my tenth birthday. Obviously I couldn't have a birthday party with actual child friends—back then I was sheltered and homeschooled—"highly protected," she'd call it. Also, we couldn't go to a normal place all out and about and free, because back then I didn't yet have the blue contacts. So she crammed a bucket hat deep over my head and brought me to a late-night diner in Chicago at midnight.

"Nobody asks questions of people in diners at midnight. Everyone wants to be left alone. So don't engage," she said as she opened a grease-smudged door on a streetcar diner.

I yawned in response.

She found a green booth. That's what I remember of the setting, a green booth in an otherwise silver space. I dragged myself to my side, fighting my eyes to stay awake.

"Do they have cake?" I asked, after reading the menu.

She looked at the counter. I followed her eyes.

"Does the menu say there's cake? Do you see cake on the counter? Aren't those pies?"

"Um?"

"Can't you read? Don't I teach you?"

"Why are you mad, Mom?" My face burned, and a scratchiness crawled on my neck.

She closed her eyes in such a tight way, her whole face accordioned.

"Sorry, sorry," she said. "I hate that we can't have a real birthday for you. I'm sorry." She rubbed her temples and then lowered her head to look up under the rim of my bucket hat. "Oh, baby, I'm sorry. I'm stressed."

I didn't know why she was so stressed. My whole life had been on the run. Back then, I thought our lives were normal. I hadn't yet gone to any schools, so I had no context. We ordered our food; she let me get whatever I wanted. So I asked for a cheeseburger and a milkshake and a large order of onion rings. She smiled and ordered the same.

A woman with a sheepdog came in, and that's when the night turned back to black. I'd never seen Mom slide so far into a booth so fast. Never saw her physical fright so deep as when that dog trotted in. Except maybe today when Gretchen said her name was Gretchen.

I didn't know what to do because I thought he was a really cute, fat, fluffy dog, nothing to be afraid of, unless you're afraid of shag carpets. Things got worse because the dog came straight up to me. I couldn't help but pet his Chewbacca face. His big, round, black eyes looked out at me through strands of white fur. The whole while, Mom shrank herself in a corner of the booth. Maybe I was supposed to be afraid of the dog, like Mom—that's what I questioned. I didn't know. The dog's owner turned after reading the specials board, I guess not finding what she wanted, and poof, they were gone. My hand was slimy because the dog slobbered while I petted him, so I dragged my fingers on my jeans to wipe them clean while the waitress served my order.

As I went to pick up my burger, Mom shot up from her coiled crouch in the corner, her back straight.

"Gah," she said, as if spitting down upon me.

I looked up.

"Do you think, Lucy?"

"What?"

"You do not realize, do you, you've contaminated that whole bun with your disgusting hands. You just petted a dog."

I dropped my meal.

"I, mean, really. What germs might be on there? Do you know?"

I didn't know. I was ten.

"We're leaving," she said, while sliding out of the booth and throwing two twenties on the table. As I walked behind her, the itching on my neck turned into a fire red, so I pulled the hood on my hoodie over my scalp because I didn't want her to see what felt like popping skin. I had learned and was learning, especially by ten, that if Mom got set off on something, it was best to shrink myself and hide.

Two mornings later, I woke to find she'd decorated our apartment's dining room as if cartoon characters were coming for a fabulous birthday breakfast. Hundreds of strands of streamers formed a raining rainbow from the ceiling, and a red and purple and blue two-part cake was perched on a stand in the center of the table: a large number one and a large zero, ten was my cake. We never discussed the diner-and-dog incident again.

Now, I run to my little white bathroom as nausea rises in my throat. Doubled over, I try to calm my breath and feel the familiar hives that erupt sometimes when I feel this way, when my heart is full of jellyfish, my brain full of hummingbirds, and my throat full of bile. No hydro-cortisone will fight this flare of hives—these are from the mind. Looking in the mirror, this case is bad: my face is popping with stress welts, the horror of which is added to the mosquito bites and blood splashes from me smashing the full-bellied suckers.

I rip out of my smelly jelly T-shirt, out of my black stretch-cotton pants, kick off my slides, turn on the shower, and focus on washing all the bug blood and mind hives off my body.

# CHAPTER NINE

After my shower, I went to my room, changed, and cuddled up and napped with Allen. At some point, Mom called my cell from her bedroom and said only one sentence: *You're on your own for dinner.* What this meant was I'd have to eat the remainder of the shitty orange peanut-butter vending-machine crackers in my backpack and wash the orange dust down with one of the comped Cokes in the turquoise fridge. We haven't, obviously, gone to any stores to stock up yet.

It's night now.

I'm lying in bed, my stomach half-full. Allen is purring and snoring next to me—I had cat food for him, lucky jerk. My window that looks upon the out-beyond field is open. There's a screen, thank goodness, so no army of mosquitoes can launch a second attack. The wind is high and loud, and this is calming, washing away the interior terror with Mom. Also, when the wind takes a pause to inhale, night crickets sprinkle the lull with chirps that sound like string instruments and heartbeats. And the pond below my window must be infested with bullfrogs, who add echoes of bass horns. An owl hoots here and there. With every minute of these sounds, wind ruffles in and tosses the curtains and then Allen's fur, then the little hairs on my arms, and I calm more. The clean air smells like the color of light green. I melt.

I've launched into a book I found on the shelf by Susan Barker, *The Incarnations*, about two soul mates who basically can't separate despite having different lives and bodies over thousands of years. In some lives, they can be pretty terrible to each other. I've dozed off a couple of times, but I keep waking because the atmosphere of my reality is so intoxicating and the world of my book so compelling. A perfect night, but for the thing with Mom. The thing that could upturn the peace I'm feeling tonight at dawn. So this is another reason I keep waking, so I can savor the night and the book as long as I can.

Midnight, the moon is high and bright, pulsing in gray shadows and bright white. If the moon's gray-white pulses were shades of red, I'd think the moon had the same skin as Gretchen. Wind whooshes and whistles and rolls imaginary pebbles in the air, crinkles leaves. I'm calm. No hives. Something about this place, the permanence of the moon in my window, like a framed painting. The force of the constant wind, its tendrils trailing through the air like giant, flying, invisible jellyfish: indestructible. The immovable field of the out beyond. The solidity of the house. Like nothing can shake this, move this.

I think of Jenny. I think of being ripped from her and ripped from a different friend, whose name I can't even remember now, from the previous school. I think of my transience and how I'm a scar in the moonlight, a blemish to a moon that won't budge. I'm an insult to the faithful wind that weaves and slides and shimmies, never leaving, as if this hillside and the forest beyond are under a dome or a cloche or a glass bell. This house could be the subject of a beautiful snow globe. We could have everything here. Things could be perfect and permanent.

Two years ago, Mom stopped homeschooling me. A girl in my first-ever school had a group of four close friends; they'd been together since kindergarten. They called themselves the Fives, and she was clearly their leader. She played soccer, and her mom was in the PTA. I used to watch the girl hop in their Range Rover after school, and her mom, who was her older clone, sometimes handed her an after-school cupcake and then put the hazards on and got out of the driver's side to brazenly, with no shades on, hand out whatever extra cupcakes she had to whoever passed. The girl was super sweet and kind to everyone; I studied her behind my blue fakes. One Monday while we waited for English class to start, I overheard her telling the Fives how on Saturday she'd gone to an aunt's baby shower and ate blue cake, and on Saturday night, she and her cousins slept at her grandmother's house and ate homemade doughnuts and carved pumpkins. She seemed so gold, so natural, in doling out her weekend facts, as if her home-life stories were normal and frequent and not extravagant, unattainable luxuries. I didn't understand any of her words or any of the places she spoke of. She was aglow with a sustained peace that itself was a whole new state I'd never known existed.

She smiled at me a couple of times when she caught me staring. She didn't know why I stared; I stared because her life was so foreign to me. I didn't understand who she was or how she could live so free. How did she walk like that, stopping and waving and smiling to everyone along the way, with her real eyes and no contacts, while I lowered my head and ran fast to enter whatever used car we'd acquired by barter or cash. How? How did her mom stand exposed, doling out cupcakes without sunglasses on, while I'd join my shaded, shrouded, shoulder-scrunched mother in the rear, rear of the pickup line. How? And I've realized now, I stared because I wanted what she had. The confident glide, the easy smile, the consistent group of friends—or at least one, a Jenny—the family parties so frequent they were like cast-off pennies, the silly laugh, the whole package of feeling whole that comes with the comfort of knowing you'll wake in the same bed tomorrow and the next day and the day after that.

Whenever we run, I always make myself believe we move to a new moon, a fresh slate where I'm not a scar yet. And I want to keep this current picture-frame moon, even if it means accepting strange neighbors. I'm exhausted from centering myself under new moons.

A clatter erupts outside, as if wood logs or something heavy is rolling. I think of the bear den Jerry warned about. But then a sudden rap-rap on the casing outside my window jolts me, and when I look, rising up from below the window and staring in at me is Gretchen's pulsing, red-white moon face. She stares through the screen, and I can't tell if she's smiling or not. I'm about to scream, but I bottle the noise, because if Mom finds out about this second window visit, I won't be able to force a stay.

I walk to the window and stare back, somewhat in a standoff. I do so desperately want to be settled. I'm digging in in my own mind, which is itself a betrayal, even though my true desperation is the center of my own self—and how can I deny truth to myself? How? I'm bad for having this truth, for wanting this and admitting I want this, and so the level at which I want this must be kept a secret. I hate me for being untrue and secretive with Mom. And I'm scaring myself by how much I think I'll do to ensure we stay—when I don't even know what that means or what I'll agree to endure. But something. There's something I'll have to endure for this betrayal. A trade, a barter, perhaps, with the whims of the universe.

As I step closer to the window, I'm accepting something, some quiet warning in the back of my mind, blinking. As I look on at Gretchen's face through the mesh of my window's screen, both of us standing here staring and silent, I extinguish an early-forming flashing, a red whirl wishing, I think, to blare. *Soak this in, brace yourself, you need to stay.* Allen is happy in this environment and purring on my new coral-print pillow. I want to work at Dyson's, which I won't need Mom to drive me to, because we're close enough to bike. I want this town. I want this rental. Mom can't know about Gretchen's night visit.

Gretchen smiles, showing all her kernels of teeth.

"Didn't mean to scare you, Lucy. Saw your light on and wanted to do a puzzle with you. I'm going to miss you while I'm at camp. It's a new

Stave, the puzzle, called Waiting for Nightfall. Eight hundred pieces, four thousand dollars."

*Gretchen is a definite boundary jumper.*

*Also, to see my little pin light on, she'd have to have walked all the way down the windy dirt road from her house and around to the side of mine. What?*

One of the important things I've learned in being on the run: set clear boundaries early with people, especially the boundary jumpers, the people who assume levels of intimacy they haven't yet put in the time to attain. The people who say they'll miss you while they're at camp when they've only met you that same day; the people who ply you with unnecessarily specific details about a puzzle's manufacturer and title and pieces and price while they stare in your window at midnight. *Holy fucking shit.*

I swallow my fright, stiffen my composure, build the emotional moat around myself I've had to build so many times, bend so my forearms rest on the sill, and now only the screen separates my face from Gretchen's. I look straight in her blues with my naked violets. I'm banking on the black mesh to wash away whatever color she's seeing in my true eyes.

"Gretchen," I whisper, "don't ever come to my or my mother's windows again. If you do, we will not be friends. Understood?"

"Oh gosh, yes. I'm so sorry," she says, and starts crying. "I . . . I . . . I . . . I'm so stupid. I don't . . . ugh . . . I don't have any friends, and I don't know . . . I . . ."

This blubbering crying is the boundary jumper's classic manipulation, or maybe she's sincere. Seems the crying came too fast to be real, though. I do think I can, and I do want, to cobble together a safe friendship with this girl. She seems so bad to want it too. But we're going to need to work on the contours, and she'll need to understand boundaries. Either way, when you're on the run, boundaries must be dredged deep and fast and clear, regardless of the boundary jumper's emotions or intentions.

"Gretchen," I say with my mother's icy tone, because ice is necessary to set the fence, "your tears won't change this rule. Go back to your house, stop lurking around mine. When you get back from camp, we'll talk about how to be friends."

"Okay, okay," she says, sniveling and backing away from the window. "Good night. I'm glad you moved here, Lucy. You're so cool."

"Good night," I say, and close and lock the window and draw the curtains.

I remain fairly pissed off at Gretchen for making it so I can't listen to the sound of wind tonight. I look forward to listening while she's away at her jigsaw camp.

# CHAPTER TEN

## MOTHER

Mag, as her loved ones call her, a loving nickname she rarely hears anymore, has violet eyes. An uncommon mutation, like the long-ago Alexandria Genesis myth, and like Elizabeth Taylor. And her baby girl, at first she couldn't tell, but as she neared age two, she started to see that she, too, had violet eyes. She caught her mother's mutation. The violet of their pupils is not albinism, which is the reason for some violet eyes.

She could have named her purple-eyed baby girl Elizabeth, after Elizabeth Taylor. She could have named her Alexandria, after the myth. She didn't. When it came time to fill out the birth certificate, and high on birthing endorphins, Mag told the nurse her baby's name was the name of a girl she'd grown up with at the Triple C camp: Laura. She respected Laura's style, her biting wit, her oddities, her damaged independence, her fierce competitive fire. Laura's outrageous, accidental shooting of the camp nurse in the ass with an arrow, which she'd learned was no accident at all—benevolent as it was, the act, if not the victim, was intentional. She also respected a danger they shared in secret, and how that secret came to be. Laura was a symbol of the dark and light of Mag's adolescence, a person who had become both challenge and motivation. Seemed to her in her cloud of postbirth hormones, such was having a child: challenge and motivation. And so, she named her baby girl Laura.

But now, in moments of untethered dramatizing of her life, Mag hates herself for naming her baby girl Laura. As if naming her Laura unleashed a tragic prophecy, like whatever it was that happened to Laura. Illogical, yes, she knows, but in the way she listens to the universe in drives around the country in a beast mobile, at least consistent.

As for herself, she thought of her own name as a nickname started at the Triple C: Magpie. It was this nickname big sis Carly contorted into Maggot or Mag for short. Mag wasn't her real name, but the loving nickname was who she thought of herself, because love is what she knew. Love is what Carly and her three other sisters bathed her in through childhood.

Mag had been going to the Triple C every single summer, like all her sisters. And, just like big sis Carly, when she aged out, she became a counselor. Several other girls did the same, so they'd become a tight sorority over the years. Ass-shooter Laura, she was among them.

In the summer of 2003, Mag was twenty and working as a lead camp counselor. Carly was visiting the camp for a week to celebrate her birthday (turning thirty-one) and to deliver some news. Over the course of the week, drastic events and news kept changing Mag's life, one after the other, so by the end of the week, Mag's life, which had been a smooth spinning top, became a top toppled on its side and rolling off the earth.

The first drastic thing was at the start of Carly's visit. Carly, whose birthday celebration would be at the end of the week, hadn't yet delivered whatever news it was she intended to give. Mag and Carly were roaming over to the breakfast hall, a long logwood cabin, when Marianne, the camp director and former camp nurse, whom Laura had shot in the cushy tush so long ago, came running up to them.

"Laura called. She took the last two days off, yeah?"

"Yeah," Mag said, affirming an obvious and innocuous fact. "So?"

"So, she just called and says she's not coming back. She was set to be back last night. Said her aunt died and she has to move to Wyoming."

"Wyoming?" Mag said, looking askew at Carly.

"She never mentioned Wyoming. And what's with this aunt? Who?" Carly said.

"Don't know," Marianne said, flipping her hands in the air. All three women looked to each other and shared confusion.

"Weird," Mag said, her mouth slack in shock. She'd been sharing bunks with Laura for twelve whole summers. The group of girls who'd done the same, they were all like family to Laura, an only child whose parents boarded her during the school year and sent her to the Triple C in summer. And above all that, Laura and Mag had shared a secret and a secret competition since age fourteen. Nobody else at camp had anything like that with Laura.

"Real weird. Laura never misses summers," Carly said.

"That's it? She's not coming back?" Mag asked, suddenly feeling the first pang of grief in her life. She hadn't lost anyone she could remember before. She didn't realize how much she loved having Laura around. Loved her as part of her oddball, patched-together family. Loved keeping a serious secret with her, and also a secret, perhaps dangerous, game involving the treetop adventure course, a game even Carly didn't know about. To Mag, her connection with Laura was a ragged orphan love, wholly bohemian and perfect in its strangeness.

"She ain't coming back," Marianne said.

"So she what, goes? No goodbye?"

"Guess not, honey. And now your load's going to be even heavier."

Just then, drastic thing number two pulled in in a white BMW, parking directly in front of the porch to the log-cabin dining hall. Paul. This first sighting of *Paul*.

And the presence of Paul in Mag's life was truly as quick as this. Drastic. He opened his driver's door, stood the long length of himself, and flipped up his sunglasses, stunning the women with his sparking eyes, rich olive skin, and lean, muscled body.

"Hi there," he said toward the trio: Marianne, Mag, and Carly.

"Can I help you?" Marianne stuttered, having lost her footing in looking at him.

"I'm with the private equity—"

Marianne interrupted him. "Ah yes, come with me," she said, jogging and hurrying him off toward her office.

Mag turned to Carly. "What's that all about?"

"Private equity, Mag, think about it. What do you think?"

"A loan for the camp?"

Carly shrugged, indicating she wasn't so sure. The sisters watched Paul pausing Marianne along the way, pointing to and assessing structures and asking questions.

Mag registered that he was handsome, knew she would, could, might for sure, be attracted to him, but was still smarting from the sting that her sister-friend Laura had up and vanished from her life. Gone. Snap. She imagined the sinking she felt must be a fraction of what it must have felt like for Carly to one second know she had parents and, the very next drastic second later, not have parents. How a life changes so fast sometimes in a slap by the universe, or rather, a twist and torque. You're driving down the road one second, and the next you're in a head-on collision with a bread truck. Twist, torque, snap.

And now, here, a man drives in and cranks the wheel in yet another direction.

Turns out, Paul was ten years older than Mag, and being chiseled and dark and rich, and working for a fancy-pants private equity firm on some uber-confidential something or other with Marianne (and neither of them would divulge what), he was a definite rarity at the Triple C, a girls' camp. Camp director Marianne fanned herself when Paul walked to her camp office, and she let him, in violation of camp security, roam unattended around the grounds to assess the land and structures. Paul could have told Marianne he worshipped the work of Jeffrey Dahmer and watched *American Psycho* for tips on face creams, and she wouldn't have heard a word.

"Girls, he makes me wish I was young again," Marianne said when a group of women later sat at a staff picnic table, ogling Paul untying a rowboat to "assess the lake."

"Marianne, you could be his mother," Carly said.

"Well, whatever, if I was young again, I wouldn't be sitting here like you useless lumps when I could be snuggling up next to him in a rowboat."

"Oh damn, Marianne, you want to *ass-ess* the lake with Paul," Carly said, laughing.

"You can kiss my big fat ass. You're all chickens," Marianne said.

The women were giggling, Mag mimicking Marianne's raspy voice. "I'm Marianne, camp director of the Triple C, grandma to three, and I'm gonna *ass-ess* Paul."

One of the women was another of Mag and Carly's sisters, a middle one whom they called the Squawk. She'd come in to visit for the day.

"You'll get in trouble with that sarcasm someday," sister Squawk warned, wagging a finger at Mag.

Carly and Mag rolled their eyes at Sister Serious and continued snort-laughing, adding a chorus of "Squawk, squawk, squawk," to which the aptly nicknamed Squawk shook her head and double-handed flipped them off.

*Sisters.*

As the group of women howled and traded lewd jokes about the camp's boy toy, Paul, off in his lonely rowboat, "ass-essing things," Mag once again felt the pang of sadness that Laura wasn't sitting here laughing too. Surely Laura would offer off-center, biting comic commentary about Paul. Mag didn't like this new feeling, this loss of Laura's wit. It angered her, actually.

But more drastic events were to happen in just this one week. Things that erased any whiplash over missing Laura. Looking back on it now, at age thirty-five, still driving around the country and acknowledging all the years between, and her baby girl being fifteen, Mag gets more than whiplash. Something more like debilitating bends.

On the night before Carly was set to finish her week visit, the staff congregated at a Carmel restaurant for Carly's birthday party. They invited boy toy Paul, and Squawk and the two other sisters came in too. Mag remembers the dinner, the cake, dancing when the band started, slow dancing with Paul, whose long body was a perfect puzzle piece to her long body, and then nothing more. Like she'd fallen off a cliff into a black void. Mag had only been drinking margaritas, using her fake ID, right? Right?

Next thing she knew, sunny light was bathing her face, and she felt cushiony, and all around her cottony. Maybe someone was whispering in her ear. A woman's voice? She's not sure. A dream? A door slamming? She cracked open an eye to see a large glass window looking upon the ocean. White sheets covered her, and a white comforter was crumbled on the wood floor—along with all her clothes, underwear, and black bra. Next came true and identifiable sounds, these ones verifiable and not dreams: the roar of the ocean, snoring behind her, and a soft and then louder and louder banging down below.

Mag flipped around to find Paul, naked and snoring. She jumped out of bed, pulled on her underwear and clothes, and ran out of whatever fucking room she was in. At a landing, she realized she was in a colossal open-floor house and now at the top of designer floating stairs suspended on hanging cables. This was like one of those ornamental homes in *Architectural Digest*. For millionaires. Or billionaires. Sleek and artistic impressions of furniture dotted the open spaces below, along with statues made of dripping metal in corners. Enormous artwork dominated the white walls.

Mag padded fast down the stairs, following the noise to the pounding front door. Her shoes from the night before were right there in the entryway, jumbled atop a neat row of male shoes and one pair of red heels—not hers. She slipped on her flats and opened the door.

It was Carly. And on sight of each other, Carly exhaled loud and bent over. "Oh, thank God. Thank God. Motherfucker, thank God. You're alive. I've called you a billion times. It's two in the afternoon, Mag."

"What?"

"What is right! What the hell were you thinking? I've looked everywhere for you. I had to practically bribe Marianne to get Paul's address. You had me so damn worried."

"Carl, get me out of here. I don't remember anything. I'm scared."

As Mag stepped onto the front porch and after the blinding sun faded, she paused, looking around the neighboring homes.

"Mag, come on. Let's go," Carly prodded.

But Mag stalled, staring at a colossal mansion next door: an oceanside estate seen through a line of cypress.

"What is it?" Carly asked.

"Wow. Um," Mag said, trailing her thought, as she walked on behind Carly, somewhat in a trance. Pointing to the neighbor's mansion, she said, "That's Laura's house."

"That?"

"Yes, that. Yes. I only ever went one time. Slept over once. Remember? I was fourteen."

"I don't remember. Really? Should we knock? See why she left without a word?"

"No. No way," Mag said, shaking her head hard and fast and keeping to herself what she could never forget happening in that house six years before. She'd never told Carly about that secret, and she wasn't about to tell her now. "No. Her parents are assholes."

"Well, duh. We know that. Who sends their only daughter to boarding school across the country to New Hampshire and then summer camp all year every year?"

Mag didn't mention how, based on what she'd witnessed, Laura was better off living elsewhere. This was their secret and was what sparked their dangerous, adolescent competitions—like they were daring each other to be the first to snitch, the first to break the bond.

"Let's just go. I want out of here."

The sisters headed to downtown Carmel. The café- and boutique-lined sidewalks were packed with the typical parades of nameless Carmel visitors. Mag considered how so many different faces always came and went in this tourist town, and nobody seemed to care to remember any one person from the next. The sisters found a two-top in the back of the darkest café, behind a tower of boxes of Colombian beans.

"Give us the stiffest espressos you got," Carly said to the barista.

Carly didn't have much more by way of details of the night before. She, too, remembered up to Mag slow dancing with Paul, and then, after going to the bathroom with Squawk, Carly came back to find Mag and Paul had disappeared. Carly assumed her younger sister was hooking up with Paul, but knowing her, assumed she'd be back at the camp within an hour. Mag wasn't one to miss a morning shift. Back at camp, Carly passed out only to awake late the next day to find no Mag. She tried calling her for a while and then ratcheted up the panic.

When Mag didn't show and didn't answer her phone, although she didn't want to start relentless camp gossip, Carly convinced Marianne to give up Paul's home address. Marianne admitted then she'd met Paul and others from the private equity firm there during the past week.

"Shit," Mag said, sipping her espresso. "What happened to me?"

"I don't trust that guy. Stay away from him," Carly said.

Mag nodded.

"I don't think he hurt you. You look fine. You feel fine?"

"Yeah, nothing hurts. He seemed real peaceful in the bed. Maybe I drank too much?"

"You had, by my count, two, maybe three, margaritas. Nothing you haven't done before."

"Yeah."

Carly scrunched her brow. "Should we call the cops? Do you think he roofied you?"

Mag didn't answer right away. "I really don't think so?" Said more as a question. "Yeah, he can't have. Honestly, Carl, I was into him last night. I must have not eaten enough before the drinks. And I know this is super lame of me, but we go to that joint all the time and use fakes. I don't want to get the staff in trouble."

Carly stared at Mag with a stern and loving patience. "Maggot, I do not give one solitary fuck about some shitty restaurant. I think we need to go to the hospital and make a report. We'll get your blood checked. Come on, after your espresso."

"Carl, no. No," Mag said in a soft but firm voice. The kind of tone that means the answer is final and assured. No more pushing.

Carly reached across to rub Mag's wrist.

"Carl. Don't go. Stay longer. Don't leave today," Mag said, her voice cracking.

"Oh, Magpie, I wish I could stay. I do." Carly paused, looked away, inhaled, exhaled, looked back, and straightened her lips. "Look. I have to give you my news. The news I've been sitting on all week. You want the good news or bad news first?"

"Just tell me. Tell it all at once."

"First off, I'm getting married. Jim asked last week. Need you to be my maid of honor, 'kay? The other sisters will be jealous, but they're always jealous. Who cares."

Both sisters giggled.

Mag was weeping, happy for her sister. "I'm so happy for you, Carl. Jim is great. I love Jim. Always have. Sisters are gonna be snit-snittertons that I get to be maid of honor, especially Squawk, but you'll let them wear nice bridesmaids' dresses, right?"

Squawk, the middle sister, was dubbed Squawk by Carly and Mag because, to them, she was always bitching and moaning and squawking and planning something. Bitch, bitch, bitch. Plan, plan, plan. Hover and worry and mother and lob questions and advice. They loved her—all the sisters loved each other—but Squawk could be a handful. Typical sister shit, Carly called it.

"We'll see about the bridesmaids' dresses. Squawk despises pink and kitten heels, so we should probably start off with pink and sling-back kitten heels, yeah? Just to screw with her, don't you think?" Carly said with a big smile. She lowered her eyes and returned to serious. "Second off, ugh. Second. Here we go. I've agreed to move to Costa Rica with Jim. It's for his career, Mag. Third off, I'm moving there soon, like next month. Wedding will be in San José, and, Mag, hear me out, I want you to consider when you come for the wedding to look for your own place. Don't answer now. But it could be an amazing life in a tropical world."

And thus was the next drastic change. Carly and Mag had always lived together with their aunt and uncle or only a block apart in separate apartments. Always together in a little town south of the Triple C. Mag's hands shook so hard, her espresso cup clattered to the table and plummeted to the floor.

But Carly wasn't finished delivering drastic changes in Mag's life.

After she picked up Mag's cup, which miraculously didn't crack, Carly plowed on with more drastic news. "And, the other thing. Marianne wanted me to tell you. Okay, now brace yourself. Paul's assessment of the Triple C apparently was glowing. This wasn't about a loan at all, but things are very confidential. We're not supposed to know. Anyway, his private equity firm is buying the Triple C. This is the last year of the camp. Did he tell you last night?"

Mag wasn't sure which part broke her most. Laura leaving so suddenly without a goodbye. Paul's appearance and her waking up a finger snap later in his bed. Carly moving to Costa Rica. The Triple C closing. But in that moment, everything boiled together and suffocated her in the dry air of the café. Mag bawled her eyes out right at their table. "No, no, he didn't tell me. Or I don't remember if he told me," she said through tears.

In the weeks that unfolded after that night, Paul had apologized, sworn he hadn't drugged her, and insisted the bartender had a heavy pour. They got close, but not for long. It was a month later when the most drastic-fast life changer came. Whatever happened the night of Carly's birthday party in Carmel, the one Mag can't remember, well, it certainly involved sex of some sort, because Paul got Mag pregnant, which ended the relationship's short tenure and started Mag's dance with the devil.

# CHAPTER ELEVEN

## LUCY

The morning Gretchen left for camp, Mom woke me at 8:00 a.m., told me to dress "nice" and "get in the car." We passed through Bottle Brush Forest, driving along the windy country road, a different way than we took to get here, passed through a seriously wooded area, about thirty seconds of driving, climbed a hill, and then, at the crest, the village of Milberg appeared in the valley below.

Mom parked on the far edge of a red-house library, where fewer people roam and, as she always does, told me to exit our brown Volvo before she did. We should not be seen together. Us getting ice cream in the park, I have been reminded several times, was a colossal mistake.

"I'm going into Scheppard's to buy bread and coffee. You go get groceries and a job." She paused a beat. "Yes, a job, at Dyson's." She didn't look at me. Didn't smile.

I startled; I'd assumed a job was off the table.

Checking her lipstick in the rearview mirror, she continued, plowing right over the startling permission she'd just granted, which is her way of holding all the control. She must hold all the control, always. "You know the drill, Lucy. Don't take off your contacts. Stick to the backstory. Keep your head down, don't engage. Don't connect. And if anyone recognizes you, tell me. That is our deal. You must tell me. I'm giving you more and more freedom. So I need more and more trust."

I grabbed the door handle, anxious to pop in to Dyson's before she changed her mind.

"Oh, and Lucy," she called as I exited.

"Yes, Mom?"

"If this goes sideways, this one's on you. You don't want to hear about red flags, don't want to listen to me. This one's on you."

"Mom, come on. Please . . ."

"Lucy, go. Before I change my mind."

Pretty remarkable that the first place I asked for a summer job, I got. The short owner of Dyson's, Sandra Dyson, seemed to measure the length of my legs with her eyes.

"Ya tall," Sandra said, in a heavy New England accent.

"Yeah."

"Good. You can reach the plantain chips. Theyah on the shelf above the kale. When can you stahht?"

"I guess, um." I roved my eyes over the artistic, rustic interior. Everything had gone so fast. I was still standing in the entrance. "I guess today? What would I be doing?"

Sandra laughed and pulled me in farther. She looked around at all the other workers who were mixed between rough wood shelves of gourmet pastas, an aisle of vintage penny candy, and a whole section of oils in blown-glass bottles—the deli guys standing behind a bulbous glass case, the woman at the meats counter with literal ham hocks and beef sides hanging, a boy stocking what I now know to be artisan cheeses in a flat, refrigerated case of bries and goat cheese and cheddars, and two cashiers in the center of the store, standing on opposite sides of a circular counter. Sandra, still laughing, called out to the workers, "New gahhl asked what she'll be doin' when workin' here. Guys, what will she be doin'? Tell her, on one, two, three . . ."

"Everything," they sang out in a chorus.

One of the deli guys belted, "New girl does everything!" He smiled and winked at me, but not in a letch, awful way, rather in a kind, *I'm your friend* kind of way. I averted my fake blue eyes. I've learned his name is Dali, and he works the deli, so the staff has lots of play-on-words jokes about that.

It's been a week since that overwhelming moment, that high. I recall beaming and my heart flooded with blood. Compared to all the other moves before, life this time with this move is the most quickly drastically different. Within one and a half days of seeing the bearded man and his Frisbee-catching son in our tenth state, we moved several states east, rented a ranch house, and I got a job at the gourmet organic grocer. The journey on a bike, I know now, is eight entire minutes between Dyson's and the ranch.

It's true, in my first week at Dyson's, I've worked the cheese case, the meat station, and the deli with Dali. I've helped roast the turkeys, which involves a ton of brushwork and basting. I've swept, mopped, stocked, and watered the red petunias and geraniums hanging from the outside eaves. Everything except the center-of-store registers by myself, which I finally get to do today, one week after moving here. Whiplash. Mental whiplash from these drastic changes.

Ah! Today! I'm trusted to run one of two registers by myself. Yes, I'm excited. Perhaps I'm weird. I stand on my side of the circular counter. Above me is the highest-pitched cathedral ceiling, the ceiling made of barn board. Two giant beams, salvaged from an old mill, cut the open ceiling in a wooden equal sign. Hanging from the apex and between the equal-sign beams is an octopus constructed out of painted reclaimed furniture. So cool. Dali said the wooden octopus is Jabo, named after a drummer who played with James Brown. Sandra, the owner, plays funk and blues from the opening minute to when she locks up at night. All in all, Dyson's is a super-happy place, and I love working here.

What I love about sliding items through the scanner is the hypnotic rhythm. With Sandra's blues thumping low in the background speakers, the music and the scanning feel timed with my heartbeat.

I'm feeling really chill. I have a line eight deep, and the other register is unmanned during the other counter girl's lunch break, which means I can slide and scan, slide and scan, scrape and beep, scrape and beep, for a good long while. The motion and the sound calm me, and since I'm required to be cordial to tourists but not necessarily the townies (following Sandra's lead, who trades friendly barbs with them), I'm concentrating on my slide-scan-scrape-beep-smile routine. No other worries on my mind. A cool breeze is just right, swirling in from the open door and spinning in the column of the center circular counter, around me, and up to Jabo the octopus hanging between the wooden beams. A bagger boy assists me, so I'm free to limit my motions to sliding and scanning, scraping and beeping, and smiling.

My next customer steps up with her basket of stuff. I slide her bag of apples over the scale embedded in the counter. Punch, punch a few keys. Beep. Next up, beef broth, beep. Locally made tomato sauce. Beep. A pound of Dyson's famous shaved turkey, *typical*. Beep. She'll go next door to Scheppard's for rolls. Everyone does. I nod. Recycled paper towels, red wine, baby Boston lettuce. Beep, beep, beep. I total her up, beep. Scan her card, ting. She's on her way. 'Bye.

I smile.

Next.

I look up.

I lose my smile.

I pause too long, holding his gaze.

I inventory my eyes. *Yes, I'm wearing my blue contacts.*

It can't be him. No. No way.

The familiar awful pattern drops writhing snakes in my gut, kills the hypnotic calm with just one look. At him. It's him. The bearded man with the Frisbee kid in our tenth state. The same one from a week ago. The same one who made us run here. He's at my register at Dyson's in Milberg, New Hampshire. He stepped from my tenth state into my eleventh. He's looking into my fake blue eyes. And as if I can read minds, I know he knows I'm a total phony fake.

# CHAPTER TWELVE

"Whoa! Are you following me?" the bearded man asks, a lame joke to him, a life-altering announcement to me.

"Um, excuse me?" I say, lowering my head. I've only been here one damn week. I've got a whole line of people stacking up. I can't stall. Can't run. Can't take a bathroom break. My heart is racing at the realization that in the past, had this scenario presented itself, I would have dropped everything and run to Mom. And we'd leave, like right now. But I remain.

He's looking over his shoulder. "Thomas, come here," he says. He waits for Thomas, who I see is the boy from the lake in my tenth state. The bearded man keeps looking between me and Thomas, who's way over by the deli and making his way to my register.

I should stop. I should walk through the notch in the circular counter. And then out the front door.

But.

I don't.

I surprise myself, because I don't.

I grab a package of spaghetti from his basket. Slide. Scan. Slow. Like giving in to a sip, a glazing taste on the lips, a pucker of a puff, just one, just one more hit of a bad, bad addiction. I slide. Another. Just one more. This feels like the time Mom coated my fingers in Vaseline and wrapped them in gauze so I'd stop sucking my fingers. Feels like those three months last year when I sneaked out to smoke cigarettes after Mom fell asleep. I did eventually stop the sucking and the smoking. I did. I should stop. *Stop now.* I should stop scanning this man's items. *Stop.* I slide one more. A jar of almond butter. Beep. And now another. A bouquet of daisies. Beep. I should stop. *Stop now.* I should run to the back room. *Run.* I should race on my bike to our rental ranch. *Go now.* I should tell Mom. Pack. Run. Leave. I slide a can of tomato soup. Beep. One more, slow. Beep. Another two. Beep, beep. *Just one more. Why am I glued here? Don't look up.* But I look up.

The bearded man shakes his head when he sees Thomas stopped to join a conversation between another teen boy and Dali at the deli.

"Ivan, man. Whatcha up to?" Thomas says to this Ivan. I tune out their conversation and sneak a peek at the bearded man, who is still shaking his head at his son's failure to join him at the register to interrogate me.

He abandons hope of Thomas.

"I saw you in Indiana," he says to me. "At the lake, just last week. I was playing Frisbee with my son. We were there for a family wedding. You were eating ice cream, on the bench. Then you, snap, up and vanished. Remember me? That was you, right? Had to be you."

I contemplate saying no. I justify to myself that denying I was indeed at the lake in Indiana a week ago would cause more alarm bells for him, if I were to so blatantly lie. I say nothing and do not answer one way or the other.

"What a coincidence!" he says.

I pause, bounce my eyes up to meet his and quickly look away.

"You look so much like this—"

"Lucy," Sandra interrupts. "Line's stackin' up. You havin' trouble?"

"Whoops, sorry," the bearded man says to Sandra. "Sandra, all my fault. Sorry. I'm jamming up the new girl. She's new, right? You're new, right?"

"Whateva, Doc. All you townies just standing round chattin' all day," Sandra says with a kind smile. "Lucy's tha new gahhl, Doc. So stop buggin' her."

*Doc?*

Stepping up to *Doc*, Sandra says lower, "I do love ya business, Nathan, but have ya chats ova at that scoundrel Scheppard's." The bearded man, *Doc Nathan*, laughs. And Sandra is smiling at him like he's her very own son.

"Sandra, you ever going to be at peace and play nice?" Doc Nathan Bearded Man says.

Sandra walks off laughing and swatting the air as her answer. Some other customer I've seen here almost every day, a regular townie, as Sandra calls him, shouts from deep in the middle of my line, "Sandy Crampy, such a grump. Always got the grumps."

Sandra waves them all off by continuing her *whatever* swat of the air.

During all this distraction, I've been working fast scanning Doc Nathan Bearded Man's items. I push bagger boy to quit with his obsessive organization of items and just stuff everything in a bag, whatever, as I total up. I have my mind back, my head down, and I'm intent on Doc Nathan leaving without asking any more damn questions.

"So, Lucy is your name?" Doc Nathan says once Sandra's gone off behind the deli. "Welcome to town. I'll make sure Thomas introduces himself sometime this summer, before school. Thomas, come on. Hi, Ivan." He's looking toward Ivan and Thomas.

"Fifty-four twenty-nine," I say.

He hands me three twenties. I give him his change. He grabs the handles on the very sturdy, old-school paper shopping bags and walks to the door. I continue with the next customer and pretend to ignore Doc Nathan stalling in the doorway. He takes two steps back toward me, apparently intent on pursuing more questions. But Thomas swoops up to him. "Dad, Ivan and I need you to take us back to his house ASAP. His dad got box seats to the Red Sox tonight. We need to go, like, right now. Come on."

"But your mother's grave. I bought the daisies."

"We'll visit Mom on the way to Ivan's. You know Mom would want me at the Red Sox."

"She was a fan."

Doc Nathan pauses, looks at me, which I catch because I gather the guts to look up at him, and his face is so serious. But he takes a step back as Thomas pushes him out of the store. The kid Ivan follows, blocking Doc Nathan's line of sight on me, and mine on his.

The other counter girl whips by on her way outside for part of her break.

"Hey, can you cover me for one second, please? I need to use the bathroom," I say.

She groans but agrees to cover for "two minutes."

I escape through the notch in the circular counter and fast-walk to the staff bathroom. When I'm clear of the main part of the store, I hear Dali's voice behind me.

"Hey, was Doc Nathan bothering you?" he says.

"No, nope. He just thinks he knows me," I say, averting my eyes because I'm so obviously lying, and I'm trying to decide whether to run to Mom or keep quiet.

"Hey, okay, just, like, if you need help or anything . . ."

I hold up a hand, look him in the eyes. "No. I don't need help."

"Okay, cool, cool," he says. Dali smiles at me in way that seems really kind. Too bad he starts college in the fall. I imagine he might make a good friend at school. He turns and heads back to the deli.

I decide to not tell Mom. This time. Maybe because I don't want to be wrong in the battle of wills we have going on. But maybe, could be, maybe because I don't know why. But I know in the very center of myself, something nobody else could ever know, I will not tell Mom. I cannot tell Mom. She'd make us run. And I'm not ready to run again.

# CHAPTER THIRTEEN

I'm at my two-week mark working at Dyson's, and I feel I've got the groove. Break time means I select one of the cheese-and-rice-cracker packets Sandra Dyson makes up for Great Katherine Lake beachgoers. They sell like hotcakes. So with my packet and a bottle of Fiji, I head to the tree out back where I lean the vanished renter's bike, which is mine now. The sky is super blue, and the day is warm with warm breezes, so it's perfect. I plan to sit in the shade of a big, draping willow tree on the grassy edge of the unpaved gravel parking lot out back—where all the delivery people go to unload and the staff who drive here park. Beside the willow is Dali's tiny red Toyota truck with a big weatherproof turkey on the roof. Apparently Sandra agreed to buy Dali this truck if he agreed to advertise for Dyson's with the ornamental turkey. One of the wings says **DYSON'S**.

On this break, I'll read *Word Freak* for fifteen minutes—another book on my rental bedroom shelves. This one is about people obsessed with Scrabble. Gretchen obviously read this one multiple times, based on all her highlighting and pencil notes and the dog-eared pages.

I step within the willow's canopy umbrella, and my heart flutters happy to pretend the leaves and limbs knit nets of sunlight lace to throw upon my warmed body. But this joy scatters, because I hear a shuffling behind the knobby trunk.

"I'm back!" Gretchen blurts while jumping out from behind and scaring the literal life out of my body. My invisible shawl of light lace obliterates. I shriek and jump-stumble-fall-on-my-ass backward, causing my crackers and cheese to explode from the packet and scatter in the gravel; my water bottle rolls to the grass. As I'm collecting myself, I notice she doesn't reach out a hand or apologize. She stands by the tree and my leaning bike with her head cocked, watching, her eyes wide and round. I determine to never flinch for her again.

"You're coming to my house tonight. BLTs and puzzles, friend!" she says when I'm standing straight within the shade of the canopy.

Like she had when I first met her two weeks ago, she's wearing the same ivory sundress with the repeated apple print. She hasn't tanned during her two weeks in North Carolina. Standing by the dark brown of the tree trunk, she's a contrast of stark white, her face flush with pulsing spots of red. Her breath is fast and smells like yeast. Her strawberry-blonde hair is thin and loose. Sweat dots her forehead.

"How long were you standing behind the tree? Were you going to hide until I got out of work?"

She bites her bottom lip and averts my gaze, like she's embarrassed to answer or unwilling to answer.

"Hello, Gretchen, hello, were you going to wait all day?"

"Lucy, I just got here. Came to tell you to come over after work for dinner and a puzzle."

"Can I tell you after I'm done with work? I need to check with my mom," I say.

"I already asked your mom! As soon as you're done with work, my house. 'Kay?"

"O . . . kay," I say. "I need to go back inside."

I collect my trash in the gravel and my water in the grass and go back inside Dyson's. I shove the book and my backpack back in my cubbyhole. This break is ruined. I nose around the corner from the staff hall to ensure Doc Nathan doesn't also appear to stress me out. As I do,

Dali comes around the corner with a new packet of cheese and crackers. He hands me the packet.

"Sorry, but I was about to chuck the trash and I saw what Gretchen Sabin did. Saw you freak and lose your snack."

"Oh."

"Look. Um, do you know her well?" He scrunches his face in a wince, like he's not sure he should say more—likely negative news given his face—about Gretchen Sabin. Dali is a townie, which means if there's scoop, he'll have it to share, but I need to be careful, because I can't give him scoop to share on me.

His question, *Do you know Gretchen Sabin well?*, translates to: *How the hell do you, new girl, know Gretchen Sabin?* I look away and bite my bottom lip. I lied on my employment form, gave a totally fake address. Mom says it's best if fewer people know our address—cuts down on pop-ins and such. So far, nobody knows I live near Gretchen, and I know she hasn't talked with anyone in town.

"That's fine. You don't need to tell me. I get it," Dali says after I don't answer, and now the silence is *awkward*.

What does he get? How could he possibly get what I'm living, my life until now, and my weird acquaintance with Gretchen Sabin?

"I mean, I don't know what you got going on in your life. I didn't mean that," Dali continues. "But I'm sensing you don't want people prying. I respect that, truly." He looks at me dead-on with a worried and honest expression. "Look, I just want to be your friend." He shrugs and steps backward, about to turn and leave.

"Thank you, Dali," I say, and smile. He nods and doesn't push anything; I thank him in my mind for leaving this scene and allowing no answers. I have zero creep-factor vibes from him. I know in my bones he's sincere.

Once he's gone, I rifle several cracker-and-cheese combos down my throat while leaning against the hall wall. Refreshed, I again check the store to see if Doc Nathan has appeared.

Still no Doc Nathan in sight, so I relax a fraction. He hasn't returned during any of my shifts since last week. But Dali did say at the beginning of today's shift that Doc Nathan came in last night asking about me. Apparently this Nathan knows everyone in town, since he's a clinic physician and has tons of family, brothers and sisters and nieces and nephews, in town. Dr. Nathan Vinet is his name. And his son's name is Thomas Vinet. So. That's them. The same ones from my tenth state, same ones with the red Frisbee, same ones who made us run here. I still have not told Mom, and at this point, it's impossible to even think of telling her.

When I get home from work tonight, I find Mom in our red-turquoise kitchen. She's pulling a single-serve pot pie from the red oven; she is decidedly *not* eating the beef-and-barley soup I made her from scratch before I left for work. We really haven't talked much at all in two whole weeks and counting.

"You should go up to Gretchen's tonight. Would be weird if you didn't" is her greeting. I notice she doesn't even attempt to discover if I want to go or if I'd rather eat prepackaged pot pie with her. She turns her back and carries the pie to the dining table, where she'd already set a poured glass of wine, sits, props the *Incarnations* book I was reading against a napkin holder, and starts to eat and read and drink her wine. I become a thing in her periphery.

*I'm alone. She won't look at me. This is the longest of any of her cold-shoulder spells.*

I take a shower and change to go up to Gretchen's. I think mostly because I need someone, anyone, anyone at all, who wants me around and in a place where the oxygen is not girded in steel.

So here I am, walking to Gretchen's, and as I hit the circular parking area, the grounds flood with light. I squint as I continue on to

Gretchen's black door and knock. I'm checking out these three weird metal shields above and on the one side of the door, one bolt in one side of each shield. The air is so much colder at the top of the hill, even though these floodlights should be baking me, geesh. I look along the edge of brick on the front face of their brick fortress and note again the odd smallness of the window slits and newer bricks around the casings. It's the end of June, so the days are long. It's not pitch-black like it probably is during winter at this time. Beyond the dome of stadium lights around the house, the sky is the light blue of summer dusk, backdropping the towering pines, which appear as black silhouettes.

The door flies open outward, and I have to jump back so it doesn't slam into my face. I stumble in the gravel of the circular driveway. Here's Gretchen, her smile beaming wide, her skin bright white. She's in her apple-print dress. A blotch of red pulses on her neck. Her hair is shiny bright, straightened to the point of being sharp. Rail thin, fragile, and shorter than I am—I'm a giant, or a shadow in her presence, especially since I'm in black jeans and a black T-shirt with an octopus screen print and my black hair hangs long and loose. Blue contacts are my only pops of color. My silver jelly pendant sparkles in all this blinding light.

"Lucy," she yells and grabs my arm to pull me in. "I missed you so MUCH at camp!"

I'm inside the foyer.

"Sorry about the alarm lights. Remember Daddy told you?"

"Uh-uh," I say, but I'm no longer thinking about floodlights. Inside, surrounding—I, I, I can't believe what I'm standing in. This is the strangest space I've ever seen.

First off, I was right that the ceiling height on the first floor is high, about fifteen feet high. Within the foyer, a staircase to the second floor is offset to the left. Three hallways lead out of the foyer: one running beside the offset stairwell and toward the back, one to the right wing of the house, one to the left. Within the column of the foyer, around the three doorways and staircase, and up the fifteen-foot-high walls, are framed, shellacked puzzles. Every square inch holds a puzzle. From the baseboards to the crown molding. The number of patterns in here is confusing, unexpected, nothing I've ever encountered anywhere, ever. I'm turning a circle to take them all in, roving my eyes, tilting my head up, tilting down. I feel like I'm riding a carousel horse, around, around, up and down, dizzying myself from the motion and the light blinding off center mirrors that turn counterclockwise to my clockwise. I think a piano plays disorienting scales of waves in the belly of the house. I'd call the song "Seasickness."

Gretchen stands to the side and watches me. She's silent as I inventory what I'm seeing: hundreds of puzzles of colorful dinosaurs, dinosaur bones in archaeology digs, the T. rex Sue in Chicago's Field Museum, which Mom brought me to once.

"A lot of the fossil puzzles I made. Some of the dinosaur ones are commercial puzzles, a Ravensburger. A rare Schmid. And one—" She's pointing to a painted-on-wood, bones-in-a-cave puzzle that I think might be a one-of-a-kind antique. "That one should be in a museum. But," she leans in to whisper, "the museums can fuck themselves, right, swearer girl?"

"You made some?" I squeak out, but I'm not focusing on her. I'm trying to estimate how many puzzles of dinosaurs and fossils are in this room. *Two hundred?*

"Sure, I made some," she says, still watching me as I twirl around and look up and down. "Did you know that the dinosaurs they find, those aren't bones, actually. You'd think they're bones, but really through a process called petrification, minerals fill in the pores, and the bone becomes stone. So they're fossils. Depends on the environment, whether water or wind speeds up decomposition, and also the acidity level of the soil. Unfortunately, bones need at least ten thousand years to be hard as a stone. Bummer."

"Oh," I say. *Was she talking about decomposition? Is she bummed by how long bones take to fossilize? What?*

"Come on," she says. "Let's eat so we can work on a new puzzle."

Gretchen leads me down the hallway to the left. We have to circum-navigate a tower of, one, two, three, I think eight boxes of brand-new Crock-Pots.

"Sorry, don't mind Daddy's Crock-Pots. He's working on some project. I don't know."

"Okay," I say.

This hallway seems unnaturally narrow. It's as if the wall opposite the exterior front wall is makeshift and built after the fact to the home's original design. I think in a normal house of this size and make, we should be walking down a wide hall with openings to fancy living and sitting rooms. But that's not what we're in. This is more like a claus-trophobic hallway in one of those laser-tag mazes (which I did once with Mom so as to break up one of our long road trips through the Midwest).

Although narrow, this hallway is not dark. Lights shine up from the baseboards and down from the crown molding the whole long length. Also, vertical rods of lights are interspersed along the way—as if Ahsoka Tano came and tacked her white lightsabers to the wall. Again, framed and shellacked puzzles cover the wall surfaces, floor to ceiling, the entire length of the hall. I pass puzzles of groups of people, massive crowds of people in each one. Some are blocks of people of one race, some are multicultural. I feel like I'm in a research wing belonging to some mad anthropology professor, one obsessed to the point of derangement. There's a puzzle of tribesmen in what I presume is an African village. One of colonial-era villagers in what must be new America. One of a bunch of faces—black, white, olive. So many others. As we progress, I note two of the slit exterior windows.

Gretchen narrates as we walk, her ahead of me as if a museum guide. "Wish we didn't have to have any windows at all, could have had a couple more puzzles hung in here. But Daddy says it would be weird to have no windows. Whatever," she says, and snorts.

I have no idea how to respond to this. Fortunately, Gretchen keeps walking and talking.

"The puzzles in this hall are from my peoples collection," she says. And I think, *This hall? Are there more narrow halls?* "These here I found at Brimfield," she says, pointing to two puzzles high up on one wall. "Bought that one, the five-thousand-piece Cockburn Village Auction, at, ha, ironic, a competitive auction in which one of my chief competitors tried to wrench it away from me." She stops short and, in a slow turn, looks up at me. I tower over her, so she literally looks up. Her face is serious. "He didn't win the auction," she says, almost in anger at whoever this competitor trying to outbid her was. "Nobody wins when I want something."

I nod. *Noted.*

She leans in. "I always get what I want," she says, staring at me.

I nod again. *Mm-kay.*

She turns back around and continues on. I consider walking backward to the front door so I can go home. *So I can escape,* I start to think. But I move forward, feeling somewhat possessed, and also not wanting to go back to the stifling, steel air of the rental with Mom. This is feeling like the part in the horror movie where I'm yelling at the main doofus to turn the fuck around and run. So I guess I'm the doofus. I hope I'm not the doofus.

"Several of these are not for sale anywhere, because I made them from scratch."

Again, I ignore this comment about making puzzles, because I'm distracted by one in which people are stacked tight in a serpentine line, one that loops on itself to take the entire space of the puzzle—much like intestines loop in a layer in your gut. The people seem to be marching to something, and all their faces are resigned and haunted. Nobody's smiling. None of the men, women, children, or babies in arms smile. They stare into the back of the head in front of them. One of the people is grotesque; he has the twisted-in-pain face of an elderly man in agony, but on a boy's body. Gretchen stops.

"Ah, interesting you'd stop for that one, Lucy."

"What is this?"

"A cult. That's the Death March. Really, a painting. A painting turned into a print turned into a puzzle. It's a rendition of a cult, all members walking to their death. You ever hear of mass vanishings? There's been a lot throughout history. Total mysteries, except some are totally not a mystery at all. Ever hear of Jamestown? The mass suicide?"

I'm shaking my head at her, not sure what to say. *Mass vanishings.*

"Anyway," she says and continues walking. Over her shoulder she says, "Do you have a grandfather, Lucy?"

*What?*

*I need to leave.*

"Gretchen," Jerry shouts from the belly of the house. The piano music has stopped.

"Come on," Gretchen says, skipping ahead.

*Death March. Wait. Wait. Death March? Mass vanishings? Cults? Do I have a grandfather? What?* I note I've walked nearly the length of the left side of the house away from the foyer. I consider turning and walking out, but Gretchen calls again, "Luce, come on," in a voice that is odd for its normalcy. Her voice is as if she's just another girl calling me to skip a rope or swing a swing. I follow on, telling myself I have no friends. Dali's just a work guy. Sandra's just my cranky boss. I've got no one else in the world to talk to except Allen, the greatest cat in the world, and all I'm doing right now is churning myself into paranoid worry, *like Mom does. Gretchen's just a weirdo. Harmless. A nerd. You need a friend. Move on.*

At the mouth of the hall, we enter a seriously dated kitchen of piss yellow and brown. The pine cabinets are a dark stain, the kind you might find in a cabin in the woods. The floor is practically antique linoleum with a yellow-and-white tulip pattern. And the yellow countertops are midcentury Formica—I read a lot of design magazines. I do not know how to understand Gretchen's kitchen. I do not know how this dated, cabinlike kitchen could be in the brick fortress-mansion of the girl who decorated the insanely fashionable and colorful rental I'm living in. Would I be rude to point this out? My confused scrutiny must be obvious.

"Lucy," Jerry says in greeting. He's walked into the kitchen from some other entrance point and deposits himself beside the yellow stove. I'm beginning to feel like the interior of this house is a maze. "Gretchen's made us a load of bacon, and the rolls are warm. Got 'em from Scheppard's, of course. Come on into the dining room." Jerry is once again wearing his white cotton gloves. The sound of a piano playing is gone, and I wonder if I heard a piano at all, since background noise seems impossible in this sealed vacuum of *Twilight Zone* outer space. The lack of noise bothers me; all I hear is Gretchen's and Jerry's breathing, and also the sound of my own heart thudding. And the lights—the lights are so bright, I'm sure I'll get a migraine.

The kitchen smells of bacon, which is a conflict, for the scent is a comfort compared to the warning sirens my other senses are blaring. My stomach growls, and yet my heart thuds in my throat. *Don't they have any ceiling fans?* No air moves in here. It's hot.

As I consider closer, the kitchen appears much smaller than I think it's supposed to be. The interior walls also appear retrofit, just like the narrow hall.

I follow Jerry, who limps ahead in the lead, and Gretchen down another narrow hall, which runs adjacent to the same hall we came down. Again, uplighting and downlighting and lightsaber lights accent floor-to-ceiling puzzles along the way. We're walking back toward the foyer. The puzzles in this narrow hall are of underground scenes. Several are ant colonies. Some are the frayed, veiny growth of tree roots in the soil; some are of plant and flower roots. Some are of burrowing underground bugs.

"This hall holds puzzles from my earth collection. Aren't they the best?"

"Yes?" I say, as a question at first. A mistake. Gretchen stops and twists to me. "Yes," I add in a more definite tone. "Really great."

We pass a puzzle of a rock cliff, a puzzle of a cave with stalagmites, or stalactites, or whatever they're called, and more of other caved or underground items. *Buried things.*

At the tip of this second hall is a small square of a room that blunts the end and blocks what should be an opening back into the foyer, if I'm oriented correctly and haven't fallen down some mind-warping, *Alice in Wonderland,* crazy dimension. A round dining table takes up nearly all the space. I'm sure all these weird walls and halls and this window-less dining nub were built after the home's original construction; this is obviously not a natural design. Jerry scootches sideways around the table and sits. I remain standing and pivoting my head up and down the fifteen-foot-high walls, like I've been doing all along. Here in the dining room, once again, are floor-to-ceiling framed and shellacked puzzles.

"The dining room!" Gretchen says. "Obviously all of these puzzles showcase foods. Had to have fun in this room. Right, Daddy? No bones or bugs or people or dirt earth in here."

"Correcto. Not in this room," Jerry says while winking at his daughter. "This is a room for eating."

True enough, a puzzle of slices of bread hangs above Jerry's head, next to one of several bunches of bananas and one of all the candy bars on the market. And so many others.

Gretchen sits, and I sit where I'm directed. In the center of the round table is a lazy Susan with a yellow platter full of bacon. A literal heaping pile of bacon on a yellow platter. There's enough bacon here to construct one hundred Dyson's turkey-club subs. Another yellow plate on the lazy Susan holds white Scheppard's rolls, which indeed must be warm, like Jerry said, because the room smells of fresh-baked bread and bacon. Another yellow plate holds iceberg lettuce, slices of American cheese—the legit deli kind—and sliced bloodred heirloom tomatoes. A plate covers each of our rattan place mats, in front of which are tepee'd napkins. No utensils or cups for any drinks.

Using his white-gloved hands, Jerry reaches behind to a skinny side table and drags over three kid juice boxes, one for each of us. The size is the toddler size that you'd find in the baby-food aisle. I get berry-berry, Jerry takes apple, and Gretchen gets grape.

"Dig in," Jerry says.

Gretchen first makes Jerry a sandwich from the ingredients on the lazy Susan, and then makes herself the fattest BLT I've ever seen. I'm sitting here stunned by how weird this is, wondering not only about the crazy puzzle halls and walls, the Death March puzzle, which for some reason is lingering on me like a stink, but also why Gretchen made so much bacon and why Jerry is wearing gloves to eat—and, not to mention, the creepiness of us drinking these tiny juice boxes. *What?* I can't get over the obscene amount of bacon. Above Jerry's head, between a puzzle of a pyramid of cheeseburgers and one of a watery ham, is a puzzle of a vintage ad for a candy bar called Chicken Dinner. My eyes are blinded by the light refracting off the glass that covers billions of puzzle pieces.

Gretchen follows my eyes, keen on my every twitch, every breath, every thought.

"They used to use old advertising to make puzzles, Luce. Make your sandwich, dig in!" She spins the lazy Susan so the warm Scheppard's rolls are closest to me. *Why is Jerry drinking from a kid's juice box? Why am I? Why does he eat with gloves on? Why am I in a maze house of puzzles? Why did they close off rooms with these walls? For the puzzles? Just for the puzzles?*

I take a roll, a slice of cheese, and eight slices of bacon like a normal person, not twenty like glutton Gretchen. Could make about ninety-five more sandwiches with the bacon remaining. I suck up all the juice in my tiny juice box, and I must be lost in bewilderment, because I suck so hard the center collapses and makes a loud cracking implosion sound. Gretchen laughs.

"Thirsty much, Luce?" She continues giggling. Jerry hands me another berry-berry. I note he's on his fourth apple. There is no ambience of soothing music, just hot silence when people don't talk. And the lights are surgical-level bright. I know Mom says all families live differently from every other family, and all families have quirks. We certainly do. And it's true, I've never in my life had dinner with any other family, so I'm not the best judge on what's normal versus quirky versus downright total horror-level nuts. Lunch in school cafeterias doesn't count, because that's more like war-zone battle, fighting for survival—that's not *dining*. And I've watched movies and read books about friends eating with friends, scenes on the screen where people improbably all sit on the same side of a table. So that's one thing that's different, because here we're seated in a circle, which might be the only normal thing we're doing—I guess. In fifteen years of life, I've only ever eaten meals with Mom, just the two of us with separate plates and no need for a serving dish in center. In all my countless hours of fantasizing about what it would be like to dine with a friend, visions of giggling through a course of perfect cheesesteaks and icy Cokes with a Jenny, I never imagined walls of puzzles and blinding lights and a mountain of bacon and baby juice boxes. So although I have zero real-life context to rank tonight on the crazy scale, I have to believe this whole situation is a runaway crazy train to coo-coo town.

Gretchen stops giggling when she looks at her father. "You're doing very well, Daddy. Do you feel weird? Want another sandwich?"

I scratch my neck, feeling a prickly heat, like I might break out in mind hives, or a centipede with stinger legs is crawling and hatching poisonous eggs in my skin.

Jerry reaches for Gretchen's arm and squeezes. "Doing just perfect, doll. Yes, please make me another."

Jerry looks at me. "Gretchen has been so good to me ever since I broke my finger. I've been too afraid to use my hands for anything. Didn't want to hold anything. No silverware, not even sandwiches. For a few weeks, Gretchen spoon-fed me everything. She's such a good girl. Tonight's my first night back to holding sandwiches."

"Yeah, Daddy!" Gretchen yells.

I concentrate on chewing whatever is in my mouth and nod to both of them. I could have swallowed a millennium ago, but I keep chewing and nodding and saying nothing. Because I don't know what the hell to say. And while I do wish Mom was here to extricate us with her sharpness and evil eye, I know I need to snap out of it on my own, finish this dinner stat, and get home—at this point, I'll take Mom's steel oxygen to this whole scene a million times over.

"I mean, I have used my hands, of course. I've had to drive to Boston and back. Been practicing with the symphony as soon as the doc cleared me. But anything beyond driving or playing the piano, not much at all. Have to be careful," Jerry says. He cradles one hand with a hand hammock the way he does, and Gretchen slides him a second BLT. "Anyway," he says, "Gretchen has been very understanding."

Father and daughter do a weird scrunchy face in mirror to each other, the kind of face you'd do to a newborn or a kitten. I'm over on the side like a third wheel eating a bacon-cheese sandwich, thinking about my escape through the maze of halls back to the foyer.

*I can't even imagine what hysterical scene broke out when Jerry broke his finger.*

"So, um," I venture, thinking on details I need to get out, "do these halls continue like this through the whole house? With all the puzzles?" I hope my tone doesn't reveal fright or plotting or judgment. I tried to ask in Mom's indifference voice.

Jerry wipes his mouth with his napkin. "Nope," he says. "Not yet."

Gretchen takes over. "That," she says and coughs, shifting her pupils to the upper left like she's scouring her brain for the right words. "Old renter. Um, Earl. The guy who lived in your place and disappeared, he was *supposed* to build a few more halls. I have hundreds more finished puzzles waiting to be hung. But no, just the two halls you walked through so far. You'll see the living room next, though, with more puzzles!" She drops her excitement into a scowl. "On the other side of the house, there's regular house rooms, blah, with puzzles, fine, but not the halls like on this side. And then upstairs, same thing, regular house rooms."

Gretchen is staring at me for a response. "Oh," I say. "So the old renter built these halls special for your puzzles?"

"Yup," Gretchen says, sucking her third grape juice and staring at me, seemingly waiting for me to give any kind of reaction. Like if I give the wrong reaction, she will metamorphose into a lethal insect and pierce my skin with the point ends of her pincher strands of hair.

She must be okay with however my face is reacting, because she sets her juice box down, Jerry hands her another, and she continues talking. "Earl, the old renter, was *supposed* to renovate the kitchen too. But now Daddy says we have to find a new contractor. Which is very hard. Very hard to find good workers. Right, Daddy?" She gives him a knowing look. Maybe a smirk? A minuscule smirk?

"Sure is," Jerry says. He's sucking on his eighth apple juice. His right arm with his Apple Watch lies on the table next to Gretchen's left arm with her matching Apple Watch, as if this pair is bound by virtual cuffs.

Again, Gretchen follows my eyes to Jerry's juice box.

"Daddy likes the width of the juice boxes, instead of grasping around a round glass. And they're safer than glass too. So we drink juice boxes."

"Oh, okay," I say. Because what the fuck am I supposed to say? There is definitely sweat on the back of my neck, and the overhead light in this windowless room is so bright, I honestly have to squint. The glare off the glass over the food puzzles creates dizzying prisms and refractions at all levels in this small, small space. The walls are not just closing in, they're inside my rib cage and compressing my lungs. I wonder if this is how captive octopuses feel in the middle of an aquarium day, when the halogens are on high at the top of the tank and all those faces and tourist cameras are flashing nonstop. My cheeks are ablaze and puffy; my eyes are dry. My throat is tight. Every surface of my skin is hot, and I want to rip off my T-shirt to cool down.

"I think I'm full," I say. I'm half done with my sandwich. When Gretchen and Jerry look at what remains, I add, "Sorry, I can't finish. I don't think I'm feeling well. I should go home."

Gretchen drops the last of her sandwich, holds her face, and shakes. Jerry rubs her back in, again, the gentlest motion. And in a literal switch, she exhales loud, which is either a groan or a hiccup of a cry, I can't tell. *Can people switch that fast?*

When she looks up at me, her eyes are red with a sheen of wet, and her bottom lip trembles.

"Lucy, I don't know how to be your friend. You want to go. I get it."

"Uh, Gretchen. I was just feeling hot. Gretchen?" Jerry's smiling at me, indicating I should keep talking. "Gretchen, hello. I didn't say I didn't want to be your friend."

Her face is warping in red pulses, but now she looks hopeful. "Really?"

"Yeah. Just, I don't know, I'm hot. 'Kay?"

"Okay," she says, seeking affirmation from Jerry.

"Lucy, maybe a bigger room with better air would make you feel better? Can we try that before you leave?" Jerry offers.

"Um," I say, shaky.

"You girls head into the living room. I'll be right there."

Gretchen cow-eyes me, waiting for me to agree. So I nod and shrug my shoulders. And again, I'm the doofus who doesn't leave the horror movie. "Okay, let's go to the living room." I fan my hands in front of my face to give myself some air.

Gretchen stands, turns around, and pushes on the thick frame of a puzzle of watermelons. A hobbit-door-size rectangle in the puzzle-filled wall opens up: a secret door.

*Mom would leave. Mom would be out of here already.*

I inventory the items in my life I'm keeping from Mom, items I never before would have kept to my core: how far I'm willing to go to live here; Gretchen's window visit; Doc Nathan, the biggest betrayal of all; and now this strange night.

*But Mom's down there, alone, ignoring me. So here I am. Here I am. Following Gretchen into her living room.*

# CHAPTER FOURTEEN

I stoop to follow Gretchen through the smallest door ever, and we enter the living room.

Bones.

Bones everywhere.

And nearly every item is the color of bone, of ivory.

Among the bones on the walls are a few square blotches of black.

I don't think I've blinked my eyes the entire time I've been in this crazy house, and I'm certainly not blinking now.

I am surrounded by brightly lit bones on the walls. Bones, high and low, all around, except for about eight blotches of black pictures.

"Daddy calls this the living room, but more like the dead room, right, Luce? With all these bones." She's twirling, as if joyous, like Julie Andrews in *The Sound of Music*.

The *dead room* is as brightly lit as the damn dining room, so the ambience is cutting and blinding, and not subdued and comforting the way Mom and I keep the lights at a calm amber. It's a painful bright light like in Best Buy or Staples, and given the subject of bones and the scattered black pictures on the walls, more like a working morgue in the hospital's basement. The fifteen-foot-high walls are filled with puzzles of bones, and no furniture takes any space against any walls. Instead, an ivory couch sits five feet from one wall. There's no rug or carpet on the hardwood floors. Opposite the couch is an ivory baby-grand piano. And on the floor between the bone couch and bone piano is a puzzle box. Sure enough, the pattern on the box is of bones, but I'm not focused on the image for specifics, because Gretchen is pulling me to walk the perimeter of the room.

"Come in, let me show you these puzzles. They're my favoritey faves!" Apparently she's done with her outburst of manipulative sad emotions, because she's exuberant and loud again. Her extreme emotions vacillate as fast as flicking a light switch.

"I'm going to be a bone doc, Lucy. Ever since Daddy got his compound fracture in his leg in the woods, and I did see his bone sticking out, gross, I've been *obsessed*. A bone doc is called an orthopedician, so I'm going to be an orthopedician. Most all of these puzzles have to do with the human skeletal systems. Cool, right?"

Gretchen didn't take one breath in the entire time she took to say this last paragraph.

"Don't you mean orthopedist?"

Gretchen snorts, a slight snarl in her nose. "Lucy, no. Please. It's an ortho *(pause)* ped *(pause)* ician." After spacing out the word in a slow education, she rolls her eyes as if I'm some ignorant, illiterate mope.

"Well, sounds like you're really into bones." *Whatever.*

"Yeah, I am," she says, and we're off again, walking the perimeter, her leading me around the room like a docent. "These on this wall are from my skulls collection. And these, here, on this wall, from my limbs collection." We keep walking, and she's talking while pointing out puzzles and collection facts. "This wall, and this is the exterior wall, which faces the forest, these are the intricacies of hand and foot bones. Twenty-seven bones in the hand, twenty-six bones in the foot. Hands and feet hog most bones in your whole body. Most all of these aren't for sale on the market, Luce. But you probably figured that out by now. Most are from photos I find on the internet and Daddy prints in high def in Boston, and then I make the puzzles with my scroll saw in my lab in the basement." She pauses her slow, instructional stride and looks back at me. "I'm really good at cutting."

I've stopped walking. "Your scroll saw in the basement?"

"Oh yeah, that's how you make jigsaws. I'm very good at making jigsaws," she says. "And I'll have to do lots of surgeries when I'm an orthopedician, so I'm getting pretty skilled at the cutting." Gretchen says all these facts in a light and informative manner, as if all she's talking about is how someday she wants to be a doctor and her father bought her—all normal-like—a copy of *Grey's Anatomy*, instead of a whole home with slit windows and retrofit maze walls to showcase floor-to-ceiling puzzles and, oh, can't forget, also a lab in the basement with a scroll saw to make puzzles. She talks like we're talking of normal things.

She resumes her instructional stroll along the exterior wall, and I follow.

On this wall, hidden among the floor-to-ceiling puzzles, are those slit windows, and when I look through, I see nothing but black night and the blackest of black pines. My skin starts to itch as I recall all those damn mosquitoes. I stall before one of the black image puzzles intermixed within the bone puzzles. This one has what seems to be an underground spiral, with different people at different levels of the spiral, which narrows to a point. Curling cursive font labels each level, so I squint to try to read.

"Dante's *Inferno*," Gretchen says. "That's Dante's *Inferno*. The only other puzzles, other than bones, in here are of Dante's *Inferno*. The different levels are layers of hell."

I abandon reading the font. I know what Dante's *Inferno* is; we read *Divine Comedy* in honors English this year.

"Did you make these too?"

"Yeah. The puzzle industry isn't into death and depressing things, like games, which are often about money and crime. Puzzles are more about fun. I had to make these. This one is an illustration titled *Inferno* from the 1400s Daddy had printed. I like the vertical alignment and composition of layered souls, stacked in hell, in this rendition."

"Oh."

Gretchen shrugs, like this is nothing. Nothing at all to have puzzles of bones and Dante's *Inferno*, normal to love the composition of souls stacked in hell. No big deal. But she's especially quiet, and her hands are clasped at her tailbone as she saunters on. Her fingers skittering on themselves. I can't tell if she truly is so nonchalant about these puzzle topics.

"So, Gretchen, question," I say. I feel my voice is finally in order.

She stops and twists fast, apparently thrilled my tone is more definite and not quivering or light, like since I entered. "Yeah?" she says, leaning in on me.

"I was wondering. These windows are really narrow. Are they the originals?"

"You're so smart, Lucy. I knew that when we met."

I wait for the answer.

She's shaking her head no. "Nope, those aren't the originals." She glances sideways to the hidden hobbit door to the dining room, and now I realize, that's the only door out of this interior space. Unless there's another hidden door. I scan quick for obscured hinges. I can't imagine this home doesn't violate all kinds of fire codes.

I'm trying to tamp down the fear rising in me, the sweat on my neck, and the closing of my throat. Gretchen appears to be checking to see if Jerry's about to enter from the dining room. Leaning in closer, she whispers, "A couple years ago, I had a 'spell.'" She says *spell* with quotation marks around the word. "Daddy calls it a spell. They locked me in a special hospital and tied me in a cloth thing so I would be still. My arms were bound."

I take a step back.

*A straitjacket?*

"Don't be scared, Lucy. I'm fine now. Daddy made me better."

As if we're ballroom dancing, she steps back into my personal space, checks again for Jerry, grabs my arms, and whispers into my face as she pulls me down to her level. "The doctors thought my spell was from lingering PTSD from finding my mom and her baby in the woods. Even though I can't really remember. They have no idea . . . Anyway, when I was in the hospital, I kept thrashing and got super mad because being tied up meant I couldn't do puzzles. And when Daddy came to visit, he saw what they'd done, and he made them free me. He gave me a puzzle, and I was better." Gretchen snaps her fingers on saying, "Just like that, in a snap, I was better."

I suddenly feel an instinct, maybe a survival instinct—perhaps this is something wild animals do to make sure they don't become some subservient beta to a megalomaniac alpha. I push my face into hers. "Gretchen, what's you having a spell and having your arms bound got to do with the windows?" This feels somewhat like when Mom tries to change the topic, but a much more unsettling manipulation.

Our faces are about an inch apart. Gretchen smirks; I smirk back. Maybe all these years on the road with Mom, living our own twisted reality, has made me immune to life's insanities. It feels like Gretchen and I are locked in a power struggle, the weirdest kind, one I have no idea how to define or how to win or shape. But I'm plowing ahead like I'm impenetrable steel. Maybe I'm steel because of my life on the run, and that's why I'm able to fight back. Or maybe I'm a stupid doofus playing with fire and I should be knocking Gretchen on her scrawny ass and escaping through that cell of a dining room and out through those crazy-town halls.

"Luce, you're no dummy. I like you. Daddy had someone change the windows so I could have more wall space to hang my puzzles." She pauses, side-eyes me, and smirks. She drops her voice. "Sort of obvious, though, right, Lucy?"

This last line is the exact type of tone Mom uses on me, the same rhetorical, grating question style she uses when she wants to assert her intelligence over mine. I bristle and twitch my nose. *Why is this conversation making me mad?*

"Oh," I say and step away from her, pulling my arms free of her grasping. "Whatever. I get it." I'm not going to give her any inches. Won't let her force a rise out of me.

Jerry walks in and flings his arms like a grand host. "How about Gretchen's puzzles, Lucy? Amazing, right? Bones, bones, bones, and more bones! Gretchen will be a great orthopedician."

I nod yes. I think about Mom's cutting humor, her way of lightening tensions or commenting on the surreality of life. She'd say something snide to lift the ominous air.

"Most dads buy their kids a copy of *Grey's Anatomy* if they want to be a doctor. Guess you're all in on Gretchen's future," I say. *I don't know who I am right now. What am I saying? Am I channeling Mom? I should haul ass out of here. Jerry is blocking the doorway.*

Gretchen bugs her eyes, and so does Jerry, and both howl in laughter.

"Oh, Lucy, of course I bought her a copy of *Grey's Anatomy*! In fact—"

Gretchen interrupts and, as she has done several times, finishes her father's thought. "Daddy got me every single edition ever printed. I keep them upstairs in my room because they're so precious. All the hardcovers with the beautiful covers."

"Every single edition in every single language," Jerry adds.

Gretchen skips to the center of the room and plops on the floor. Her apple-print dress pools around her legs. She directs me to sit opposite her. I don't know why, but I do.

"Now. Here we go. Daddy, drumroll. You need to play tonight," Gretchen says, directing her father in a tone not unlike a mother reminding her child, it is *time now* you must *go brush your teeth and go to bed.*

Jerry obeys and sits on the ivory bench to his ivory—bone—piano. He pinches ever so lightly on the tips of his white cotton gloves to pull, easy, shoulders scrunching, as if the action hurts, his gloves from his hands.

He begins to play.

In what is really fluttering pings of piano keys, Jerry doles out a "drumroll." While he does, Gretchen pops the top of the puzzle box. The homemade title on a stick-on address label says in black Sharpie, ONE THOUSAND SKELETONS, 1,000 PCS. She dumps all one thousand pieces on the floor. The image on the box is a literal pile of one thousand skeletons.

"This is going to go right there," Gretchen says, pointing to a square of space at the top corner of the wall behind the baby grand.

"First," she says, "we must turn them all picture side up. If we had different colors, we'd need to sort by color. But this is a very difficult puzzle, a monochrome, and highly difficult because where there's variation, the pieces are cut on the color line, corners are split too. And lots of pieces. But we can do this. Anyway, flip up, then find all the edge pieces, then we start. That's our methodology. I'll impose a rule on myself, okay. I'm not allowed to place a piece unless I know exactly where it goes, because I'm an expert. You can just, you know, start. After we sort first, though, as I said."

"Gretchen, I think I can stay only another half hour. I won't be able to finish this game with you tonight."

Gretchen snaps her head up. "This isn't a game, Lucy. The Supreme Court ruled that puzzles are not games." She looks down. "It was a tax case . . ." She trails off. "Whatever."

Again, I think I can't give her an inch, can't let this last abrupt lesson cause a visible rise in me. I pause, let the silence hang a second. "That's fine. I just can't be here long enough tonight to finish."

Gretchen considers my response, nods, and drops her head to study the spilled pieces. As she begins to shift pieces around, starting her idea of what to sort, and without looking up at me, she says, "No problem. Do what you can. I won't be able to stop, so I'll finish for us." She fans her fingers over the puzzle pieces and dives in to create different piles. "Daddy," she says, while keeping her fingers fanning and sorting.

"Yes, sweet pea?"

"We'll need some Nocturne Number 2 in E-Flat Major."

"Whatever you want, baby doll."

Jerry proceeds to play Nocturne Number 2 *in specific, as commanded, friggin' E-Flat Major, holy hell*, which is a slow, haunting piano song ricocheting around this bone-dead room in a way that, oddly, almost in an instant, compels me to listen, one note at a time. The crystal clarity and volume and the hypnotic, slow timing of how he plays is something I suddenly crave to hear. So I do as Gretchen instructs, and flip and sort. I'm clinging to my intention to do a little and beg out of here as soon as possible—just after a little more of the song.

As I sort, and as Jerry plays, my intention slips. I give myself another couple of minutes. And then, another couple of minutes more. The way he plays the nocturne and the next song and the next song, the very realness of the piano and the live rhythm in the room, intoxicates me, hypnotizes me, makes me feel drugged and slipping. Maybe my brain was primed to guzzle the melody, given how starved it was in the preceding awful background silence. Somehow I feel displaced from my mind, and my physical actions are commanded by the music.

This is what I feel like in working the register at Dyson's, a sedated physical hypnotism.

Gretchen and I sort and link pieces, and Jerry plays bewitching live classical. His music and our actions form an incredibly intoxicating, addicting bubble, but one edged with black, of darkness and fright. Like an addiction or an obsession you can't stop, even though it's bad. A vice. This is what I imagine watching and listening to a train hum and hum on by would feel like, in that rhythmic motion and that constant sound, like constant waves, knowing that, because you somehow know the future, the train is about to collide with a truck full of people. You can't look away, but you know you should.

At some point, I'm not sure how long I've been mesmerized, I notice Jerry has stopped playing his hypnotic songs. My phone is ringing.

"Lucy, your phone," Gretchen says, but she's not taking her eyes off the puzzle pieces. About one-eighth of the thing is already complete. Gretchen's fingers rove and flutter above pieces we've sorted, as if furious spider legs working to weave a web.

I answer but need to shake my head to have clarity and switch my thoughts back to reality. I don't even need to wonder who's calling. It's Mom. She says to come back to the house. I hang up.

"I need to go. Can I use the bathroom on the way out?" I say while standing. My legs are cramped, so I bend my knees a few times and shake them. I close my eyes from a head rush.

"Daddy will show you," Gretchen says. She's on her knees, leaning over the various sorted piles of pieces, her face scrunched in thought.

Jerry rises off his ivory bench, gently pulls his white gloves on, and walks back through the hobbit door into the cell of a dining room. "Come on, Lucy, bathroom's this way."

I follow Jerry through the dining room, down the hall with Gretchen's "earth collection" puzzles, into the kitchen, take a U-turn at the yellow island, and head back up toward the foyer through the first hall. All of the glass over the puzzles is still glaring and blinding in the bright lights that accent the length of the hall. I wince when I pass the Death March cult puzzle.

At the end of the hall, we weave around Jerry's weird tower of boxed Crock-Pots. Jerry points across the foyer to a normal-width hall in the right wing of the house. "Bathroom's at the end," he says. "You can let yourself out when you're done. I need to grab something upstairs. I appreciate you giving us a chance, Lucy."

"Okay, thanks," I say, not sure what else to say.

As I head toward the bathroom, of course passing many more puzzles on the walls, I hear Jerry climbing the stairs in the foyer to the second floor. Walking down this hall, I note all the doors are closed. At the end, I find the bathroom, and it's normal enough. Super dated with piss-yellow toilet and piss-yellow sink and piss-yellow tub, but normal. I hear Jerry walking around above me.

I'm glad Mom called. I'm glad I'm leaving. I don't know why I lost myself in working the skeleton puzzle. I finish and exit the bathroom, intending to walk as fast as possible to the front door, leave, and sprint down the hill in the dark to my house.

But I stall in walking to the foyer because I notice a door closest to the bathroom is painted ivory. All the other closed doors are wood doors. What pulls me to do this, I don't know, but I set a hand on the gold knob and clench my fist to turn.

"Don't, Lucy." I hear her voice. "Where's Daddy? He let you down there by yourself?" I look up to see Gretchen standing in the spotlight of the foyer. Light amps the glow of her white and pulsing skin and the red apples on her dress. I'm in the darker end of the normal hall. Her tone is of frustration, and she's looking up at the ceiling, as if burning anger to wherever Jerry is.

I pull my hand away from the knob. She continues talking.

"That's my special room. I'm working on something in there," Gretchen says. She grinds her jaw, again looks at the ceiling. "Daddy? Hello, Daddy, where did you go?"

She looks down to me, closes her eyes three beats, shakes her head, and when she opens her eyes, she smiles. "It's a surprise. And I want you to see it when it's all done. Okay?" Her tone is one billion octaves sweeter than when she just maliciously yelled for her "daddy" and said this was her "special room."

I walk down the hall, nudge past her, open the front door, and step out. Once outside, the *alarm lights* blaze again. Facing Gretchen in the doorway, I put on my indifference voice and ice my nerves like Mom would.

"Oh, Gretchen, question."

"Yes?"

"Why so much bacon? Do you always cook so much?"

Her eyes move past my eyes, settle somewhere adjacent to my face, off to a middle space. Her closed-mouth smile spreads. And in a snap, she's locking her eyes with mine.

"The rest is for my doggo in the basement, Luce! Old Mr. Snoof. He likes to sleep in dark and cool places. Sleeps all day next to my scroll saw. See you tomorrow, friend!"

"Good night, Gretchen," I say, and run down the hill in the dark.

I'm panting when I enter our rental.

"Mom?" I say, as I walk through the red-and-turquoise kitchen, in which no lights are on.

"Mom?" I repeat, entering the darkened living/dining room area.

Mom lifts off the couch and walks to her own room. "Good night," she says. And she's gone. She didn't wait for a response, didn't ask for a recap of my night. Nothing.

*Why was she sitting in the dark?*

I lock my bedroom window, close the curtains tight, grab Allen, curl into him, and hide under the blue-pink covers. I don't think I'll sleep tonight.

# CHAPTER FIFTEEN
## MOTHER

Thirteen. Thirteen years of driving. *Thirteen.* Her baby, *her baby, God, her beautiful, violet-eyed baby*, is fifteen. *Fifteen!* Sometimes in the dark dead of night, nights she can't sleep, she sits in her beast vehicle and stares into the void outside the windshield. She imagines she's peering into her daughter's dreams and wishes in doing so, she's able to push happy scenes and also, lessons on specific self-defense maneuvers. If only she could lord over her baby's body every single second of every single day her daughter graces this planet.

It's the summer of 2019, and here she sits again in the dark dead of night, staring into the void beyond the beast's windshield, wishing, thinking, remembering. She white-knuckle grips the wheel as if the engine is running and her foot is stuck firm on the gas, plummeting herself down the single lane of a rocky mountain road, and not as she is: parked and going nowhere, only racing in her mind.

What was it about Paul? How was it she allowed herself to black out at age twenty and allow him, allow Paul, *awful Paul Trapmore*, to impregnate her? What was it about all those drastic changes in that one week in that one summer when she was twenty? *I was only twenty.* What was it about the way she ignored some signs in the beginning? Was it her grief over Laura vanishing and Carly moving to Costa Rica and the Triple C selling that made her fail to see in real time, and only in hindsight, how Paul would suddenly appear after the sale of the camp became common knowledge to assess structures where girls slept and showered? How he took so many pictures of the property, but when girls were out playing. What was it about Paul's explanations in those few weeks of dating after the blank night, but before she knew she was pregnant, that made sense after a strange event, but were always needed to be given? *Every question I asked him, he had a vague answer.* Who was his family? *They were in a foreign country.* Where did he come from? *America, but had grown up in a foreign country.* Who were his closest friends? *Guys from college, they live all over. You'll meet them soon, babe.* What did he do on that silver laptop? *Business, nothing. Something I'm working on.* Why all the pictures? *They're needed for the redevelopment.*

Why?

Why!

As Mag sits in her beast vehicle, staring into the dark void of night, her baby girl now fifteen, an anger at herself grows so deep, she often finds herself punching her own legs. The answer as to why is obvious in retrospect—blazingly, glaringly obvious—and only a fool wouldn't have seized the puzzle pieces and built a picture in real time. Although nobody could have predicted the extent of Paul's evil. But it's her fault, all her fault, for bringing her gorgeous girl into the world by way of a blank night with a monster. She'd let her guard down, was foolish and young and whiplashed by changes, when she should have had a clear mind.

When Mag told Paul she was pregnant, Paul showed his true colors and solidified Mag's nascent suspicions that he was a monster. She remembers standing with her back to his bedroom's glass wall, the one framing a view of the sea.

"I'm pregnant," she said.

Paul jolted off his white-on-white bed, slapped her across the face, and shouted, "How many men have you fucked in the last month, whore?" Mag kneed him in the balls, ran down his floating stairs, and fled.

That night, Paul, getting nowhere with unrelenting calls and messages in which he spit his cold brutality, demanded an abortion in a very public way. Banging on Mag's apartment door and yelling he was there to drive her to the "whore clinic"—the neighbors heard, as was his intention. As for an abortion, Mag wasn't quite sure exactly why she refused, but *her* true choice in *her* core was to have this baby.

Mag alerted Camp Director Marianne, who in turn alerted Cord, the Triple C's retired marine who ran the camp's archery, tracking, and clay shooting. Cord "ensured" Paul knew he was banned from the camp "forever and irrevocably" and also banned from "any location Mag might be in or thinks she might want to be in or even dreams she's in." Cord and Mag were already close; he acted like the father she couldn't remember having, and with Paul's swift expulsion by Cord, she felt secure.

Nine months went by, and Mag's Laura was born.

Paul insisted on paternal visits; Mag insisted they be supervised. Paul threatened a lawyer but never hired one. As time wore on, he spent two hours in a park with baby Laura (and Mag watching nearby) every other Sunday and never demanded more.

Two years burned by, faster than one night.

On the day that monster took Laura, as soon as the cops were done with Mag at the station, while detectives pulled street CCTV and store video, Mag asked if she could please go change her clothes back home. The sheriff said he'd drive her and that forensics would meet them to pull her computer, per protocol.

*Of course. Of course. Go right in. My computer's on my desk in my apartment.*

Once the sheriff was done with her apartment, Mag stole away to "walk the beach." She knew in listening to the sheriff that the cops had called around and found Paul in the ER about to undergo an emergency gall bladder removal, all of which detectives verified with the surgeon herself. One detective would wait in the waiting room, and the team would later convene at Paul's Carmel house after the one detective acquired Paul's consent and house keys. This, they said, would be faster than getting a warrant, seeing as they'd already confirmed, in looking through his glass home's glass walls, that the place was locked and empty. Plus, they'd confirmed Paul was in an ambulance on his way to the ER at the very moment toddler Laura was taken at Bing's. They didn't have any physical proof or anyone's stated concerns about Paul vis-à-vis baby Laura, and so probable cause to enter without a warrant was weak. At that point, he was just the barely present dickhead father of the baby, stolen by a stranger in plain sight.

So. Mag had a short window.

And a mother's instinct is all the probable cause one needs.

After breaking into Paul's and finding his laptop, but not knowing the password, Mag hit herself in a fury to find something, anything. She sensed he was involved but had no proof. Every creak, every ocean wind shaking glass, was Paul with baby Laura, hiding in a corner.

And then she saw the note. Stuck under a pile of bills, a Post-it: *Saturdays, groceries, Bing's w/ Laura. Distracted. Crowd cover.*

So, yes, she'd been targeted. Tracked, all right. Tracked by her baby's father. Paul had sold her details, her pattern, the very ones written on the Post-it, to a person—*who?*—and that person snatched her girl.

It was simple after that. Had Paul not required an emergency gall bladder removal, the authorities might never have known. Might never have gained access to his damn computer, which showed quite clearly what Paul had done. He likely was on his way to toss the laptop and rip up his notes but doubled over in pain and was rushed to the hospital.

The timing was shocking.

Still.

*How? How could someone be so evil?*

*Why?*

Thirteen years she's been asking herself these questions, and now her baby, her baby girl, is no baby. She's fifteen. *My baby, my baby, my baby is fifteen. It's my fault, all my fault. I should never have trusted Paul. Never. I am a monster for being so oblivious. Knowing I was falling for a dangerous temptation, but going forward anyway. Ignoring signs like a fool.*

This merry-go-round with herself, these unanswerable insomniac's questions and self-recriminations have gone on unabated for thirteen years. And so, Mag once again exits her beast vehicle with no relief and no promise for sleep. She chooses instead to train her body, her only way to take her mind off horrors, and drops to her palms and toes to hold a three-minute plank. She breathes in the damp dirt; she listens to crackling fireflies and chirping crickets.

# CHAPTER SIXTEEN

## LUCY

It's noon on a Saturday, and I don't have a shift at Dyson's today. Gretchen has dragged me back to her creepy house, through her front door with the weird metal shields around the doorframe, and insisted on showing me her lab in the basement where she makes jigsaws. A week has passed since I had dinner here, and I haven't been back since. I told her we can go to her basement as long as we spend the rest of the day in the summer field in the out beyond, painting, playing Scrabble, or doing puzzles. She's agreed. She even packed us a picnic basket, which waits for us in the fossils-puzzle foyer beside Jerry's box tower of Crock-Pots.

"Why are the bags under your eyes so dark?" I ask her.

"Oh," she says, squinting in the bright light of her own foyer, "couldn't sleep last night." She doesn't expand with a litany of unnecessary facts or lessons, like usual.

We proceed down the back hall off the foyer and walk down a normal set of stairs into an unfinished basement, which is mostly huge open space—the length and width of the whole gargantuan brick fortress—except for two sealed-off rooms on each end. The lighting down here is minimal, so although the space is open, shadow pockets and draping blackness close in the sides. Feels like we're walking down a narrow hall under the line of tiny bulbs in the ceiling. Of course one bulb is buzzing and zapping and flickering. Of fucking course.

Gretchen, who is again dressed in her apple-print dress, leads me to an area under the left side of the house. Here's her lab. On a worktable is a flattened, blown-up picture of deconstructed arm bones, which are yellowing and some parts crumbly, on a gray background. Next to the picture is a dry-mount press like we had in media club at my first high school. Also on the table: several plastic jars of Mod Podge ("sealer, glue, and finish," the label says); a line of mason jars full of wide bristle and foam brushes; apothecary jars, each with different-size blades; a gigantic pair of murderous silver scissors; several X-Acto knives; a metal squeegee thing; a can of polyurethane; and rulers. A pegboard serves as the headboard to the worktable, and on the pegboard hang at least a hundred rolls of blue painter's tape, one roll per peg. Beside the worktable is a gunmetal-gray, industrial-looking mechanical tool with one blade, which looks like a buck tooth. Leaning against the metal legs of its support stand are several cuts of thin plywood and foam boards.

"Here's my scroll saw. A vintage Rockwell with a twenty-four-inch throat," she says, indicating how past the buck-tooth blade, the space goes twenty-four inches to where the neck of the arm curves and bends to hold the blade. Looks like a skinny-headed, alien-type creature in a *Star Wars* bar folding his head to his chest.

"Need the long throat to be able to turn, turn, turn a mounted picture and cut puzzle pieces with loops and voids."

"Oh."

"Don't put your fingers under the blade. That's a fine but sharp blade. You're too smart for that, right?" She gives a malicious grin, like when I left her house a week ago.

I scrunch my face and steel myself to not flinch. "You know, Gretchen, here's a rule to follow if we're going to be friends. Don't give me that creepy look anymore. And when you say creepy things, like how you're good at cutting, and how I shouldn't put my fingers under your saw blade, those things don't help our friendship."

No switch this time to manipulative emotions from her. This time she raises her eyebrows as if saying touché, or as if swallowing a game rule and accepting it. She pops her lips.

"Well, then, just wanted you to see where I make the puzzles. Oh, and in that room at the end, that's my painting studio. I know you like to paint too, Lucy." She's pointing to the far, far away end on the right side of the house. Zero light down there; I see nothing. A black hole.

"Where's old Mr. Snoof?" Seems nothing's down here but me and Gretchen.

"Who?"

"Your dog? The one you said you give the extra bacon to?"

Gretchen laughs. "Oh right. Old Mr. Snoof. He's sleeping," she says, pointing with one hand to the closed-off room in our end. She brings a finger to her lips to hold in a giggle.

That imaginary centipede is hatching poisonous eggs in my neck skin again.

"'Kay, then. Let's go outside." I start to walk back to the stairs. I'm fanning my face from the sudden flash of burning inside and out.

"Oh, wait!" Gretchen has jumped into a dark space and is rummaging in a cabinet I hadn't noticed because it's hidden in a shadow drape. She pulls out two wrapped boxes with big red ribbons. "I made you these gifts. But let's drop them at your house on the way to the field, and you open them tonight when you're in your room. Okay?"

After an afternoon in the out beyond of picnic and painting (I dragged *my* easel and paint case and a blank canvas from Peterson's Craft Store, and Gretchen seemed dismissive and judgmental about my subpar material) while Gretchen did a puzzle (and we didn't speak much)

and two games of Scrabble (in which we bickered over timing and rules, and she won one round and I the other), I'm back in my bedroom. The window is open, the breeze is wonderful, the temperature just-right warm, with dashes of blowing cool. Crickets and bullfrogs and the owl offer their night song, and the wind! The wind is rolling pebbles in the river of leaves. I'm in the amber-lit bubble of my colorful room, green in the mermaid wall puzzles, the blue and pink of the bed and curtains, and the giant red ribbons on my unopened presents from Gretchen.

Mom is reading in her bedroom. We ate separate dinners in separate rooms.

I pull on a tail of the red bow on the top box; the ribbon unfurls and slithers to the floor. The wrapping paper is plain white, and I rip that off quick. The box is a white rectangle. I pop off the lid. Within the box, and I can't believe she did this, is another box on which is pasted a print of an oil portrait of *me* scowling. *Me.* A homemade label says, **MAD LUCY, 500 PCS.** I shake the box, and sure enough, pieces rattle and slide inside. So to sum up, Gretchen oil-painted my mad face, then cut me up. One million poisonous centipedes take over my body. I throw the box on the bed, my fright-anger adrenaline driving me. I rip the red ribbon off the larger box, tear at the paper, and my mouth drops open. *I can't . . . what?* Here on this box top is a print of another oil painting. In a corner, she added a sticker label with her handwriting: **DEATH MARCH, 1,000 PCS, 2ND PRINT.**

I drop the box on the bed. Because sure enough, here she's made me a copy of the creepiest puzzle—that I've seen so far—in her house. The damn cult Death March.

"Do you like them?" I hear from the window.

I look to the open window, and here is her damn face against the screen.

*Gahhhhhh.*

"What the hell!" I yell, clawing my hands in instant fright.

She steps back from the window.

"I know. I know. Your first rule. No windows. But I had to watch you open."

*She could have watched me earlier. She wanted to make me flinch. Wanted to scare me with the topics of the puzzles and her creeping face in the window.*

"Don't do that again," I say, and slam the sash. Again, I'm furious; because of her creepy lurking, I can't listen to out-beyond noises tonight.

*And what the hell with this massacre of my face and this demon cult puzzle? I can't give her a reaction about them. Can't ever mention them.* I throw both boxes under the bed. I can't tell Mom. I won't tell Mom. *Am I trading one evil for a new evil?*

I could tell Mom. I won't tell Mom. I could refuse to see Gretchen. *But if I do, Mom will know something's up; she'll make us run. And who else do I really have?* This isolation, this suffocation, of a life with only one, a person who won't speak to me when she's a middle console away from me in a car. A person who asks me if I'm capable of thinking when I ask if a diner sells cake. A person who hovers over *her* iPad to ensure I watch only an approved show or movie and don't surf the web. A person who could, this very minute, barge in this bedroom and demand I pack, drag me by my arm, push me out the door, and tell me I'm *foolish and reckless* for wanting to keep a *meaningless* job at Dyson's—never mind how happy working the register makes me feel. *Hush, hurry, don't speak, move. No lights, take everything. Leave nothing. Hush, don't speak, before anyone sees,* she'd say.

Perhaps my sin is seeking life outside our box, because now the drug of freedom, of *engaging* with others is, is it? Is it an addiction? To want to break away. If I can control Gretchen, if I can prove to who? Prove to myself? If I can prove I can control Gretchen and make her a comfortable friend, or at least understand her creepiness, measure the doses of her into doled-out vials of time—a constant buzz and not spikes of craze—such that her sudden appearances and taunting gifts don't scare or anger me, maybe I'll prove I'm capable of protecting myself. And I can be free of running.

I won't tell Mom. I will make this work with Gretchen. No matter what.

# CHAPTER SEVENTEEN

Late July, and it is "wicked hawt," as Sandra Dyson declares all day, every day now. Milberg is packed with tourists. "Gawd love 'em and theyah Masshole, New York, big-city money."

She's gone off with her husband, the chief of police, for their anniversary and left Dali and me to close up Dyson's for the night. As soon as she left, Dali switched Sandra's constant jazz to Ice Cube's "Good Cop, Bad Cop," and even Jabo the hanging octopus, made of reclaimed parts and named for jazz, is relieved about the faster beat—this is how I interpret the glint of moonlight off his big, watchful eight-ball eye. Perhaps the fat moon shoots a ray through the skylight, hitting Jabo's literal pool-ball eye just right—but I do take it as his wink of approval, and also encouragement, which I need tonight. I'm smiling, Dali's smiling, even though we're so hot and sweaty. And I've got a secret burning fissures on my lips that I want, no, I need, to tell Dali before my mouth breaks, or my heart breaks, or my mind dissolves my resolve.

Dali and I are sweeping up the remains of the workday: literal Great Katherine Lake beach sand from the soles of tourists' flip-flops. The front doors remain open for a stubborn breeze that won't show, so the interior is thick with the scent of roasting turkey, which normally disperses in moving air. We dragged the outside planters, stuffed with massive, flowing red petunias, to block the doorways, and stretched a rope across as well, so all these late-night customers who keep pulling up know we aren't selling any more fancy cheeses tonight. Plus, we already squared the register drawers with receipts, and I am not about to go do ugly math all over again—especially not when I need to *say something*.

I've never worked alone with anyone before. Especially not Dali. Sometimes, he and I have taken breaks together. Sat under the lace-sunlight-throwing tree out back and shared a pack of cheese and crackers for the fastest fifteen-minute allotments known to physics, but not talking much beyond whatever store gossip was swirling around in the given day. In other words, he hasn't tried to get personal with me ever since that day he caught Gretchen scaring the shit out of my exploding crackers when she came back from puzzle camp.

And because he hasn't pushed, and because he has kindness in his green pupils, and because I've caught him thrusting his hips while mouthing Ice Cube lyrics into the broom handle like it's a mic because I think he thinks I'm not watching, I'm pretty sure I can trust Dali. I'm pretty sure he's a Jenny, which is a new concept for me, because he's a boy.

Watching him dance and sing and sweep is like getting a hit of my current addiction: freedom. The truth is, if I'm being really, truly truthful, I've been emboldening myself all summer for this chance—a chance I now realize I want to take with an alarming desperation. I'm standing in the belly of an open plane about to jump, and I don't care whether there's a parachute or not—this is how bad I want *this, this freedom, this, whatever this is*. And yet, because the moment is here, a clotted, curdled feeling clogs my throat.

*Do this, say it, don't stop.*

I force my feet, which feel thirty yards away from my pulsing, over-active brain, to take a physical step toward him, as though the physical step will clear the clot in my throat. I must, I want to take this step, this definite betrayal of Mom. Another in my series of betrayals. Perhaps, I justify to myself, she wants me to betray her; she is pushing me away and expects me to defy her, because she still has not talked to me much all summer. She still eats alone, ignores my efforts to cook for her.

Dali sees me approaching. Stops his dance routine and smirks.

"Whoops, you caught me," he says.

"I need your help," I say.

I close my eyes, shocked I would trundle ahead so fast. In my mind, my brain is skipping, as if my feet are skipping, tripping me on the floor.

He stands straight, leans his mic-broom against the shelves with mouth-blown bottles of oils. A rainbow confetti of light sprinkles the aisle's floorboards from the moonlight shooting through the colorful glass. *What is Dyson's like at Christmas, when fluffy white snow softens outside and Sandra decorates the door with green wreaths wrapped in red ribbons? I bet it smells like cinnamon-spiked cider in here. I bet, I bet she decorates a fragrant balsam in the corner by the penny candy. Will I experience Christmas in Milberg? Will I be gone?*

I can tell Dali's unsure what to do next. So I repeat, "I need your help." This time my voice cracks, and I can't believe I said it twice. I can't believe I really mean this. It's like my intentions are sick of me stalling, unwilling to wait for me to be ready. Like some instinct is demanding that time is of the essence. *And I don't know why.*

Dali pulls his iPhone from his back pocket and turns the Bluetooth volume down on the music. I look up at Jabo, and his eight-ball eye is still winking, encouraging me to take another step. This is so monumental, I am no longer in control of my secrets, and my eyes tear up, shocked that I would betray Mom so fast, scared in thinking on Christmas at Dyson's and how I don't think I'll be here—I won't have that warmth of a cozy season, a fireplace with stockings like in the movies. This is overwhelming. This act. This act of defiance.

*What am I risking if I speak? What am I risking if I don't?*

*It's not specifically Milberg I want. It's a settling I want. A free life lived in truth.*

I'm crying when I acknowledge this desire so full and deep in me, it is me. I see myself.

Shivers, like ice shards, are on my inner wrists and in my veins, shake my arms. But I'm not cold, I'm crying. I'm truly crying.

"Oh my God, what's wrong, Lucy?"

"I don't have blue eyes," I say, but more like a choke of words and not a fluid sentence.

What I've liked about Dali since I met him are his quick assessments. Like when he very first saw me and gave me a respectful wink of friendship. Like when a pregnant lady's water broke by the artisanal breads two weeks ago and he didn't rush to her, like everyone else did, tripping over themselves like a rash of fools. Nope, not Dali. He whipped out his phone and dialed 911 before even raising his eyes to the chaos.

"Okay. Come here. Actually, go out back. Let me lock the doors. It's okay. Whatever is wrong, I will help," he says. "Go. I'll be right there."

In this moment, I'm happy Dali is a couple of years older than I am. And now I'm recalling, he's got years on his mind he shouldn't have. I'm reminded of one personal conversation Dali and I did have under that lace tree out back. He was a foster kid, and his family adopted him after fostering him for a year. He hasn't had a rough or abused life, he said, but he's felt "displaced" in a "borrowed family." In the boys' home, he'd seen bad things happen to good kids. Even though he's been with his foster-adoptive family since he was five, he still remembers, because watching a friend leave for a foster all happy and hopeful only to return a month later with greasy hair and a permanent withdrawn stare, night terrors and screaming from any amount of touching, haunts you forever, he says. So he knows, he knows, he said that once—maybe he planted the seed, actually, waiting for me to be ready—but he did say once that he knows "how important it is to respect someone's secrets, because they own their secrets, and you own yours."

This is how Jennys speak; this is how damaged people speak. They don't have all the answers, and the best part is, they never pretend they do.

I scrunch my shoulders, wipe my eyes, stand up straight, and pull all of Jabo's moonlit, cosmic strength into my core. I'm going to do this. I'm going to at least do half of this. I won't quit. I will be strong. I walk fast to the back as I hear Dali dragging the planters outside and shutting and locking the doors.

The floorboards creak as he runs to meet me where I stand, leaning against the hall wall, across from the staff cubbyholes, where Dali now lands and leans. He's smart enough to not touch my body or condescend to my weakness from a couple of minutes ago. I'm no longer wet in the eyes, and my face is set on my intention.

He nods.

"Go," he says.

"Okay, then."

He folds his arms, solid in watching my eyes and my mouth for when I'm ready to begin.

"Right. Wow. I really pulled off that Band-Aid," I say.

He waits, still not speaking unnecessary words, nods again, like a wise confessor, ready for anything. *He's a bona-fide Jenny, all right.*

"You can't tell anyone. I mean it."

"No shit."

"No shit?"

"Lucy, I'm not an imbecile. Whatever it is you got to say, it's between us."

"All right. I'm trusting you, then."

"Good. You should."

I suck in my lips, scroll through the pick list in my mind of items I need help with. The biggest of all is my true identity and the location of my birth father. Another item on the list is a core angst I'm willing to acknowledge in the center of myself that I no longer believe Mom's stories, but I ache to even consider that angst, because although I know I'm living a surface lie, I refuse to believe the lie is subdermal, that she is a lie, and thus, my whole being to my core is a lie. The idea of exploring such an option makes me physically cringe in front of Dali, and now I'm feeling a clotted throat again.

"Hey," he says. "Look. Whatever it is you think you need help with, if it's hard to say, maybe just start with the easiest part?"

It's almost like he can read my mind. *Is this what it means to have a real friend?*

"Um—" I'm pressing my lips together. "So." I breathe in hard. Exhale. "Right. Look. How about this. Can you help me look up someone on the internet? And um, I like your idea of the easiest part first. Maybe don't ask why?"

Left unsaid is that I don't have an iPhone, just a shitty flip with no internet. And left doubly unsaid is that I could go by myself to the library and do the research on a public computer. But really, I need someone to be my proxy fingers and type the words. I need help—that's the truth. I need someone. And admitting that much was the biggest, hardest step. Last night, hives formed a necklace around my neck in thinking of this moment, knowing we'd be working together tonight. But I showered off the welts, and I keep them away now. *I need help, I need someone: the toughest six words to say in the very center of myself. But I did it. I did.*

"You got it. What's the name?"

"Gretchen Foulin. *F, O, U, L, I, N.*"

Before I can think further on whether this is a good idea or not, he's jamming the name into Google. I don't want to tell him this is the name from my birth father's family or my birth father's last name. I actually can't believe I'm finally taking the step I promised I would never take to investigate my own past.

*How many betrayals am I willing to allow? How far will I go to keep this? This place?*

"Hmm," he says. "Weird."

"What?"

"I'm not finding anything. Not even a profile on Facebook. And that's weird. How do you spell Foulin again?"

"*F, O, U, L, I, N.*"

"Yep. That's what I did. Let me try just the last name."

He's typing and pressing, and I've moved to his side of the hall. We're shoulder to shoulder, watching for mysteries to be solved by one click. He's tall, I'm tall, but he's enormous compared to my frame. He smells like turkey and spices, and so do I.

Ancestry sites and name-origin lists pop up. Dali scrolls, and we read the synopses together.

"Seems Foulin is a Scottish or French name. Does that help you?"

"Scotland and France don't really have laws against women, right? Like they're not exactly uber-patriarchal societies where women have no rights, right?"

"All of modern society is patriarchal," he says. "Unless you're a bee."

"But I mean like oppressive in a bad way where women have zero rights and are trash."

"Definitely not France. At least laws-wise. And Scotland is wicked religious, but they're not exactly known for stoning women for driving, if that's what you mean."

I'm so confused right now. None of this makes sense. For years Mom has beaten into my brain that my birth father's ancestral country treats women as chattel, third-class citizens, sometimes lower than livestock. I'm pretty sure I've read about women in France in open relationships. They don't dream of getting married as the end-all, be-all happy ending like in America, is what I think I read somewhere. So. Pretty sure French women are free. I don't know much about Scotland, but like, they're free too, I'm pretty sure.

"Please try Gretchen Foulin again," I say.

He does. And still nada.

"Try," I hesitate. "Try Foulin and kidnapping," I rush out before my hives stop me.

Dali shudders, stalls, looks at me. His forehead is dancing between furrowed brows and a twitching eye. "Lucy?"

"You promised to not ask or say anything."

He winces his chin to the side and swallows, appearing to accept a promise he now realizes he might have made with a devil, and to which he is honor bound.

My heart expands to take up my whole body and is beating inside my arms as Dali types.

Just like Mom said, there are no kidnapping reports involving any-one with the last name Foulin. I walk away from Dali, cradling my skull, so completely disappointed at finding nothing. And now I'm startled by how disappointed I am. I don't know what I expected to find. What specific answer about myself I thought was going to be so easy to uncover once I finally got the guts to look. But I know for sure, like an unrelenting need, I must find the truth. Right now, though, I have no other clues, or none I'm willing to tackle tonight, and I'm exhausted, wishing my heart would slow the fuck down before I puke. There is that metal box Mom keeps, the one I've never opened, that she guards like an archangel, guarding the meaning of life.

I could expand on what I'm thinking and say all this to Dali, who I feel waiting for me to turn and speak, but I squat to the floor, still cradling my own head. I could tell him about the metal box, ask him his thoughts. I could take out my contacts, show him my violet eyes.

There is one thing tonight did prove. To sum it up, finding noth-ing on the name Foulin, confirming my suspicion that the name has no apparent origin in a country unfriendly to women, means my sus-picion is true: Mom lied. I've studied her construction of lies for years, and now I'm sure, Foulin and the way she told me, wanted me to be distracted by the name, yeah, Foulin is a fucking lie. Proving Mom a liar to me about me, that was the one item on my pick list of items, the core angst I have, that I wasn't sure I was ready to face. But now I know. I know in my jellyfish guts.

And I can't go further than that tonight. Can't open any more boxes, real or figurative.

Not tonight.

I turn around to Dali.

"Lucy, what is going on? Why would you have me look up kidnapping? And what is this with your eyes not being blue?"

"My eyes are my eyes, Dali. Please don't say anything."

"Come on. I'll drive you home. You're too upset. I can't let you leave like this."

This is kind of Dali, I know. But I can't have him driving me home. I bolster all the strength I have left tonight to make him think I'm fine to ride home alone. I switch to a false levity. "Oh, you think I'd be caught dead in a truck with a turkey on top?" I've been teasing Dali all summer about his tiny red truck with the Dyson's mascot turkey on the roof. The truth is, I love that damn truck. I would gladly be caught dead in such whimsy.

He flips up his hands and smiles, knowing best not to push.

I could tell Dali where I live, that I lied on the employment form. I could tell him the bargain I made with myself to control Gretchen Sabin's creepy lurking so as to stay in Milberg. I could tell him how my life is a lie. I am a lie.

But right now I'm grabbing my backpack out of my cubbyhole, and I'm walking to the back door toward the bike that used to belong to the Sabins' old renter, the vanished one. And my mouth is sealed.

Core strength, I'm finding, the kind to withstand hurricanes of hurt from your closest loved one, is not available like an easy-peasy bag of quick-set cement. It doesn't magically appear when you start your period, and thus your womanhood, or just like that when you want, when you imagine you need adult fortitude. No. Core strength and conviction require me to slow down. Require layers of rebar and steel mesh, after finding ground of granite rock bed, and waiting for framing and then the setting of concrete, the kind that takes hefty mind machines to mix. I've done some groundwork, I've set what should be an achievable, albeit difficult, goal: living in freedom and truth. It's just I need to calm and set, wait for the frame of my strength to find shape. No more work tonight.

# CHAPTER EIGHTEEN

A whole summer has passed. All of July and now most all of August, and life has been generally okay, with an undercurrent of odd and awkward patches. Gretchen and I are like two adversaries, stuck on a deserted island, who must cooperate in order to survive. I can't say our time together is wholly unpleasant, although most often it is horrible or horrifyingly creepy. But I do enjoy constructing puzzles. The hypnotic rhythm, the satisfaction, the meditation, the reward of making a disconnected picture come together.

Not once have I mentioned the puzzles Gretchen gifted to troll me; they remain under my bed. With her, I have to constantly set stark and deep and definite boundaries. I am always making rules of engagement and pushing back on her aggressive stares. One rule is that I will not go inside her house, and she may not come into mine. I require we meet in the out beyond, where I can bring my easel and case of paints, and she can do her puzzles on a quilt. We usually end an afternoon in a sort-of-civil Scrabble match that actually often ends in her screaming and me storming off. I warned her to never come to my window again or we'd move.

She hasn't tried to sneak up on me at Dyson's again, and frankly, she never, ever goes to town, that I know of. So all her prodding to go bike riding for snickerdoodles when I first moved here, I'm not sure what that was about. It might have been her way of trying that out with someone, and when I rejected her, she came up with a new game in her mind.

I've watched Jerry bring home bags of groceries from Boston, which I suspect someone else places in the trunk for him. And I've watched Gretchen carry them inside. Jerry drives to town early in the mornings, I notice, and comes home with to-go coffee and a wax bag of snickerdoodles, which Gretchen leaves the house to take out of the car for him.

Anyway, because she doesn't go to town, and apparently Jerry doesn't talk to anyone, nobody knows where I live—I never corrected the address of my falsified employment application—nobody knows I have any connection to Gretchen or Jerry Sabin. Except Dali, but it's been a month since the night I asked him for help, and I haven't been ready to discuss any more with him, and he hasn't pushed. We just sit together during breaks under the lace-throwing tree in a silence I'd equate to medicine, medicine for me, and medicine for him too. It's possible, maybe, he knows where I live and isn't calling me out, because I think he might have followed me home that night I left so upset—he may have trailed me to make sure I was okay. Maybe.

But I trust him to keep my address a secret if he did. Like a true Jenny, he's willing to accept who I am as is and the little I can offer. I own my secrets; he owns his.

Also, at Dyson's, four times this summer, I've had to duck and run to the back room when bearded-man Dr. Nathan Vinet came in. Nathan's son, Thomas, he's around town all the time, so I lurk in the shadows of the eaves when I leave Dyson's, find my bike fast, and race home. But I've avoided both of them so far this summer. I work a scattered schedule of part-time hours, so he can't have tracked me, if he's tracking me.

School is going to be a challenge, but not impossible, because Gretchen won't be going. Dali advised that Gretchen, as I suspected, indeed has no friends. Apparently, people consider her a freak but stay away from her, which is easy, because she's never away from her brick fortress, anyway. They think she's cursed and can cast spells or is otherwise bat-shit crazy. And the "spell" she had a few years ago. Well, the *spell* got her expelled, for "the safety of the students." According to Dali, she freaked out at school and stabbed a girl in the back with a No. 2 pencil and then stood on a chair and screamed about how the girl was screwing the devil in visits to hell each night.

Word is, after her hospitalization, Jerry Sabin chose to allow Gretchen to educate herself through online courses. Nobody understood the structure, the management, the oversight of such a situation, because he wasn't homeschooling her, so the local coalition of homeschooling parents couldn't certify his curriculum was on the up-and-up. But then again, nobody cared to push too hard. Gretchen was gone away from their kids, and that's all that mattered.

So to sum up, seems some of the kids in this town really do believe all the *Blair Witch* crap about Gretchen and the brown hermit house behind Gretchen's brick fortress. I've told Dali whoever believes the *Blair Witch* crap is immature, and he agrees. But I can't get into any of that, so I work at Dyson's, sit with Dali on breaks, go home, read at night in my room with Allen on my lap, and meet Gretchen in the out beyond for blips in the in-between daylight times. We're not together all of the in-between daylight hours either. Gretchen naps a lot during the day. The bags under her eyes are often black and frankly, fixed now, having gotten worse over the summer. She says her face looks tired because she can't stop doing puzzles and can't sleep.

Mom still won't look at me. In fact, if she catches sight of my face straight on, she definitely winces. We live on separate islands in the same house. Her limited sentences in my direction are terse, using the least number of words possible for a complete thought: "I'll leave tuna casserole for when you're done with work"; "I'll be in my room, working on my book. Be quiet"; "Cash your paycheck, put the money on the counter. I'll stow it in the metal box."

Today is the start of our last week of summer vacation. I'm on my way to the out-beyond field to paint while Gretchen does a puzzle. In walking through our red-turquoise galley kitchen with my easel and paint case in hand, I pass Mom buttering toast by the stove. She doesn't look up, as I turn sideways to slip past her. I say nothing and take great care not to allow the long apex of the easel to brush even a hair on her—don't want any eruptions. She doesn't move to open the door for me, so I juggle all my stuff and bumble my way out.

It's been like this all summer between us.

A whole summer of not talking with Mom, a whole summer of Mom imposing her steel, ice silence, her mood, is the longest we've ever lived through one of her cold spells. But that's not the only thing that's different about this cold spell. Normally, I'd sweat this tension, suffer hives, and cry alone at night. I'd find ways to make her relax, fall on myself to make sure she knew I knew she held all the control. I'd make her big, happy, homemade lasagnas and plated chicken masterpieces, displayed like artistic sculptures on heated plates with perfect garnishes. I'd cook her reassurances. I'd serve my subservience. But ever since Dali proved my worst fear, that our life is a lie and the lie is subdermal, I've been living with a low-grade, growing anger in the very center of myself. Like I'm some iceberg, staring down the hull of a boat I aim to gut. So perhaps it's possible this cold war steeling the air between me and Mom is a mutual division between us. Perhaps this time, I'm holding the line too—and I note, I haven't erupted in hives this summer, despite her chills on me. I know my reason for being cold, and I suspect Mom knows I have a reason and knows she's not the only one to divide us this time. Maybe she's guilty. Or maybe she's frightened. I still don't have the resolve to discover more.

🐦

Gretchen and I are in the out beyond. I'm standing at my easel with a canvas, painting the fern garden that I imagine is full of fairies. My case of paints is open and on the ground. Gretchen's sitting on a quilt, working on a puzzle of leg bones. She's again in her apple-print sundress, clean and crisp, like always. I know she wants me to ask why she wears only this dress. I don't ask; I don't give her inches.

"My dad didn't break his leg in a rock trap," she says. "I was mad when he said that to you. You don't need those details."

All summer, Gretchen's and my relationship has been in bursts in this field, blips of time during the day, when I'm not working at Dyson's and she's not napping. So Gretchen hasn't had much of a chance to say weird things to me. And when we do meet up in daylight hours, once she gets into a puzzle, she's transfixed. She's always brought a puzzle with her to our meetings in this field, so we actually don't talk much.

But she's agitated today. She's mentioned twenty times how I start school in a week. This is the first time she's abandoned a pile of puzzle pieces to say much at all.

"What?" I say, dropping my brush away from the canvas. A plop of green acrylic hits the toe of my sneaker. I lower my other arm, which cradles a palette with a well of water in a cup holder. The water spills over the edge and onto the grass.

Gretchen stares into the wedge of woods where the trespassing signs and electric fence and traps start.

"I could show you," Gretchen says, still looking to the woods.

"Show me what?"

"Where, how, Daddy really broke his leg."

Gretchen's expression is stone. And her skin isn't pulsing. The bags under her eyes are so deep, her face is like a rotting jack-o'-lantern. Her typical loose hair is limp.

"There's so much you haven't seen in the woods yet, Lucy. So much you don't know. Don't you want to see where Daddy really broke his leg?"

"Just tell me, Gretchen." More green plops on the toe of my sneaker. More water spills from the well in the palette, which is basically vertical, since my arm has gone slack.

*How did Jerry break his leg? Why would he lie? I remember Gretchen seemed bothered when he explained the rock pyramids. Why does she want to drag me to her creep-ass mosquito forest?*

Gretchen looks down at her puzzle and shakes her head. "Nah. You have to see."

I stare at her, she stares back, and neither of us blink, because this is a standoff. It's feeling like I need to set another rule. I tighten my arm back up, making the palette horizontal again. I raise my green-drenched brush and dab paint where I'm painting thick ferns.

"Well, I'm at Dyson's in about a half hour, so if you're not going to tell me, then I guess I won't find out," I say. "In fact, I need to get ready to go to work now."

"Do you know who you are, Lucy?" Her eyes seem vacant, and she casts them, in a somewhat lethargic manner, back to her puzzle. She strokes a piece. Meanwhile, my entire insides have flared awake, and I could shoot off like a rocket.

"What?"

"Nobody knows you and Susan live here. Some people might have a vague awareness Daddy and I have renters, but everyone's too consumed to track the comings and goings of transients, like you and Susan, and tourists. But will that change once schools starts?" She doesn't appear lethargic anymore; now she's like an overpopulated beehive on a weak branch, full of nervous anger. Her eyes are beaded, her body twitching, skin pulsing. She's huffing short exhales through her nose.

*Why is she so confident nobody knows we live here? Why is she desperate and angry?*

"I'm leaving for work."

"I think you should call in and come see where Daddy broke his leg for real."

I can't give her an inch. I can't let her get a rise out of me. *She's fucking with me and wants to scare me in her horror woods full of rumors and mosquitoes—this game is actually one-sided: Can she make me flinch, not who will flinch first. Am I focusing too much on her crazy world and not the fact she questioned my identity? My real life? Did she ask if I know who I am?*

Why do I put up with this craziness? Why do I meet up with her? She feels like a tempting game. Or she and I are a tempting game. Two trains about to collide. A beautiful horror. An irresistible, bad, bad addiction. I can't look away. Who else do I have in my life, anyway? I'm no prize. My own mother is a liar and winces to see me. Nobody knows we live here. Dali kinda does, but he's about to leave for college. Do I know who I am? Yes, I know who I am. *But I don't know who I really am.* I'm not sure I have the core strength to find out yet.

# CHAPTER NINETEEN

I packed up my paints, folded my easel, and when I hurried past Gretchen on the quilt, she bit at me, chomping on the air, and then forced a haunting laugh when I jumped. As I fast-walked to the uphill path between the fairy fern garden and the cattail patch, she kept watching me. I played at ignoring her, even though chills shook my arms. I nearly dropped all my paints.

I'm at my register at Dyson's. Been here a half hour.

"Lucy," someone says behind me, across at the other register in the center circle, the one to my back. I turn and see Mom, checking out with the other counter girl.

*Why didn't she come to my register?* She's buying flounder and a block of swiss cheese.

"Mom?" She hasn't come to Dyson's once this whole summer. She's left me notes to pick things up and bring them home in my backpack. And actually, why is she even here? She's always so strict about not being seen together in public.

"Lucy," she says. And now the other counter girl is leaning to the side so Mom can see me straight on. I'm ignoring my own line of customers. "I forgot to grab olive oil. Can you please grab a bottle? You have your backpack with you, right?"

"Yeah. No problem," I say, but I can't hide the confusion in my voice or on my face.

Sandra had commented when I clocked in, "Mutha natcha's bitchin' with wind taday." So the two store doors that are typically open in the summer are shut. Which means every time a customer comes in or out, a bell jingles. As I go to ask Mom if she wants me to grab anything else from the store to bring home, the bell jingles. I reflexively look to the door.

It couldn't be worse. My greatest fear is true.

In walks Dr. Nathan Vinet with his son, Thomas, the two damn people I've been avoiding all summer. Of course they waltz right in on the first day Mom comes to visit. And the first time all summer she's looked me dead in the eyes and not winced.

I have nowhere to scoot to, can't shrink, can't crouch behind the counter, can't slink to the bathroom to hide—I'm a jellyfish in a tank, an octo in a pool, Jabo fixed to the ceiling, stuck. Dr. Nathan Vinet has caught my eyes and is walking right up to the circular counter in the center of the store. Mom follows my sight line.

"Well, well, well," Dr. Nathan says, walking toward me. Thomas meanders down the vintage penny-candy aisle.

I inventory my face, remind myself I have my blue contacts in. I wish Jabo would swoop me in his eight wooden arms and swallow me into the ceiling. My silver jellyfish pendant isn't transporting me to another dimension, so what good is it to believe in magic.

*Fuckkkkkkkk.*

"The girl from the lake in Indiana a few months ago, and here we are again. Finally. I tried to ask the last time I saw you. I've been trying to find and ask you all summer." He pauses to snap his fingers. "I remembered who you look like. My son, Thomas—Thomas, come here. Anyway, the resemblance is remarkable. Do you happen to know—"

Mom cuts in. "Lucy, can you come here? Sorry to interrupt your work." She's paid the other counter girl and walked backward to stand between the breads and the cheese case.

Nathan and his son, Thomas, are dangling at the edge of the circular counter, the place where we keep all the tourist brochures. Nathan's mouth is open since Mom interrupted him midsentence. Thomas is standing by his side with a fistful of Pixy Stix. They're duplicates, father and son. One with a beard, one without.

I motion for my line to move over to the other register, and I exit out the notch farthest from the door, and thus, farthest from the brochures and Dr. Nathan and Thomas. Mom is waiting for me by the cheese case. I wish Dali was watching all this from the deli, but he finished his shift an hour ago so he could pack for college. Some slack-jawed new dude mans the deli, and he's not paying attention. He's slicing Dyson's famous turkey in such a mindless drudgery, I think the guy thinks he's being tortured. *Tough day at the deli.*

*Yeah, well, New Dude, it is a tough day at the deli, but not for you. For me.*

My heart is thumping, and I'm sure I'm about to break out in mind hives. Mom has gone all glassy-eyed. The oxygen in Dyson's is aerosolized steel.

"Lucy, honey," she says, with a fake smile and in a low volume so no one can hear, "you didn't mention you saw the man from the lake again, here. Why?" Her smile is so phony and fake, but nobody would know that watching us.

"Don't lie, Lucy. I see you reeling around, trying to come up with an excuse. Why would you keep this from me?" Her tone is homicidal.

I don't dare look back at Nathan and Thomas. And neither does she.

"You know what," she says. "Never mind. Lucy, you'd be wise to go in the back and take a bathroom break. Until this man and his son leave. Now. Let's not make a scene."

158

A whole week goes by, and Mom doesn't speak to me. I've avoided Gretchen completely by upping my shifts at Dyson's or hiding in my room with the window locked and the curtains drawn. Mom doesn't make me any meals or eat any of mine. And I try hard to make her favorites from scratch. She leaves me no notes. No terse comments in passing. She is always in her room and quiet, so she's plotting.

Sure enough, today, a week later, as I'm strapping on my helmet to go to work for my last evening shift before school starts on Tuesday, she calls me over to the ranch's front door. I walk the bike toward her, the helmet on tight.

"Lucy, this will be your last day at Dyson's. We'll be leaving tomorrow. I trust you will stay away from that man."

I don't try to avoid running over her toes when I pop on the bike to pedal off. She jumps back into the doorway just in time.

# CHAPTER TWENTY

The sickening anxiety, the nausea, the horrible clotted throat I get, the hives on my skin from worry—all of the dread rushes over me in waves as I continue to work my *last* shift. She wants us to up and flee again, leave for our twelfth state. But I can't live like this anymore. I can't breathe her steel air anymore. I recognize how much I don't want to run by the fact that I realize I'd rather live in Gretchen's crazy fortress and stay locked in our *Can she make me flinch* game than get in that damn brown Volvo with Mom.

I think I must be the reverse of a runaway. Stressed in a situation so bad, I plot to stay, while finding a way to make her run. When I think this, worry hives erupt on my face, and my scalp itches so bad, I have to use all ten fingers to scratch. I've had to race to Dyson's staff bathroom three times this shift. Here comes Sandra.

"Lucy, if yah sick, I'd prefer yah go home," she says.

"No, no. I'm not sick. Not sick at all. I think I'm just hot with the doors closed tonight," I rush to say. "Has the wind died down? Can we open the doors?"

For a full week, ever since Dr. Nathan busted me in front of Mom, Milberg has been trapped in a strange, hovering weather pattern of relentless wind. Today the wind is the strongest it's ever been, and the forecast says tomorrow might be worse.

Sandra looks at me like I'm a lunatic for asking to open the doors. The wind is so loud outside, whenever a customer walks in, the pressure drops and sound swirls in the song of a hundred Dementors sucking air and rattling their breathing, as they swoop in and fly circles within the circular space above the registers up to Jabo, whose eight arms spin as a constant fan around his center head—since that's how the artist designed him to function. Normally, I'd be intoxicated by this sound and the whirring motion of Jabo. Rocks pin the stacks of tourist brochures so they don't blow down Penny Candy Lane.

I'm not ready to go home yet. Not ready to force a stay instead of a run.

As I work, I consider how much I'll miss this rhythmic hypnotism. How I'll miss my chance to find another real Jenny at Milberg's high school, which starts on Tuesday, so close I can almost touch Tuesday. I can't wait for Tuesday. I want to start school so bad and seek out a real Jenny so bad, I find I can't think of anything else. I'll put up with anything to not have to run again. Even Gretchen. Even Gretchen and her weirdness I can live with, like she's a diabolical sister I have to put up with—like in a beach rom-com I've read. *She's just weird family* is how I'm telling myself to think of her in this untethered and unrealistic fantasy I'm holding of staying while Mom leaves. At least I have some semblance of some real life here in New Hampshire. *I have a job. I have a home. I have someone to hang with near my house. A nice field with a fern garden of fairies. Allen is comfortable in all the colorful rooms. The wind plays symphonies for me at night. I'm so close to finding out if there's a Jenny at my new school. I don't want to leave.*

My anger grows. Grows so high and screaming in my brain, when I pedal home in the dark at the end of my shift, I think I reach speeds as fast as the Tour de France. Riding under the dark canopy on the country road between the village and the dirt road to our rental ranch, I don't flinch from any noises in the woods along the way. I don't worry about the fact that there are no streetlights and the only things saving me from a car hitting me are my bike's reflectors, several reflector stickers on my helmet, and a light I mounted on the handlebar.

I hit the dirt road that leads up to the ranch. I pass through Bottle Brush Forest and over the little creek. I stand on my pedals and arch forward to ride up, up, up the dirt road. The lights are on in the big picture window on the back of our rental, the light throwing an amber cloud over the blueberry and holly bushes below. Wild wind washes out whatever sounds my gnashing teeth are making and the roll of my tires on the gravel.

I throw the bike and my helmet on the ground by the Volvo. My black hair whips all over the place as I take hard, pounding steps to the ranch's front door. It's 9:30 p.m.

I note the chains are off the roller doors to the long, low shed, which makes me pause.

*Did the old renter come for his tools?*

*I don't fucking care if the old renter came for his fucking tools.*

I storm to the house and slam the front door so hard it hits the kitchen wall and bounces back in my face. I push hard again, step in, and the door crashes closed behind me.

"What the hell are you doing?" Mom shouts. She races in from the dining/living room.

"We are not moving!" I yell.

"Yes the hell we are. And lower your voice."

"You lower your voice."

When she sees me, when she looks at me this time, me glowering and standing tall, she winces. She shrinks and takes a step back toward the red stove, like a recoiling snake.

"You look just like . . . ," she hisses.

She turns quick and storms deeper into the house. The grapes lamp and the red cardinal lamp are lit, creating bubbles of amber that feather the dividing line of houseplants. The giant green paintings hang in shadows. I race after her as she passes the red love seats with no sign of slowing down. When I reach the end and am about to turn to her bedroom, she slams the door in my face. I hear the dead bolt lock.

"Don't," she says through the door. "Don't you dare come closer, Lucy. You go and pack. Go to your room and pack. I'm going to pack, and then I'm driving to get our cash at the place in Connecticut. I'll be back by eight a.m., and you better be rested and packed."

"No."

"Dammit, Lucy, we are leaving in the morning. You better be good and ready. I'm leaving in a half hour for our cash."

She's never let me drive with her on the nights she leaves to collect our cash from the multiple places she says she's stashed it around the country. When we left our tenth state, we didn't need to get any cash, and I suspect that's because she'd already planned to leave and had taken off on a day trip while I was in school one day—some cash hiding place in Chicago, I think. She's always made me stay behind and locked away wherever we're living when she goes to get cash. If a detective were to ask me for incriminating details, I wouldn't have one clue where or how she gets our cash. And right now, I give no fucks about any of that business.

I think I stand a good, long, literal five minutes outside her bedroom. I listen to her throwing things. I hear her scraping hangers on closet rods and pulling boxes off shelves.

"No," I say again. And I think she must be surprised I've been standing here so long.

"What?" she shouts through the door.

"You go by yourself this time." Which I realize is an irrational thing to say, because I can't afford the rent on my own. I'm just a girl.

I walk back down the hall, turn into the red-turquoise kitchen, and open the front door. I hear her racing toward me.

"Where are you going?" she yells.

But I've stopped short, because standing and staring at the front door from the middle of the parking area is Gretchen. Her hands are behind her back. It's not like I caught her close to the front door about to knock. She's standing smack-dab in the dark space between the ranch and the low, long shed. She stands still and staring, like she's been lurking and listening this whole time. Of course she's in her apple-print sundress, which, in this wind, swishes and swirls around her knobby knees. Her stringy hair slithers around her neck.

An angry train is roaring up on my backside, and creepy Gretchen is ghosting in front. I don't flinch. I do not flinch. *Don't flinch.*

Gretchen waves and offers the goofy, grinning smile she gives whenever she sees Mom.

Poised between the most fucked-up versions of Scylla and Charybdis, I make my choice.

"I'm sleeping over Gretchen's tonight!" I shout, while jumping out of the doorway. My hair is writhing in the wind.

"Lucy, get over here," Mom says.

"You've got your errand you need to do. I don't want to be alone tonight."

Gretchen pivots sideways, watching me and Mom. She says nothing. But then, catching on, says in the sweetest tone, "Ms. Smith, I hope it's okay for Lucy and me to have a fun sleepover before school starts. I'm sorry if this upsets you. Sorry."

"Come on, Gretchen," I say. "Let's go."

I. Do. Not. Fucking. Care right now to know why Gretchen was in violation of Rule No. 1 to not creep around the ranch property. I'm already halfway up the dirt road to Gretchen's brick fortress, and Gretchen's trotting to me. My black hair flies everywhere in frying strands. In this moment, I like feeling like I look like Medusa, and that fits. Gretchen's oil portrait of Mad Lucy is tame in comparison to the rage on my face tonight.

# CHAPTER TWENTY-ONE

Gretchen's bedroom is the first room at the top of the stairs. This is only the third time I've been in this house. On the way up, she suggested we go down her weird puzzle halls and into the bone-inferno "dead" (living) room again, but I told her, while stomping mad up the driveway, there was no way I was going down weird halls with her. Things are better between us when I'm frank and blunt and brutally honest. She knows exactly the things she says and does and the items in her life I think are creepy. So I'm not a phony fake with her. And as long as she can take my honesty and boundaries and rules, and keeps coming back regardless, then she and I can continue our kinda-like-tolerate-hate, who-flinches-first relationship.

Whatever.

I'm furious tonight, and I need to find a way to convince Mom we're staying.

*We're staying!*

Gretchen's bedroom is just as fucked-up as the left wing of her house. Big surprise.

One whole wall of shelves is dedicated to the hundreds of hard-cover copies of *Grey's Anatomy* Jerry bought her. The *Grey's Anatomy* wall serves as a wall-size headboard to her twin bed. I guess I'll be sleeping on the floor. Although there should be about ten more guest rooms in this joint, so maybe I'll sleep in one of those. Across from Gretchen's bed is a wall filled with puzzles of Dante's *Inferno*. The exterior wall is filled with puzzles of creep-ass porcelain horror dolls with soulless black eyes. Great. So to sum up, when Gretchen goes to sleep at night, she has human muscular and skeletal systems behind her, hell in front of her, and possessed dolls on her right side. The opposite wall, the interior wall with the door into the upper hall, is the only normal thing—until you look inside the open closet. Hanging on a long rod are twenty-five versions of the same apple-print sundress Gretchen has been wearing since I met her.

Fucking lovely.

Gretchen follows my eyes to the closet of same dresses.

"Einstein and Steve Jobs, and Obama too, said that wearing the same outfit cuts down on decision fatigue. More brainpower for my puzzles and games and painting," she says.

"Can I take a shower?" I ask.

She directs me across the hall to a bathroom, which, like the one on the first floor, hasn't been updated since the seventies.

When I finish, I see Gretchen's left me one of her nightgowns: white cotton and several sizes too small. But I'm a rail with mosquito-bite boobs, so her glorified napkin fits fine enough up top. The length, however, is all wrong; the hem lands between my knees and my crotch, like a minidress. I wear my obligatory bra—which is more like an Ace bandage—because the fabric on this white nightgown is sheer. I'm afraid of running into Jerry.

I scooch across the hall to Gretchen's room, but she's not here. I think I hear noises in the belly of the house, maybe the piano playing. I would have figured she'd be up here and in my face all night, excited to have me finally sleep over. She's been asking me to sleep over all summer. I think she's asked a thousand times.

There's a note on Gretchen's bed.

*"Lucy,"*

*I don't want you to move.*

*I hope your mom chills out.*

*I heard you yelling in the house.*

*Oh, and p.s. Sorry, but I know who you are.*

*I figured it out. Do you know who you are?*

*I think you don't know who you are.*

*Come to the "dead room" if you want me to tell you what I know.*

*I'm doing a puzzle. We can do a puzzle all night.*

*Or you can sleep in my bed.*

*—Gretchen*

What?
*What?*
*Do I know who I am? Does she know who I am?*
*And she's down there doing a puzzle?*
*Why did she put my name in quotes? Like Lucy's not my name.*
The silence in this room is weird silence, like the first night I came here. And there is no piano, like I thought I heard. No noise. Nothing.
I can't breathe in this soundless house.
*Wait a minute. What?*

I read the note again.

My hands are trembling. This is sinking in.

*Does she know who I am?*

*Who am I?*

*Aren't I fake-name Lucy? Mom's never told me my real birth name.*

*I never did get the guts to run any more searches on Foulin. What's that Dickens quote—"We forge the chains we wear in life." Is that the quote?*

*What did Gretchen discover?*

I sneak down the foyer stairs. I'm not quite sure what I'm going to do, where I'm going to go. But I'm walking down Gretchen's stairs on tiptoes. When I reach the second-to-last stair and am about to step into the fossil foyer, a noise bangs at the end of the hall to the right—the one that's a normal width. Another bang from within that hall, and I'm pretty sure the noise is from behind the ivory door Gretchen told me not to open on the first night. The piano starts up in the belly of the house to my left.

A haunting echo of her note plays in my mind: "Come to the 'dead room' if you want me to tell you what I know." *She wants to bait me down her mazes. She wants to trap me. She wants to make me flinch.*

I jump to the foyer, nearly collide with Jerry's tower of Crock-Pots, which hasn't moved all summer, pop open the front door, and dash outside in the wind.

Some instinct is pulling me back down the hill to Mom. I suddenly need to find her.

*Do I know who I am? Who am I?*

I left my clothes in Gretchen's room. I'm in her white mini nightgown. No shoes. My pendant bangs on my chest.

I'm running down the dirt road to our rental ranch. The wind howls around, in and out, up and over the blueberry-holly hill between Gretchen's and the low, long shed, the sounds morphing into blooms of screaming, as if each blueberry bush is a blowhole, exhaling agony inhaled through the mouths of the holly mounds. The hill is the earth in death throes, dying.

When I reach the parking space between our ranch and the long, low shed, I see the Volvo is still here and my bike and helmet are dumped on the ground. Meaning Mom hasn't left to grab a stash of cash in Connecticut yet. This may be a good sign. Maybe she'll listen.

The chains are back on the long, low shed, and I'm not delusional. I'm not seeing things because I'm emotional. I know for sure they were not there when I got home.

Everything is all wrong, and the wind is raking so hard through the cattails, I imagine a machine speed-grating aluminum foil. My hair whips in my eyes and mouth.

I find the door locked, so I kick the brick by the door where we hide the spare key. I enter the red-and-turquoise kitchen, which is darkened but for the pin lights on the stove hood.

*Is Mom sleeping?*

There are no sounds inside this house, but at least here I can hear the whipping wind, unlike inside Gretchen's airtight, soundproof brick sarcophagus. I'm barely dressed, and my bare feet track dirt through the kitchen. Mom's not sitting in the dark on either of the red love seats. All the fun lights are off. I head down the hall toward Mom's bedroom, and Allen races under my legs, startling me, making me trip.

"Allen," I hiss-whisper as I catch my balance by palming a hall wall.

I turn to Mom's room to find the door open, a small lamp by the chair in the corner on, her bed made, and no one here. The key to the metal box is on top of her dresser. Every article of clothing of hers is packed in the open suitcase on top of the bed; her closet door is open to show it's been emptied. Our two boxes of keepsakes are packed and stacked on the bed. The metal box is on top of one of them.

*Mom is never separated from the key to this metal box. She never leaves the box out in the open. Where is she?*

I race through the house to my bedroom. No Mom. She's not in the kitchen. Not in the dining room. Not inexplicably crouched between the row of potted plants. Not in the living room. Not in either of the white-tiled bathrooms. She's not in any of the closets. And she didn't hide herself in the hipster-antique armoire. I look out the front door toward the long, low shed, which is dark and shut and still chain locked. Nobody's out there. She's not pacing the parking area. Not stalking around the cattails, which whip against each other and the lime snake-grass like the patch is in a melee of a gang-on-gang sword fight. Mom's not waiting in the brown Volvo. I race back to her bedroom.

Next to the metal-box key on the dresser is her burner phone. I realize I left mine in my pants pocket up at Gretchen's. *Mom vanished. Left her phone and the key and the box.*

I think my heart is going to explode.

I grab the key and the metal box. Everything is wrong: Mom's missing, Gretchen says she knows who I am, and the damn shed was unlocked, now locked. I pop the lock on the box and lose my balance when I see the contents. I've stumbled backward to the chair in the corner and fallen to sitting. The open metal box is on my lap.

There's no cash in this metal box. None at all.

What I see are papers, lumped up as if covering bulky items.

I unfold the first paper: a birth certificate for a baby girl, born March 16, 2004. *My fake papers put my birthday at March 26, 2004.* The baby's name is Laura Bianchi. The mother's name is Gretchen Bianchi. The father's name is Paul Trapmore. *Is my real name Laura Bianchi?* I thought my birth father's name was Foulin, not Trapmore. And, and, and, oh my God, *Gretchen. The mother's name is listed as Gretchen. This is why Mom freaked out. Liar.*

Under the birth certificate is a newspaper clipping. The headline says, Two-Year-Old Kidnapped from Bing's Superstore. There's a grainy security photo of a person in a hat and a mustache. I push past all the other folded papers and newspaper clippings in the box because I feel lumpy, nonpaper objects at the bottom. Sure enough, I pick out a fake mustache and a squished baseball cap tightened into a roll, the bill crushed and held rolled by several rubber bands. I remove all the rubber bands, expand the hat, and hold the bill. In comparing this hat to the one in the security picture in the newspaper, although the picture is blurry and features undefined, they are the same. The same exact hat. The same embroidered *B* on the cap. The caption on the picture says, If you have seen a person matching this image, please contact Carmel Police Department at 1-800-555-1533. I scan the article for details. The mother, Gretchen Bianchi, was shopping with her two-year-old daughter, Laura Bianchi, when a man or woman in disguise snatched Laura. There's another color picture in the article, and this picture is high-def. The caption says the woman is the mother, Gretchen Bianchi, like on the birth certificate.

Gretchen Bianchi has violet eyes.

The baby, Laura, has violet eyes, the article says.

Gretchen Bianchi has long black hair.

Gretchen Bianchi is tall.

Gretchen Bianchi looks like me.

I look like Gretchen Bianchi.

Gretchen Bianchi is my mother.

Susan Smith, the woman I know as Mom, has brown hair. She always said I look like my birth father.

Who is the woman I call Mom?

Who is the woman I call Mom?

I clutch the box to my chest, suck in all the boiling air, close my eyes, bend at the waist, and fight through a panic so fierce, the pressure might pop my arms off at the rotator cuffs. My face is fire hot, and I'm sure I'm full of so many mind hives, my skin will melt off my skull.

Still clutching the metal box as if I cradle my own actual head, I race out of the house, down the dirt driveway, through Bottle Brush Forest, and to the country road. My bare feet slam onto pebbles, and

I'm sure I'm cutting them. But I don't slow. I don't stop. I'm wearing just this white nightgown. I'm immune to whatever chaos the wind is throwing, because I am chaos itself.

I'm on the pitch-black country road now. A thick forest surrounds me on both sides of the windy road, but I move on. I move fast. I ignore howls of wind through the trunks, the sounds racing in the trees beside me. I ignore the scraping and scratching I'm sure I hear, screechy animals keening louder than the wind, so they can't be real. *They're not real.* They could be real, though; they could be screaming fisher cats, could be a hungry mountain lion, could be a pack of coyotes. Could be a nursing cub and a growling mother bear. Could be Gretchen, racing like a beast in the woods, driving a motorized scroll saw, aiming to pin me on the flat plate and cut me into a human puzzle. Could be a whole team of serial killers and rapists. All of them. All of nature and all of evil, running beside, astride, behind, everywhere around me in the dark forest.

The road dips, and I'm tripping, I'm running downhill so fast. I don't slow. Soon I'll have to use this momentum to hurl my body up the coming hill. I can't see a thing in front of me. Can't hear anything but whooshing wind and screeching and scratching. I know which way to go by the feel of tar on the soles of my feet and the momentum of going down. Down is the correct way. Soon I should be heading up. Up the hill, which will lead to a view of the village.

*Where am I going?*

I'm racing to the police station. *Go to the police.* I didn't take time to dress or put on shoes or pop on the bike. I left Mom's cell on the dresser. *I left whose cell on the dresser?*

*Who the hell am I?*

*What am I clutching? I'm clutching a metal box of lies.*

Still on the downward part of the country road, that scrabbling in the woods to the right is not only getting louder, but is morphing, I think, maybe, into a recognizable, single sound, and not just a cacophony of night noise in high wind.

But it is so nasty dark, the wind hissing loud and wild, pricking hair in my eyes, and my emotions so insanely untethered, my senses are scattered. I can see nothing, and I hear no individual sound in singularity.

And yet.

This one single noise in the woods will not be denied. It's busting through whatever environmental mental soup I'm in and is gaining closer, racing through the trees. Snapping sticks while shouting, "Lucy," the noise rolls to me in a scream-groan-crackle.

And now that the shouting is distinct above the howl and hiss of wind, I see a pinprick of light bouncing, extinguishing behind trunks, returning, and bouncing more. Whatever the light is, it is affixed to whatever is racing through the woods and toward me, scream-groaning, "Lucy!" as if pulling my name from a deep, scarred throat.

The scream is malevolent, bloodcurdling, and guttural. It is not bellowed in caution or fear for me. The scream is a mad ache, murderous, one meant to stop me from leaving at all costs. I imagine spit accompanies each utterance of my name from this frothing mouth in the woods. A half-formed demon.

My body moves before my brain accepts danger. I'm hop-skipping to a backward run.

# CHAPTER TWENTY-TWO

Whatever concocted fears of being alone in the dark, on a forested country road, I may have engineered in sane times have come true in this night of total insanity. Somehow I've fallen into an evil black hole. The only thing I see is a pinprick of light that moves along with a racing demon, who aches out my name as if my name is an eternal pain.

Whoever is screaming my name, whatever is screaming my name, could kill me, drag my corpse to the gangly pines, and feast upon me there, because there are no streetlights, and nobody's on this country road except me. My bare feet are covered in sticky pine needles, and several pebbles jam my toes. Even if the wind wouldn't drown out my screaming, there are no homes close enough to hear. Maybe the demon wishes to frighten me. Maybe the demon wishes to save me. Steal me. Hurt me. Kidnap me. Kill me. I'm running backward. My bare feet burn.

The demon with the light breaks through the line of forest on the right, and as it is lit sideways to me, I watch it scamper to the uphill portion of the road. But because it is just far enough away, I can't make out the person wearing the light. The light goes out. I hear running toward me in total dark.

Skip-stepping backward up the hill I just came down, my feet slam into rocks; I'm sure my soles bleed. I'm too frightened to turn and run properly, too frightened to place my back to whoever comes my way.

I'm a slow-frozen, frightened rabbit; this person is an unflinching predator.

I stumble when the person nears enough I hear her breathe.

The light flicks back on, and I fall on my ass, but I clutch the damn metal box to my chest with one crooked arm like losing it would be to lose my own head. My protection of this box makes my fall that much worse, because I've got only one hand to brace myself.

Lording over me is Gretchen in a headlamp. She's exhaling through an open mouth, dragging phlegm and a dark hiss as she does. If she had saber teeth, I'd be punctured to death for sure. The bruised bags under her eyes are horrible shadows on her near-translucent face, given the bright light of her headlamp. I'm sure her pupils are pools of blood, she's so worked up in a rage.

"Lucy, stop! Why would you run away? Why would you steal my nightgown? Why would you leave while I'm making you a surprise in my surprise room for you? Why?" Her tone is hysterical, her voice so hoarse and so full of bitter hatred, and her body shaking so uncontrolled, I honestly think her insides are burning.

I'm crab-crawling with three limbs backward away from her, still clutching the box.

"Why would you leave me? Why would you run from your friend, Lucy?" Spit does indeed fly from her mouth when she groans out my name. "Stop!"

But I don't stop, I keep half crawling. I don't have the time it would take to stand before her, because now I notice, she's holding a long, white stick. Or is it a bone? A leg bone? Is she raising it so as to clobber me? I can't tell precisely what this object is because she settles it behind her back as she walks in a lean over me; I'm still crawling backward on the road.

"What's in the box, Lucy? Is that why you ran? I'm not an idiot. Does it hold who you are? You didn't need a box to tell you. I searched for 'violet eyes and lost girl' the first night I went to your window. I've always known."

I stop.

I swipe-kick at one of her scrawny ankles so she trips. She drops whatever long stick, or bone, was in her hands. It clatters to the ground and into the dark.

While I stand, she picks up her weapon—I'm sure a weapon—and races into my space. I tower over her. Her headlamp shines in my eyes.

"You knew?" I ask, bewildered. "You didn't tell me? Didn't call the cops?"

"You're an idiot. You really never looked, did you? You could have always known."

"You kept me to yourself. You could have helped me."

"I am helping you. You need to come back to my house now. There's things for you to see. I am your friend, Lucy. I am your only friend."

"You strapped on a headlamp and ran through the woods to stop me, Gretchen? Screaming like a psycho to scare me."

She closes her eyes and shakes her head, mouthing, "Psycho, psycho, psycho. Gretchen Sabin is a psycho. Psycho." It's as if she's reliving a taunt by swallowing the taunt, over and over. She slits her eyes open and, tapping her headlamp, says, "How else would you move through the forest at night, Lucy? Huh? I told you. There's things for you to see. We can go back the way I came. Remember? The logging road that leads to the hermit's house? There's other forest paths to other surprises. And in my house, there's a surprise for you there too."

I'm walking backward again. And I think I must be near the turnoff to the ranch, near Bottle Brush Forest, when she raises the stick-bone, and, at the same time, a car appears from the direction of the village. Its headlights illuminate its distinctive shape, a shape familiar to me. I jump up and down and wave my one free hand.

"Here, here," I'm yelling.

I may have taken a lifetime to look inside this damned metal box for truth, but I know enough to take an escape hatch the second it appears. Because I know if I don't fast-grab this chance to leave, I'll vanish for good. Gretchen's eyes are firecrackers, her lips are wet with spit, and a low growl gurgles from her throat.

She lowers the stick-bone, shuts off her headlamp.

"You'll be back, Lucy. What about your precious cat, Allen?" Gretchen says as I feel her whisk past me in the dark and run up the dirt turnoff through Bottle Brush Forest.

The familiar car, a tiny red Toyota truck with a turkey on top, is gaining on me. It skids to a stop on the other side of the road. The door opens. And my big, tall savior steps out.

"Lucy, what the hell is going on?" Dali asks.

I'm not going to the cops. The only thing I know is how to run. I want the whole world to disappear away from me. And Dali will keep my secret. He's honor bound.

# PART II

# CHAPTER TWENTY-THREE
## MOTHER

Gretchen Bianchi, that's who she is, and that's who she reminds herself she is every dawn as she push-ups and knee-bends and planks through her first daily routine. Her sister Carly calls her Maggot and Magpie and Mag, so she thinks of herself as those names too. But her name is Gretchen Bianchi. *Gretchen Bianchi.* And she's been searching for her precious daughter ever since that monster took her thirteen years ago from the baby-food aisle at Bing's Superstore. Hasn't seen her since. *Who took her?* is a question she asks herself a thousand times a day. *Who did Paul sell details to, to steal her? Who? Who on the dark web bought those details?*

Ever since bankers turned the Triple C into an upscale, year-round resort for people of all ages, added the luxury hotel as well, Mag has served as second-in-command at the Activity Center—in the summers only—supporting the lead instructors. She socks away her summer pay to use as gas money for her beast camper so as to drive and search for her baby girl the other nine months of the year. It would be easier to tell her four sisters, her special Carly, this is where she is each summer, but she can't bear to hear their arguments that she should return to them. Rational arguments that she should stop her search. *No. Never.*

Cord is his name, and he's the master archer. A seventy-three-year-old marine and law-enforcement veteran with hearing loss. Cord had started as the recreation director in his early-fifties retirement when the Triple C was a girls' camp, so Mag has known him forever. He's the same old Cord who bounced Paul out of the camp with "stern warnings." The VA outfitted him with state-of-the-art hearing aids, twin Cs that cuff each ear and match his thin, but still-present, sandy hair. Mag loves working with Cord most out of all the marine veterans.

At the end of this last June, Cord waited for Mag at the mouth of the Activity Center driveway, waving her on where to park her beast camper, which was her regular summer spot, right next to his one-room log cabin, the one he's lived in all along. The hydrangea bush he planted over his beloved dog's grave years ago was the height of a mature elephant and divided Mag's camper and his cottage with a wall of blue floral pillows.

This last June, Mag was a week late in starting her summer shift.

She parked and jumped out to hug Cord. He's been like a father to her all these years.

"Where you been, lady girl? I was afraid you wouldn't return this year," Cord said, stepping back from the hug but holding her arms. He had to look up to see her face-to-face, her being all legs and torso. The man was still fit, tanned, and appeared twenty years younger. Mag looked forward to the steak frites and red wine they'd have for dinner, as that was how they always kicked off their summers.

"Had some camper trouble in Colorado and, while I was waiting on a part, got mixed up in a course on clay impressioning and sculpting. Real cool. Sorry I'm late," she said.

"You're insatiable, lady girl. I'm just glad you're here. Reservations are booked solid all summer, and I need you. Also, we need to talk serious over our steak frites tonight."

That night, the start of her summer, Mag and Cord enjoyed dinner at the staff campfire pit, which overlooked the resort's lake from a high bluff—as if they were king and queen on their thrones, presiding over their subjects: the water's surface and a loon couple with their three hatched chicks. The night sky was bright blue with a full moon and no clouds. And the air was warm, a perfect match to her own body temperature.

Cord fried potato wedges in a seasoned cast-iron pot over their campfire. So perfectly crisp and salty, Mag devoured them fast.

"Cord, we need more fries, 'kay?" she said while cutting into her slab of fire-cooked steak, which took up most of the steel plate she rested on her sitting legs.

"Got a story for you on those loons," Cord said, pointing at the loon family cutting Vs on the glassy surface of the water.

"Here we go."

Cord laughed. "Yeah. Here we go is right. That bastard eagle tried to snatch one of them babies last week, yep."

"I'm pretty sure she's a mama eagle, Cord, and she probably just wants to feed her own. Nature," Mag said, chewing her steak.

"Yeah, yeah, nature. Look, here's the drama you missed. Eagle comes swooping, flying circles over those babies and the mama loon. And from right there, right by where the river washes into the lake, that dope father loon comes screaming, walking across the water, wings spread as wide as a pterodactyl. He was honking mad, so loud he interrupted a fancy hotel wedding up in the field. Seriously, the minister had to stop the ceremony."

"Wow. Wish I hadn't missed this," Mag said, smiling at the way Cord spread his arms to mimic the dope loon father. "Why are you calling daddy loon a dope?"

"He's a dope sometimes. Keeps dropping fish. Not efficient like the mama loon. Watch him this summer. But look, when he protected those babies from the eagle, he was no dope. Guess what he did after he came screaming in and after breaking up the wedding?"

Mag misses these dramatic nature stories from Cord all nine months of driving alone around the country. She settled her hands to brace the plate on her sitting knees and waited for him to tell her what happened next.

"So," Cord said, "that crazy loon son of a bitch takes his loon wife and three babies and nests that night under the eagle. Tree right next to the eagle and the eagle's baby chicks. You know what the loon's message was, right?"

"What?"

"The message was 'Look, bitch, you come around my baby loons again, I will take your baby eagles.' Now that is your nature right there, lady girl."

"You serious? What's Audubon say about this?" Mag asked, showing skepticism.

"Girl, I saw the whole show with my own eyes! I might be a deaf motherfucker, but I'm not blind."

"You are a deaf motherfucker." With a grin, she took a swig of her red wine in the copper cup and set it back on the top of the white Yeti cooler she was using as a side table. "Where's my fries, old man? You can't stall cooking to tell me these stories."

"All right, all right. First, we need to talk serious. I warned you this morning," Cord said.

"You better not tell me you're dying or some shit. I'll track you down in hell if you try to leave me."

"Oh, don't I know. No, no, nothing like that."

Several fireflies flashed reds and yellows in the space between their L.L.Bean camp chairs. Cord paused from fussing with his fry pot, and Mag stalled her knife and fork. They smiled.

"Seems the fireflies are happy you're not dying on me, Cord."

"Sure do. I'm going to miss those fireflies," Cord said, pausing to create a serious and solemn mood.

"Miss?" Mag dropped her silverware to the plate. It felt to her like her heart had crawled straight into her throat. She couldn't do the Triple C without Cord. She lived for her summers, teaching with Cord. There was something, she didn't know quite what, but something about allowing herself a couple of summer months at the Triple C seemed *permissible, forgivable,* maybe even *necessary. Important.*

"So listen. Now hear me out and don't say no right off. Okay?" Cord said.

Mag reached to her copper mug of wine on the cooler. She took a swig as her answer, a way to settle the loud beating heart in her throat.

"Okay?" Cord said.

"Go on with it already, old man."

"Look. I get it. You know I get it. I know you need to drive around searching for your girl. I've always supported you. You know that. You're like Mr. Loon, doing all the crazy shit to protect her baby. I know you think you need to drive around."

"I do. And yes, I need to keep searching." Mag shifted in her chair, balancing her plate of steak, straightened her back, and clutched her copper mug with both hands to her chest, preparing herself to weather another lecture from one of her loved ones on why she needed to stop this driving around already, searching for anything that would lead to her baby.

"Now, hear me out. You owe me that much, especially if you want more of my world-famous camp fries tonight. Look. It's been thirteen whole years, Magpie, and your detective has your phone number. You check in with him all the time. It's gotten to the point where it's just plain senseless to keep living the way you are. And I'm sorry, this is Cord's Tough Love 101, and you know I think of you as a daughter. Honey, this has gone on too long."

Mag interrupted with a groan.

"Okay, okay. Here's my point. Stop the groaning. I see you fidg-eting and you're about to jump in the lake and join the loons. I get it. Hear me out. Hear me out. Here's the thing. I have a job offer to run the, what do the owners call it, yeah, their Games and Ground Division, year-round, on this real wealthy family's estate. Drumroll. Outside Milan."

"Italy!" She slammed her mug back to the surface of the Yeti-cooler table.

"Yes, Italy."

"You're nuts. You're going to, what? You don't even speak Italian."

"Don't need to. They're fluent in English and, I'm told, so are all their many guests. I want you to be my lieutenant. They're paying huge, Mag, and you'd have housing covered. A nice little villa in the Italian countryside. And look, nothing would change with respect to your contact with the detective."

"Oh, Cord. Yeah, no way. No way I'm leaving the States. I could never live with myself."

"But you always say that you listen to the universe on where to go next. And maybe this is what the universe is saying to you now: go to Milan."

"No. Nope. Detective doesn't think they took my Laura out of the States."

"Detective Clue Bag doesn't know his dick from his thumb, and you know I'm right."

Mag breathed in deep, stared out over the movements of the floating loon family. Normally, she'd have laughed over the dick-versus-thumb comment. She shook her head.

"I do love you, old man. And I'm honored you'd ask me to be your lieutenant. Means a lot. A whole lot. But I can't stop searching for her. Not until the day I croak, and frankly, I'm still going to haunt this earth searching for her for eternity after that."

"Oh, girl," Cord said, setting his hands on the arms of his chair. "All right, then. Okay. I understand. But fair warning, I'm going to try to wear you down by the end of the summer."

Again, Mag looked out over the lake and considered the ripples around the movements of the loons. In rising from her seat, she patted Cord's knee with one hand while holding her plate in the other. "Night, old man. See you in the morning on the range."

"No more fries?"

"Nah. I'm full. Night."

The next day, Cord and Mag readied the hay bales by tacking fresh paper-linen targets, organized the different-size arrows in different buckets, tightened bow strings, and worked several resort groups through their archery lessons. Cord didn't raise Italy again, not even when they were alone at the staff picnic table, eating from a fancy charcuterie board, left over from a day wedding on the resort's upper field.

For the next week, Mag drove her designated golf cart to the end of the Activity Center's dirt road to the clay shooting range, because the lead instructor, a big bear of a man who went by one letter, D, had had an appendectomy. Cord was off working other jobs around the resort.

In her second week, Cord raised Italy again, and she brushed him off with a sigh and said she was going to work that week in the staff fave: the treetop adventure/bird bingo course. But when Cord raised the topic, slightly, just the word *Italy* in the third week, she met his eyes and didn't wince.

On August 9, Mag asked Cord if they could have a steak-frites dinner at their campfire pit, without the other instructors. Again, the night was bright blue with a full moon, and the lake was calm, except for Frank, the resident beaver, who was doing figure eights in a back float. The night was warmer than in June, and there were no biting bugs. A piney scent with a dash of cinnamon plumed in the air around their camp chairs, due to the spices Cord threw on the fire.

Mag once again rested her steel plate of steak on her lap and a copper mug of wine on the Yeti-cooler table, and Cord was again fussing with his pot of fries off to the side, so it was as if their June conversation had frozen in time and here they were again, resuming in August.

"So when would we have to leave for Italy, if I said yes? And if I'm miserable after a week, I can leave, right?"

"This isn't slavery, Mag. You can leave whenever you want."

"Well, not really. I'd be letting you down, and you'd have to start looking all over again if I go and then quit."

"I haven't spent a second considering anyone other than you, and so far, you've said no. So probably wouldn't change my effort. This ain't the kind of gig you post on some job board."

"Oh, so you think I'm going to break down and say yes, then, don't you?"

Cord nodded and winked. "Here's what I know, lady girl. I know you're smart, and I know you're fearless. I know you follow what the universe tells you. So yeah, I do think you'll say yes. And I also think that in that never-resting squirrel brain of yours, you've fixated on the fact that I said this wealthy Italian family speaks English and will have lots of English-speaking guests. I bet you think there could be a lead in Italy with as much potential as all your random driving around this country. And I happen to know—I know you, okay—I know you're tired of the life you've been living and you're lonely. And lastly, I know you have a thing for hairy, bearded men, and your quarry in Italy will be abundant. Plus, you're an Italian Greek."

"You think you know me, old man?"

"Did I say that?"

"Yeah, you fucking said that."

"Oh yeah, I did say that."

They both laughed.

"I'm chewing on all this, so don't push me. I'm probably going to stick with a big fat no. Okay? But you can make me extra steak fries tonight, thank you very much."

That night, Mag changed into her black bamboo-cotton pj's, bent to enter her low-ceiling bedroom, crawled into her camper bed, and lay awake, staring at the faux-wood ceiling. She thought on Cord's comments about how she always followed what the universe said. In other words, she always followed her instincts. And because she always followed the universe, her instincts, Mother Nature, whatever, one way to look at her life, she considered, was positive. The freeness of it. The constant new landscapes. Living out the wild idea that she could pick up and go wherever her beast camper would take her upon any whim she might have.

She still paid for her apartment—which she kept practically empty—with her share of the wrongful-death settlement for her parents' deaths. She needed her home base to stay frozen to the time her daughter was taken. The settlement also provided enough spending cash, enough to get by. So . . . yeah, looked at one way, her life of following instinct and whim was ideal.

One time a whim told her to attend a Ray LaMontagne field concert and somehow, she's unsure how exactly, she made friends with one of Ray's groupies and found herself watching Ray from backstage. She thought she could marry Ray, for his solitude alone, and pile on his attractive, brooding aura, his obvious genius, his poetic lyrics, his medicinal voice. Sometimes she thinks she could settle down again, with a man with a beard like Ray's, seriously sexy tattoos on his forearms like Ray's, with a man who condones silence and nature and freedom and equality. Absolute equality. This mythical, perfect man would not mind the opera and would be as irresistible in a tux as he would in faded jeans and flip-flops. She could maybe picture settling down with a man like that. And wasn't there such a guy once, or close enough? Some bearded man who stayed at the Triple C with his young son years ago. Hadn't she talked with him late at night on an overnight camping trip along the river, Mag their paid guide? And wasn't he one of the one hundred souls she'd trusted to tell what she was really doing with her life? Told him about her stolen daughter and how she would look just like her.

Wasn't there such a man? And wasn't he bearded with blue eyes? And didn't she mean to give him her full name and phone number the next morning, but then a resort emergency called her away and another of the staff had to guide the man and his son back to the Activity Center? Right? And then he was gone? What was his name? Was he a doctor? From the East Coast?

Maybe another mother would have shouted constantly in the media, social media, to everyone she saw that she was in search of her stolen daughter. Maybe another mother would have plastered posters everywhere of her baby's age progression. But Mag concluded that doing so would only drive the monster deeper, would lead to her baby's appearance being altered, to her being hidden farther away from her. No. Being loud and stomping in the woods and emitting your scent was no way to hunt. She'd decided to let the monster grow complacent; she'd decided to trust her true identity and true motives to a select few who passed her trust test. The bearded man with the young son on the overnight Triple C camping trip, he was one of the ones who'd passed her trust test.

She rolled in her camper bed, this way and that, and couldn't find any comfort, so she found herself straight on her back again, staring at her bedroom ceiling, which was only three feet from her nose. Her toes hit the base of the bed, and her head scraped the headboard.

She strained to stay on the idea that her nomadic life had been good, positive. How she's alone, sure, but no hermit. She's no nun, no saint, at least by puritanical American standards. She tries so many things. So many pursuits—intellectual, strange, physical, and otherwise. The surf lessons in Santa Barbara. The hip-hop classes in Boston with the real hip-hop teacher at a real dance academy. The winter she joined a jug band in Savannah as an unnecessary accessory to clink a triangle at the end of their songs. The spring she cut strips of squid as bait for a crew of fisherwomen off Martha's Vineyard. This June's visit to Colorado when the whim of the universe told her to take a key-clay impressioning and sculpting class. Random. In the fall she audited a college course about the political history surrounding the creation of the Bible and the simultaneous obliteration of pagan literature. Why had she taken that course? No idea. Something about the syllabus intrigued her, and the professor was captivating. Did she sleep with him? Yes.

Chess in Tennessee parks with retirees. The hula-hoop contest in Chicago. Author readings. Burning Man. Anything, everything, that had her out and about and searching for her daughter and the monster in every single face, but also experiencing everything.

Yes, looked at from one angle, she's had an enviable life.

And to top it off, she thought as she ran a finger on her camper's ceiling, she's thirty-five and fit and skilled. And ready.

Really ready to destroy whatever cretin purchased her baby girl from Paul Trapmore, the devil himself. That's what the cops said after they raided his place and scoured his computer. All after Paul had fled to the off-the-path part of Ecuador, which he did the very second the detective left his hospital bed on the day baby Laura was taken. Who had Paul sold Mag's details and patterns to for a price? The cops were not sure. The transaction encrypted and too coded. Identities falsified. The wired money in some offshore account that had long been emptied, information scrubbed.

Lying in her camper bed thirteen years later, Mag didn't want to think about the dark day when she discovered this truth, so she skipped the facts, but the familiar cycle of dark feelings came all on their own. The dreadful regret, the guilt, the lost chance, roiled in her as an unstoppable emotional tsunami. She rolled to her side and shifted her stare to the faux-wood paneling on the side of her bedroom. The white lace curtain on the screened window fluttered in the breeze. In the fetal position, she opened the floodgates to a different view of her life, the view that showed her life as utterly depressing.

Practiced in this emotion and knowing it was best to let it crest and not to suppress, she hit the menu on her iPhone on a side table and scrolled to Ray LaMontagne's "Till the Sun Turns Black." Ever since hearing him sing it live, this song has been a bloodletting, a mournful surgical tool that allows her to dredge and drain the blackest of melancholy that, if she tries to fight it, if she doesn't control the course, can grab hold of her throat and choke her, even blind her. In her early years on the road, she didn't know how to manage this mourning, and she'd go blind while driving, unable to breathe, only to have to pull fast to the breakdown lane, slam on the brakes, and crawl to the back bed to hold herself through a debilitating and scary panic attack.

But at age thirty-five, she's better at managing herself. Listening to "Till the Sun Turns Black" in her camper, still in the fetal position, the song on the fifth repeat, the bloodletting began. When Ray hit the middle of the song with his aching refrain and sang a question asking who we are, Mag cried. God, how the song's aching cadence and unanswerable question fit her dark heart. Indeed, who is she? *Who am I?* Who is she when the tires roll on the tar, town to town, alone? Where is she? Where is her baby girl? Where is she? *Where is she?* Is she in a shallow grave? A corpse? A skull and broken bones? A pile of bones? Has her baby girl forgotten her mother? Yes, she must not even know her mother exists. The sun is indeed black, the roads are black, her heart is black, her mind is black. The air is black. Her bones, her baby's bones, her guilt, her failure, her fucking utter failure as a mother. All black. Who are we? *Who are we? Who am I? Where is my girl?*

Mag swung her legs out of her tiny bed and, while wiping the tears from her face with her forearm, walked to the front of the camper. She sat in the driver's seat, turned on the overhead light, and fingered an inspirational, maybe aspirational, picture she'd taped by the rearview mirror: an image of Sarah Connor from *The Terminator*. The one in which Sarah is holding a machine gun, wearing aviators, and dressed in military-style black pants and a tank top. Sarah Connor's arms are cut and muscled. One time Mag found a rack of those same black pants at an army-surplus store in Salem, Massachusetts, and bought all five in her size.

Still sitting in her driver's seat, she pulled out a piece of bright-blue clay from a drawer in her driver's console, one of several leftover rectangles of molding clay from the course she got caught up in in Colorado that delayed her from starting this summer's Triple C shift.

She ripped off a corner and squeezed the blue clay in her hand, pinching the square to warm and make it more pliable. She worked the blue piece into a palm-rolled ball while meditating on the hugeness of Cord's beloved dog-grave hydrangea bush, smack-dab in view of her windshield. Sometimes resort brides asked to cut a blue bloom for their bouquets, and Cord always said, "Something borrowed and something Blue," meaning Blue, his dog, and thus offering his reliable and coded sentimentality.

Mag tried to go to sleep but couldn't stop cycling, round and round, the same analysis of her life, the different views of it, the positive, the negative. Turn, turn, turn from one extreme to the other, good and bad, good and bad, like her life was merely binary, good or bad, positive or negative, only those two extremes blended together.

Near the end of August, Mag sauntered over to Cord's one-room log cabin and knocked. It was 6:00 a.m., right before she knew he'd be heading out and up to the resort concierge to collect the day's itinerary.

"Fine," she said as soon as he opened the thick log door.

Cord smiled. "Your passport in order?"

"Of course."

"We leave next week, you know?"

"No shit, old man. Who do you think's been planning your retirement party?"

The next week, on the day of Cord's retirement breakfast—for Cord's, and now Mag's, flight was scheduled that evening—Mag readied her bags and called her detective. Of course he had nothing to report, and of course Mag thought he didn't know his thumb from his dick. *Find my baby, you idiot.* She told her dick-thumb detective she'd call later with a local Italy phone number, because she wasn't sure her cell phone would have service where they were going. As he always did, the detective said he'd scour the deepest ocean to find her if he ever had news to share. She hung up and finished packing.

During the day, as she and Cord rolled fishing line, repaired flies for fly-fishing, restocked bird bingo cards at the base of the treetop course, picked up clay-pigeon shards in the range, and tightened arrows and hay bales, a sense of dread descended upon Mag. A deeper dread than the one managed by Ray's song. Something she hadn't felt so severe in many years, maybe not even since the day the monster took her baby girl. At one point, while walking to dump a bucket of orange pigeon shards in a dumpster, she had to drop and place her head between her knees because a wave of nausea struck so fast and deep. Wind cooled her neck, which allowed her to stand and tell herself, but not fully convince herself, she was simply suffering travel anxiety. She went about her day, coaching herself she was only going a plane ride away—well, actually, two or three plane rides away—from her beast camper in California (the resort had agreed she could park for a year), and just a phone call away from Dick-Thumb.

*Okay, okay, okay.*

She told herself the job in Italy wasn't going to work out anyway, and that this was a way, a step, to allow herself to move to Costa Rica and be with Carly again. A testing of the waters on allowing herself forgiveness and to be able to settle down.

The gun-range veteran, who everyone called D, the one who'd had his appendix removed, drove up to Mag's camper and honked. Cord was already in the front passenger seat, so Mag threw her duffel into the back seat, sat down, and shut the door.

"Don't pack much, do you, Mag?" D asked.

"Don't need much, and whatever else I need, I'll get in Italy," she answered.

As they drove away from the Triple C, a dark, ominous dread descended again. Sweat broke out over Mag's forehead and on the back of her neck. She rolled down her window for cool air; a car whizzed past going toward the Triple C. Mag swore the man driving was the same bearded man from a handful of years ago. The one she guided, him and his son, on an overnight camping trip. The one so close to being like a Ray LaMontagne.

Mag shook her head, told herself she was inventing mirages, but something about the possible sight of her bearded man connected with the deep feeling of dread that had been haunting her all day. Some instinct told her this feeling, *this instinct*, had nothing to do with travel. She'd been on her own for thirteen years traveling all over everywhere. And it's not like in these thirteen years she hadn't taken international flights because the universe told her to check something out in London or France or Spain or Mexico, and one time a hike in Peru. And of course the time she tracked Paul in Ecuador and . . . well . . . *handled* her demon. No, no, she wasn't experiencing mere anxiety over international travel.

Then another thought sent a wave of panic through her. She grabbed her duffel, rip-zipped it open, dived her hands in, and riffled about.

"Shit," she said.

Cord turned and looked over the front seat.

"Dammit," she said. "Forgot my passport."

D slowed, pulled a U-turn, and drove back to the Triple C.

"Good thing you remembered so close to base, lady girl. We're already in a hurry for this flight."

"I know. I know, I'm sorry," she said in a disconnected whisper. She stared out the open window, not focusing on her passport or her words. Not focusing on the passing trees or the trip she was about to take. Rather, she grasped around in fractured, random thoughts. Like her mind was ahead of her, knew something she hadn't accepted yet. Like her brain was in transition to entering a whole new reality.

Instinct. Maternal instinct was screaming in her mind.

D drove back to the Triple C Activity Center and up to Mag's camper. Parked by Cord's cabin, in front of Blue's grave hydrangea, was her bearded man in an obvious rental, a black Mustang. This time he was alone, without his son.

Mag got out of D's car.

"Ray?" she said to her bearded man.

He shook his head confused. "My name's not Ray. I'm Nathan. Nathan Vinet. Do you remember me?"

"I took you on an overnight. You and your son. The doctor? You're a doctor, right?"

"Yes, right. Back in 2014 you took us camping. My son, Thomas, he was ten. He's fifteen now. I know this is weird, but can we talk? I'm on a business trip to San Fran, from New Hampshire, and I drove here to find you. I couldn't remember your name, and I had no number to call, and when I tried the resort, they had no idea who I was talking about."

"Idiots," Mag said under her breath. Her heart was thumping loud as she wondered why someone who was in her life for just a short night would go to such lengths after so long to find her. Thinking, too, on how fractured her thoughts seemed, how transitional she felt, she found she was holding her breath. Her fingers tingled in some primal instinct, but she forced herself forward. "I'm Gretchen, but I go by Mag. They know who the hell I am. They know better."

"Gretchen, right, right. Thomas, my son, he said it was a *G* name."

"I didn't tell you my name back then. I said to call me G. I say that to all the guests. That's why you can't remember. Why are you here?"

"Mag, you all right?" Cord interrupted, now standing behind her and listening to the conversation.

Big D stood in flank to the scene, arms crossed, legs A-framed, ready for battle. "Mag, remember, five will get you ten, ten will get you killed. Tell him," D said in her direction, loud enough for Nathan to hear.

Without looking to Cord or D, Mag held up her index finger, indicating this situation did not threaten her, this was a Level 1. She did note, however, D's reminder of an important self-defense move he'd trained her on. *Five will get you ten, ten will get you killed* was a twist on popular betting parlance, the meaning reconfigured to fit D's invention of a rather specific use of the hands in combat. If she'd raised the ALL RED alarm of four fingers, this bearded Nathan Vinet would be tossed in the lake and *swimming with the loons* in four seconds flat.

"I didn't mean to alarm you," Nathan said. He seemed confident, strong, unwavering in what he needed to say, despite the very trained guards surrounding Mag. He stood eye to eye with her, matching Mag's height and straight posture. "It's just, you said you were looking for your daughter. And that, I did the math, she'd be fifteen by now, the same age as my boy. And she'd look just like you. You said she'd been taken, and if I ever saw someone like that, she'd likely live closeted up, or living on the run in multiple places. And Gretchen, Mag, I mean, I've had the strangest encounters with a girl who fits, I mean. Oh wow. Looking at you, I have no doubt. I know she has violet eyes. I know it. And violet eyes are so damn rare. She tries to hide her eyes. I believe she wears contacts."

Mag gasped. Took a step closer to Cord, reaching for him. He grabbed her arm, as if preparing to hold her up.

Nathan continued, his intention like a steel bow slicing through icy waters. "It so happens, I had business in San Francisco this week, so I thought, maybe this is not crazy at all. Maybe there's some connection. Whatever it is, I can't seem to shake this feeling, keeps gnawing at me. I even felt nauseous for trying to ignore it. Anyway, something told me to drive here and find you. Maybe I'm all wrong, but what the hell. I don't know. It's like the universe demanded I come. So I listened to the universe."

Like any good father would, Cord stepped closer behind Mag in time to catch her as her legs failed and she crumpled to the ground. Cord's role was simply to slow the fall, because nothing could stop her hard collapse. On the ground, Mag shook Cord away and held up a hand, telling all the men around her to stop, stop the fussing.

"Stop!" she yelled. "Stop. Step back."

She dropped her head, breathed in hard, closed her eyes. She got to her knees, pressed on her thighs, and stood. Standing tall, dirt on the front of her black military pants and on her palms, she faced Nathan, himself standing in a bracing position, readying to help her but not daring to touch her.

"Are you sure?" she demanded.

Nathan flicked his fingers, a motion that told her to hold on. He fished in his pants pocket, pulled out his phone, clicked a few times, and turned the screen to her. "I took this picture in the store she works at. They didn't know I took the picture. That's her, the one who might be your girl. She goes by Lucy. And the woman is her mother, they say."

Mag made a choking sound. "Oh my God. Oh my God," she said. Her throat full with an instant concrete. She brought her hand to her mouth. "Oh my God. Laura. Laura."

Mag wandered off with Nathan's phone, bent over her knees, and leaned against her camper. Her back heaved up and down. "Laura. Laura. My God. Laura." She appeared like a wounded animal, taking dying breaths.

Cord stepped to her, tried to place a hand on her back, but she winced and moved away along the side of her camper, still bent.

"Oh my God. Oh my God," she whispered. "Laura."

"Your girl, Laura. That's Laura?" Cord tried.

"Yes, my God. Yes. I'd know my own daughter if she were eighty." Mag tilted her head up to Cord as if she were pleading to him from the bottom of a well. She remained bent over her knees. The phone and phone screen obscured and in her hands.

"That's Laura, my baby." Her voice cracked. "The woman. That's Laura Ingrace, Cord. Fucking Laura Ingrace from camp days. I named my girl after her. Oh my God. What? What? How can? Oh my God. Laura took my baby girl. What? What the fuck? What?"

Mag shot up and walked fast to Nathan. Standing tall and one foot from him, she steeled her face and emotions. "She goes by Lucy? My girl?"

"Yes."

"In New Hampshire?"

"Yes."

"Take me there now."

# CHAPTER TWENTY-FOUR

## LUCY

Everything in my life is the literal Upside Down like in *Stranger Things*, which "Mom" let me watch on her iPad and I binged. To sum up: tonight I figured out Mom is not my mother; I ran away down the country road wearing Gretchen's white mini-nightgown; Gretchen ran through the frickin' woods like a rabid beast to stop, or I don't know what, me; and then Dali drove over the hill, and she fled—which is super sketch and confusing and ugh . . . I don't want to think about it!

Dali saved me, and nobody knows, and nobody's gonna know, because I'm in triple hiding now: hiding from my real past and hiding from my fake kidnapped past and hiding from Gretchen Sabin, who—I don't even know. I'm underground. Invisible. And Dali keeps secrets as if breaking even one would crush the whole world to smithereens. He'd weirdly forgotten his laptop and had to drive five hours from Princeton to get it, and since he was home, he said he felt he couldn't leave things unsettled and things unsaid between us—he was worried. And, miracle of miracles, he came in the nickity-splits of time to save my almost-naked ass.

Dali's hiding me in his bedroom above his parents' garage. We've been talking all night about my situation, and I've told him about Gretchen's house and interactions with Gretchen. I'm just giving facts,

facts, facts, because I need to cut through all the cockeyed, crazy emotions, which are flying around me in a clockwise tornado mixed with a counterclockwise tornado. When I'm reciting facts to Dali, I'm able to avoid flares of stress hives.

It's 3:00 a.m. now, according to the red digital numbers projected on Dali's wall.

"Hold on," Dali says. Since he's standing, he runs his hand up the slanted ceiling of his above-garage bedroom. Having changed into Dali's gray T-shirt and big-ass boy jeans, I'm sitting crisscross on top of his platform bed. "Jerry Sabin told you he broke his leg in a hole filled with a rock pyramid that teenagers built, and *then* he put up all the fences and traps? And the teenagers did this rock-pyramid hole to trap his dead wife's and kid's ghosts? That's what he said? That's the timeline?"

"Yeah. I'm pretty sure he was real clear about that."

"Can't be true."

"What?"

"Gretchen and Jerry Sabin said that?"

"Yes, well, Jerry Sabin did. Gretchen . . ." I shoot him a confused look as he interrupts.

"Yeah, no way. So if Gretchen was at least four when her mother was shot, and *then* Jerry broke his leg, that means I was at least seven. And let me tell you, yeah. No. I'm certain about this. From the time I came to live here, I know, I know for sure, my fosters, parents—hell, all the parents in town—used to yell at us constantly to never trespass on the Sabin property because it was rigged with traps and an electrical fence. Rigged for decades, Lucy."

"Why would they lie, though? They must have known I'd find out, right?"

"I don't know. Don't know. I have no clue." He bit his lip, closed his eyes in thought, knuckled the slanted ceiling a few times. "Yeah, I'm not sure. Tell me more."

"I mean, looking back on it and knowing Gretchen better now, I think Gretchen was pissed Jerry told us how he broke his leg. And then last week, right before I left for work, she very creepily told me Jerry did not break his leg in holes with rocks and she wanted to show me where and how he broke his leg in the forest. I thought she was messing with me. And tonight, her urging me to go in the woods . . ."

"Uh-uh, uh-uh. Okay, tell me more."

So I give Dali more facts. Just whatever other facts I had in living by Gretchen. And I gave facts about Mom, about all the places we've lived. About the metal box. About Gretchen's halls. Her puzzles. About Gretchen's and my unstated, but definite-for-sure, who-flinches-first game. About the creep-ass cult Death March puzzle she gifted me and how a painted boy in the painting's serpentine line had an old man's face. About the crème-de-la-crème Jenny in Indiana who I left behind in my tenth state. About anything I can talk about that is pure-grade, verifiable fact. No emotions. No organization on my ramblings.

We trail off talking and both fall asleep, me on his bed still fully dressed, and Dali half on his beanbag on the floor, because he's not a creeper who takes advantage of a girl in distress—he's a Jenny. A solid Jenny.

Now some ringing is waking us both up. Dali answers his iPhone, and his face goes white. He's bulging his eyes on me. He's stammering, saying things like, "No, sir. No. I don't. Uh, uh, I'm not sure," and staring at me. Whatever this call is, is about me.

And then he breaks his rule about holding secrets. He gives whoever's called my rental ranch's address. He hangs up. I jump off the bed and run to his door, but he pops in front of it, stopping me. I can't believe he betrayed me.

"Stop. I had to. That was a cop. They were going to come here. I didn't say you were here. I couldn't deny I knew your address. They thought I might have taken you or hidden you because, whatever, because they did. Sandra saw how we were friends at the store, and I shouldn't be home from Princeton. I mean, I did drive home the night you disappeared. If I didn't give your address, they were going to come here. We need to go. Let's go. I know where we can hide you."

*Maybe I should just go to the cops. They can help.*

*No, I'm not ready. I don't know if I'll ever be ready. I'm trained in being invisible, being on the run. It's all I know.*

I understand the bare facts. I can intellectualize what I found in the metal box.

But it doesn't mean that accepting all this is easy-peasy beautiful pie. Hell no.

I'm mad. I'm sad. I'm scared. I want to scream-cry and hide. I'm raking my nails so hard through my scalp, I think I might wash my hair in blood.

Nobody can fix this for me. Nobody can make this easier for me.

Pacing a circle between Dali's bed and beanbag, I try to catch my breath. I need to become an indestructible jellyfish, but with a spine, all on my own. A silver solid jelly like my pendant, which, shit, is the only thing except my bra and underwear I have from my—*old? real? former? stolen?*—life. While pausing to stare at Dali's poster of the Cat's Eye Nebula, I'm finding on some level—a little level somewhere deep inside me nobody could ever know about, and I didn't even know about until now—I think I might have sort of known something wasn't right in my galaxy. Truth is always crying inside us, never truly muzzled by denials.

I think this is what they call a surge of adrenaline.

Or flight or fright or fight, or whatever that saying is.

Or some other kind of delusion that allows you to power through trauma.

I don't know.

What I know is, at some point in the last few seconds of me being trapped in the whirl of my own mind, I allowed Dali to pull me out of his above-garage bedroom, and now I'm following him to some far-off garage on his massive property.

Dali and I jump in his older sister's black BMW, because nobody knows her car since she's been traveling in Europe for three years and she never drove the thing anyway. I know all this because through the haze, Dali is narrating facts to me. Fortunately, his parents are off to work and think Dali brought a faceless girl home from college for the night and apparently said they'd leave him be and to have fun after handing him a six-pack. Rules seem different for boys. Dali gives me his dad's extra-huge fishing hat with hooks and pins all over it. I stuff all my long hair inside and drag the brim over my forehead and ears.

"There's a place at Great Katherine Lake where nobody will find us. But first we got to make a quick stop."

We park in a shadowed spot behind the village's hardware store, and I scrunch down real low when he insists on going inside the red Victorian library with gold shutters across the way. The BMW's windows are tinted black, and I lock the doors. Despite being sealed in this car, I can smell the hot baking bread from Scheppard's next to Vinet's hardware store, which, oh yeah, of course Vinet's, because Dr. Nathan Vinet is yet another haunting in my life. I'm getting it from all sides.

Dali returns with some papers he says he printed off microfiche and copied from a reference book; he says we can discuss what he's found out about the Sabin property once we're settled at Great Katherine.

At the lake, the wind is awesome and fierce. But we don't care—we're safe under the cement roof of an abandoned waterworks station. Dali brought along a cooler with peach iced tea, a jar of peanut butter, and a loaf of bread. When he packed this, I don't know. Maybe I went catatonic in his bedroom after the call from the cops—I think I was literally spinning circles into his carpet for a bit. We don't have any utensils, so Dali uses a Snapple cap to scoop the peanut butter, and he uses the Jif lid to spread, and because he's infused the preparation with thoughtful care, my three separate sandwiches taste like a whole new world. Dali is a good friend, definite Jenny-level material. And he's freaked out, too, but he acts super calm and lets me stare off into space.

The waterworks station is a gutted shell. What remains is a cement square in a gully with both ends open, about seven feet tall and twenty feet from the lake's edge, nestled in a grove of saplings that's taken over since the place was abandoned. The station reminds me of a stunted version of one of those huge cement tunnels in horror movies where psychos chase and chainsaw the morons who run there. But this is square, not a circle. Inside, Dali sits on an overturned five-gallon bucket, I sit on another, and Dali unrolls the papers he's printed at the Milberg library. He holds the first page against a graffiti-decorated wall and lights it with his iPhone flashlight.

"The Death March cult puzzle Gretchen gave you."

"Yeah."

"So here, that jogged something for me. Nobody ever talks about the Sabin property all that much anymore. I mean, yeah. Agree. There are rumors. But the place has been off-limits for so long, it's old news, and nobody can breach the electric fence, and nobody wants to be hung up in those tree traps. So. Look. And with all the changes in town with the tourism, nobody talks about the Sabin place anymore. But." Dali holds up one of the pages. "Look."

"What am I looking at?"

"This was an article in the Milberg *Times* in 1952. I think that's a picture of a pyramid rock trap that a hunter tripped on, again in 1952, and broke his leg. But they didn't call it a pyramid rock trap. Read it."

Sure enough, the picture, albeit grainy, shows a one-foot-wide hole filled with toppled rocks. In the forest. I read the lead paragraph:

Gary Musterson, visiting from Rhode Island, broke his leg in a one-foot-wide hole full of rocks while hunting the Taylor property. He claims the hole is a "dangerous trap, unfairly placed there by the property owner."

I looked up to Dali. "Taylor property?"

"The Sabin property was owned by the Taylors then."

"Right."

I kept reading below a picture of this Gary Musterson with his broken leg.

Mr. Musterson had in his Peterman knapsack a brand-new Kodak Brownie 127 and was able to take this picture of the hole with rocks, and several others in his vicinity, while he waited for his hunting partner to find him. The hunting partner was a Miss Sarah Felmore, an unmarried woman, who was carrying a loaded Remington rifle she received for Christmas from a male family member. When Miss Felmore came upon Mr. Musterson, they were disturbed by Alton Sams Taylor, current owner of the Taylor property, who threatened to shoot Mr. Musterson "in the face" and Miss Felmore in her "[female body part]" if they, as Mr. Musterson averred in a police report, didn't "crawl off Taylor grounds [in the direction Mr. Taylor pointed] stat."

Standing on his front stoop, smoking an Old Gold cigarette, Mr. Taylor would not permit this reporter to enter his secluded home or inspect the woods surrounding it to document Mr. Musterson's and Miss Felmore's account. However, Mr. Taylor offered this statement: "Everybody knows to stay off my property or they'll get hurt or dead or shot in their privates. This [expletive] Mr. Musterson and his unnatural woman with her own gun are fool out-of-towners come to hunt on land they don't own, cause (sic) they got no sense, and to kill God's creatures, because they got no respect. They weaseled in cause (sic) the storm knocked the power off my electrical boundary fence. Well it's back up now, so all your [expletive] readers should be reminded to not come near my property 'less (sic) they want to fry. I know the law. I can protect what's mine."

When asked about the holes filled with rocks, Mr. Taylor stated, "You're all a bunch of nosebleed cubes with your poppycock. Rocks and leaves in a forest, good grief. You gonna get a Pulitzer for this one?" Mr. Taylor then asked this reporter to leave his property.

"They used to write articles like this?" I ask.

"Yeah, I know. I did a paper once for school on the town's history, and some of the old articles are hilarious. So much weird specificity and seemingly irrelevant facts and embedded judgment and weird quotes and weird redactions of things we wouldn't redact now. Anyway, see what I mean? The fences were always there. I mean, they've certainly been upgraded over time, sure. Seems to me your Jerry Sabin stole this hunter's story, changed some things, fast-forwarded in time, and made it his own. Right?"

"I mean, yeah, I guess."

"But what sticks out to me is the date of the article, and that's what got me to thinking it's connected to your cult puzzle. Look at this."

Dali holds another document to the graffiti wall. "I copied this out of a reference book I remembered some kid in school mentioned when he did an oral report on cults. Look. I paid an extra two bucks to copy this page in color."

The color print has much better clarity. This shows another one-foot-wide hole in the ground, but with an intact rock pyramid inside—not the fallen jumble as in the grainy 1952 Musterson black-and-white. Page 345 out of a book titled *American Cults, Truth & Lore.*

Dali interrupts my reading. "This page is from the chapter titled 'Rumored Sects and Mysterious Vanishings.' Go ahead, read it."

According to the printed page, a Wyoming couple found this particular rock pyramid in a hole when they'd purchased an old farm and decided to build. Reading further, I learn about unsubstantiated rumors about rock pyramids in holes found in several states leading east. Some speculate, based on what amounts to a very obscure conspiracy theory—built on a significant game of telephone and bar talk with no footnotes or actual quotes—that a quickly assembled group of people started following a "charismatic minister named Jonny Guile." With Guile in the lead, they moved east like a pack, collecting followers along the way, sometime in the 1950s. Rumor has it the followers dug holes and built rock pyramids within them in order to capture "earth breath," which they believed was the literal breath of God. Earth breath would give them immortal life. Not one surviving member of this rumored cult has come forward to verify whether anyone named Jonny Guile ever existed or any of these accounts.

When I'm done reading, Dali says, "I had never heard of these rock pyramids in the ground before. But then you tell me what Jerry Sabin tells you, calls them rock pyramids, so I vaguely recalled this weird hunting story from the fifties involving the Taylor property. Not from the Musterson article, but something my foster grandma said once. Doesn't matter. That's how I knew to search for this Musterson article in microfiche. But without you saying 'rock pyramids,' I never would have thought the 1952 article was telling me anything other than old Mr. Alton Sams Taylor was a crazy nutjob who dug ankle twisters on his property to stop trespassers. So from there, I thought about the Death March cult puzzle, and it was a total lucky guess, but I remembered the cult book that that kid used in his oral report. And bam. Right there. I mean, it's even in the index, 'Rock pyramid, 1950s.'" He flicks the page in a motion of pride. Leaning back on his upturned bucket, he says, "You can call me Detective Dali."

"So to sum up, Detective Dali. From all the vomit stew of facts I've been throwing on you, what you boil down to is page 345 from this weirdo cult book, and you're saying Gretchen and Jerry Sabin are running a cult on their property, even though I didn't see any mass of people all summer? Is that the story?"

"Well, when you put it that way." He gathers the papers and rolls them up. "But you have to admit—"

I cut him off. "No, for real, though, it is kind of messed up. Thanks for looking up these articles. And I know you're doing this to take my mind off the real horror in my life."

Dali shrugs and sets the roll of printouts in his back pocket.

"Wait," I say, as something hits me. "Wait. So do you think Gretchen was mad that Jerry mentioned the rock pyramids because those words might lead to someone like you piecing this together? Like maybe Jerry doled out that factoid as a distress call or something?"

"I don't know. It'd be a pretty wacko distress call. And a dad needing help? What help? From a waif daughter? I mean, she wasn't running a cult in the 1950s."

"What the fuck."f

"Yeah, what the fuck."

A howling train of wind whooshes through the tunnel and knocks us off our buckets. We crawl to the water station's mouth and watch a tornado rip a path through a lake island, toppling bull pines in thundering booms. Our buckets roll out and plunk in the lake, float away.

It's scary and magnificent all at the same time, and I'm captivated in watching, huddling next to Dali, who huddles next to me. We lie on our bellies all afternoon and theorize about Gretchen Sabin and nothing real, like my fake lie of a life.

It's late afternoon. I'm sick of not having my own clothes. And I need Allen so bad I wish I could fly like the hawk I'm watching circling above the destruction from the tornado.

"Dali," I say as he takes inventory of whatever food we have left in his cooler.

"Yeah?"

"Do you think we could park near the ranch in a hidden spot and I'll sneak in and get my own clothes? And I want to get Allen too. What do you think?"

"Well. We can try. Let's case it out. You want to go now?"

"Yeah, let's go now."

# CHAPTER TWENTY-FIVE

## MOTHER

Mag waits in the Milberg station for the Milberg cops, the Boston FBI, and Detective Dick-Thumb to execute an "inquiry" at the rental house that law enforcement *finally* uncovered as the place where Mag's baby girl, Laura, now called Lucy, is living with Laura, Laura from camp, meaning Laura Ingrace. The very Laura Ingrace who disappeared the day Paul Trapmore appeared at the Triple C. The exact Laura Ingrace Mag had named her baby girl after.

Roaming and listening all day in the U-shaped, one-floor, industrial station house, Mag learned that it is rarely used for anything beyond soothing angry tourists into paying parking tickets. She's also learned that the station's one holding cell is typically used for station-house poker games and that the chief of police, Sandra Dyson's husband, in fact, is proud of the interior's mint-green cinder-block walls and Pride rainbow painted in the arch over the dispatcher window. This is that kind of town: progressive and inclusive and full of mixed-everything-paying tourists. Good tax base and good tourism dollars, given the flocks of foodies who come to the village and the people who camp and swim and water-ski at Great Katherine Lake.

Mag's relieved Boston FBI and Detective Dick-Thumb have joined forces, because she's pretty sure Milberg's finest are in over their water skis.

At one point in the *painstakingly long* day of *planning a controlled inquiry at the property in question*, Mag walked with Sandra Dyson, who loves "that gahhl, Lucy," to Dyson's in order to collect what they already knew to be Lucy's falsified employment record. Mag had to wait out in front of Dyson's disguised in a heavy jacket and baseball cap, but she'd needed the air, so she begged the chief to let her walk with Sandra to the front of his wife's store. Along the way, she saw in a boutique window Milberg's trademark poster of a champion water skier waving to her shoreline friends while slicing a slalom on the surface of Great Katherine Lake.

Mag paced in front of Dyson's, waiting on Sandra to collect worthless evidence, and noted how all the window-shoppers wore bright-colored Vineyard Vines T-shirts and Lilly Pulitzer dresses. In a frame store next to Dyson's, Mag noted the display of paintings of Milberg in the fall, the next season to come, revealing the park to be a leaf peeper's dream: a white church spire spearing the blue sky and casting a pointed shadow on a wishing well, which bubbled beside a gazebo in a park full of trees bursting in red, green, yellow, and orange.

The library across from Dyson's was a red Victorian with glistening gold shutters. Mag studied the quaintness and considered the postcard vibe, until Sandra bumped her shoulder. A black BMW with tinted windows drove past, whooshing the air with its kitten-purr engine, anonymous in a sea of other luxury vehicles in town.

"Great little town we got here, ma'am," Sandra Dyson said.

Mag nodded agreement.

*Of course Laura Ingrace would pick a perfect town like this,* Mag thought, and then shuddered to even consider such a thought. They walked back to the station, passing a hometown hardware store named Vinet's with a giant cardboard key in the window that said LOCKSMITH.

It's all such a blur, every minute melded together since Dr. Nathan Vinet found her yesterday at the Triple C. After that, just last night, they flew across the country, met with the Boston FBI, and drove to Milberg. Dick-Thumb made the same trip. It was a miracle their red-eye landed at all, the region's week of wind dying down at dawn for touchdown and resuming almost the second they landed.

At some point, an FBI counselor joined Mag in the mint-green cinder-block Milberg "multifunction" room. The doe-eyed counselor had warned Mag that her girl, Laura, would have difficulty going by any name other than Lucy, even if Lucy was a false name, so it would be best for Mag to accept Lucy as her name. Could she do that? Mag asked herself all day, *Can I do that? Can I call my baby by a name that monster gave her? Her stolen name?* And then she'd fist the thick cotton of her black Sarah Connor cargo pants and flat-palm the mint-green wall while commanding herself, *Yes, you can do this. You will call her Lucy.*

Law enforcement's day of surveillance filtered to Mag in pieces, but she heard enough to put the puzzle of their planning together into a coherent picture in her mind:

- Sandra Dyson's confirmation that Lucy worked at Dyson's as late as yesterday.

- Some college kid named Dali, reached by cell, who sounded sketchy or high or obtuse, apparently, not wanting, at first, to divulge that he knew where Lucy lived, finally did.

- Officers couldn't drive up a dirt road to "ascertain a direct visual" of the now-identified "subject dwelling" without tipping anyone off. The secluded hilltop area concerned them as prime for a hostage situation or ambush.

213

- A drone confirmed a brown Volvo in the property's "parking area," beside a dumped bike and a helmet five feet closer to a long shed.

- The drone detected no movement in or around the ranch.

- The presumed landlord, Jerry Sabin, was a reclusive concert pianist who lived in a colossal brick home (mansion) overlooking the "subject dwelling." His daughter, Gretchen, did not attend the local school, and nobody had seen her all summer.

- Verified accounts of the Sabins' electrical fence and traps kept them from involving the Sabin property in any sharpshooter surveillance staging.

- Nobody wanted to involve the Sabins for fear of involvement or that they'd send up red flags. Law enforcement would craft a controlled inquiry, knocking on the Sabins' and the ranch door simultaneously.

With every hour of the day, things grew more tense. They grew especially more tense when a few resources were diverted to deal with the aftermath of a tornado that ripped across Great Katherine Lake in the middle of the afternoon. Electrical lines had fallen across roads around the lake.

Evening now, and the overthought *inquiry* is underway.

Here Mag is in the Milberg police station, waiting on Dick-Thumb, the feds, the local cops, anyone, to return from the overly cautious, overly planned *inquiry*. Only one day has passed since Nathan Vinet showed up in California. Thirteen whole years since Laura Ingrace stole her baby. What's another hour of waiting? *Another fucking hour is a fucking eternity.*

"Let me go storm in there right now," she'd yelled several times in the station throughout the day.

"No, no, Ms. Bianchi. We don't want a hostage situation. We don't want anyone hurt. We don't know if she has any weapons."

Mag nodded then, hanging on the word *weapons*. Admittedly, she couldn't shoot down the notion. Couldn't deny that Laura Ingrace might indeed have weapons. Sure, everyone else at the Triple C might know Laura as a bumbling clod when it came to sports, might know her for the quiet presence that would lob biting zingers and dry jokes at precise times in group conversations, might know her as a total nerd who was always tracking birds. But, and Mag had never shared this with anyone, Mag knew some secrets about Laura Ingrace.

*Could Laura have weapons on her? Now? Now with weapons?*

*Yes, detectives, officers, agents, Dick-Thumb, Ms. Counselor with the doe eyes, I understand. I'll wait here and bite my nails to the skin and then down to the knuckles while you delay me, mollify me, in your nauseating, mint-green, windowless hell room—I will literally eat my own hands from the nerves while I sit like the useless, dumb, unplugged fax machine in the corner, because, okay, maybe, you're right, I guess, it seems unthinkable, but not really, Laura Ingrace might indeed have weapons. Fine! Stop looking at me and go save my girl.* Mag didn't say any of this out loud. Instead, she nodded and skulked off to punch buttons on the unplugged fax machine, just so she had something to stab.

Was Laura Ingrace's impossible tree-banked arrow shot that hit Marianne—the camp nurse at the time—in the ass really a fluke? Mag knew it was not. She'd never told anyone else when she learned the truth years later. Not even Carly. *But that was all innocent, right? Laura never intended to hit Marianne. Right?*

"Ma'am, you're going to need to calm down and stop pacing. Maybe take a nap here in my office. We cannot have you attacking the suspect if we bring her in," a man with badges said at some point in Mag's fog-filled, station-house day.

"I'm not taking a nap. You take a nap," she barked back.

The officer didn't push, but he did send in the damn doe-eyed counselor again.

Did the odor of violence seep from her? Was murderous rage blazing from her eyes? Was her brain screaming a war cry? Yes, perhaps. Mag indeed had visions of murdering Laura every time she looked at Nathan Vinet's picture of her in Dyson's with her daughter. She planned the physical moves it would take to snap Laura's neck with her legs. Could be over in four moves and four seconds. *Swoop. Squeeze and fall. Torque. Crack.* She imagined executing D's famous *five will get you ten, ten will get you killed* and sending Laura off to a permanent nap. *You take a nap, bitch.*

Dr. Nathan Vinet walks in to find Mag still waiting in the same mint-green multifunction room she's been roaming in and out of all day. The fax machine is still unplugged; perhaps the number pad's faceplate is newly cockeyed and cracked. *So sue me,* Mag thinks. She sits in one of two green molded chairs. Nathan takes the other, handing her a to-go coffee from Scheppard's. He keeps his own to-go coffee along with a wax bag of something that smells like hot cinnamon.

"My cousin is the baker at Ferry Farm & Fudge, and he gave me an unauthorized bag of contraband snickerdoodles. You're supposed to only get them hot at four a.m. Anyway, hope these help with the wait," he says.

"Your family is all over this town, aren't they?" she asks in a disconnected tone, revealing a deep wish that she, too, had family all over some town where she lived.

"Yep. One of my brothers owns the hardware store next to Scheppard's. Small town." He digs out a hot cookie for her.

"The locksmith. The one with the big key in the window," she says, staring forward and taking a bite of the offered cookie.

"Yes." He opens his mouth to say more, perhaps recite the litany of relatives in town, but chooses to respect quiet.

Mag, appreciative of the cookie and the quiet and his presence, finishes the cookie in three bites. She knows that in some distant reptilian part of her brain, she's logging the perfect blend of hot butter and granules of sugar mixed with a dusting of cinnamon sticking to the roof of her mouth. Nathan hands her another cookie, and the two sit side by side in mutual shell shock. They eat cookie after cookie and sip coffee, which Scheppard's calibrated just right with steamed milk and sugar. They eat and sip and stare at the green-and-gray linoleum floor. Mag had earlier climbed on her green chair and unscrewed several of the long fluorescent bulbs, so the lighting is less eye-stabby and more like a lonely hospital wing after visiting hours. The merciful aroma of cinnamon and coffee masks the otherwise relentless scent of bleach.

"I settled Thomas with a friend for the night. I'm staying with you," Nathan says. "Okay?"

Mag nods a yes, chewing her fifth cookie. "Thanks," she reinforces.

They'd already chatted on the plane ride here, so she knows Nathan's pertinent biographical details: he's a family physician, Thomas is his only child, he's a widower, his wife died earlier in the year he took Thomas to the Triple C to go camping. Five years ago. He and Thomas had vowed not to discuss his wife's/Thomas's mother's death during that one trip—and they damn well near succeeded. Nathan had considered Mag's late-night-campfire words a relief, and he's sorry to admit this, but a relief to listen to someone else's woes. And when Mag disappeared the next morning, Nathan said he'd returned to his fog of grief, focused solely on consoling his young son. He somehow forgot about the abrupt clarity this woman named G had brought into his life, about the comfort of talking to her, and even about the shocking story she'd told him about the kidnapping of her daughter. Looking back on that dark time, Nathan explained, when your ten-year-old son shakes so hard in grief he seizes, when medicines and counselors can't calm him, everything else in the world disappears. But Thomas is much better. Both of them so much better now.

Mag again thanks Nathan for the coffee and the hot cookies and for staying with her.

Cord had called a billion times and said he'd delayed his trip to Italy, as he now considered himself "on standby, awaiting commands." Mag told him not to fly out but to hold base at the Triple C. Gun range D was so amped over the whole event he was about to explode into a million tiny D-soldier clones. Unafraid of vigilante options, Mag felt she had enough cover if things went sideways. Big sis Carly would fly in as soon as Mag said the word.

Sitting with virtual stranger Dr. Nathan Vinet was the only consolation Mag allowed. He didn't look at her with pity. Not with history. Not judgment. Not directives on how she should feel or think. He looked at her as an equal, himself equally bruised, and with solid—forged from his own battles—strength. A tarnished and honed and experienced strength. Like the finest polished silver on the table, with smooth handle, earned nicks, and storied scrapes.

"I just, I just, I'm sorry. I keep saying this, but I just can't put this all together. Why would Laura disappear that day from camp? And then, when, somehow, why? Why did she come back three years later and steal my baby?" Mag rubs the tips of her fingers to remove the film of sugar and cinnamon from her cookies. Nathan hands her a napkin.

He obviously has no answers, and he wisely remains silent. He doesn't offer clichés or overwrought speculations. He sits and listens to her questions, hands her the last cookie, and takes back the spent napkin when she's done.

"I just don't get it. I just don't get it," she says.

Nathan stands, tucks the empty wax bag under the wing of his biceps, and offers his non-coffee-cup hand to pull her up. "Let's walk outside. We can sit on a bench by the door. The wind is crazy. That tornado ripped across Great Katherine today, but wind is better than this bleach smell." With the cookies gone, the bleach is back and won't be denied.

Mag doesn't refuse or even hesitate or appear to give Nathan's directive a thought. She takes his hand and rises and continues talking as if she were still within her previous train of unanswerable questions.

"I mean . . . how can you explain this? Laura was always odd, true. And I knew, even saw, experienced, some things about her that others would find shocking. But, this? No. No . . . How?"

"You know," Nathan says, as they reach the station's all-glass double door entrance, "I haven't asked for details, and you've been pretty darn busy all day. But what about this Laura? Who is she? Tell me a story about her, anything to paint who she is. Do you want to?" He holds the door open while Mag moves outside. They match in height and stride and sit on a bench by the door in a series of easy motions, a tandem-gliding, ice-skating duo.

While trying to tame her long black hair in a clip, fighting with a wind yanking tufts in different directions, Mag considers Nathan's questions about Laura Ingrace and whether she has an illustrative story about her. Yes, she has many. And one fairly profound story—in terms of personality shaping and relationship staging. So where to begin? She'd spent, what, one, two, three, yeah, fourteen summers with Laura Ingrace. Age six to twenty.

*Are those sirens in the distance?* She thinks. *No, I'm wishing, fearing sirens.*

There's the one time she slept over Laura Ingrace's house at age fourteen, and things Mag witnessed there, and even became party to.

*Maybe sirens?* She's straining to hear but telling herself it's the wind.

And, stemming from that one night at Laura's, there is the one activity she shared with Laura in secret: a nighttime treetop competition, more aggressive than was ever intended by Triple C management. And nobody but Mag and Laura knew the rules they played by.

*Those are definitely sirens.* Mag and Nathan rocket up from the bench.

A mushroom cloud of shouting in the station and interior doors banging blooms over the howling wind and mixes with definite sirens growing louder and louder. Mag and Nathan step away from the bench, drawn to flashing lights between a line of dark pine that divides the parking lot from the adjacent main road. A blurred river of red, white, and blue streams toward the station entrance.

Mag is frozen. Officers and dispatchers who were inside run outside. They look at Mag with collective bewilderment. Mag doesn't know how to read this sudden crowd or the sirens or the flashing lights. The doe-eyed counselor bursts out the front door, clattering the glass-in-steel frame against the cinder-block facade. And just when the counselor is about to grab Mag's arm, a cop car speed-turns in at the entrance at the end of the line of pines. This was an unmarked car that now has one of those stick-on-the-roof lights. The same car Mag's dick-thumb detective had been in when he drove out with a Milberg deputy so as to execute the *inquiry*. The deputy pulls up to the station's front curb. Mag is five feet away. Nathan behind her. The station crowd behind them.

Mag's detective is in the back seat.

Next to her detective is a girl in a gray T-shirt.

Mag's detective opens his door.

The girl slides across the seat and scootches out. She's wearing jeans rolled at her slim waist, too big for her there, but fitting okay in length. They're men's jeans.

The girl stands tall. She's wearing no shoes.

She has long black hair.

She has violet eyes.

She matches Mag in height.

"Dali's shoes don't fit me," she says in a disconnected tone, her gaze starry and staring into Mag's. She seems bewitched. She seems lost on some other plane of reality.

"Baby," Mag bumbles out, her voice cracking. She fights tears.

Mother and daughter are clones, and two feet apart.

"Lucy," Mag forces out, using all the maternal strength she has to say the right name. "Oh baby—" Her voice broken, tears erupting.

An ambulance hauls in from the fire station across the street. Officers and agents and dispatchers crowd around, gasping, murmuring, a couple of them crying. A beat-up Ford pickup skids into the lot.

"Son of a bitch, friggin' press already!" someone in the crowd blurts.

"Damn local Joe. *Milberg Press*. You know he listens to the scanners. I'll deal with him," someone else says.

The wind is wilder now, wilder than it's been in a week of wild wind. Howling, whipping, twisting in the bowl of space between the cinder-block station and the line of pine along the adjacent road. Everyone's hair is literally on ends. Papers are pulled off clipboards and fly in mini cyclones. Empty plastic bags and takeaway food containers are strewn and tossed around parked cars. Numerous empty soda cans clink and scrape as they bounce and skid and roll, banging off tires and rolling more. Tomorrow is recycling day, and some "friggin' nitwit" put the bin out early, someone is saying.

But all is still in the bubble of the mother-daughter reunion. Everything else disappears for them as they lock in, seeing each other eye to eye. Neither one winces. Mag doesn't blink, even though she's seeing her baby girl through thirteen years of tears.

# CHAPTER TWENTY-SIX

## LUCY

Earlier today, Dali had tried to drive me to the ranch so I could get Allen, a few hours after the tornado ripped across Great Katherine. But the damn tornado blew electrical lines down on the roads so we were trapped until Dali figured out some back-ass, long-ass way, which led us all the way around the lake through nine hundred other towns and over a zillion endless mountains. And then it grew dark, and my anxiety to see Allen grew so bad with the delay, I think that's why I lost my mind and gave in when we saw the cop by the ranch.

I miss Allen so much.

And also a pair of shoes and a change of clothes. Dali's jeans are too big for me, and his Converses are the size of boats. I was going to sneak in or send Dali in, somehow try to avoid Mom, who is not *my freaking mother*. I don't know. I don't know! But when we got close to the ranch, we saw two weird cars parked on the country road. And Dali's not a moron. He said they were unmarked cars and recognized one of the drivers as a town cop.

I set my hand on Dali's arm. "I'm ready," I said. Because I don't know. In that moment, I felt ready and I needed some relief.

"You sure?" he said.

"Yeah." *No. Never. I'll never be ready.* "Sure."

So Dali drove me right on up to the unmarked car with the cop he knows. And that's how I came to be standing here, looking at a woman who looks like me, on the curb of the Milberg police station.

This woman is my mother.

I don't need the birth certificate that's burning a hole in Dali's borrowed jeans' pocket. I don't need a video of my birth. I don't need a DNA test.

This is Gretchen Bianchi. This crying woman who stares in my violet eyes with her violet eyes from a height that is level with mine—she's my birth mother.

The wind has been blowing for a week, and today's the strongest. I could choose to believe we're a pair of black-haired witches who flew into town on broomsticks and whipped up these cyclones to accompany a ferocious reunion. Or I could believe the army of fairies in the fern garden answered my secret wish to feel safer and fuller and without all the mind hives and anxiety. Because right now in this bubble of time with the older twin of me, I feel a sudden rush of safety. *Who's the real monster I've been avoiding all my life? Who? Do I really have a father who's a monster? Where's Mom? Did they say someone's checking the ranch? Right after Dali left me with these cops? Where's Mom? Stop. Look at the woman in front of you.*

I'm choosing to allow this rush, even though, even though I know other parts of me tremble, and other parts of me boil, other parts of me cry, and other parts of me hide. Right now for a blip bubble of time, I'm allowing some strange happiness to bloom. My brain feels illuminated and full of floating glitter. She breathes, and the air smells like chocolaty coffee and sugary cinnamon.

I could accept this as simple reality, and this indeed is my mother, Gretchen Bianchi.

My mother.

My real mother looking at me. She doesn't flinch. She doesn't wince. I think I see a whole ocean of love in her eyes.

I do not want to step out of this bubble. I don't want the wind to stop. I don't want this, whatever this is, to end. I don't want to deal with what comes next. *Please don't take this lightness away, Mom. Please don't take this woman, my mother, away and make me run again.*

*Mom? Mom? Who are you? Where are you? Please don't drive into this lot and take me away. But where are you? Did you leave me?*

*Where are you? Who are you?*

# CHAPTER TWENTY-SEVEN

## MOTHER

The cops haven't found Laura Ingrace. She's vanished. And all Mag can do is relive events from their childhood together as she waits for Lucy at Boston Children's Hospital. For two days now, Lucy has been enduring rounds and rounds of checkups, tests, and psychoanalytical interviews with doctors and law enforcement.

It was the weirdest moment that brought the whole defining event from so long ago into Mag's mind. She was waiting in Boston Children's Hospital for another round of doctors—a psychotherapist and nutritionist this time—to clear Lucy. Sitting beside a large fish tank with several orange Nemos and at least one blue Dory, a woman in a lemon-print sundress walked by holding a stuffed-doll English sheepdog with a pink ribbon around his neck. Presumably, given the pained look on the woman's face and her hurried pace, the stuffed dog was for the keeper of her soul: her sick child. A mother knows the unmistakable look of torment on another mother.

But it was not a connection to the mother's pain that was so jarring to Mag. What was jarring was the almost uncanny match to the items in her present field of vision with those at play in her memory of sleeping over at Laura Ingrace's house at age fourteen: lemons and an English sheepdog. Mag stared, in awe that the universe would so blatantly throw memory talismans in her face. It was time to consider this memory, the defining moment of when she thought she'd learned what she needed to learn about who Laura Ingrace really was—a dark, damaged version of Laura that Mag would know from age fourteen on up to the moment a few days ago when she learned her assessment was disastrously wrong: Laura Ingrace was not dark and damaged in an interesting way; she was dark and damaged in a dangerous way. Back at fourteen, however, there was a romanticism in thinking of Laura as a benign demon, a reluctant pirate lobbing witty banter, a secret weapon of a friend who came with challenges and secrets.

In the fall of their fourteenth year, Laura called Mag at Mag and Carly's, and their other sisters', apartment outside Carmel, California.

"Magpie, it's Laura, calling from school. How's school for you? Do you miss camp?"

"Laura?"

"Yeah, Laura Ingrace."

"Oh wow. How are you? What's up? Aren't you in your boarding school in New Hampshire?"

"Yeah. Crap. Here comes our RA. I've got, like, one second. Look, it's my birthday this weekend, and my grandbones are coming in from France. My parents said I could have a friend sleep over Friday night. I'm flying home for the weekend. Can you come?"

"Uh, sure. Okay."

"Cool. Our driver will pick you up on Friday at four. Be ready, 'kay?"

"Okay. Um, so my address . . ."

"I don't need your address. I know where you live. Gotta go. 'Bye."

Mag hung up, wondering how Laura Ingrace from camp would know where she lived. They'd been bunk mates, cabin mates, had generally hung out, but with everyone else, since age six. Until then, they'd never been one-on-one friends, so this was odd. But fourteen is a weird age of binaries: immediate and irreversible rejection or immediate and unquestioning acceptance. On this occasion, Mag went with the latter.

That Friday, Laura and Mag sat in the back of a Bentley while Laura's driver drove them to Laura's home—the same colossal mansion Mag would much later identify as the one next door to Paul Trapmore's glass home. But back then, back at age fourteen, Mag had no clue a monster lived next door to Laura Ingrace. Instead, she was soon to learn that monsters lived inside Laura's home.

The Bentley pulled into Laura's pebbled driveway. It wasn't until the driver opened the trunk and began removing luggage that Mag learned Laura herself had not yet been home, had landed from her New Hampshire boarding school and gone straight to collect Mag.

"You came straight from the airport to pick me up before coming home?"

"Yeah. Nobody really wants me here. This is an obligation for Mother to showcase me to the French grandbones. So whatever. I have you with me this time. Can you be cool with that?" Laura stalled in dragging her suitcase, cutting lines in the pebbles, which troubled the driver, who hurried along behind, smoothing stones back into their spaces with his polished shoes. The swish of the pebbles and the swish of the sea beyond the house made for a feeling of swirling. The scent of sharp cypress and salt intoxicated Mag further.

"Hello, Gretchen, can you be cool with that?"

"Sure? And Laura, call me Mag. Okay. I don't go by my real name."

Laura stepped up to Mag, both girls standing by the home's cedar fence, about a foot off a gate to what looked like a back garden. "Gretchen, look. Mag, okay, fine. I don't have a happy little house all wonderful like you. So can you please just be cool with my weird family? They don't like me. I just want to have a nice birthday for once with a friend. Which I've never done."

This was the most heartbreaking and honest thing Mag had ever heard come from Laura Ingrace. Mag and Carly had discussed how sad

Laura's life seemed, always at boarding school or camp. But they'd never talked with her about it, and Laura had never before opened up.

"Laura, I'm so sorry." Mag placed a palm on Laura's arm. "I'm so totally here for you."

Laura stared at Mag's hand on her arm and closed her eyes, as if soaking in a warmth she felt from her touch. When Mag removed her hand, Laura startled and shook. And then her eyes switched to a cold stare.

"Whatever, Gretchen. Thanks. Come on. Leave your bag here with my luggage—the maid will get them. Let's go out back to the greenhouse, and we can get the whole encounter with my mother over with."

Mag bristled when Laura called her Gretchen again. She'd remind her to stop if it happened again, but let it pass this time.

Laura opened the gate in the cedar fence, and out before them stretched the greenest side and back lawns Mag had ever seen. Perfectly curated turf rolled upward to a cliff's top, and down below, Mag couldn't see but heard from the distant laughter, the whistle of high-flying kites, and the roll of the tide, the beach. A line of twenty-foot-high cypress trees bordered one side of the property like stick-straight green crayons, and beyond that green boundary was a large glass home—years later to be discovered as Paul Trapmore's home. The other side, the side to which Laura was walking, went along the back of Laura's house, which was a wall of glass for a breakfast room that met upon a greenhouse. As they neared the greenhouse, Mag saw the blurred image of a woman working away at a tree.

"My mother has three lemon trees she keeps in giant pots on rollers. She makes the gardener roll them out in the better weather, as if they're precious, elderly ancestors in wheelchairs who deserve a view of the sea."

Mag bit the side of her lip and said, "Hmm."

Laura continued. "This is what Mother does every day. She inspects those fucking trees, picks dead leaves, and prunes. I've always had a full-time nanny when I'm 'in residence,' as my bitch mom calls it. Do you think she ever cared to make sure the nannies were getting me enough sun like her trees? You know what else she has in there with her?"

"Other than the lemon trees?"

"Yeah, Gretchen, other than the lemon trees." Laura shook her head.

"Seriously, Laura, call me Mag. I mean it."

"Right. Sorry. So you know what else she has in there?"

"You got me." Mag was holding back a smirk, but also feeling a falling, a calling, maybe, that perhaps the dark, ominous feeling she'd had in the Bentley on the way here was true, or partially true, and not, as she had switched to thinking, just Laura being nervous about coming into an unwelcoming home.

"Mother has in there with her the only true loves of her life, a glass of vodka and her dog, which she named, of course, because she's a drunk and incapable of an original thought, Lemon. A fat-ass, fluffy mope of an English sheepdog."

Laura stopped and turned Mag by the shoulders to look upon the cliff wall toward the sea. The greenhouse was about fifteen feet to their sides now. And then, as if Mag's skin had burned her, Laura pulled her hands away from Mag's shoulders with clawed fingers.

Squeezing out whatever tension had seized her, rolling her hands together, perhaps as a way to move past something that startled her, Laura said, "There, on that rock wall. One time a movie producer rolled Mother's trees to the edge where the sunset over the Pacific can bruise the whole sky in a washy lilac. And it did this one day, the washy lilac sky, the blue of the ocean, the true green leaves and true yellow of Mother's lemons made the perfect backdrop for a movie wedding they filmed on our property—which ended up winning an Oscar. Lemon was the corny ring bearer in the film. What a crock of cliché horseshit."

"A movie on your property is kind of cool, though."

Laura folded her arms. "I knew you'd say that. No, it's not. It's Mother's stupid ego on display is what it is, and that is ugly, and that is evil. Come on, let's get the encounter with Mother over with so we can go play with the only thing that makes me happy here. My parrot, Copte. He's a total rainbow, and he talks. Come on, we can hurry."

The girls walked into the greenhouse, finding Laura's mother, a woman in red pants and a light-green T-shirt, with bleached blonde hair and pruning shears in one hand and a clear glass with a clear liquid and olives in the other. A fat English sheepdog sprawled on the floor beside her.

"That's Lemon," Laura said, pointing to the floor. Her mother twisted her torso, keeping the shears pointed at the very full lemon tree in front of her. Laura's mother glared, no greeting.

Lemon said hi by lifting his fat, furry, black-and-white head off the floor and plunking it right on back down, his long fur spreading like a throw rug.

"Mother," Laura said, "I'm home. This is my friend Gretchen, but people call her Mag. Got my grades. All A-pluses. Top of my class. Where's Copte?"

Laura's mother nodded to Mag and then set down her large glass of drink on a wood workbench, pointed her clippers at the lemon tree even higher, and glanced up. "Laura, you're home, I *hear*. Ripping the peace with that voice of yours."

Laura narrowed her eyes on her mother.

"Mag, is it? Mag, how lovely for Laura to drag you into this soiree, I guess. You girls need to get ready. Your grandparents will be up from their siestas in an hour." Taking a pause to look Laura up and down, she added, "You're fatter. I'll tell the school to watch your diet. What the fuck am I paying for?" She sniffed the air. "And, Laura, you're damn right you got straight As. I'm not keen on throwing more of *my* money away on you, it's bad enough already. But you keep gaining weight like this, grades won't matter, because you'll end up a sniveling average spinster working middle management. Oh, and Copte died. Your father burned him in the firepit. Fucking rainbow parrot feathers went everywhere."

The woman turned her back and continued clipping. Laura stood and stared, glared, boring lasers into her mother's back. Mag had backed herself into the doorway and a step beyond to outside. She'd never in her life witnessed such wickedness.

"Leave," Laura's mother said while keeping her back to the girls and waving her hand with the clippers over her head.

Laura spun around, faced Mag, looked straight into her eyes, and didn't blink. Pure, unadulterated hatred filled her blackened pupils. No tears. Just hate. Naked, barbed hate. Mag wasn't sure if Laura was trying to speak telepathically with her, but she, too, didn't blink. The girls walked to a side door into the glass breakfast room and stood shoulder to shoulder looking out over the lawn. Mag was stunned, couldn't speak.

They stared a good long while saying nothing. And then Laura broke the silence with a hushed, almost gravelly, monotone. "If there is *one* thing Mother knows about me, it's that I despise death," she said. Her tone was such an even cool, it was like her beloved parrot had died a decade ago and she was merely in a solemn nostalgic moment. Mag already knew this was true of Laura anyway, thinking on the time Laura discovered a Triple C cabin mascot, a goldfish, belly up in his bowl. Laura had stayed up all night, sitting in a corner of the bathroom alone, unable to flush him down the drain.

"This nonchalance of hers over Copte, the brutality of burning my beloved pet in their fancy firepit, changes things. Things are different now, Mag," Laura said, grinding her teeth. "So I'm going to need you to hang in my room, okay? I just need to do a few things for my birthday dinner. Are you okay with that? The maid will bring you."

Just then, a maid, in a literal black-and-white outfit like a Halloween costume, appeared.

"Hey, Laura, I think I'm just going to go home, okay? I'm sorry about your parrot and real sorry about your mom," Mag said.

"Just give me a half hour, Mag, please. Promise. I'm going to work on something with the chef for my cake, is all. I'm the one sorry about my mother. Okay?"

Forgiveness again appeared, but this time was covered in flashing warnings. Mag would give this tortured night one more shot, but one more thing and she'd call Carly and split. Laura disappeared for a half hour, while Mag waited in her white-on-white bedroom.

That night, after a stilted formal dinner of the worst foods possible—bloodred, rare filet; hard, cold carrots; a lukewarm cream soup with mushrooms and onions; and disgusting coconut cake with cream-cheese frosting—Mag and Laura joined Laura's French grandmother in her guest suite and watched rom-coms and played with her furs and silks and ate an entire two boxes of contraband macaroons. That part of the night was fabulous, making up for all the wickedness and weirdness and awkwardness, and also the terrible, horrible meal that came before. They woke the next morning, strewn upon huge pillows and giant down comforters on the grandmother's suite's plush carpet. The whole house woke, in fact, to the sound of screaming, which did not fit the gorgeous Saturday outside the suite's large bay window that faced the sea.

Laura and Mag ran downstairs to find the grandmother already there in the glass breakfast nook, standing behind Laura's mother, who was screaming upon viewing the back lawn. And on that stretch, on the part tipped up to meet the cliff wall, was a total massacre.

Laura and Mag backstepped into the pantry and watched Laura's mother discover her first horror. Lemon did not bark at her side. Lemon wasn't within the crowd. Laura's mother turned and searched everyone standing behind her, which now included the grandmother, the grandfather, and a maid. Laura's father was out on the lawn. Like a bloodhound, Laura's mother tracked to Laura in the pantry. Clenching a fistful of Laura's hair and yanking, she said, "You fucking monster." The caps on her front teeth glistened pearl white.

French Grammy pushed past Mag to pull Laura's mother away. "Patrice, calm down," she said in a very French accent. "She's a little girl. She didn't do this. Look. Look out there. Maury has found something pinned in this, this, this, ah, this mess. Ze girls were with me all night. We were watching movies in my room very late. Leave the girl alone."

Laura kept her head down and primed tears. Mag rewound the night they'd spent with the French grandmother and how Laura was so keen on loving and snuggling and complimenting her traveling silks and French hats and soft, taut skin. *Grammy, I want to be as beautiful as you one day,* she'd said. They'd been up all night; in fact, they'd chugged Mountain Dew in order to watch every possible movie they could. When they woke, it was only after a fifteen-minute nap. So there was no way Laura could have done what was out on the lawn.

"Lemon!" Laura's mother yelled to no one in particular, moving away from the pantry and toward the glass wall of the breakfast room. Looking upon the massacre, everyone inside watched Laura's father navigating the disaster. With all eyes on the lawn, and French grammy drifting in that direction, Laura winked at Mag, leaned to her ear, and whispered, "It must be weird for Mother, not having Lemon with her. He should be with her to see this special horror, designed just for her. Gee, wonder where he is," she said, and nudged Mag's arm.

Mag had no idea where Lemon had gone. No idea what game Laura had played.

French Grammy circled back to the pantry and grabbed the girls' hands. "Girls, come now. Let's go see what this is about outside."

Laura's mother ran ahead to Laura's father, Maury, who tiptoed around the yellow mash in the grass. Holding a piece of paper he'd found stabbed to the ground with a gardening spike, he kept shaking his head in disbelief.

The sloped lawn to the cliff wall was like a propped book, open to reveal pages to read. And on the opened green pages, spelled out in blotches of mashed lemons, was a ransom note:

## $2 MILL FOR LEMON

Every single lemon had been plucked from the lemon trees and smashed with a mallet to spell out this lawn note. The bright lemon rinds cracked like yellow eggs, and the lighter lemon flesh squished into the greenest of green grass. The sky was such a perfect, uncorrupted, smooth, cerulean blue with a wash of lemon above the horizon line on the navy ocean. And jagged against the blue sky were the three, now black, lemon trees. The trees had been torched in a controlled fire and left at the top of the cliff wall; the stubs of their black trunks and remaining limbs stood like broken-down zealots burned on the cross. Wisps of smoke billowed, as if the aftermath of a war battle. The only things missing were severed heads on spikes.

Maury, the father, read aloud the paper he'd found: "If you want Lemon back, leave a duffel of $2 mill cash on the cliff wall when you go out today. Because you'll go out today. If you leave someone behind to watch, we'll kill Lemon. If you install a camera, which we know you don't have, we'll kill Lemon. If you call the cops, we'll kill Lemon. If you use anything other than the cleaned cash in the safe in the basement, we'll call the IRS and drop a tip about your tax evasion. We know who you are. We know your secrets. If you do anything other than leave cash in a bag on the cliff wall when you leave today, we will kill Lemon and call the feds."

Laura's mother vomited on the lemon mash of the letter *E*. Grammy gasped and clutched Laura tight into her stomach, and Laura primed more tears.

Tall Mag, black-haired Mag, with her violet eyes, standing in a shadow of a towering cypress, in awe of a witchcraft so dark and foreign, felt frightened that she'd be blamed just for the inner act of holding admiration. She had no clue how all this came together, but she did know why. Casting her lightning eyes to Laura, she hoped to send the following telepathic message: *I know you did this. I know why you did this. And I won't say you did this, as long as you tell me how you did it and that Lemon's okay.*

Laura winked as if she read Mag's mind, and indeed, later that morning, when Laura stood with Mag at the end of her driveway waiting for Carly to pick her up, Laura said, "There are three things I'll tell you if you'll compete with me, just me, in the Triple C treetop course next summer: one, where Lemon went; two, who helped me pull this off; and three, why they did."

Mag sucked in her cheeks, considered the offer. "Before I agree, is Lemon okay?"

"Holy shit, everyone worries about the damn dog. Yes, for fuck's sake, not any clumps of his stupid fur were harmed. He's happy. Okay? Do we have a deal?"

"So whoever helped you wasn't anyone in the house? Not your grandparents, maid, chef, father, driver, nanny?"

"Nope. None of them half-wits. Well, Grammy's not a half-wit."

"And when you say compete in the treetop course, what do you mean?"

"That's up to you, Magpie. You're the camp champion at everything. Come up with some challenges for us. Deal?"

Mag, never one to shy from a competition, and beyond intrigued by this strange game with a baked-in secret of revenge on an abusive mother, and also fourteen, stepped into Laura's space. "You better prepare yourself to lose and tell me everything. I never lose," she said.

"We'll see about that."

Mag snapped out of her reminiscences in Boston Children's Hospital when she felt a tapping on her shoulder.

"Excuse me, excuse me," a girl's voice was saying.

Mag looked up to find a skinny, strawberry-blonde girl in an apple-print dress.

"Hi," she said. "I'm Gretchen. Gretchen Sabin. Lucy's landlord, or her landlord's daughter. You're Lucy's mom, right? Your name is Gretchen too! How cool. I saw on the news. They, the cops, didn't let me meet you the other day."

"Oh, right, yeah. Hi. I'm Lucy's mom, yes. You can call me Mag," Mag said, her voice unsure on the words *Lucy's mom*, it being such a true title, but also false: her baby's name was *Laura*.

"Mag is such a cool name. I'm happy you guys are together again. I can't stay long. My dad's waiting on me outside, and the reception people won't let me visit Lucy anyway. I tried. I just wanted to tell her not to worry about Allen. I'll keep looking for him. Okay? Will you tell her? She can Skype me every day, and I'll give her reports on my searching."

Lucy had been frantic to find Allen, her cat, but like Laura, he'd disappeared.

"That would be wonderful, Gretchen. Thank you," Mag said. Mag knew near to nothing about this girl. Lucy hadn't talked about her, as far as Mag knew beyond whatever she might be telling counselors and doctors and law enforcement.

Gretchen scrunched her shoulders around her neck and swayed. "I'm so happy for Lucy," she said with a sweet, sweet, innocent smile. And then in a snap, she stopped swaying and jammed her fists on her sides and switched her tone and face and posture to that of an exuberant, confident game-show host, and, emphasizing words, wagged a finger as if a person decades older. Talking out of one side of her mouth with twisted lips, she said, "Okay, 'bye, but only for now. Because I'm going to find Allen. I promise you that." It was an odd, possibly shocking, affect on such a tiny, young girl, an intimate comedy that breached boundaries between strangers—uncharacteristic of the sweet little girl Gretchen portrayed with the innocent smile and scrunched shoulders. In a word, the moment was awkward. The quick switch of personality, creepy.

As Mag watched Gretchen walk away, she couldn't tell if the cold shock crackling up her spine was from her memories of Laura Ingrace at age fourteen, or the present vision of an odd, awkward teen in an apple-print dress who shared her name.

# PART III

EIGHT WEEKS LATER

# CHAPTER TWENTY-EIGHT
## LUCY

I've been in California for eight weeks. I'm about to Skype-call Gretchen Sabin, my *super-creep* neighbor-landlord, in New Hampshire, sure to once again hear a negative report on her continuing search for my lost love, Allen. I miss my cat so bad my full-size heart feels compressed enough to fit in a thimble.

I can't make sense of the night I ran from Gretchen's house and discovered the truth about my life. And there's no way to make sense of Gretchen turning into a demon and slamming her body through the forest to come screaming up on me on the road—holding a bone. I think it was a bone. I don't know if she meant to beat me with it. Honestly, though, my perceptions of that night are so warped, blurring with the insanity of everything that came right before and right after. Of the disappearance of Mom, Laura Ingrace. Of being reunited and moving to California with my real mother, Gretchen Bianchi. I believe whatever Gretchen Sabin had in mind that night, as she burned a hole in her throat in screaming at me, was malicious, but since I'm so confused about everything from that night, I focus on just one thing: *checking in with her from afar on her search for Allen.*

Events over the past eight weeks have been a blur, but I think, maybe, they are starting to come into focus. When I think about the last eight weeks, snippets and scenes and conversations pop into focus with blurred edges around the beginnings and ends and around the actual physical place, like all I can remember is very specific details within the very circle I was in, such as sitting at an oval dining table as opposed to whatever the actual room or house looked like—blurs. I'm not sure if I have the series of events in chronological order, but I also don't care to organize my life since finding out Mom is not Mom and Gretchen Bianchi is my mother. The feds still don't know where "Mom"—Laura Ingrace—is. They believe she's on the run. So she left me, stole me, and abandoned me.

Special people in Gretchen Bianchi's life call her a variety of names: G, Maggot, Magpie, Mag, lady girl. I've chosen to call her Mag because I can't call her Mom. I just can't. The blip-bubble of me that allows myself to love her thinks Mag could be the most perfect Jenny. Maybe Mag is the queen of Jennys. But that thought is hidden in the secret blip-bubble inside me that I don't let anyone know about. It's not safe yet. We've got boundaries to overcome. I have to be sure.

We could have driven—not flown like we did—to California in Mag's "beast" camper because a guy named Cord, who acts like he's my grandpa but he's not, and a big burly guy named D took shifts and drove Mag's camper literally day and night to New Hampshire. But after what later happened at Nathan and Thomas Vinet's house, there was no way Mag would make me drive across the country. Cord and D were worried that Mag and I would be stuck in New Hampshire for a long time and she'd need her comfort space. They seem like really nice, but also really scary, guys, especially D, who showed me this self-defense move he calls *five will get you ten, ten will get you killed*. Mag thanked them, and they flew back to Carmel. Mag wouldn't let anyone else, except Nathan and Thomas Vinet, be around us during all the initial turmoil, not even any of my aunts—I guess my aunts, right? "Carly, please. When things are settled, please come meet us then . . ." is one such conversation I listened to while Mag thought I was sleeping in some bed—a hospital bed, maybe? Or the bed Dr. Nathan Vinet gave us in his guest cottage at his lakefront property, where Mag was staying while I was tested and interviewed and prodded at Boston Children's. A bed. That's what I remember.

When all the "preliminary" work was done and I was "cleared," I joined Mag at Nathan's for a night. Once again, some odd blip-bubble let me lower my shoulders while we ate a goodbye meal. In the center of the Vinets' oval dining table, they set out a blue bowl full of spaghetti and meatballs. Glistening glitter filled my head as I sprinkled fresh-grated Parmigiano-Reggiano from Dyson's over my steaming pile of pasta. During the short time the four of us sat together, everything seemed happy and normal, even though that dinner was so sudden in the grand scheme of things. Just days since I'd found the truth in the metal box of lies.

I think it was Thomas. Thomas took away all the awkwardness by being super funny during dinner. He's a strange kid. First of all, everyone else had full glasses of soda. But Thomas poured himself a literal half gallon of whole milk into one of those leftover 7-Eleven Extra Big Gulp jugs. And when he took an overpour sip and milk sloshed not in but around his mouth, he said, "Guess I'm full," in a very dry and matter-of-fact way.

I don't know why, maybe I was thankful everyone's attention was on Thomas and away from me, but I thought it was the funniest thing anyone had said in the longest time. When I started to snort-laugh, like a pig snort, Mag and Nathan snort-laughed too. Encouraged, Thomas didn't wipe away the milk, which surrounded his mouth in a mustache and goatee. Instead, he stood, went to a closet, found a top hat (who has a top hat at the ready?) and an umbrella, pulled a quarter from his pocket, stuck it in the socket of one closed eye, and pranced back to the table, saying he was the Monopoly Man. I guess the umbrella was supposed to be his cane.

"The Monopoly Man doesn't have a monocle," Nathan said, laughing.

"Yes, he very well does, Dad." The quarter plopped from Thomas's eye and splashed into his giant jug of milk. "Now you made me lose my eyepiece."

"The Monopoly Man does not have a monocle. Prove it. And be careful with my top hat."

"That's your top hat?" Mag said.

"Yeah," Nathan said.

Then the two of them stared at each other so long, both of them with twinkling eyes, pupils searching around the other's face like spotlights, Thomas and I raised our eyes at each other, saying "wow" with our expressions.

"So you would be up to going to the opera in a tux?" Mag asked. She hadn't blinked. And neither had Nathan. The only way I can think to describe the moment is this: Nathan's blue eyes were like diamond-studded sapphires when he looked at her.

"The opera?" he said in a dreamy tone. His pupils grew even wider.

"Yeah, the opera," Mag said in a voice that sounded drugged.

"If you want to go to the opera, I want to go to the opera," Nathan said.

Double wow. I was grinning wide from within my secret blip-bubble. I think I allowed the grin, the blip-bubble itself, probably out of self-preservation: it was exhausting to be so confused and angry and anxious and scared all the time. And I probably allowed the blip-bubble because nobody was peppering me with questions. And this dinner, with the perfect ingredients and the organic laughter over unexpected silliness and even the lighting and the background James Taylor Spotify station, this, like a sudden blip in a perfect dream you never want to leave, was always the fantasy I had conjured when I pictured what it was like to dine with other people. Sitting there in that blip-bubble at the Vinets', I realized just how much the structured dinners with Mom led me to crave a comradery I had never experienced, only dreamed could happen. Certainly hadn't happened in my first attempt at Gretchen Sabin's house. And meals when Mom was in a "dark space"—weeks of her mind-numbing obsession with some bird project or editing job—I'd eat alone, not allowed to turn on any lights, for lights burned her brain, she'd say. So I'd eat alone by battery candlelight and silently tiptoe into her room, careful not to disturb her "thought process," to collect her finished dishes of items I'd made for her—otherwise, if I hadn't, she "starved" for her "art." She could be dramatic. She could be relentless. She could be sharp and unloving and cruel. But after a spell of dark obsession, she'd emerge my mom again, and we'd eat tandem dinners with the lights on and discuss books and my homeschooling homework. Sometimes she'd splurge on a hug or rolling my hair in her fingers, but as I think on those moments, she did always seem to cringe in pain at the touch. Like I burned her.

Thomas circled his lips in a silent wow and whispered, "Dad hasn't dated anyone since my mom died. Whoa." Thomas seemed excited about the prospect. "I thought he was a eunuch or a priest or something."

Nathan overheard Thomas and told him to go find the Monopoly game. As Thomas left, the blip-bubble popped, because Nathan said to me, "Well, Lucy, so tomorrow you and Mag will start your drive across the country. That should be exciting, right? Make all the stops."

All my brain heard was "drive across the country" and Mom's—I mean Laura Ingrace's—face floated into my field of vision, overlaid Mag's face, and an anxiety so fierce gripped my throat, it caused me to run from the table and hurl in Nathan's kitchen trash.

Sandra Dyson let Mag keep the camper in the back lot behind Dyson's. Mag said we'd fly home. "I understand, Lucy. We've talked with the counselor. I know what driving across the country means to you. We'll get the beast some other time. When you're ready. If you're ready. No rush. No worries. It's all good," Mag said.

When Nathan dropped us off at Logan Airport, I rolled the luggage they bought me to enter the terminal. I didn't realize Mag wasn't behind me until I stopped at the automatic doors, turned to say something to her, and saw her long, tall body sealed against Nathan's long, tall body in a mutual full-body bear hug. When they separated out of the embrace, he pulled her back to him, closed his eyes, set his hands on the sides of her face, and pressed his lips on hers, which she reciprocated even harder. This went on, them kissing and touching each other's faces, for, I think, a literal eternity. I believe this was their very first kiss. That's one of the other blip-bubbles of very specific, telescopic memories I keep from the past eight weeks.

Every time I hear the doorbell, every time I hear a creak outside my window, I think Laura Ingrace has come to claim me. And when that happens, I seize up in fear and hives grow, but also my heart explodes in excitement to see her. It's very confusing. They tried to give me meds to deal with the hives and insomnia from all this. But I said no. Maybe I'm wrong.

"I've always gotten these hives," I said to the counselor while sitting in some blurry space with red chairs and a brown couch, I think. Sometimes the counseling memories, and there've been several, shift to an amber-lit room with a green hanging chair and lots of plants. And sometimes a hospital room with no color. All the sessions blur together in a potluck of sessions.

"Didn't your mother take you to a doctor for these hives?" the counselor asked.

"You can call her Laura. I get it. She's not my mom."

"But you called her Mom for thirteen years."

"Yeah, I know. I get it. Let's call her Laura, okay? I think calling her Laura would help me separate things and help me to make sense."

"You're very brave, Lucy. That's astute of you." The counselor paused, dangling her smart-doctor glasses from her thin fingers. "Can we talk about these hives more?"

"I guess."

"Why didn't Laura ever take you to a doctor about these hives?"

"I never told her about them. I hid them."

"Why?"

Silence.

"Lucy, why didn't you tell Laura about these stress hives?"

"Because, because, it was, mainly, it was her words."

"Her words?"

"I mean, her words is what I think would sometimes make the hives. But it was after I provoked her."

"Hmm. We'll talk about that, how you think you provoked her. But first, maybe some medication could help with the stress and the hives? Would you be open to that?"

"Maybe later. Okay?"

So on. Numerous counseling sessions like this, especially after I've clawed at Mag and screamed at her to step away. But I don't want to push her away. I want to love her. The counselors say the roller coaster of ups and downs is normal.

But none of this is fucking normal.

Trust, they said. Give Lucy trust. Trust and time and space, and then give her more trust and time and space. I'm not sure whatever Mag did to nuke-bomb all the reporters, but she keeps them well away from me.

Right now, I have the Apple laptop Mag bought me on my lap. There's no restrictions or spyware, and she doesn't monitor like "Mom" did, I mean, *Laura*. I'm sitting on my new bed in my old baby room. The wind is rustling through the leaves in the canopy right outside my high window, and the sound soothes me, as this sound always does. Mag says my treetop bedroom always sounded like this when I was a baby.

I launch Skype and wait for it to load and my credentials to clear. Gretchen usually answers in two seconds.

I miss Allen so bad I can't sleep. Why is everything about my life before the box of lies stripped from me? Even the keepsake and metal boxes, the feds took those for evidence. I miss snuggling into Allen's fur and his purrs so bad, I've considered running away in the middle of the night and trekking across the country to Gretchen's so I can search for him myself.

Every night for eight weeks, Gretchen's reported that she can't find Allen. I had looked for him before we left New Hampshire, after the cops cleared the ranch, saying Mom-Laura wasn't there, and neither was her roller bag or phone, the two things I know I for sure saw when I opened the metal box. Jerry and Gretchen told the cops I left their house to leave with a friend, so they weren't alarmed. Gretchen said she didn't see I'd left my phone and clothes behind. They also said they had no reason to check in on Mom during the day. And it's just now, this very second, I think some fog is lifting, but I shiver at the thought, but it really doesn't make sense that a dad would have no alarm that a teen sleeping over his house just fled to meet up with another friend. Right? Why would they lie about that? To keep people from searching their property? Wasn't Gretchen screaming that night about surprises on trails in her forest? *Stop. Stop. Stop. Call and find out about Allen.*

I shake my head. I'm allowing conspiracies and horrors. Mom's burner last pinged in New York City, the feds say. Here's what had to have happened: Mom came back after I took the box—*where was she?*—figured her jig was up with me, grabbed her roller and burner and ran. That has to be what happened. She abandoned me. I need to accept this.

It's time for my fifty-sixth Skype call to Gretchen Sabin to see if by some miracle she's found Allen. I'm telescoping on my desperation to find Allen. Needing him is more acceptable than needing Mom—*Laura Ingrace.*

"Hi, Luce," Gretchen answers as her moon face pops on my screen. She's in her room, sitting on her bed, and her wall headboard of *Grey's Anatomy* books is behind her. In last night's call, she again reported no Allen. The fifty-fifth report of no Allen. I'm assuming there's still no Allen, and tonight's will be the fifty-sixth negative report.

"Hi, Gretchen. How's things?" I ask.

"Oh, the same. Want to see the new skulls puzzle I'm working on in the dead room? I can walk down there with the computer."

Do I miss this? Gretchen's constant attempts to corral me, keep me, set me in a barricaded room, surrounded by puzzle mazes? Not really—I've never liked the unnatural creepiness of her need for me. But, in the very core of myself, which nobody could know, there is something about her naked—terrifying—need, which matches my need to be needed, and so, Gretchen remains a dangerous addiction. Truth be truth, I know these nightly Skype calls are a subterfuge, vain attempts to find Allen, for I think I must accept he's gone. It's been too long. I know what I need are doses of Gretchen's wicked desperation, and this is not healthy. I've got to break this cycle. Accept that Allen is gone. And let Mom go. As I always do, I will refuse going to the dead room, even virtually.

Before I can answer, she twists her head to the left, which is toward her door, and she shudders, surprised by what she's seeing, but then scrunches her forehead like she's mad. She looks back at the screen.

"What's going on? What's that?" I ask.

"Oh, nothing. Nothing. What were we talking about?" She shifts her computer so her camera is angled away from the door, and now I can see the corner where the wall full of porcelain doll puzzles meets the *Grey's Anatomy* wall.

"You asked if I wanted to see your new skulls puzzle in the dead room," I say.

Again, Gretchen twists her head toward the door. Red blotches pulse on her neck and chest. She is, of course, in an apple-print dress. This time she stiffens her body, freezing her torso straight against the wall of anatomy books. A flash of orange and white jumps between her and the computer, and then it's gone. Gretchen throws her computer on the bed. Now her camera faces the wall opposite her bed with all the Dante's *Inferno* puzzles. I hear her wrestling and scrabbling around in the background and muttering. I can't tell if she's angry or in distress.

Then in a flash again—the orange and white is back. This time it freezes before the screen and blocks my view of the *Inferno* wall. The orange and white is fur. His face fills my screen.

"Allen!" I yell. "Allen!"

I must yell really loud because Mag barges in my room, which she's never done before without knocking.

"Are you okay?" she asks.

"Allen! Mag, Allen is back!"

She swoops up to my bed, bends, and peers at the screen. Gretchen has grabbed Allen and is throwing him on the floor.

"Gretchen found Allen," I yell. "She found Allen. Allen!"

"Hi, Gretchen," Mag says.

"Hi," Gretchen says, putting on a quick sunny tone and smile, which doesn't match the scowl I know I caught on her face when she threw Allen on the ground.

"Why didn't you tell me you found Allen?" I interrupt.

"Didn't I?"

"No, you didn't."

"Oh, well, surprise! I found Allen!"

"Are you taking care of him?"

"Of course I'm taking care of him," she says, sparkling her eyes toward Mag. With that, Mag moves away from the computer and to the door. In the doorway, she pumps her long arms in the air as if in victory, mouths, "Yeah, Allen," and softly closes the door. I know she's following the motley crew of counselors' directives to give me space and then give me more space.

But I don't want Mag to give me space. Things aren't right. As soon as Mag leaves, Gretchen switches her cheery smile to her weird eerie stare down, the kind she used to give when I lived there as a way to make me flinch. But this time she has my cat, and I'm helpless, sitting on a bed clear across the country. So this time I do flinch.

With a tremble in my voice, I say, "Gretchen, please tell me you'll take care of Allen until I figure out how to come get him. Please."

"Silly, I'm very busy, you know. So I guess I can try to feed him between puzzles and computer school when I can and all. You shouldn't have left what you love behind. It's sort of a breach of the lease. You should come get him ASAP." Her tone is a clear warning, completely disconnected from the—I know now, phony—sympathetic tones she gave over the last eight weeks when she'd report she'd looked everywhere again, called for him, left food for him outdoors, but just couldn't find Allen.

My heart is clogging my throat in beats that ricochet all the way up to my brain.

"Please, Gretchen, don't hurt Allen."

"Ope!" she yelps, smashing her hand against her chest. "Me? You think I'd hurt Allen? Lucy, you're being paranoid." She loses the smile and winks in her wicked way. "You know I want to see you again, Lucy. And, remember, I always get what I want." Gretchen stares another beat with no smile and then shuts the lid of her computer to close me out.

I'm frozen. I can't move. I can't believe she said that. I can't believe she did that.

*How long has she had Allen? When was she going to tell me? What is this game?*

My iPhone beeps. An incoming text:

Can't wait for you to come get Allen! Don't worry, he can snuggle with Old Mr. Snoof in the lab until you get here. Xoxoxoxo —G

My fingers pop straight and grow ice-cold. I drop my phone. A chill runs up my spine and causes a brain freeze. An instinct tells me to send nobody but myself to get Allen. Something about Gretchen's awful, eerie face and words and tone were a warning, a ransom message, unspoken but blaringly loud: *Lucy, only you may come to get Allen, or Allen disappears.*

# CHAPTER TWENTY-NINE
## MOTHER

Lucy steps out of her room with a face so ghost white and scared, Mag's not sure she's prepared to do whatever she's supposed to do. That creepy-awkward girl Gretchen in New Hampshire found Lucy's cat, Allen, so Mag is confused as to why Lucy looks scared out of her mind.

Mag's at her computer, sitting at one end of their two-top table in the kitchen. Green curtains flutter around her from a breeze through an open window. She'd already made an instant decision after leaving Lucy's room. She hopes she's right. She hopes this will knock the fright out of her girl.

"Lucy, I'm booking us tickets to leave in the morning to go get Allen. We'll get your fur-love tomorrow, lickety-split. Okay?"

Lucy collapses on the floor, wailing, "Thank you, thank you, Mag. Thank you."

Hovering over her fifteen-year-old daughter, Lucy is her baby girl again. Her infant she failed to protect. And now, Mag folds over her as an impenetrable tent. She hopes Lucy feels all her motherly intentions seeping into her, her unwavering commitment to never, not ever, allow another fiber of her being to hurt. Not on her body and not in her mind. Mag will give everything of herself to her girl, every last minute she's on this earth. If Lucy needs her cat, they'll fly to get him tomorrow.

If she needs counselors, she'll buy her twenty. If she needs food, water, shelter when she's fifty and grown and long married, Mag will give her hers and sleep under a bridge.

Whatever Lucy needs, Mag will give double. Mag is irrelevant as a separate being. She's only on this planet as a sentry to her child.

"Hush, Lucy. Hush. I'm here. I will get you whatever you need. Always. You are safe."

And in her mind, she bites back a hatred brewing so fierce, she's afraid she might explode. *Laura Ingrace, if I ever face you again, I fear for you. I fear for what will become of you for doing this to this beautiful child. For raining your wreckage upon her and reducing her to fear and crying and hives and terror, you will pay. I promise you that.*

# CHAPTER THIRTY

## LUCY

I'm knocking on Gretchen's brick fortress door with the weird metal shields around the frame. Mag is taking a call with my aunt Carly down in her beast camper, which we parked at the rental ranch. She's giving me space to handle the collection of Allen on my own. I must have made her think I need "agency" and to "advocate for myself" and "more space" because I wasn't talking the whole flight here. But she's 100 percent wrong. I want her with me. Maybe I'll advocate for myself by telling her outright I've grown to like, could see myself love, her being around. And her strength is something I aim to have. Like she's that missing wedge of me that would complete my own almost-strength.

"Lucy!" Gretchen yells as she opens the door by pushing outward. I know enough now to step to the side.

"Where's Allen?" My tone is back to steel, showing I'm not flinching anymore, and she's crossed too many lines, broken too many rules, for this friendship to lift and fly. We, as a we, are dead. She's in her apple-print dress. I grind my teeth. Her hair is frizzed out free, forming a halo of thin hair around her face, a cloud of wispy, frayed hay.

"Oh, Lucy, is that a way to greet an old friend?" She lifts her eyes so the pupils are at the top of her eye sockets, and the whites of her eyes show the below-lid veins. She has the darkest bags under her eyes I've seen on her yet. Another late-puzzle night, I suppose.

I inhale through my nose, close my eyes. "Where is Allen, Gretchen?"

She pops her lips. "Guess you'll have to come in and find him. I'm busy."

I open my mouth to stammer out a protest, but she turns and runs up the staircase, leaving the front door open to the fossil foyer. I can't leave Allen in this horror house. I have to find him. *Dammit.* I should turn. For sure turn around and run and leave a man behind. But I can't leave Allen. The thought of Gretchen brutalizing him, leaving him alone, possibly starving him, throwing him on the floor, not lavishing him with hugs and pets and combing his fur and giving him treats and treating him like Prince Allen kills me. I can't leave my entire past behind. I step inside and pull shut the door so Allen can't scoot out and get lost all over again. *Was he ever lost? Did she have him all along?*

As soon as I step inside, I note the box tower of Crock-Pots is gone. I jump when I hear metal swinging and clanking outside the door. A swoosh and a clink. Another swoosh and clink. And another swoosh and clink. I swirl back around and grab the knob. While it does turn and is not locked, when I push, the door opens only a half inch and jams. I slam into it with my shoulder, and I'm met by a solid wall.

*Did she lock me in?*

*What?*

*How?*

*What was that metal swinging? Those weird metal shields?*

"Gretchen!" I scream.

She pokes her head over the railing of the top landing.

"Shh, you'll wake Daddy, Lucy! Don't be so rude. It's time for you to find Allen. Isn't that the game we're playing today? Or do you want to do a puzzle in the dead room?"

*Wake Daddy? It's noon.*

"Where is Allen? And did you lock me in? What the fuck, you bitch!"

Gretchen is howling laughing. Her frizzed-out hair scratches the air around her moon-bright face. Red pulses pop on her exposed arms. Her eye sockets merge with the bags underneath and appear like two black bruises.

"Oh ho." She tapers the laugh. "Actually, let's do something else first. I wanted to wait to show you. But now's the time. Head on down the hall toward the bathroom, open that ivory door you tried to nose into the first night you came."

"Is Allen in there?" I ask, staring, not flinching.

"Maybe."

She steps slow down the stairs like she's Pepé Le Pew and I'm her unwilling cat lover. She slides her left arm with the Apple Watch along the railing, making her own limb a trailing veil. Because I can't stand the thought of her being close to me, I walk toward the ivory door.

As I do, I hear that metal swing and click outside the front door again. *Swing click, swing click, swing click.*

I turn around in the normal hall to see Gretchen in the foyer. She opens the front door and pushes outward, easy and fine.

"Maybe you're having a spell, Lucy? Are you stressed about finding out you're not who you thought you were and losing your cat? Look, honey, the door is not locked."

I tilt my head and raise an eye to her. I do not flinch. I flip her off.

I place my hand on the gold doorknob, push, and find a blackened room.

"Allen," I call into the darkness.

She pulls the front door shut.

"Reach in. Wall switch is on the side," Gretchen calls down to me.

As I do, I hear running behind me, and before I can turn, hands push hard on my back and I'm shoved inside. I stumble forward and fall to the floor. The door is pulled shut, and I hear the turn of the lock. I'm screaming.

It is pitch-black in here. I continue screaming and feeling for the door. Palm over palm, I climb myself up, and finally when standing, brush my hands on each side until I feel a plastic plate and switch.

Just as I flick the light on, my body pressed against the locked door and me still screaming, a voice comes over an intercom. "Lucy, nobody can hear you. The walls are soundproofed. I left you a note."

I turn around to a whirl of horror: blue pools, bones, and the brightest lights.

There's no furniture. No windows. The walls are white white. The lights are huge industrial halogens you might find over a factory floor, so bright my eyes sting. And in two rows of five are ten blue kiddie pools on the wood floors. Beside each pool is a rectangular gray mat. In each pool is an assortment of human skeletal bones. In the closest pool, a human skull, which is missing some teeth, sits atop a pyramid stack of longer bones, possibly leg, possibly arm, I don't know. A rib cage is set to the left, several other smaller bones, and flat ear-shaped pieces—I think hip bones—fill all the other spaces. In a nook on one wall is a piss-yellow toilet.

On the floor closest to me and at the start of the two rows of bone pools is a printed page, I think from a book, and a note on top of that.

### Dearest Lucy,

*These are human bones and they are puzzles! Each pool is a puzzle of a real dead human! You can use the page I ripped from Grey's as a guide to put them back together. Use one gray mat for each one. When you have correctly assembled all of them, then you can go find Allen. Hint: he might be playing with Old Mr. Snoof in the lab.*

*I feel like I created a really great game, and I even gave you a guide and the best of my latest specimens! Be careful with them! Don't you think the pressure of being locked away makes it more challenging?*

*Toot-a-loo! This will be fun!*

*—Gretchen*

# CHAPTER THIRTY-ONE

## MOTHER

They told Mag to give Lucy space and then give her more space and to make sure she was allowed to advocate for herself so she had agency and self-confidence. Fine. But something is wrong, and Mag's instincts are blaring a four-alarm fire. If one thing is ingrained in Mag so deep, it's that she will follow her instincts.

Mag had secretly trailed Lucy up the driveway to the Sabin house, and she stood at the bend in the road, listening. When the door opened, she heard Lucy demand Allen, and while she smiled proud at her daughter's *agency*, she also detected that this was all wrong. A girl shouldn't have to pound on someone's front door and demand her own cat. To have this level of anger. To sound as if she were fighting for what belonged to her. Wasn't this Gretchen girl watching Allen until Lucy came for him?

Still standing at the bend in the road, Mag hears the door on the brick house shut. She stalls and listens, and within a few seconds, hears a metal swishing and clicking sound. She creeps out of the bend to see the door being pushed out a half inch and banging into three metal rounds that have dropped into place around the door. Lucy is yelling behind that door.

Mag sprints up the hill but is stopped at the start of the circular parking area by a man in khakis. He's wearing white gloves. To her side is a small excavator under a green metal roof on four poles. She notes how as soon as she got within twenty feet of the house, floodlights shot on, which is apparent, even though it's noon, given the dark shading of the tall pines. And now, as she steps backward away from the man, and out of the twenty-foot perimeter, and he walks toward her and out as well, they switch off.

"No farther," he says.

"What the hell is going on?" She steps toward him; he backs up within twenty feet of the house. The lights flood back on.

"What is going to happen is very simple," he says in the calmest tone. "My daughter is going to play with your daughter for a few days." He turns to the front door when the metal plates grind and roll and click into spots around the doorframe, no longer blocking ingress and egress. The door opens for a second, a girl speaks, and then the door is pulled shut fast.

"It's all a game, see. I'm Jerry, by the way."

"I want Lucy out here right now," Mag says, trying to push past him.

Jerry extracts a tiny silver gun from his pants pocket, and Mag jumps back. Jerry walks to her, and the lights are off again. Mag notes that each time the lights turn on or off, a flash appears on his Apple Watch.

"This life," Jerry says, scraping his house slippers on the tar of the circular drive, "has gotten away from me. I can't control Gretchen anymore. I can't keep her happy. She is not well. And I am tired. My girl has bags under her eyes so dark, she looks dead. So here is what we are going to do, Ms. Bianchi. Here is what we are going to do. This watch—" He lifts his right arm and bounces his wrist toward her.

"With this watch I control several things in the house. Smart-home appliances, locks, temperature, et cetera. You don't need to know the intricacies, but the whole house is rigged." He pauses to breathe in while closing his eyes. When he opens them, his eyes are dead, like he's lost whatever soul he had. A rabbit runs across the parking area, but no floodlights switch on.

"See," he continues, "I've lost control of my life. And there's no way out for me, or for my Gretchen, and I need to end all of this, but I can't hospitalize her again. I need to give her this game. I need her to finish her project out back. And part of that is having Lucy for a few days. Because this is Gretchen's wish. My Gretchen wants to play with Lucy one last time. Things, oh—" He pauses. Shakes his head. "Things were pretty bad before. Then when Lucy moved in, there was a small window when I thought we'd turned a corner and things might improve. But no, no, actually things have only escalated." He pauses and shakes his head again. "Anyway, this house"—he gestures to the house—"this house has no exits. The windows . . ."

Mag notes the slit windows and questions the phrase *finish her project out back*.

"All of the windows are like that. There's no basement bulkhead. No other way in or out. The attached garage, sealed. We walled off the interior door, needed the wall space. Okay?"

Mag flares her nostrils and is biting her bottom lip. She's considering Big D's *five will get you ten, ten will get you killed*.

"Anyway," Jerry continues, "this house is a dormant oven. With my watch, I've set up a few things. Gretchen has the same watch, sorry. She thinks pressing the commands I set would bring trusted help if I'm ever hurt. She doesn't know. We don't have any trusted help. So, so, thing is, if Gretchen's game is interrupted, if even one cop comes near this property, if she can't finish her project out back, or if she sees me harmed, one of us will use our watch and torch the whole place with all of us inside. Yes, murder-suicide. A grand finale for our little cult of two, I don't know. But yes, Lucy would be caught in the middle. I'm tired, Ms. Bianchi. And my Gretchen deserves this game and to finish her project out back and Lucy to play a part. Got it?"

"You are sick. We can get you and your daughter help. Let's do that now."

"Yeah, no. Nope." He's shaking his head. "We've had too much trouble in our family for any healing. Things just need to see their way through. Look, Ms. Bianchi, don't fight this. Don't push this, just wait for the game to play out."

*You are both mentally unwell. You're suicidal, homicidal. Wake up!*

Mag considers him a second and decides getting facts is more important than fighting. You can't talk reason into someone who feels he's got nothing left to lose—she should know. "If Gretchen has a project out back, then how can you torch the place with all of you inside?"

Jerry raises an eyebrow, stares at the ground, and then looks up. "Oh, right. Right. Um. Sure. I meant she has a project in the back rooms. We won't be leaving the house. Much. And, you know, if we were to leave the house, and you or the cops got close, an alarm would trigger, and I'd torch the inside, and anyone inside, like Lucy, sure, the second the alarm flashes. Or my Gretchen would. Lucy would be stuck inside. Sorry."

Mag is fairly sure this sick man hasn't thought through his plan, because he's clearly lying about this alleged project out back. Whatever the truth is, she needs Lucy out right now. She's not going to "let the game play out." Fuck that.

She notes the rabbit is frozen and on his haunches now, well within the twenty-foot perimeter. The lights still do not flood on for him, and Jerry's watch does not flash a warning.

Jerry walks away, turns his back to Mag. She follows. The floodlights blaze, and his watch is flashing. She suspects it vibrates too, given the low hum. He turns and points his gun.

"Listen, Ms. Bianchi, I'm serious. You need to let the game play out. It won't be long. Be patient, maybe a couple of days, maybe a week, and Lucy will be fine. If you push, she won't. Simple rule to follow, I think. Just stay out of our way and down in your camper, and wait."

*I won't fucking wait.*

He reaches the front door, enters, pulls it shut. And within three seconds, as Mag races to pry her way in, those three metal rounds swing and click into place: *click, click, click.* Mag grabs one and tries to yank, but the thing won't budge. She sees no keyholes, just solid metal with one bolt on one side. And as she inspects every square inch, she hears the door being locked from within at the knob, and then higher, at a dead bolt. The doorknob and dead bolt do have keyholes, if only she had the keys, and if only there weren't metal rounds blocking the door from opening.

# CHAPTER THIRTY-TWO

After being locked out of the Sabin property, Mag ran to her beast camper, which she'd parked in front of the ranch, and paced a good half hour, muttering to herself, kicking at the beast's middle sofa area, trying to tease out what the hell was going on. Next, after grabbing her high-powered hunting binoculars and a corner of blue molding clay, she climbed up to the roof of her camper, sat crisscross, and stared at the brick oven at the top of the hill. Watching with binoculars in one hand and rolling her blue clay in the other, she set her intention on never leaving, never blinking, waiting out a moment when she could fly up the hill and snatch Lucy.

She was a crazy loon, nesting below a psycho eagle with brain worms. She considered calling Cord and D for help, but no way they'd get here in time. She considered calling Chief Dyson, but she knew how these Waco-type cult freaks with dual psychosis killed whole communities in one swoop. She didn't want to test her luck that she could call Jerry's bluff. He seemed pretty dead inside. He seemed willing to torch his whole world, literally.

She glared on, sitting on the roof of her camper. Hatred, anger, and rage were pushing her mind to wild, impossible solutions she had to keep casting aside. Through her binoculars, she watched squirrels scamper in front of the brick house, but no floodlights beamed on.

Same was true when a flock of wild turkeys paraded through the lawn all nonchalant, the leader strutting four feet tall.

*I'm safe crouching below knee height,* she thought.

Staring for a second at the roof of the low and long shed beneath her camper, a potentially valuable balloon of information floated out of her memory bank: she recalled the cops on the day of their *inquiry* and how they studied drone images of the forest around the Sabin property. She recalled the cops talking about all the electrical fencing and traps. A segment of the east side, however, had no electrical fencing; instead, that side was bordered by a 150-foot-deep gorge with granite walls. There had to be a notch of some sort that would allow for ingress and egress somewhere at the far side of the gorge, the cops had speculated. But they ultimately decided that to explore the area and come up with a plan would take too long for their purposes, and abandoned using the Sabin property in any way for the *inquiry.*

Mag would exploit that gorge now.

She slides from the roof and enters the camper through the door that faces the rental ranch, and thus is obscured to the Sabins. Lifting the storage cubby in the rear of the camper, she inventories her various Triple C staff camping, hunting, treetop-course, and expedition gear. Gathering the items she thinks she'll need in the New Hampshire woods, she packs her black Osprey backpack with night-vision goggles, her high-powered binoculars, her expandable fly-fishing rod with the thickest of unbreakable line, paper and pen, a headlamp, dry matches, pods of water, two bricks of her blue molding clay from that June course in Colorado, a fistful of PowerBars, tissues, a first-aid kit, a lightweight portable hammock, dry socks, a knife, her collapsible bow and arrows, a Gore-Tex jacket, bug spray, and two microfiber blankets, in case she needed warmth or a canopy. Already in her Sarah Connor black pants and a long-sleeve black T-shirt, she laces her lightweight hiking shoes and shoves all her hair under a tight black cap. Black gloves too. Deet sprayed on top of all that.

Using her positional advantage with the camper blocking her, she creeps to a trail to the side of a patch of cattails. Following that down to a field, she then slithers on her belly across the top hem of the field that borders a small pond. From the viewpoint of the brick house at this angle, and also given how the slit windows are situated, it would be impossible for anyone in the house to see her. She looks into the canopies of the dark trees as she approaches the edge of the field and sees no cameras. She presumes, like with the house, that any motion detectors, if they're bordering this field, are set to about waist-high and higher, to avoid constantly going off for animals and ground fowl.

She drags her backpack along her side, remaining as low to the ground as a rabbit on his haunches or a proud turkey. Can't have a humped back.

She takes care not to cross the line of trees with all the big orange trespassing signs. And true to the report she'd overheard in the Milberg police station, she can't anyway, because, sure enough, electrical fence wires are strung tree to tree to tree, from ground to chest-high.

Still on her belly, she turns and snakes along the long edge of the field until she is out of the wedge of dark pine. Once she tops the crest of a rolling hill, she rolls her backpack down to the base, and she, too, rolls. Out of any possible visual view from the Sabin house above, she stands and runs to a point where she feels safe she's out of Sabin property range. No electrical fences here. She sees no traps. She turns left, enters the woods, and, albeit from a blurry memory, tracks as best she can to where the drone picture showed a gorge.

# CHAPTER THIRTY-THREE

## LUCY

On my first day in this shit-hole bone-pool prison in Gretchen's house, Gretchen set up a pattern with me. At 1:00 p.m., her terrible voice came over the intercom, and she said she could see me through some camera in the ceiling among the blinding bulbs. And, she said, she knew I was flipping her off, which I was. Then she moaned about how I hadn't made any progress in the one hour I'd been her captive and she was "disappointed." I yelled back, "Fuck off, you crazy bitch." Then she laughed. Anyway, she said I needed to step all the way to the far side of the room and sit on my hands, and if I did, she'd throw some food in for me, as my lunch. Not knowing when she'd offer food again, I walked to the far side of the room.

"Sit on your hands if you want food. This is the last offer for lunch today."

So I did all that stupid shit she said, and she threw in a loaf of Wonder bread, a bottle of water, and a package of presliced ham—the gross, wet, oil-slick kind.

"I'll be back at five before I leave to work my other bones into their permanent place out back. You better comply then and sit on your hands again if you want more food for the night, because after a couple of hours out back, I'll need to leave straightaway for the pit."

No clue what working *out back* or *the pit* means, but this is the pattern. My brain is in survival mode, and I'll pay emotionally someday, but I'm stripping out all horror aspects and straining to stick to facts, facts, facts.

And here she is, 5:00 p.m. on the dot. My first dinner. I've completed exactly zero skeleton puzzles, because fuck if I'm going to touch dead bodies with my own hands.

I've been sitting in the same spot, still as a statue, inventorying everything I might use in the room to get the hell out. Am I pissed? Damn right I'm pissed. What's in here? Nothing beyond what I saw when I entered: ten blue kiddie pools, gray mats, bones in the pools, a printout page of skeletal structure, a crazy-ass-insane note from crazy-ass-insane Gretchen, a dumb yellow toilet, cameras in the ceiling, ginormous industrial lights, a damn locked door.

And me.

And a bag of Wonder bread.

And disgusting fake ham that looks like shaved face skin.

An empty bottle of water.

I don't have my phone; that's charging down at the camper. *Because I didn't think collecting Allen would take longer than three minutes. And I didn't predict I'd be taken as a hostage in a lunatic's brick prison of puzzle bones. FUCK.*

I'm wearing clothes, whoop-de-doo. Jeans. A T-shirt. Underwear. Consolation bra. Socks. Sneakers. My silver jelly pendant.

I've got nothing else. No weapons. No tools.

"Oh whoa, Lucy. You didn't make any progress today," Gretchen's saying through the intercom. "I don't know. Gee. And with your lack of progress and my concern that my pit workers haven't found you the right bones yet, hmm, would be a shame for you to have to wait until my pit workers find any missing pieces. Could take weeks! Would really be better if you got a jump on it so we can see if any specific pieces are missing for your puzzles."

*Pit workers?*

I crack my neck and look up at the cameras in the lights. I am not flinching.

I extend both middle fingers. "This bone's missing, Gretchen. And this one too."

"Oh, Lucy! You're so funny. Go sit on your hands if you want some bacon for dinner. I know you love lots of bacon!"

I sit on the floor on my hands on the far side of the room and watch her toss in three tiny juice boxes and several pieces of bacon, directly on the floor, like I'm a literal dog. I suppose I'm supposed to make a sandwich with more of my Wonder bread.

After she locks me back in, I rewind her words and ask myself who these pit workers could be. *Mother of all fucking hell, why didn't I tell Dali sooner, like way, way sooner this summer, how loony tunes this bitch is? Maybe I would have avoided all this. Instead, I played her game, and now I'm a stupid doofus in a horror. I'll work all night on a way out. I won't sleep.*

# CHAPTER THIRTY-FOUR

## MOTHER

The winter owl banked just in time to pass

And save herself from breaking window glass.

—*Robert Frost*

After a full afternoon of trekking and hiking, Mag finds the gorge by evening. Standing atop a 150-foot-tall granite wall, she looks across the cavern between and to another granite wall on the opposite side. On the floor of the gorge is a thin soot valley with trees and shrubs. She sets down her backpack to take a break and collect her flashlight and night-vision goggles, intending to search out a trail down into the gorge's valley and back up the opposite wall into the Sabin property.

But voices moving into the floor of the gorge from the opposite side stop her.

Lying flat on her stomach, camouflaged in black within the black night, she slips on her night-vision goggles. The cavern of the gorge is like a bullhorn, so voices within are as if she is down below with them.

"Move it. Move it. Move it," a girl says. Focusing her goggles, Mag recognizes the girl as Gretchen Sabin; Gretchen holds the rear of a train of people walking along a far trail onto the floor of the gorge, a headlamp strapped to her forehead and a gun in her hand and pointed to the back of a woman in front of her. Focusing further on the train of people, Mag gasps, quickly shooting a hand to her mouth to bottle the shock. In front of Gretchen, wobbling and struggling to walk, is Laura Ingrace, outfitted in ripped and soiled sweatpants and a sweatshirt, obviously forced to march, although slowed and pained on what Mag perceives to be broken or severely injured legs. In front of Laura is Jerry Sabin, who wears white gloves and holds his piddly little gun to the back of an old man. Jerry, too, wears a headlamp. The captives, Laura and the old man, do not.

*Holy shit.*

Darkness drapes on the train of people, folding darkness between the Sabins with headlamps. The whole trek and their practiced gait seem like recurring drudgery. Also apparent, when Mag zooms in, are the biting bugs peppering Laura and the old man, as well as the pain on Laura's face, the excruciating wince each time she grabs a pine bough to pull herself forward or grasp a skinny sapling to stable her wobbling ankles. Something has happened to Laura to become a broken-leg captive, but what? A beating? A fall?

Mag watches from her far-up perch as the train progresses down the final switchback of the opposite trail and onto the gorge floor. Laura, as if choreographed, slides, palms a tree, turns, steps, slides more, palms a tree, and so on. She walks the jangy way a stilt walker walks, but without the excuse of stilts. Her legs are atrophied and crooked under her tight and grimy sweatpants, and based on the picture on Nathan Vinet's phone, she's overall lost about twenty pounds. Her face skin sinks into the shape of her skull. Her hair is a knotted nest of dry-brush hay.

"Lucy's come for Allen," Gretchen taunts Laura, the train now snaking along the floor of the gorge toward an end capped by a line of pine and what appears to be a wide-mouthed granite cave. "Maybe she can work the night shift too. Would you like that, Laura Ingrace?"

Mag, calculating, listening, hears the name of her daughter come off this demon child's tongue. *That apple-print dress of hers will be a rag of blood.* For now, bottling every motherly urge in her body to fly off the top of the cliff and into the gorge to eradicate Jerry and Gretchen and take their watches, Mag pulls on all of her tracking and hunting training with Cord and D. She sets her intention to listen. Assess. Collect information.

She closes her eyes. She exhales.

*Listen. Assess. Gather information. Get those watches.*

The train of captors and captives reaches the capped end, and in a click and hum, lights powered by a now-visible generator bloom, illuminating an open cave that nubs the end of the gorge. With her point of view now illuminated, Mag rips off her night-vision goggles and switches to her high-powered binoculars. Laura and the old man, again in practiced drudgery, allow the Sabins to place headlamps on their heads before they drop to their asses and slide into a pit in the floor of the cave.

"Grandpa, I need that femur tonight," Gretchen says to the old man. "If you finally finish these excavations, you can go back to being our renter again. But move it."

*Grandpa?*

"Dad, do you think you can do it? Can you get that femur for Gretchen out tonight?" Jerry asks the old man.

"Trying my hardest, son," he says.

"Earl, how about I help?" Laura says to the old man.

"Bitch, work on your own bones," Gretchen snaps.

Industrial, caged construction lights surround the top edge of the pit within the open cave. Around the mouth of the cave, Gretchen and Jerry move into place various items set aside presumably the last time this motley crew came down here: a folding table, which Gretchen sets a puzzle atop; a tent behind that; two chairs; and a tripod holding a pot over a firepit, which Jerry is lighting. Once lit, he takes a water jug, fills it from a stagnant puddle to the side of the cave, and dumps it in the pot. A larger tripod is set up over the pit; dangling from its center is a rope from a wheel, around which the rope winds, leading to a winch set up beside the fire.

Earl and Laura settle into the pit, the tops of their heads visible to Mag through her binoculars. Their voices are now even more amplified, the cave acting as a bullhorn to the bullhorn of the gorge walls.

"Go on, Earl, please recite the facts again. Need 'em to work," Laura says.

"If you're going to talk boring science again, make it fast, I want to do a puzzle," Gretchen barks into the pit.

"Well, now, Laura, happy to go over the science again if that helps to settle your mind. Our work pit here is the result of a convergence of rare factors, making it near impossible to have occurred, but it did. A sinkhole within the floor of a cave at the nub end of a gorge of granite."

As Earl talks, Mag skates her binoculars around the interior of the pit. From what she can tell, and based on Gretchen's command, Earl is set before a femur embedded in the pit wall, and Laura is set before a skull, a quarter protruding out of compacted dirt. White pieces, presumably more bones, dot more of the pit walls.

Earl continues his night lesson, apparently one given as a regular bedtime story to dull the horror of their work. A captive's routine of forced archaeology. Mag feels whiplashed by the oddity, by the sheer horror. The inexplicable situation to find her baby girl stuck in—but she doesn't have time for a stunning. She must listen. She must gather facts and plan. Recalling her summers of survival trainings with Cord and D, she settles her mind with a trick they taught her: *Pretend there is a knob on the right side of your head, by your temple; turn the knob off. Literally turn off the worry and the fear. Listen, recite what you hear in your mind as if you're saying the words yourself. And catalog every single little thing you see in a constant running list.*

"The pit, fifteen feet wide and thirty feet deep, so far, is the result of loose sediment giving way and sucking further to the core of hell, as if the earth has inhaled, and thus, revealed these hidden secrets. These vanished people," Earl says.

Gretchen, having set up her table with a puzzle, grabs two items out of a crate. She drops one to Laura and one to Earl. After the captives unfurl their packages, Mag can see they are satchels, each containing a plastic trowel, a toothbrush, several wooden skewers (typically used for dices of chicken and vegetables), and a separate cloth bag with a hook.

The captives hook their cloth bags to the end of the rope that dangles from the center of the larger tripod over the pit. Once attached, the bags hang deflated in the center space. *Presumably for bones they extract?* The operation is somewhat like sending an advance team into a well to test for oil. Except Earl and Laura work the sides of this hole for human bones.

"More facts, Laura?" Earl asks.

"Yes, please."

Laura holds a toothbrush and a wood skewer, alternating between the two tools to pick away at pebbles and dirt around a tiny skull she appears to be working to extract.

"But skip the part how these people died. I don't want to hear that part tonight. Get to the science part about the bones," she says.

"All right, then," Earl says. His voice is an elderly, authoritative, rumbly gravel, like big rocks in a tumbler. "Assume a mass of people died in the floor of this gorge decades ago. Assume the manner of death also helped with preservation of their remains. All in one day, one died, then another, then another. So on. The very next day . . . It's crazy. But the very next day, with all those dead bodies on the floor of the gorge, a flash flood far off pushed a mudslide to rush in a funnel through this long-dry riverbed, causing mud and silt with plenty of fine sediment mixed with clay to cover the bodies and carry them into this cave. This then becomes an anoxic environment, no oxygen, and, with the way the people died, which part you want me to skip tonight, well, a perfect storm for preservation. With the bodies deprived of oxygen and under layers of mud, the skin, muscle, and fat decomposed, but no predators were able to carry off the bones. Then . . ." Earl pauses to cough.

He's stopped talking and is brushing at the femur he's been trying to extract.

*Just watch. Get intel. Make a plan.*

"Pull yourself together, Grandpa! Get back to work," Gretchen yells at Earl, who is barely breathing through the coughing.

Laura edges closer to Earl as if to help him.

"Back away from him, Laura. Do you want me to drop boiling water on you two again? Keep apart, no whispering. Only talking loud enough for us to hear. No plotting, you two."

"Fine," Earl says. "I'm fine, ah, fine," he repeats, between catching his breath.

Earl points up to Gretchen, *his own damn granddaughter*, to indicate he hears her. He shows her his brush and that he'll begin work again.

"I need that femur tonight."

"Oh baby, you'll be the best orthopedician. I'm so proud," Jerry Sabin says.

"Tonight, Grandpa!" Gretchen shouts.

"Yes, Gretchen. You'll have it tonight," he says.

As Earl brushes at the femur, he continues his recitation of scientific facts. "Then, in the most perfect of storms to collide, a minor, minor sinkhole began beneath this pit, much like a pinched-in nozzle on a funnel. But real pinched in and tiny. So anyway, sediment starts sucking into the core of earth, and I imagine there's some kind of rock bed with crevices below us here making this happen, revealing the bones. Now they haven't had time to fossilize, obviously. And you know we need to be careful. Some are in good shape, preserved pretty well, some brittle, some yellowed, so on. There's a ton of variation in the preservation of bones in here. But all these rare factors came together all right, and this pit's the proof. Now the wildlife?"

"Yes, please," Laura says, brushing away dirt from the small skull's cheek. "Go on." She's pick, pick, picking at a stubborn cluster of pebbles.

"Did you ever see a bear den, Laura?"

Mag listens and watches and logs and catalogs all night.

Dawn now. A mist haze hanging in the colorful fall treetops acts as a low ceiling above the cliff walls. Mag scans the face of the granite ledges and notes ravens' nests. All around in trees and in rock crevices are homes for black-capped chickadees, tits, the Northern cardinal, and sparrows. Mag thinks back to how she and Laura and all the Triple C girls were trained on bird-watching, especially as part of their treetop–bird bingo course. Birding was the key, number-one theme, a core tenet, at the camp for "adventurous girls."

On the top of a dead tree in the base of the gorge is an eagle's nest. A woodpecker greets with his morning hammer, and joining his drum comes the orchestra of several birds braiding their calls into a symphony of chip-chip-chips, dee-dee-dees, trilllllls, and caws.

"Send up your tools," Gretchen yells to her captives in a chipper morning voice.

Earl and Laura place their respective tools in the pouches attached to rope, cinch the tops, and yank to let Gretchen know she can pull. Up the sides of the pit, the tools go. Next, Gretchen cranks the wheel that winds the now-empty cloth bags up the center space. Earl had sent up the femur hours ago to a silent audience, which Mag noted, for at that time, Gretchen was napping in the tent.

*Jerry and Gretchen nap in turns in the tent.*

Earl and Laura climb out of the pit, Laura struggling and pausing and grunting with the effort of using her mangled legs.

The songbirds chitter and dee-dee and pick and hammer and caw, a song to accompany Laura's literal crawl through the valley to the trail that slopes up and up and winds in serpentine curves onto the Sabin property.

Mag monitors and logs the entire trek, timing when she herself will add to the birds' symphony. She has a plan.

Once the train of captors and captives reaches the joint where the valley floor meets the serpentine, upward trail, Laura Ingrace shifts her crawl to a wobbly stand. This joint is also where Mag had last night watched Laura struggle to reach during a guarded pee break. Now, in daylight, through her powerful binoculars, Mag notes a bright-orange mushroom in a hole in the base of a large pine that marks this very turning point.

Higher up in the orange mushroom pine, a female long-eared owl nests in a cavity. She's nocturnal, so her round eyes are closed. Last night, Mag had noted her yellow globes glaring out, searching for a midnight snack skittering on the gorge floor.

And now, trusting Laura would have also noticed the long-eared female, given their similar experience at the Triple C, and given what the feds have since told Mag of Laura's bird-photography business, Mag adds to the birds' morning symphony. "Whoo, whoo," she sounds out from the top of the opposite cliff wall, sending the imitation call from the back of her throat, using her stomach to push the air as a singer would, as trained in birding, as practiced for years.

Laura pauses in her wobbly stand. She's beside the orange mushroom pine, the long-eared female above her, sleeping in a high cavity.

"Whoo, whoo," Mag signals again.

Nobody else in the train pauses; nobody else notices a different birdcall among nature's morning clatter.

But Laura does. And Laura looks up to the long-eared's nest and then around and up toward Mag's cliff wall. There is no way Laura can see Mag, camouflaged so far away and up and flat on the surface of the cliff top. And yet, Laura most definitely heard her.

"Whoo, whoo," Mag signals to cement the call.

Laura tips her head up, indicating an answer, an *I heard you. And I know you're not the gorge's one resident owl.*

Anyone trained on birds, like Laura and Mag, would know a *whoo whoo* would not come on an October morning from a *nocturnal, female* long-eared owl. Laura would know. She's been paid big bucks to capture snaps of *male long-eared owls who whoo whoo during breeding season, February to July.*

A *whoo* cannot come from this female, in the morning, while she's snoozing, in October.

In the train of people in the silt valley, only Mag and Laura know her *whoo whoo* is not natural. Another *whoo whoo*, and only Laura reacting, confirms to Mag that everyone else hears only an owl hooting. They don't even look up into the tree they stand beside, apparently not knowing one was ever there the whole time.

Before turning back to the task of hobbling and struggling and grasping pine boughs to pull herself up the trail, Laura shoots a look of pure hatred to the top of Mag's cliff wall. She is in the rear now, Gretchen ahead, waiting for Laura to find her feet and step into her second-from-the-rear spot in the train. And it is at this point, as her face is free to stare up to the top of Mag's cliff wall, when Laura mouths, "Fuck you, Magpie."

*Laura is sick,* Mag thinks. *She's deranged. She's captive and sick and broken. But she's going to need to get her shit together and help me save Lucy. And then I will think on punishment and revenge. Then. Only then.*

Mag is frightened and confused, but she turns that invisible survival knob on the side of her head. Turn, turn, turn of the knob, fighting through the horror and panic, because what other choice does she have?

*At least Laura recognizes my voice, our old game of birdcalls. Our old camp training. Part of our secret game.*

Once the valley of the gorge is clear—presumably they're all back on the Sabins' property—Mag finds a precarious trail down the side of the gorge wall. In clear daylight, she logs the intricate details of the silt floor. The slate-colored inchworm on a slate rock. The lime brightness of lichen on light-gray stones. A carpet of moss bordering the edges, dotted with fallen crimson leaves. A lacy cobweb strung between the lowest boughs of a Douglas fir, like the low-hanging ornament a toddler hangs. The smell of dirt. Twigs that look like stick-insect soldiers for fairies. A white-tipped gray-and-black tail feather from a wild turkey. A blue feather from a blue jay for good luck.

She extracts pen and paper from her backpack and writes a note. Once done, she slides to the skull—an infant's skull—Laura is working to extract but hasn't cleared yet. Having rolled her note, Mag sticks the scroll in an eye socket.

# CHAPTER THIRTY-FIVE

## LUCY

The first night was a long one of me whipping myself into a fruitless fury. I kept slamming my body into the damn locked door, locked good and tight. Jamming on the solid knob. Nothing. Stupid, wasteful efforts, along with unfocused pacing. Dumb. I tried to find a way to climb on something to get to the big halogen lights, thinking I could smash one apart and create a tool or weapon. The yellow toilet is no help, as it's in a nook and not near a damn thing in the ceiling. So I dumped all the bones out of the kiddie pools and stacked the pools on top of each other upside down. But that was an obvious stupid waste of time, because when I took a running jump to the top of the plastic tower, the top pool ate the one below, and that one ate the one below that, and so on. Friggin' crumpled to the ground, and now I have a huge bruise on my forearm.

Then I got all worried Gretchen would return from her stupid work out back and her supervision of pit workers, whatever the fuck that means, and see all the dumped bones and freak out. The fact she wasn't saying anything over the intercom told me she was truly not in the house—I don't think she would have been able to keep her flapping mouth shut had she seen what I'd done. And certainly she would have mocked me when my pool tower collapsed and I fell.

Anyway, I put all the dumb pools back in their two lines next to the gray mats, filled them back up in a way that looked even, but now all the stupid bones are mixed up, and who cares, because I am not going to ever finish all these skeletons. I am going to find a way out. I wasn't kidnapped and kept from Mag for thirteen years to wind up kidnapped by Gretchen Freakshow Sabin for her personal horror show.

It's our second day now, and about elevenish, I'm guessing. I'm judging from this morning when Gretchen's sickening voice startled me over the intercom and said, "Lucy, it's dawn. Daddy went to go get his coffee and snickerdoodles, as usual. I see you made no progress with the bones."

I didn't look up at her. I slumped on the floor.

"Well, poopsie-doo. You better get on it. No cookies for you this morning."

Then she was gone.

Now it's a few hours later, so I'm saying it's eleven, and here's her horrible voice again.

"Shoot, Lucy, darn. Your moth-errr is insisting on video evidence that you're okay. She's such a psycho. She's sitting on top of her camper holding up a big poster that says, 'Proof of Life Call Now. Or I Call the Cops. FaceTime.' And then her dumb phone number. So here's what we're going to do. I'm going to hold my iPhone up to my screen, and we'll do a proof-of-life call. You say you're fine. And that is all. If you do anything more, I will snap Allen's neck. Ready? Oh, and you can stand now, walk to the center of the room, and look up to the cameras. Ready?"

I'm reminded how when I came up here, I stupidly left my own iPhone charging in the camper, and then once I was locked in, Gretchen made me strip and prove I had no phone before she turned her Wi-Fi back on. That was humiliating. All I had on was my jelly necklace.

I do as she says and emit no emotions for a proof-of-life call to Mag. No emotion of fright or anger or anything. I do exactly as Gretchen says, because now I'm plotting; some kernel of a plan is bubbling in my mind.

"Lucy, are you okay?" Mag asks. "I see you. Where are you in there?"

"Room. First floor—"

"Enough," Gretchen interrupts.

"Sit tight. They say it's a game. They'll torch the place if we don't play along," Mag says.

"Enough," Gretchen says, harsher this time.

"Wait. Wait. Put her back on the screen now or I swear to God, I'm calling the cops," I hear Mag yell.

"Lucy, I'm back. I see you. What level are you at?" She stresses the word *level*.

*Level.*

A calm washes over me, because she's speaking code. I love that I have a secret code with my mother. When we were in California and visiting Cord and D at the Triple C, they taught me how in their search-and-rescue-and-extraction practice—in case any resort guests ever went missing (they like to overprepare)—they have signals. A number-one pointer signal meant "Level 1: no danger." Four fingers meant "Level 4," and shit is going all haywire.

Obviously this shit show is a Level 88, maximum haywire, so Mag asking is her way of saying she's working a rescue-and-extraction plan. If there's one thing I trust, it's that there's no way Mag is sitting still, so I want her to concentrate on whatever she's doing on the outside of our trap and not worry that I'm falling apart on the inside. We're fighting this together, I can feel it. She is the very wedge of me I was always missing, and with her, I am whole now. I need to work the inside while she works the outside. We're a tandem team: mother and daughter.

I'm scared as all hell, but my past makes me hard. And I will not be a simpering girl. I will not weaken this team. I won't fall and fail. I'm going to be tough as nails.

It is so hard to do, but I do not smirk at our sly code in holding up a single pointer finger, meaning, *Sure, Mag, I'm cool. I'm at a Level 1. And I trust we'll work this out together.*

"What the hell is that?" Gretchen yells. "That's it. You're done with this call."

A long silence comes over the room.

All day I hear clomping around above me and outside the door. And now it's dinnertime again. Gretchen just threw in a fistful of loose peanuts and a bottle of water.

"You need your protein. Oh, and Lucy, I do hope you'll be okay again tonight. Daddy and I will be out back as usual a few hours, and then Daddy and I will leave for the pit. Won't be back until morning. *Ciao, bella.* That's Italian. Nighty-night. Hope you find the courage to start your puzzles soon! Pacing around all day is doing you no good."

Does she realize how imbecilic it is to tell her captive that she and her freak father won't be here all night? Maybe she's confident I can't escape this locked room and then out through the sealed door. Maybe she's right and I'm overconfident. After all, this is her game, not mine. Maybe she's tempting me into a separate trap.

I hear her walk away from the door, and I take inventory of the contents of the room *again*. I run a hand over the solid door and door-frame and newer, and more unpickable, doorknob. I set my tongue in my teeth and consider solutions.

They want me to demonstrate agency? To advocate for myself? Well, I'll show you self-advocacy. I'll show all y'all what it means to take charge.

# CHAPTER THIRTY-SIX

## MOTHER

Night again, and Mag is hiding within a grove of trees, off to the side, within the valley and atop a boulder. Her vantage for view of the trail on the Sabin side of the gorge and of the pit within the cave is perfect.

The train of captives and captors has arrived and set up in their spots. Lights. Table. Tent. Tripod over pit. Boiling pot of water. Captives in pit. Check. Check. Check. Same as last night.

Through her binoculars, Mag watches Laura positioning herself to the baby's skull, and by the way she sits straighter in her spot and looks up to the top of the cliff wall, where she'd heard Mag's owl call this morning—but where Mag is not tonight—Mag knows Laura's found her note in the eye socket.

"Earl, need you to go over the facts again, please," Laura says, especially loud tonight. Mag assumes Laura needs a distraction so she can read her note.

"You got it," Earl says.

Remembering Laura's caustic barbs, her quick temper, her biting wit, her open, relentless competition with Mag after the lemon-tree night when they were fourteen, Mag imagines Laura's fingers trembling to unscroll her note. And she knows Laura will soon know nobody else could have written this note, because it is written in the same pattern the girls always wrote notes in order to set up a night's secret challenge in the Triple C treetop course: first the stakes, next the object of the night's game, next the rules, and last the timing. The pattern of tonight's gorge challenge is irrefutable evidence of Mag's identity and presence, more so than if she'd left verified DNA.

If this were their secret treetop challenge, one would be up in the tree course—with safety clicks, lifeline, carabiner, harness, transition cables—jumping to high platforms, crawling across log bridges, climbing up ladders bolted to trunks, swinging on ropes to nets spread between canopies, and one would be assigned to the ground. And whoever's turn it was to write out the night's challenge would set the stakes and the rules—like Mag has done here tonight. And since it would be night in the forest and dark—their vision thus blocked or blurred—and they had to keep their game a secret, only birdcalls and no speaking marked where one was in relation to the other.

Mag recalls the spitting tirades Laura would give upon reading her challenge notes:

*Oh, you want me blindfolded, Magpie, yeah? Fuck you, I know this dumb Triple C course blind. Oh sure, walking backward while holding a brick paver from the main lodge's walkway that I have to extricate with a spoon before I can start the ground course beneath you, while you rope swing in harnesses high above? Bite me, bitch. You in the trees, me on the ground, again, rolling a bowling ball with one hand and no sleep for two days? Whatever.*

Laura's endurance had allowed her to compete with Mag's athleticism.

But.

All that's in the past.

*Focus. Stay sharp, Laura. Read the note. Tonight's challenge is not a game. It's life or death. Focus,* Mag thinks, hoping telepathy exists.

Tonight's particular challenge doesn't need to be in sync, like their secret Triple C treetop night challenges. And, knowing Laura and how desperate she was to secure Lemon the dog after she stole him from her mother, and how bereft she was upon the death of Copte the parrot, and believing the psychoanalysts' opinions that Laura truly loved Lucy in her twisted way, Mag is banking on Laura executing tonight's challenge so they can together save Lucy.

Given the way Laura crouches down in the pit, Mag knows she's reading her note.

*Stakes: Baby bird trapped in house. They'll burn her alive.*

*Object: Raven needs ring of keys.*

*Rules: *Emus can't know.*

*Leave keys in Owl's tree, the one where you turn to piss, the one with the limbs that look like a goalpost, eighty crawl-steps from pit. Set keys next to orange mushroom.*

*After you piss, pick keys back up and return to Emus.*

*Again, Emus cannot know! They've rigged things. Bird will burn.*

*Timing: I'm watching, so you set timing. But tonight!*

Emus have been classified as the dumbest birds on the planet. Mag knows with Laura's caustic temper she's calling the Sabins far worse than emus in her mind, and she can almost hear her, hear Laura's retort to this note. She'd say something like, "You think you're so clever, Magpie, with your lame bird jokes. Ha, ha, ha," and roll her eyes. "Your challenge is impossible. But I won't let you beat me."

# CHAPTER THIRTY-SEVEN
## LUCY

What I really need is a screwdriver. The house has been stone quiet for a couple of hours now. And I did listen for and heard both Gretchen and Jerry leave after she threw me a fistful of stupid loose peanuts. So yeah, a couple of hours alone. It's safe to work.

I don't have a screwdriver, but I do have my titanium-hard jellyfish pendant. All in, with the floaters, the thing is as long as my pinkie. The head is silver and domed, and the floaters from that are pointy. It'd be fantastic if the damn thing had a handle, but it doesn't, so I'll have to deal.

Guess what, this is good. The jelly head fits right on in the screw head of one of three screws in one of the three hinges holding the door to the doorjamb. The screw head is that pain-in-the-ass plus-sign kind that requires the Phillips screwdriver, and the grooves are worn, so my jelly pendant head keeps slipping. Also, this first screw is sunk deep in the wood, so she ain't budging. But she will. I'm not giving up. I've got all night to work my jelly in these nine screws.

I will rip your door off the hinges, Gretchen.

# CHAPTER THIRTY-EIGHT
## MOTHER

Whenever Mag wrote a challenge for Laura for their treetop games, Laura would read it fast, say one of her caustic lines, and ultimately finish, "Challenge accepted," all within five to ten minutes, tops. For their first few challenges after the lemon massacre, Laura had written the night's rules so that Mag could "win" the answers to the questions she'd raised: What happened to Lemon the dog? Who helped her murder the lemon trees? And why did they help her?

Although Mag had completed Laura's initial challenges, it was only ever the first question Laura agreed to answer. She'd keep moving the goalpost on what Mag had to do to get answers to the next two questions. So in between, Mag wrote treetop challenges for Laura to complete, the difficulty and danger increasing every time.

And now, watching Laura in the gorge, Mag waits, hoping Laura will accept this current challenge and help save Lucy.

*Please get those keys. Do this. Help me save my baby.*

Mag waits, camouflaged, at her post on a boulder by the long-eared's pine. She listens; she watches. It's been two hours since Laura found Mag's note in the skull's eye socket. The silence in the gorge is deep. Night wind whooshes, Jerry reads, Earl's done with his bedtime stories of gorge and bone facts, and, importantly, Gretchen has entered the tent for a nap.

"Lady problems. Need to use the bathroom," Laura yells up to Jerry Sabin.

By the tone of Laura's voice from the pit, the pitch, the authority, the volume, Mag knows Laura has figured out how to execute the challenge.

"Hurry," he says.

Laura then trills her tongue in what Mag recognizes as a wild turkey call.

"What the hell was that?" Jerry says.

"Just clearing my throat, asshole," Laura says.

Game is on. Mag pops to her feet but stays low on her boulder. Watching.

Laura must know Gretchen Sabin is napping, given the lack of her squawking voice.

"Oh, Laura, did I ever tell you about how I came to be on this property ten years ago?" Earl says as Laura is maneuvering out of the pit.

Mag is unsure, but she thinks, given Earl's volume and tone, and the way Laura nods at him as she rises out of the pit, that whatever Earl is about to say is meant to distract Jerry Sabin. Mag zooms in to watch and strains to hear every word.

"Many times. But tell me again, Earl. Will help me scoot up out of the hole. Keep talking," Laura says.

"Oh, so, see, I had known about this property since I was a boy. I fled one day long ago, in the fifties. I was ten. Oh yup, a boy. My daddy ran a cult here. His followers called him Jonny Guile, but his real name was Alton Sams Taylor. He was terribly ill in the mind. He's your reason, all right, we got all these bones. But I escaped. I did. I was just a boy. A boy. He made me photograph that day, what he did to these people that day. Anyhow. I got away. Raised myself on the streets. Got married, had a son, Jerry here, but then got divorced. Apparently Jerry listened a little too close to all my stories of growing up with my cult daddy, and he got himself obsessed. A little deranged, and he knows this. He admits this now. Don't you, Jerry?"

Jerry moves to the lip of the pit. Earl keeps talking. "When Jerry was a grown man, he came here, bought this property. But I didn't know. I was estranged from him after the divorce. Anyway, so one day, ten years ago, I had to see the place again. Had to see my son again. Curiosity got the better of me. I crept in, oh, I'll tell you where, how, anyway. Ten or so years ago . . ."

Earl is droning on about ten or so years ago, and Jerry Sabin appears addicted to this story, given how fixed he is at the lip of the pit. Laura emerges topside, cracks her knees and shakes her legs, which appear made of crooked bone on bone. She stands, not straight at all; her ankles toggle.

On the Sabins' topside folding table, which Mag watches Laura approach behind Jerry, is a ring of keys lying beside Gretchen's latest puzzle-in-progress. This one is a blown-up picture of a creepy brown house in a forest, which Mag can tell from the box's standing box top.

Laura hobbles toward the table, which she must pass on the way to the gorge floor to get to the "bathroom" behind the long-eared owl's pine.

Earl's voice is louder now. "Ten years ago, I snuck in. Ayup, Jerry, you, right? You caught me; at first you didn't recognize me, but then you had me stay the night. The next day, I was walking in these here woods with my gun, when out of nowhere . . ."

Laura grabs the keys. Mag cringes when Earl tells the next part of his story: how he accidentally shot Jerry's pregnant wife.

"But I tell you, was a trap, a frame-up. Because . . ."

Laura tucks the ring of keys in her disgusting sweatpants pocket. She drops to the ground, hands and knees, and begins *eighty crawl steps* to Mrs. Owl's tree.

Jerry Sabin is laughing, engaged with his dear old daddy, Earl. *Laughing about his father shooting his pregnant wife.*

"Dad, you old dummy! You did fall for my trap. And look at you, doing the Lord's work for your son and granddaughter. Paying your penance!"

Earl, apparently in an effort to keep Jerry distracted and engaged, maintains a chipper tone. "Jerry, you and little Gretchen are indeed the smart ones here. Oh boy, and after that day, what with little Gretchen's mental state, I have to be honest, was easy for you to convince me to stay longer. I had to be sure you were both well. A'course . . ."

"Of course, you didn't really have a choice in leaving, now did you, Dad?"

"No, Jerry, I suppose I didn't. You made that very clear."

Laura has crawled onto the gorge floor and is winding her way around the obstacles of stones and boulders and scrub brush and bushes. Jerry is trailing behind with his prissy little gun, but his attention is on Earl's voice, booming up and out of the pit.

"Things never did improve, now did they, with Gretchen? Maybe I should have ran, got you both help, after she found my pictures from that Death March day and painted it. Or when she made us come out here and find the pit, and things, well, escalated. I never should have ever returned to the old place and stepped back into your life, right, Jerry?"

"Oh, well, now, you were a good worker for ten years, though. Was good of you to stay on after your tragic trespass—our deal's been good, no? We've sure lived up to our end. I still haven't told anyone you're the bad hunter who killed a pregnant woman and her baby and fled. Haven't said a word to anyone about your part in your father's mass murder. And you've lived up to yours, working hard for us—the metalwork, the construction, the brickwork, the digging, doing the Lord's work. You have. I think the deal's incredibly fair."

Laura's crawling along the gorge floor. Jerry's trailing behind, holding his gun toward her but stepping sideways to keep up his conversation with Earl.

"Gretchen's gotten so much worse since the day you shot . . . well, her mother."

Earl says something Mag can't hear; her attention is now fully on Laura, who is making a turn at the owl's tree.

"Well, anyway, definitely agree things have escalated. I do need someone to do the manual work, though. Look what happened when I fell in the pit? Broken leg and finger!" Jerry is gasping now, reliving a reverberating personal trauma he cannot handle.

Laura sly-drops the keys in the hole of the owl's trunk, beside the orange mushroom. Does she sense how close Mag is to her? Is this why Laura pauses behind the tree, scrunches her shoulders around her neck, closes her eyes, and whispers as if in prayer, "Touch my skin. Please just touch my skin."

Mag slides silent down the backside of the boulder. Crouching into a space on a thin trail she made herself, free of crunching leaves, she slithers on her stomach toward the base of the owl tree.

Jerry yells back to Earl, "Dad, hold on. Hold on. Hard to hear from here. Hold on." Jerry, now paying attention to wherever Laura went off to, walks toward the owl's pine.

"Hurry up in there," he yells. He must know Laura can't hobble off and up the serpentine trail; he doesn't seem too concerned. Yet he does want confirmation, because now he shouts, "Tell me you're in there or I'm coming in."

"I'm in here, fuckface," Laura shouts. Mag is frozen on the ground between them, low behind shrubs and therefore hidden. But if Jerry walks any closer, she could be cooked.

Laura crawls to and crouches where she usually pees. Jerry stands midway between the pee point and the pit so he can guard both Laura and Earl.

A whoosh of air brushes Mag's cheek, a funnel of wind through the valley. She's about five feet off from grabbing the keys, but frozen on the spot, afraid Jerry is too keen on the area behind the owl's pine.

Laura must sense that Mag needs a distraction, because she begins to make disgusting grunting noises, as if groaning through a painful shit the size of a sideways football. Priss-ass Jerry is cringing out there, turning his face and nose the other way.

Mag slithers, grabs the keys, presses them into her blue clay to make impressions, sets the clay in her back pockets, and sets the keys back by the orange mushroom.

"Whoo, whoo," she calls out, once she's slithered back behind her boulder.

*The coast is clear.*

Now Laura must return the keys without the Sabins seeing.

Laura whispers in resignation, in pain, "I can't believe I let you in again. You never touch my skin. I'm always alone."

*What is this? Was she always obsessed and I didn't see?*

*Focus.*

*Just focus for now.*

Laura crawls out, slower than need be, slower and dragging. She re-collects the keys from the mushroom hole.

As she begins her crawl-steps through the valley floor toward the pit, the keys in her pocket, and now Jerry stepping behind her with his gun, Gretchen emerges from the tent. She stands behind the folding table with the brown house puzzle, right where Laura needs to return the keys. Mag sees only Gretchen's head and torso; her lower half is severed for her. In her quick nap, her apple-print dress corkscrewed around her body.

Mag's heart is about to beat out of her chest.

The boiling pot of water and the folding table are the items that divide Laura from Gretchen.

"Daddy! Didn't you remember I forgot my earplugs tonight! Why are you letting him talk so loud and you're yelling!"

Gretchen scowls when she sees Laura.

And then the worst happens: she looks at the table. *Like she knows.*

"Where are the keys?"

Jerry trots around Laura, leaving his lame gun limp at his side.

"Daddy! Where are the keys?" Gretchen yells again, more panic in her voice.

"I don't, I don't," Jerry is saying. Patting his pants pockets.

On her hands and knees, Laura cranes her head up, looking away from Gretchen and to the far cliff wall. A glint on the rock wall catches Mag's eye, something like a silver flashing fish from where she believes she saw a raven's nest.

Laura stands fast, grasping the keys in a closed fist. Her legs wobble, but she fights through. "Coyote!" she yells, pointing with her left hand toward a crop of bushes in the dark, while she stumbles forward. Gretchen, standing before her, and Jerry, off to the side, follow the direction of Laura's left pointing hand, so they don't see what Laura's doing with her right hand. Only Mag, behind them and hidden atop her boulder in a grove of trees, watches as Laura thrusts the keys. They land above Gretchen's head in a long line of pines behind the Sabins' tent.

Laura does not watch the keys' silent arc in the air because she keeps her head and left hand directed to a phantom coyote in the left-side bushes. She intensifies the bloodcurdling scream while still stumbling forward. And just when Gretchen and Jerry seem about ready to look at Laura and not left, Laura amps the distraction by free-falling toward the boiling pot of water on the campfire, grasps the lip, and pulls the pot down. She torques her body as much as she can away from the flood of boiling water and crashes into the folding table, whereupon brown house puzzle pieces explode around her. The table buckles and flattens to the ground, and boiling water splashes her legs. The searing pain must be unimaginable.

For a sweet second, everyone is still and silent.

But nobody is looking to the pine trees behind, where Mag sneaks a peek through her binoculars. Five feet above Gretchen's head, thank luck of all lucks, that damn ring of keys hangs like a glorious Christmas ornament on a pine bough. Laura will have to keep screaming and pointing left or at her legs until the bough stops bouncing from the keys' landed weight. And her screaming is authentic, because her busted legs are now scorched in splashes of boiling water.

Lying in dirt with open wounds, Laura could die of sepsis. Considering this fate, Mag is in conflict, for she hates to see suffering. And yet, Laura deserves death for what she's done. She deserves Mag's hatred and her revenge, all of which is in conflict with a sliver of respect Mag's feeling for how Laura's pulled off this challenge—how far she's willing to go to save Lucy, a pact playing out not by verbal agreement, but by Laura's actions tonight. There's no helping Laura, no moving into the valley off the boulder and showing herself as a savior against the Sabins. Mag must remain a ghost in the trees, ensure there is no question about the keys, and then be off, for she has more work to do tonight.

Puzzle pieces stick to the hot water on Laura's legs. More pile on her hands in the dirt.

Gretchen grabs a sharp switch, appearing to prepare to beat Laura.

Laura aches her arm out to point to the pine bough above Gretchen's head.

"You should be careful with your shiny objects, Gretchen. There's a raven's nest up in the cliff. Don't you know they like shiny objects? They steal them. You're lucky this time. Seems like the raven was playing with you and passed them back to you."

It's more like a New Zealand Caledonian crow, *Corvus moneduloides*, endemic to the islands of New Caledonia, would do this, not a common New England raven, *Corvus corax*. But what difference do scientific facts make to this dumb bird demon child? She doesn't know. And frankly, a common raven might have done this, maybe. Who cares?

*Did Gretchen buy this story?*

Gretchen stalls. Looks up to the tree.

"Daddy, a raven is playing with me!"

*Laura Ingrace, I swear to God, if you fail your next challenge, which I'll deliver tonight, if you, by God, fail to help me save my brilliant bird, an infinity more brilliant than this useless dingbat shit bird of a girl, I will outlive eternity and haunt you forever. But good job tonight. I still don't forgive you. I'll never forgive you and you'll pay. But good job.*

# CHAPTER THIRTY-NINE

## LUCY

I'm giving up on this first screw. I've been at it a whole hour. I wore down the damn screw grooves too much, and now she won't turn at all. And also, I realize I didn't sleep last night or today, and my eyeballs feel like they're filled with those metal threads in one of those magnet Wooly Willy games. I need to nap if I'm going to survive and work the inside of this trap. Just a quick nap on one of the creepy gray mats. Then I'll be more careful and more forceful in working the second screw. Just need to rest my eyes and fingers.

# CHAPTER FORTY
## MOTHER

With the molds of the Sabins' house keys in her squares of blue modeling clay, Mag notes the trail she's spied this train of captors and captives take in and out three times: in last night, out this dawn when she *whoo*'d to Laura, and in again tonight. She listened, too, when Jerry had said, "The weather is going to be good all week, so we've got to do night shift every night, before the colder weather hits upon us. We're already past Columbus Day."

And so, knowing this is the week's pattern, believing Lucy is okay from the weird Skype call she'd demanded when she trekked back and sat upon her camper's roof all day like a perched loon, and presuming there are no trip wires or alarms on this trail they take back toward the Sabin house, Mag treks on the trail with her key molds tucked in her back pockets.

Somewhere at the start of the switchback portion of the trail, and nearer the flatter top of forest, high above the gorge, there is a bend in the trail, a winding around a grove of trees, something similar to a bend in the ground course below the treetop platforms at the Triple C. She and Laura used to call this spot Heaven's Knot. And like Triple C's Heaven's Knot, this Sabin property Heaven's Knot allows for a person in the bend to be hidden from whoever might be in a train of people ahead and behind her—not for long, maybe four seconds, but hidden long enough. Mag takes note, thinking on the next, and final, challenge she must leave for Laura.

She continues on. Along the way, as she gains closer to the house, her night-vision goggles expose locations off the trail where there are, indeed, several trip wires and also inner electrical fences—short spaces between trees, more like gates, enough to zap anybody who was unaware and had breached the outer ring of fencing. She notes the trip wires leading up into the trees, such that one wrong step and a person would be whisked in a net—hidden by ground leaves—up and up. She wonders how many animals have tripped these traps. And she presumes in this area closer to the Sabins' brick house, with the short electrical gates between trees and the hidden trip-wire nets, the animals have adapted. She presumes nature has learned not to cross into this part of the forest. This also means that the trip nets must require more weight than a squirrel or mouse or rabbit or other woodland creature.

In her mind, she is mapping the locations of the obstacles in this ground and treetop course.

Once she has the Sabin brick home in her sights, she notes a piece of plywood over a hole and an open padlock, lopped to the side. She lifts the wood, looks inside, and sees stones set in the earth as a ladder down. With her headlamp on, she sees what appear to be underground dirt halls.

*Later,* she tells herself. Given the location of this underground access, directly at the end of the trail, and given the open padlock on the exterior, she wonders if this is where Laura and Earl are kept during the day. The direction of halls appears to run to the side of the Sabins' brick house and then, she presumes, down and under the blueberry and holly hill that leads to the back side of the shed that sits opposite the rental ranch and where Mag's camper is parked.

She stands and, from her spot closer to the edge of the forest, looks down at the plywood cover and then to the back of the Sabins' brick house. With her night-vision goggles, she notes within the forest to her right a separate trail, one leading to something else entirely, possibly a house in the woods about 250 or 300 yards in. Hard to tell with all the trees in between. She can't identify the house's color at night, but it must be dark: brown or black.

She removes her backpack and sets her goggles inside. She drops to belly-crawl into the strip of lawn behind the Sabin house; again, she drags her black backpack. She's in all black and presumes she need only stay as low as the animals, slither on the earth as a shadow demon. Since no lights trip on, she believes she's good to go. She continues through the Sabins' backyard, a black mamba in the grass, until she reaches the side by the excavator.

Slithering this way leads her to think of the time she sneaked up on Laura when they were fourteen. Laura was holding a bow and arrow and pointing toward the back side of a staff cabin—Cord's, to be exact. The night before, Mag had won their secret treetop challenge to do the course backward, with no harnesses, the one in which Laura tried to down her by shaking the sky bridge. And because Mag won, Laura told her to meet her at this spot in the field the next morning. Mag looked to the cabin, and there was Cord, then a new camp employee, a recent marine retiree. Cord was beyond his cabin, walking toward a far tree; tied to that tree was an English sheepdog: Lemon. Laura let go an arrow, sending it to stab square into the back side of Cord's cabin—a place he'd obviously planned on spending much time in residence, given the table and chairs he'd set up there. Behind the blade was a note, which was now pinned to the back of Cord's house.

It was shocking to find Laura skillfully handle a bow and arrow, mind-blowing to find her point an arrow at Cord's cabin. Nuts that she'd left Lemon for Cord.

"Holy cow, what are you doing, Laura? You can shoot? Why are you shooting at Cord's cabin? Hello?" Mag asked.

Back then, Laura lowered her bow, looked into Mag's big violet eyes, which in this moment of amazement and the sun shining on her, Mag actually felt. She felt her violet eyes ablaze in a purple glow.

"Hello? Laura? Holy shit, holy shit. You can actually shoot? You meant to shoot Marianne all those years ago. I knew it. Holy shit."

"I did not mean to shoot Marianne. I would never shoot to hurt someone. I just, whatever. I just wanted to shoot the Emily Dickinson statue in the ass, for fun. For respect. A joke. Friggin' Marianne got in the way, like always."

Mag lent a solemn "wow" of awe. "Why do you pretend to suck at archery? Why do you pretend to be a clod?"

"I just want to be left alone to track birds. Really, nothing more. Nobody wants me in group activities anyway."

"Then why do you insist on night challenges with me? Makes no sense."

Laura stared at Mag, shook her head. "Someone like you would never understand, Mag. You have everything. You're everything. You'd never let me into your tribe all natural, without me forcing the issue. So whatever. We have a secret game, us. Can't you just play our game?"

"What's on the note?"

Laura shrugged.

"Come on. I won last night. You called me to meet here. So what's on the note?"

"It says, '*Hey Guy, Can't care for Blue anymore. He's yours. —A Traveling Man.*'"

"Hmm." Mag lowered the glow she felt in her violet eyes. "So Lemon is Blue now?"

"Yep."

Mag stared into Laura's eyes, looked over at Cord, who was petting Lemon, now Blue, and twisted to stand shoulder to shoulder with Laura, them both watching, obscured to Cord. Girls on a hill, watching a man below, like witch twins observing, assessing. Judging.

"Well," Mag said, "I agree that Lemon deserves living at the Triple C instead of with your horrible mother, who doesn't deserve him. This is our secret now."

"Good," Laura said.

"You still owe me answers on how you did what you did to the lemon trees and who helped you with that and bringing Lemon here and why. Wasn't anyone in the house? Not your maid, grandfather, father, driver, nanny?"

"Nope."

"Who and why?"

"You need to win more challenges first."

"Fine."

Now, twenty-one years later, Mag belly-crawls down the Sabins' driveway. Relieved this worked, she takes a second to bend and breathe behind her camper.

Once settled, she stands, straps on her backpack, grabs the bike in the lean-to, puts on her headlamp, and pedals down the dirt drive. As soon as she hits the country road, she takes out her iPhone from her side-zip pants pocket and dials.

"Mag?" He answers on the first ring even though it's midnight.

"Nathan, get your brother and meet me at his store. He's a locksmith, right?"

"Mag? Are you here? I thought I saw that your camper was gone from Dyson's. What's going on?"

"Just meet me at your brother's shop with your brother, ASAP. Please. I'll explain. And don't tell anyone. I have key molds and need duplicates, ASAP."

Mag is hopeful Nathan and his brother understand the importance of keeping a tight lid until she can set some precautions in place tonight and during the day tomorrow. She can't have psychos freaking out and tripping their cult finale and burning her daughter. She doesn't trust anyone but herself to get this right. If Nathan can follow through and hold his word for one more night, she may indeed continue along the path of whatever relationship they tried to start weeks ago. He did honor her request to leave her be with Lucy for the past eight weeks, to allow them solitude to heal and bond.

But she can't wander in thought on romance bullshit now. She has work to do before the train of captors and captives returns at dawn.

She's slithered back onto and around the Sabin property and has jumped to standing within the forest on the trail that leads to the plywood cover and then to the serpentine trail. With backpack on, she climbs an oak she previously detected without any traps. The oak happens to have a long, long limb that leads to a maple with a long, long limb.

This is so dangerous, what she's about to do. It was never like this on the Triple C tree course, with all her safety clips and harnesses. At age thirty-five, Mag pulls on all her years of experience, all the way from age six up to even this last summer in counseling resort guests through the Triple C course. Her steps across the tree limb are fast and sure, because it is always best to move fast and not pause on a sky bridge. Below Mag on the forest floor are those inner electrical gates and big-game, springed net traps. Mag needs to stay high in the trees in order to reach a few of the net-trap cables because she needs to do a few things with the cable cutter, pliers, cordless drill, rope, and bolts she gathered at Nathan's brother's hardware store. A couple of the nets aren't located quite right for Mag.

After her renovation work on this crazy obstacle maze, Mag treks to the plywood cover that leads to stone steps into the earth. She drops her lit flashlight to the bottom and descends. Once secure underground, she stands and flashes her lights to find dirt halls, weaving to the side of the Sabin house and then beyond, webbing under the blueberry and holly hill.

As she walks, Mag reads names, numerous names, etched in rocks sticking out of dirt walls, which appear to have been hand-dug decades ago. Here and there on the floor are lit battery candles. She passes dug-out rooms, one with a hole drilled deep into the earth and a pile of leaves beside the hole. At the bottom of the hole is an underground stream. The room smells of human waste. This must be the captives' bathroom. Only a fetus could fit down the hole, so there's no escape.

Mag passes numerous dug-out rooms—many to explore, and none have an exit.

In awe, Mag pauses, flashing her flashlight around, shining on dug rooms and engraved names, nearly knocked senseless to find herself in a catacomb prison.

# CHAPTER FORTY-ONE

## LUCY

I don't know how long I was asleep. It feels like it might be three in the morning, but I could be way off. Gretchen never turns off the blinding, torture halogens, and there are no windows, so I have no clue. I want to start working on the second screw, but what if it's dawn? Or almost dawn? What if Gretchen's about to look down at me from the ceiling camera like she's some evil angel?

Now that I have a plan on how to deal with the door, I need to make sure Gretchen's comfortable leaving me alone again tonight. And the only way to do that is suck it up and attempt to put a skeleton back together. I'm thinking progress will keep the bitch away and feeling comfy in her sick game. Here we go.

# CHAPTER FORTY-TWO
## MOTHER

It was easy for Mag to explore and map the catacombs. Eight connected halls, twenty dug-out "rooms" (really eight-by-eight-foot cubbies). At the stunted end, directly beneath the low, long shed, was a covered hole in the roof. Mag examined evidence here: a feather earring mixed among shards and slivers and the full mouth of a glass vase and corpses of wildflowers. The debris, scattered on the greatly disturbed dirt floor, below the covered hole in the roof, created a collage with an unmistakable story: someone holding a vase of flowers had fallen through that hole. Mag, having hunted and tracked for years, surmised this was where Laura had fallen in, how she was taken. Racing back out of the warren through the other end, the trail end with the stone steps, slithering back down the hill, and breaking into the shed opposite the rental ranch, sure enough, after moving a heavy metal tool bench, Mag gained access to the hole into the stunted end of the catacombs. She was careful not to land on the shards of glass and dead wildflowers when she dropped in.

Next, back in the catacombs, Mag found a dug-out room with two wood pallets covered in piles of matted leaves. A place for captives to sleep. A bottle of pills with a warning showing *X*s on eyes, presumably to induce daytime sleeping, sat between the pallets.

Following obvious footsteps on the catacomb floors, Mag returned to find that same bathroom with the hole to an underground stream, and across from that, another dug-out room with heavy foot traffic. She followed the foot traffic. Within this compact space was a protruding underground boulder that looked like a giant gray nose. Inspecting further, Mag poked her hands and then head around the nose's sides, and sure enough, shining her flashlight into a back crevice, Mag found a captive's calendar.

On a flat space within the crevice was a makeshift calendar of rows of pebbles. It appeared that someone had been creating this pebble calendar for months, far longer than Laura was in captivity. Which meant, tying things with things Earl said last night, Earl had been a captive for months before Laura. So this whole calendar was his idea, and that meant, Mag presumed, Earl could be trusted.

She stood a moment and calculated. She needed to be sure both Laura and Earl would comply with her plan. And the only way to be sure was to look in Laura's eyes and ask. Once settled, Mag went to work and waited.

Dawn now, and Mag is roused from her vigil by the sounds of feet scraping and scrabbling down the stone stairs and into the catacombs. She'd already returned the plywood cover on the trail end and the metal tool cabinet in the shed at the other end to their almost rightful places. The tool cabinet was slightly off the mark, a portion of the hole now covered with a thin, and movable, black metal sign she'd found. Enough to make it appear as if the hole were wholly blocked, enough for Mag to push the sign aside and slither back on out once she was done with her confrontation. Exhausted from no sleep, but jacked on enough adrenaline to power a Super Bowl stadium at halftime, Mag feels as if she's levitating on her own vibrations.

"Here's your breakfast. Then sleep," Demon Girl Gretchen shouts down into the catacombs from up top. Mag hears a thud and then the slamming of the plywood back over the hole. They're locked in from that end now.

Footsteps shuffle near her. One set enters the bathroom. The other enters the calendar room, where Mag stands in a dark corner, a place shrouded from the battery candles glowing on the floors. Laura has no idea Mag is behind her when she takes two pained steps toward the nose rock. But she stops abruptly midroom and swings around.

"Magpie," Laura whispers, somewhat in a hiss.

Mag stares back at the woman who stole her baby girl. If her violet eyes could change color, they'd be murder red in this moment, and monster Laura, with her skeletal face and black-hole eyes, nasty, gnarly, knotted hair, sunken stomach, and crooked legs would be sliced to shreds and ground to pulp.

"Tell Earl to take your breakfast and his sleeping meds and leave us be, Laura."

Shuffling sounds approach them from the bathroom, and Laura doesn't budge. Twisting her head to the side but keeping her body poised at Mag in the shadowed corner, she says, "Earl, head back to the bedroom. I'm handling business."

Earl pauses, murmurs approval, and shuffles on.

"He's no trouble. He'll do what I say," Laura says. "He's a prisoner of these assholes too."

"I know," Mag says. "But thanks for the confirmation." Her tone is pure sarcasm, telling Laura she can't tell her anything she doesn't already know. And she does this on purpose so as to pluck at the one thing she knows infuriates Laura: attacks on her intelligence. She needs Laura to remain at a high degree of rage today and into tonight; Laura will need rage for her challenge.

"You know everything, don't you, Mag? You're the genius among us, right?"

Mag steps out of the shadow toward Laura. With her hands in her black pants pockets, and through gritted teeth, she says, "Funny how these emus don't follow your feet prints down here. I found your calendar in two minutes. Next time, try to brush away your tracks. You know better. Do you know better?"

Intentional taunting. She needs to dig into Laura's chronic insecurity. She needs her to rage. And if she's honest, Mag wants to hurt Laura deep—physically, mentally, existentially. Murder her ten times and then ten times again.

"We're not all perfect like you, Mag."

"Why did you do it? Why did you take my child? Why?" Mag has stepped closer into Laura's space. She can smell her; the stench of BO and rot is awful. Laura's breath is a thick cloud of fleshy, rotting meat. Mag could destroy Laura's shaking body with one knee to the groin and one power slam to her bent back. She pushes into Laura's face, ignoring the stench of her living death. "Why?" she asks in low, cutting anger.

Laura closes her eyes. Breathes in. Doesn't step back, doesn't retreat. With a sigh and after dropping resigned shoulders, she says, "I didn't want to keep her."

"What? What the fuck. You took her, Laura, why?"

"I didn't want to keep her. That part was a mistake."

"Holy shit. Why?"

Laura closes her eyes again, shakes her head. And for the first time ever, when she opens her eyes, she forms tears in front of Mag. Mag, stunned, realizes she's never seen Laura cry before. Not in any of their years at camp. Never. Not even after Laura learned of Copte's death and after her mother called her fat. She didn't cry. She had just flipped into a cold rage. Here before her now was a woman showing she was broken.

"I honestly couldn't believe the turn of events. Of all the two people in the world to come together: my rapist and my . . . what are you, Mag? What are you to me?"

"What are you talking about?"

"Paul. Paul Trapmore. My next-door neighbor. You never knew, did you? His parents gave him that house when he turned twenty-one, and they trotted off to their grand chalet in Ecuador. You never put together that Paul in his glass house next to mine, he was the one who helped me with the lemon trees and moving Lemon. And do you know why?"

A pause fills the space between the women, so tense it could detonate a bomb.

"I'm waiting," Mag seethes.

"I just said. He was my rapist. He'd been raping me since I was nine, Mag. Nobody knew. My parents didn't give a shit that their little girl went next door to the twentysomething neighbor. Can you imagine? Well, you can't. Can you? You could never imagine because you're perfect. And you never came back to my house after that night with the lemon trees because I'm nothing to you. I never was."

"I named my daughter after you, Laura. You're sick. Why did you take my girl?"

"That night." Laura pauses. "That night of the lemons. I snuck away for a half hour, do you remember?"

"Of course I remember. What does this have to do with Lucy?"

"I went to Paul's. I told him he could fuck me if he ruined the lemon trees and took Lemon and grabbed the two million the next day. And he did, and I kept the cash. He had to, Mag. I threatened to turn him in. I was fourteen. You were fourteen. He's a predator."

"Well, I fucking know that." Mag holds up a hand to stem Laura from a retort. "Look, I know that, okay. He sold my baby to you. Did he know he was selling her to you? Did you plan this? You planned this."

"No, he most certainly did not know. You know me, Mag. You do. I didn't plan this. And I have to say, I was shocked when you two came together."

"I'm not following you. You're making no sense. Back up. Why did you leave town? Three years before you took Lucy. Two years, the day before Paul came to the Triple C, in fact. Please, Laura, how am I supposed to believe this wasn't all staged?"

"It absolutely was not staged. Do you honestly think I would plan this out? Plan for you to meet Paul, get knocked up, just so I could take your baby two years later? That's insane. So many variables in there I wouldn't be able to control. Think, Mag. Do you think? How insane. That's totally insane."

Mag raises her eyebrows. She can't help it—she says, "Laura, this situation is mightily insane. You know that, right? You're a kidnapper. And now you're a captive underground. So pardon me, but yeah, I'm thinking you planned all this because you're sick."

"That's fine. Think what you want. But I didn't plan this. The day I left, yeah, fifteen-some-odd years ago, I was with Paul. My rapist. I am sick. I did still visit with him all the way up to the day I left when I was twenty. The day before you met him. I don't know why I was with him. I don't. And fuck you for looking down on me like that."

"I'm not looking down on you. I have only pity. I'm sorry you were raped, and son of a bitch, Laura, I would have done anything for you, anything against him, had you told me. And trust me, he's been dealt with. On my terms. But shit, Laura, you stole my child. You stole my child. You've ruined lives. I can't forgive you for that. And I won't."

Laura closes her eyes, inhales, slowing the room. "You done preaching? I told you. I didn't want to keep her. That was a mistake."

Mag flips up her hands, frustrated.

"Look. That day I left town. That day. I told Paul I was going to use my trust fund and part of the Lemon ransom money, which at that point I had stashed in hidden places all over the country, to buy the Triple C. You know, Ms. Gretchen Bianchi, it's always good to plan ahead. A woman should ensure a financial means of escape."

"Laura, I swear to God, get to the fucking point."

"I was going to invest and own the Triple C because I loved that place. I had inside scoop because I'd been listening to Marianne squawk in her office. She always had such a big mouth. They were looking to sell off for a low price and fast, given the owners' massive debt. Do you know what Paul did when I told him my plan? He hit me. Slammed my face against his glass bedroom wall until I bled. Face cut and bruised."

"What? Why?"

"He's a predator, Mag. Hello."

"He hit you because you were going to buy the Triple C?"

"Who knows why he hit me, okay? He's a sick prick. The point is, my face was bashed up bad and I couldn't, I just couldn't . . ."

Laura closes her eyes, steps back. Her breath is shallow. "I couldn't . . ."

"You couldn't what?"

"I couldn't face you, Gretchen Bianchi. I couldn't show up for work at the Triple C and let you see that I'd allowed myself to be beaten. That I was a weak woman. A pathetic girl. Vulnerable. It was you. The thought of facing you. The thought of this face you have on right now. That's why I ran. You have no idea the effect you have on people, Gretchen Bianchi, because you're reckless. You're reckless with love, with friends, with playthings, with family, with your own daughter. You're reckless. And what do you do? What do you fucking do when I leave town? Holy hell, of all things, you go and screw Paul Trapmore! You have his baby! I knew from spying from afar with his passwords." She pauses to force a chuckle. "Do you honestly think

I didn't spy and get all his passwords when I was a girl in his house all those years? Please. I knew I'd have to hold things over his head. I never predicted, however, that I'd have to spy to protect someone else. That was a surprise."

Laura pauses for a deep breath but continues her tirade. "The morning I left town with my bruised and bloody face, I told Paul I was never coming back to Carmel. And son of a bitch if that bastard didn't go straight to his private equity firm and give them my inside scoop on the Triple C. You know by now he's a predator. You should have been smarter and not so reckless. Do you think, Gretchen? No, seriously, do you think?"

Waving her hands at Mag, Laura doesn't give any seconds for any response to her questions. "Oh, Paul didn't hesitate. That's what psychopaths do, Gretchen Bianchi, they don't hesitate. They pluck. They take. They take, take, take. They don't plot and plan and spy for years, like I did.

"And noooooo, no, no, no. Oh no. I am not a psychopath. I did not *take* Lucy! I *saved* Lucy. In all my spying, I saw him post our baby bird in a dark forum. I paid the price to get the specifics on where and when to take her."

"You could have just called the cops, called me, Laura. This is insane."

"Maybe. Perhaps. Doesn't matter now. I bought Lucy for fifty grand so no one else would have the chance. And then I fell in love with her, which was a mistake. And I couldn't give her back. I finally had someone. I wasn't alone. And she needed me. She loved me. You were too blind to pay attention and protect our baby bird. Too reckless."

"She is not *ours*. She is not *yours*."

Laura exhales in a way that sounds like a warning hiss. Her tears are burned off now, and so are all signs of vulnerability. Laura's rage is brewing back up, and fast. "Oh, how I hate you, Gretchen Bianchi. Funny how my thoughts of you braid with those of Mother. I do so loathe you." She stumbles toward Mag with clawed hands as if she's about to choke her, but trips on her own useless ankles. As she tries to balance herself, Mag takes an easy step out of her way and slips her hands into her pockets in a calm gesture, showing Laura she is unperturbed by her violent words and violent lunge.

"What happened to your legs?" Mag asks in an indifferent tone, not rising to meet Laura's emotion, which she knows galls Laura as a show of superiority. Mag knows how to push Laura's buttons. And she needs Laura's rage to keep on boiling. She sneers, chuckles.

Smiling, Mag taunts, "You fell for their trap like a sucker, didn't you, Laura? You were tempted to pick up a vase of flowers that suddenly appeared in the open shed, and when you did, you fell into a hole and busted your legs. Hmm?" Mag's tone is pure, open, joyful judgment. Standing tall, hands deep in her pockets, she does look down upon Laura, literally now.

Laura claps. "Woo, hoo, hoo, Agent Starling. Look at you, solving mysteries."

Mag winks. "I'm right, though, aren't I? You fell for the old phantom-vase-of-flowers trick. Sucker."

"Sure did. I'm a sucker. Ayup. You're just so smart, Mag. And Earl, old Earl, cast up my blown knees, busted tibias, and twisted ankles with puzzle backboard that bitch gave him. He carried me from dirt room to dirt room for six weeks. And here I am. So you see, I might look like a half woman, a pathetic, pitiful loser to you. But I'm relentless—my endurance is boundless. You know. So let's get this over with. What's my next challenge? I might detest you, but I will not fail Lucy."

Mag considers further discussions. Questions. Fighting. But she knows all she needs to know: Laura is in a rage, Laura is committed to her endurance, and Laura will not fail Lucy.

"I've left your instructions on the pebble calendar," Mag says, and slips out, passes Earl in the bedroom, who nods to her in a way that says he's compliant with her lead, slithers up through the opening in the shed, and pushes the tool cabinet back over the hole. She knows Laura is raging as she reads the note she left her belowground.

*Ostrich,*

*Got the keys. But that was only Phase 1. You know there's more, right? Right?*

*I have to admit, you did a good job keeping them distracted and occupied tonight. Meanwhile, I handled the keys and then tracked to this crazy lair. Did some other important tasks too, all for Phase 2, which must be tonight.*

*Now pay attention.*

*Stakes: Baby bird trapped in house. They'll burn her alive.*

*Object: Disable, distract, and delay front Emu and take his watch before he can set remote fire. While I handle back Emu. Whatever you do, do not step off trail. You get out through notch in gorge. Earl knows. He's always known. Listen to him. Can you listen, Laura? Are you capable? Get to cops in case I fail. Warn of Waco-style cult trap.*

*Rules: In Heaven's Knot, grab weapon behind point-tip tree. Bank it at front Emu, like w/ Marianne. I repeat, do not step off trail.*

*Timing:* Must be timed exact with Raven. Clock starts when you leave catacomb. Takes a normal person 14.5 minutes to trek to Heaven's Knot. For you, with your defective legs, I estimate it takes 17.2-18.2 minutes. I haven't been able to monitor that part of your journey. 17.2 is my best charitable guess. You need to make sure it takes 17.2 minutes to reach the crook of Heaven's Knot. That's when we begin.

*Personal Note:* Are you furious, Laura? Are you raging right now? So mad I condescended you about the owl tree, gave you all the minutiae of where it was, as if you didn't pin it the very first day you were dragged into that hell gorge? Are you furious that I suggest you "listen" to Earl, as if you don't listen? As if you don't understand? For sure you're clawing your hands because I've demoted you to Ostrich, a reflection, you think, of my impression of your intelligence. Are you spitting reading this because I know your triggers? Well, good. Good. Because I need you mad. I need you furious in a homicidal rage. You cannot fail this. You cannot let her burn. Let me boil it down real simple in case your atrophied brain still doesn't understand: I do not know if my opening their doors with these dupe keys will set off an alarm and he'll just trip something and burn my baby. Or his baby Emu will. They both have watches with remote capability. You have to figure out how to distract and disable him, WHILE I disable her from behind. And then I can enter their house, if I'm able to open the metal barricades. Get it? You cannot fail my baby. My baby, my baby, Laura. I'm never going to forgive you for taking her. I hope you rot in hell.

Are you mad? Are you furious? I would leave you for dead in the desert for the buzzards to pick you clean.

*Would you throw your body into a house of flames to save her like I plan to do if I have to, and not flinch? Would you live in hell for endless years and walk deeper into the depths to search for her, save her, protect her? Would you? How much pain would you endure? Because I would endure all of it. All of it, plus all of yours, and all of everyone else's pain. Everything they throw my way, I will take for her. What would you do? Would you ostrich out?*

*Yours never,*
*Magpie Raven*

# CHAPTER FORTY-THREE

## LUCY

Like the last two nights, it's 5:00 p.m., Gretchen's left me a weird dinner of a day-old snickerdoodle and cold ramen noodles in the microwave carton, and she's off with her fuckface of a father. Before they leave, Jerry intercoms in to check my "comfort." I yell, "Let me out," and he, as he did the last two nights, says, "Just play the game out, Lucy." Then footsteps away, the front door slams, and also, because they're loud enough and I know the sound, those three metal swings. Now I'm alone in their crazy horror house. Except for Allen. And I need to get to Allen and out.

Last night I tried and failed to remove the hinges on the door. After failing at one screw and falling asleep, and then waiting again all day for her to leave, I was going to start screw two. But, counting all the screws on all the hinges, nine, it would take me ninety-nine years to remove all the screws. So last night was a total bust.

I'm glad I took time to rest and to meditate in working a whole entire skeleton together today, which was totally so much harder than it should have been, since I'd mixed up all the bones in all the pools. But the concentration was a good distraction, because I realized sometime after lunch, and after another proof-of-life call and me flashing another

Level 1 pointer finger to Mag, that I'd made things way too hard for myself last night. There's an easier way out.

It's nighttime. Gretchen and Jerry are "out back"—whatever. I'm free to work.

I walk to the nook in one wall, take the piss-yellow porcelain top off the toilet tank, go to the door, and smash as hard as I can into the gold knob. I keep smashing and pounding with all my strength, twenty times I bash; pieces of knob fall everywhere. Once I expose the inner mechanism, I pick and pull using my fingers, my multifunctional jelly pendant head and floaters, and that metal rod thingie that holds the toilet stopper in the tank—which I yanked out. Hopefully the toilet runs over and floods this whole ugly house. Eventually, the pieces of the knob are on the floor within the room, and within the hall—which I see through the empty hole. I open the door. I'm out.

I don't hesitate. I run to the basement door, flick on the line of lights, run down the stairs and down the lit strip to the closed-off room where she said Old Mr. Snoof slept, and where she's "hinted" Allen might be. Everywhere outside this lit strip is dark and black, and anything could be hiding.

I have no idea what I'll find behind this door, but if Allen is in there and he's hungry or cold or scared, I need to be brave enough to save him. I need to salvage something good from my past. And Allen is all good, only good.

I take a deep breath, close my eyes, and open the door.

Allen jumps on me, and I stumble backward.

"Allen! Oh, Allen! Buddy!" I say, hugging him tight. There's almost nothing in this room. In the middle is a wooden chair, and on the chair is a stuffed animal beagle, covered in what seems like dried black paint. Or blood? A note card sits on his lap. I don't trust walking into doorways in this house, so while cradling Allen in one arm, I position sideways and slide one foot inside the closed-off room. My other foot is safely out, and I keep looking over my shoulder to ward off anyone creeping behind and pushing me in. This closed-off space is totally empty, so nobody can pull me in.

I snatch the note and jump back out in three hops. Now I'm standing within Gretchen's puzzle lab. I won't let Allen down, so it's a little awkward trying to open the note card with my nondominant hand. But eventually . . . .

*Lucy!*

*You are so smart! You finished all your skeleton puzzles! And, see, I did make good on the reward. You're reunited with your Allen! Old Mr. Snoof kept him company. Tee hee hee. My stuffed doggo from long ago. Don't mind the dried blood on him. That's Mummy's blood from when that "bad hunter" shot her. Old Mr. Snoof was such good company that day for me. He was supposed to be my new brother's toy when he was born. But I was playing with him until he wasn't inside her anymore, and until he wasn't dumb anymore. Like other babies. I remember wanting Mr. Snoof so bad. I remember him being good company for me. I remember thinking that a stupid baby boy wouldn't be able to play with a doggo for a long time anyway.*

*I knew Old Mr. Snoof would be good company for your Allen.*

*Xo, Gretchen*

I drop the note and shake my head, trying to make any sense of this. I know upstairs is blocked by whatever those swinging things are I hear when they leave and after they've returned. I know when they come back together at dawn, Gretchen will enter and she'll come straight to check on me. She'll say, like she did this morning, "Daddy's gone for his morning coffee and some snickerdoodles. If you're good, I'll give you one. Depends on your progress."

So I know there's a window of time when I'm vulnerable, but alone with Gretchen. And I need to both delay her and figure out how she locks the door from the outside, while she's inside.

My free hand is scraping against her vintage Rockwell scroll saw. I turn to her workstation and inventory the tools here. The wood worktable, the silver scissors. I look again at the scroll saw and recall Gretchen's lesson about how the saw's deep throat allows one to *turn, turn, turn* a mounted picture so as to cut the loops and voids of puzzle pieces.

I grab the silver scissors, arm-bar Allen to my chest, and run upstairs.

I've got work to do.

# CHAPTER FORTY-FOUR
## MOTHER

During the day, Mag sat on her camper roof again, and again demanded and received a proof-of-life call. Check. After that, she allowed herself a three-hour power nap, for she'd need a clear head tonight. And now, dressed again in all black, she awaits the train of captors and captives by hiding high up in a tree, near the trail opening behind the Sabins' house. It took a lot of hard physical work, camouflaging herself in the shadows, crawling and slinking on in through the gorge side. But she's here. Her night-vision goggles are strapped on tight. Her legs are strong. No shaking. She's allowing no emotions to enter her panther brain now.

Here they all come upon the screechy calls of Gretchen Sabin into the hole, Jerry Sabin to her side. First comes Earl topside, next Laura, after painful grunting and yelling at her by Gretchen to move her "busted ass" up the stone stairs "faster, bitch."

Nobody notices Mag above them watching in the dark canopy, a calculating crow.

They fall into their regular spots: Earl in front, Jerry with his gun and headlamp behind him, then wobbly Laura, and last, Gretchen with her gun and headlamp. Mag starts her stopwatch. She can't fall in line right now and follow on foot just yet—she's concerned her footfall will attract them. She must wait and swoop in fast. She watches Laura grab pine boughs and hurl herself forward. Within minutes, the train is no longer in Mag's line of sight.

At the 15.9-minute mark, Mag runs down the limb of the oak she's hiding on, jumps to a wide Y crook in the next pine, hops to that tree's fattest limb, above which is a crosshatch limb upon which she'd installed a rope. She grabs the rope and swings forward as far as it will send her, flying dangerously close to electrical gates between trees below, but keeping aloft with legs out straight, using all her core strength. She drops off, sticking the landing in a soft thud on the trail. Hopping fast forward, a curl of blowing leaves in a train's wake, her feet are like feathers on a lake. This is why she and Laura had to be timed. To minimize noise. Reduce the period of time in which Mag could be detected.

As she approaches the train entering Heaven's Knot, she hears Laura coughing, likely to mask Mag's slight leaf crunching and tree shaking, the noise these two emus might register as something beyond forest wind. And now, at marker 17.2 minutes and entering the crook of Heaven's Knot, Mag leans far to the side to see Laura kneel, straining her broken legs, reaching around the point-tip tree, feeling under leaves, and extracting a bow and a fistful of arrows. All courtesy of Mag, courtesy of Triple C gear in her camper.

As Laura loads up one arrow and shoves the remainder in the waistband of her ugly, awful sweatpants, Mag choke-holds Gretchen from behind, clapping her mouth with a black-gloved hand. She cranks Gretchen's scrawny arm, the one with the gun, behind her back, takes the gun, and tosses it to the safer side of the trail, the one spot Mag hadn't moved a net trap to.

Although choked and muzzled, and much smaller than Mag, Gretchen drags Mag forward enough such that Mag can watch Laura shoot Jerry Sabin square in his watch hand.

The fool is screaming like a newborn out of the birth canal—angry to be forced into this life. He's not pressing anything on his damn watch; he's too distracted by the blood spreading on his stupid white glove.

"Earl, get his watch," Laura shouts as she barrels forward and rams straight into Jerry. In her charge, she grabs the shaft of another arrow, and now that she's upon Jerry on the ground, she jams hard into another part of Jerry's hand. The arrowhead stabs through to the ground, so, one, two—that's two arrows pierced in Jerry's watch hand—he's a voodoo doll of himself. Laura pushes in on one while keeping a knee on his chest and another knee on his other arm.

Earl removes Jerry's watch.

"Go, Earl, run. Run, don't let him get the watch," she's yelling.

Mag is still struggling to contain Gretchen, whose bottled screaming is nonstop under Mag's hand, as is her unbelievable strength to torque under the choke and grip. Mag didn't want to hurt the girl, but she's going to have to hurt the girl. And she must, at all costs, keep her from pressing anything on her damn watch.

Jerry knees Laura in the tailbone, and she falls to the side. He pulls on the arrows with his free hand so he's not impaled in the ground, but the arrows remain in his flesh as he rolls away, stands, and screeches something awful, "My hand. Gretchen! Trigger the alarm!"

He kicks Laura in the ribs, jumps on her stomach, and now she's backside on the ground, like a dumb, upturned turtle. As she gasps for air, because Jerry can't get around her—she's blocking Heaven's Knot—he grabs his fallen gun and runs off the trail to the side, calling out to Gretchen to "Press the alarm, press the alarm."

A click and a fast *swoop, swish* up is heard in Jerry's direction. When Mag looks into the forest off the trail, she sees Jerry's headlamp high in the canopy. His headlamp gives enough light to reveal Jerry suspended and netted, arrows in his hand. He's scream-crying a death howl.

"Gretchen, Gretchen. Get help. My hand. Trigger the alarm," he's yelling.

Mag removes her choke hold so as to clamp Gretchen's wrists and begin the work of extracting her watch. But as she does, Gretchen does the unexpected. She stomps Mag's foot while breaking Mag's wrist grip by torquing her arm, not pulling away. *Self-defense 101.* Next, the girl drops to the ground, rolls sideways and then forward beyond Mag, like a course-correcting BB-8. Once clear of Mag's commanding space, Gretchen pops to standing and sprints back toward the house. She's still wearing her watch.

Mag jumps over Laura, who's still panting on the ground, and grabs Jerry's watch away from Earl. She doesn't stop to give any more directions. She turns and races toward the Sabins' house without pause. No pause, no slowing, no hesitation, even when a gunshot fires behind her.

A yelp is followed by Earl screaming, "Laura! No, Laura! My God, Jerry, you shot a woman on the ground. My God, my God, my God. Laura!"

Mag sprints and sprints and sprints, and as she nears the rear of the Sabins' house, Jerry's watch begins to shine and vibrate. The screen flashes and text pops up to tell her, "Movement Rear House." The vibration intensifies with the next brighter flash. "Movement Side House." Vibration continues with more flashing. "Movement Front House." Light alarms and vibrations keep flashing warnings. A dome of light covers the brick fortress like a stadium.

# CHAPTER FORTY-FIVE
## LUCY

I'm standing in the foyer, all the fossils on the walls around me. And parts of the big surprise I've created are piled on the floor. I hear the *swing click, swing click, swing click* of the metal shields. Someone is here. I had anticipated going back up to Gretchen's room, stealing a pillow, and sleeping here in the foyer beside my surprise, to wait for her until morning. But here she is, back so soon. I think she's here, but it could be Jerry. Could be both. I don't know. I actually hope it's Gretchen Sabin, unless someone else is here and about to save me, but I know nobody's about to save me. They'd be yelling my name.

Good thing I escaped and did my project as soon as they left at five. My fingers are aching; using those heavy silver scissors was hard work. My hands and fingers vibrate; two hours of cutting with the scroll saw was also hard work.

Someone inserts a key in the knob, *turn, click.*

Someone inserts a key in the dead bolt, *turn, click.*

And, sure enough, here she is, Gretchen Sabin, hair frizzing out in clumps. Several locks are not frizzed, just limp and greasy and thin. Her apple-print dress is soiled. Dead leaves stick in her hair and on her pulsing skin. Something's happened.

She stalls in the doorway, sees the pile I've left on the floor.

"Back so soon," I say. I'm grinning, watching her take in the massacre.

Yelling behind her fills the foyer: Mag yelling, "Lucy!"

Gretchen turns, pulls the door shut, locks the lock, and cranks the dead bolt. Next, she slams her palm on the wall beside the doorframe, and a hidden panel pops. Within the panel are two buttons. She presses one fast, and here again, I hear the swing clicks, *swing click, swing click, swing click.* And during that noise, the face of her watch flashes. *She can control the outer locking with her watch and this panel.*

Gretchen doesn't appear to have any weapons, and I'm so much bigger than she is. So I could barrel into her tiny body and knock her out to get out. But I don't need to take violent measures. I know how to remove her from the foyer, cool and easy.

Mag pounds the door and screams my name—all of which Gretchen ignores as she turns to the pile on the floor. She flinches. I see the quiver. She flinched. And now she snarls. "What did you do? You fucking whore!"

I'm not sure why I'm a *whore* for silver-scissoring all the hardcovers off her *Grey's Anatomy* books and then cutting each one into puzzle pieces on her scroll saw. Not sure how making a puzzle makes me a whore. But Gretchen hasn't quite mastered the art of swearing.

"Gretchen. Here are the rules," I say. Because I know she can't resist a game or a puzzle. "I won your challenge by breaking out. And now you're the loser. I've scattered all the pieces to your *Grey's Anatomy* covers all over the house. Did you know you had two hundred fifty-five copies? First editions and first runs too. Multiples of some editions. I saw the labeling. Rare collection. Wow."

I lop my head to the side, watch her taking in these facts. Her whole body pulses. Blotches upon blotches of red pulsing.

"Anyway, you should start. You have three hours to find all the pieces. I'd start in the dead room if I were you. I know you like to sort the corner pieces first. So that's my gift to you, a hint. And then you have eight hours to put all the separate covers back together. Tick, tock, I've already started the timer." I tap my head. "Tick, tock, tick, tock. Get going, Gretchen. Tick, tock."

Gretchen Sabin cannot resist a challenge or a puzzle. No. She runs down the Death March hallway. I wait until I hear her slamming feet coming back up the earth-puzzle hallway toward the dining room. I run to the front door, scattering the pile of puzzle pieces on the way. I jam a button in the panel, and those three swing clicks swing open.

I've unlocked the doorknob, and I'm about to crank open the dead bolt, when from my side, she's racing toward me. She must have heard me shuffle through the puzzle pieces or heard the shields swinging, and here she is. Damn, this snake is fast. She takes me from the side, and we've slid to the middle of the foyer. *Grey's* puzzle pieces jam into my back, and pieces stick to our arms.

She's pinning me, sitting on my stomach, and she has a knife raised high above me. She's about to double-fist plunge. *I should have hidden all the knives in the kitchen.*

I wince, I do, I flinch.

But now she's yanked up and off me and is flying through the air to the far wall. The knife drops and clatters somewhere at my feet. And the sound of Gretchen's flung body slamming a wall filled with glass-covered puzzles is a loud bang and then the shattering of glass.

Standing over me is Mag, who entered, I don't know how, and ripped Gretchen Sabin off my body by gripping a clump of her limp, thin hair.

The clump is now in Mag's hand. That's how hard she gripped and threw.

Mag, head to toe dressed in black, stomps toward Gretchen, who's crumpled on the floor, broken glass from framed puzzles all around her. Blood, which drips from where her hair ripped and from a glass shard stabbed in her shoulder, stains her apple-print dress, such that the red apples are bleeding. Mag steps on the knife, bends, picks it up, and throws the bloody clump of hair on Gretchen.

When Mag turns to look down at me, when she offers a black-gloved hand with her long, black-cloaked arm, I think, *My mother is the queen of Jennys, so that makes me a Jenny too.*

I jolt up.

Gretchen's not done. Behind Mag, she charges toward us like some rabid beast.

I jump around Mag and recall D's lesson. With one hand, I punch Gretchen in her windpipe, *five fingers in a fist*, and while she's stunned and gasping for air, I raise my other hand, intending to choke her out with *ten fingers. Five will get you ten, ten will get you killed.*

# CHAPTER FORTY-SIX

Everything in the last half hour has been insane. First, Mag bolted in and ripped Gretchen's hair out of her skull while throwing her off me. Next, Mag helped me stand. Next, I performed half of *five will get you ten, ten will get you killed*, because Mag intervened and said I didn't *need* to do the second half—I didn't *need* to kill Gretchen. With some minutes now beyond the blowup, I accept Mag made a fair point. I didn't *need* to kill her. Next, Mag whipped a plastic zip tie out of her backpack and cuffed Gretchen, while she demanded I run away from the house and call the cops. She handed me her phone. I did what she said, and next thing I knew, I heard Mag dragging Gretchen down the hill. "Tell the cops they rigged the house to burn. I don't know how."

Next, the whole entire police force of the world and all of the firemen in the galaxy showed up, at least a billion cop cars and twenty million engines. And now, so soon, news helicopters have mobilized, likely upon all the police-scanner talk of a "Kidnapping at the Sabin Property," and the need for a "bomb squad," et cetera.

Firefighters and some GI Joe–type woman, who I swear rappelled in from a cloud upon a bat signal, are huddled with Chief Dyson.

Gretchen Sabin, who was foisted off on the cops as soon as they screamed in here, is long gone in some squad car. I didn't say good-bye. Good riddance. Some kinder-voiced person in the crowd said something about getting her the mental-health care she needs—after they stem the bleeding. Fine. Whatever. Fine.

Right now, sitting in the camper, someone beyond the bubble of my consciousness, someone in a haze, is talking *at* me about how paramedics and a child psychologist need to check me. This snaps me awake to my current surroundings.

"Yeah, nope. My counselor is in California. I'm not leaving Mag's side," I say. Mag's handing me a Vitaminwater from the camper fridge. The orange flavor, the flavor she saw me select at a café by our California apartment and, without asking, went out and stocked the apartment fridge with. And here, she magically stocked the camper fridge too. She takes a seat next to me and stares at whoever this official is who's trying to move me out of the camper and into an ambulance.

"You heard her," Mag says to the official. She cracks the tab on a Coke she got for herself.

Carbonation sizzles to soundtrack the pregnant pause.

The official looks us up and down and shrugs. "All right, all right." She turns and leaves.

Mag stands and shuts the door behind the official, sealing off all the other cops and Chief Dyson, who want to talk to us. Mag already told them where she thinks Jerry Sabin is netted up or wounded. Told them about the catacombs and the trail to the gorge. She whispered something else to him too; I heard the name Laura. But I can't deal with that truth right now.

We're alone. Just me and Mag.

"What's up with that brown house in the woods? Do you think there's more kidnapped people?" she asks me.

"No. But I do think Gretchen's got something going on in there. I don't know what. Something with the bones."

"All right."

Mag opens the door and calls Chief Dyson over.

"The second trail, the one to the brown house I mentioned. Can you let us know what the hell's going on in there when you find out? And did you find, um—" She pauses and looks back at me. Then back at the chief, she whispers, "Did you find the others yet?"

"We've mobilized and outfitted the team. They're heading out now. And the catacombs are clear of any incendiaries, like you reported, so we won't need to back out the trucks or your camper.

"About Laura," Chief Dyson says.

"Not now," Mag says.

"Understood," Dyson says, and nods as he leaves.

I hug into Allen and shake. Mag had retrieved him for me.

Mag shuts the door when Dyson steps out; she crouches and looks in my eyes. I shake my head, indicating I really can't listen to any more facts right now. She says nothing and hugs me instead.

I'm bawling in her presence, and I know I don't need to be strong for her. She has all the strength, and I am allowed to be weak, and this makes me feel, oddly, stronger for it.

I fall half-asleep with my head on her lap, something like a barely conscious delirium. At some point, she whispers to someone who knocks to "Piss off and stop knocking." I can't deep sleep with all the activity going on around the camper: we're at ground zero.

Mag keeps raking my hair with her fingers, my head on her lap. She doesn't wiggle or move or try to adjust anything. Her leg must be prickly from lack of circulation. I'm in and out and in and out of consciousness.

A knock on the camper door startles me, and I must have truly fallen asleep, because a dawn light is warming the camper's windshield, and a blanket has been laid upon me, a pillow exchanged for Mag's leg. I sit up, and Mag materializes from the back to open the door. Chief Dyson steps in.

"Well, everything's cleared now. They cleared all the smart Crock-Pots," he says.

I rub my eyes. "What?" I ask. The chief looks to Mag. Apparently they've had updates throughout the night.

"Jerry rigged the house by taking out the crock parts in ten Crock-Pots and stuffing the ends of discarded drapes inside, so the very flammable fabric was touching the heating unit. And he added fire accelerant too. All he had to do was use Wi-Fi on his Apple Watch to crank up the heat. Very strange. Rooms with doused and rigged drapes were all over the house," Chief Dyson reports.

Once again the chief looks at Mag. She nods. "Look," he says, "Lucy, we wanted to see if you wanted to see what's inside that brown house in the woods. The team has cleared all around the place, and you'll be safe. But we have some questions about what's out there, and if you see the inside, you might help us understand whatever this is. Maybe Gretchen Sabin said something to you. She refuses to speak to us. Jerry too. Lawyers. What do you think? No pressure."

"Yes," I say, because I have to know what the hell she had going on out there.

I put on my sneakers and follow Chief Dyson up the hill. Mag is by my side. She hands me a bottle of water. "Morning, Luce. Someone's bringing you an egg, bacon, and cheese breakfast sandwich from Dyson's," she says. I take the bottle and nod at her. "Your friend Dali, actually. He'll be here in fifteen. Drove up when news hit the fan. Cool?"

"Cool," I say, smiling at her.

We follow the winding trail; the cops follow us. Once we reach the brown house, Dyson leads me along a marked path that he says a forensics team cleared overnight. White-suited folks mill between pines beyond a clear plastic tarp erected off the rear of the house—like they're containing a ground-zero zombie patient. Huge drum lights hum and shine and light up the whole space.

When we enter a tunnel in the plastic tarp, it's hard to describe what I'm seeing ahead; it's just so strange. The back of the house has a garage door–size door, which is hinged up. Someone cut this out of the back side and created a hinge-up door.

"Big enough to fit the arm of the excavator scoop in," Chief Dyson says to me. He twists and points to the old logging road. "A witness tells us he drove that excavator in and around down the side of their property to do the digging work inside for them."

"A witness? Who says he dug this for them?" I ask.

"That man Earl, the captive with Laura, Lucy. He made it to the police and . . . ," Mag says.

I hold up my hand to stop her from speaking. I hear only the negative aspect of her last sentence—the black part about how Earl "made it to the police" means Laura didn't. "I don't. No. I don't . . ."

Mag holds up her hands, showing me her palms. "Of course. Not now. Chief, let's just show Lucy the hole and clear out."

Chief Dyson directs me to designated pads I'm permitted to step on. We enter through the cutout, but only about a foot, where we are stopped by a railing the cops must have installed.

We're standing above a spiral pit into the earth, within a house.

Yeah. So.

To sum up, someone removed the interior guts of the first and second floors, all the floorboards, even the ceiling above, and dug and dug and dug a deep, spiraling pit into the earth. In other words, this crazy house is a shell, a big wooden tent, obscuring a spiraling pit.

And on the sides of the pit, at different sculpted levels that appear to have been formed after all the digging, are intact skeletons of all sizes—child, adult, teen, baby. Layers of lying skeletons on the different levels down. Gretchen added painted signs on stakes as well, labeling each layer.

"Dante's *Inferno*," I say.

"Excuse me," a woman in a white suit with a clipboard says.

"Gretchen is obsessed with Dante's *Inferno*. She must have been re-creating it here," I say.

"She seems obsessed with a lot of things," Chief Dyson murmurs.

The woman in a white suit stops writing and joins me in staring into this macabre scene.

"Too bad she's sick," she says. And walking away while resuming her writing, she adds, "She might be an artist." She shakes her head while going about her work.

*She might be an artist.* I think that's what you call an understatement.

# CHAPTER FORTY-SEVEN
## MOTHER

After two weeks of interviews with the cops, giving in to some medical/mental reviews, meeting a prosecution team that needed details if ever there was a trial, and having a dinner or two with Nathan and Thomas—including a fun intermission of handing out candy to trick-or-treaters at their house—Mag and Lucy are in the beast camper, on their way to cross the country.

The Ingrace family made arrangements to burn Laura's body and throw her ashes in the Atlantic. Lucy cried enough tears to fill the Atlantic after she was told of Laura's abusive childhood, why she says she kidnapped Lucy, her horrific eight-week captivity, her tragic death, and her heroism in saving her. Lucy will be dealing with the facts and emotions of Laura Ingrace her whole life, but she feels, she says, when she looks at Mag, that she has great support.

Today, though, is not about anger or fear or grief. Today is a good day. A happy day. And the girls are on the road.

"Did I ever tell you about the time I was in a jug band?" Mag asks.

"I don't think you've told me about any times yet," Lucy answers with happy sarcasm, because, indeed, Mag has slipped in a few of her endless stories in the bright skies of happy times in their few months back together. And now Lucy has taken to saying she's never heard her tell any stories yet, as part of a running joke.

"Oh. Well. Let me tell you about the time I clinked a triangle at the end of this song." Mag presses her iPhone in the holder on the dash of the camper. "Play 'Knockin' on Your Screen Door,'" she voice-commands.

Mag turns up the volume as John Prine's classic begins. Banging her thigh with a free hand, the other tapping on the steering wheel, all in keeping with the country-music rhythm, she sings one of the lines about a sailboat and a fur coat.

She hums along to a few more lines. Lucy is sitting quietly, not asking questions, just watching her mother and seemingly waiting for whatever story her mother will tell. Her face is patient, waiting, like she *needs* her mother's story. Mag feels both awash with deep gratitude to have this responsibility, but also a tinge of fear. She doesn't want to let her baby girl down. Ever. Not ever again. She'll tell her a trillion stories for eternity and then start from the beginning, if stories are what her baby girl needs.

In turning down the volume, Mag looks away from the road and to Lucy.

"So, November 2014. Everton, Pennsylvania. I'm at the local Laundromat. Weirdest name, Suds O' Tons O' Funs. Crazy, right? So I parked my camper, did a load, bought myself some Fritos from the vending machine, and in walks the Depravity Jan Jug Band. The DJ-J's, ha. Anyway, they were on their way home to Savannah, Georgia. Seems they were one triangle player short of their full band. So . . ."

Mag pauses to turn up the volume. She sings the final line and pantomimes along to the final drum send-off. She turns down the volume again. "So I said I'd be happy to fill in for eight weeks if they signaled to me when to clink that triangle. And that, my darling, was the time I joined a jug band."

Lucy keeps watching her mother, who smiles back with a look of love.

A ding on Mag's iPhone, which is mounted for easy view of the Google Maps navigation, indicates an incoming text. The font is *huge*, so they both read out the name of the sender: Dr. Nathan Vinet.

"Hmm," Mag says with a smile.

Lucy leans forward and reads aloud from the iPhone from its mounted holder:

Mag, how about Thomas and I meet you wherever you both are for a long weekend after Christmas? Thomas and I will get our own hotel, of course. I'm going right out over the edge here and being as direct as I can be. Hope you'll say yes. I like, no, I love, our talks.

Lucy giggles. "Oh my God, Dr. Hot Pants has flaming hot pants for you."

"You think he's hot?" Mag says in a nonchalant ease.

"Hell yeah. I mean, for people into dads."

Mag laughs. "Not sure I should be into a dad here. Do we really want some guy and his son intruding on our new life? Should it be just us for a little while longer?" Mag regrets saying it as soon as she says it, for Lucy shivers. Mag yells at herself in her mind that of course her baby doesn't want to be shut in anymore, kept away from the world. "I mean. Sorry. I didn't mean . . ."

Lucy doesn't answer. Instead, she takes Mag's iPhone from the holder and starts typing a text back to Nathan.

"Oh no," Mag says. A devious smile takes the place of her worry. "What did you do?"

"Okay, here's what I wrote." Lucy reads aloud:

Nathan, if you can travel internationally, then let's plan on you and Thomas coming for New Year's. There's good surfing on the coast and Monopoly. In our board, the guy has a monocle. We can text and FaceTime until then.

Lucy looks to her mother and doesn't blink. "Is that okay?" she asks, cringing her face into her neck, widening her mouth and scrunching her eyes, shielding herself from reproach.

"Is that okay?" Mag says with a cool calm and a slow, easy smile. "It's bloody brilliant." Mag holds up her hand for a high five, and Lucy high-fives back.

Lucy beams and sits straighter.

A happy-face emoji dings back from Nathan, followed by a separate text:

Deal. Anywhere. Anytime.

And then, after a couple of seconds, another text:

I'm sorry to say this, but I'm going to miss you. Talk soon.

Sorry to be so direct, but you're basically perfect.

A ten in every single way possible.

Mag smiles and offers noiseless laughter, subconsciously stroking her long neck.

"Oh. My. God. Get a room already," Lucy says, laughing.

Mag tapers her smile and hums a *Hmm*. After a pause, she says, "Maybe we don't write back to that one quite yet, yeah? I'll send Dr. Hot Pants something a little later."

Lucy bites her bottom lip and sets the burning phone back in the holder. "Yeah, Mag, you need to take this one from here. That's all you. Thomas needs to teach his dad how to text like a normal person and not write a whole dissertation of slobbering lust. Whatever. It's awesome. I hope he keeps texting and baring his soul. This is entertaining."

"Oh, babe, you're the best. This is fun. I'm having fun. You having fun?"

"I'm having fun." Lucy smiles and says, "Cool. Um. Oh, but wait."

"Yeah, babe?"

"Um. So. I wanted to ask." Lucy rolls her hands in her lap, her face dropped to watch them. "So do you think we could make a stop in Indiana? There's a real-live Jenny there who I never got to say goodbye to when we left for New Hampshire. And, um, I'd like to be long-distance friends with her. I felt bad for never saying goodbye. I don't know her phone number, and I guess I'd like for once to say goodbye in person and for real."

"First off, of course. Yes. Absolutely. Let's map the coordinates when we stop for lunch. Also, and we've talked about this, but you know the feds found one of the places where Laura stored money, right? In Chicago. And she's left you a note. FBI is holding it in their office there, so are you still okay with that stop too? Right after Indiana and before your aunt Squawk's big party in Riverside? But wait, also, a real-live Jenny? What's that mean?"

Lucy lifts her eyes in a careful glance at Mag. "Yes, I'm still okay with getting Laura's note in Chicago. It's fine. Fine. I mean, it's going to suck hard to have to read it, but you'll be with me, and whatever, I can deal. I've got to deal with it sometime. And a Jenny. Well, it's like, well.

"There's a certain kind of girl, could be a boy, too, like my friend Dali, but often I find it with girls—because they become my friend even though it's always with some distance between us, because I always have to run, had to run. Anyway, she's just so self-aware and assured, naturally at peace, even though she's had trouble. And she's beautiful, but she throws nothing in your face. She's quiet but explosive when you know her. She doesn't pry or judge you for anything, and she'll listen if you decide to talk. If you're not afraid of her independence, you'll learn to see how crazy beautiful the world seems to her. Anyway, I call girls like that Jenny. And this girl in Indiana is really named Jenny." Lucy pauses. Mag is nodding her head like she fully understands 100 percent what Lucy is saying, because she does. To her, her big sis Carly's a Jenny. She gets it. Lucy seems encouraged, because she keeps talking. "And um, well, Mag, I hope this isn't weird, and I truly mean it as a huge compliment, but I think you're a Jenny too. Maybe even the truest Jenny."

Mag closes her eyes; her eyelids tremble. Instant tears flood her face.

Lucy starts crying too, which turns into a full-out sob. "Ugh, I guess I popped the blip-bubble," she says.

"What?" Mag says, sobbing.

"Never mind. Never mind."

Mag pulls over to the side of the road and pulls Lucy into an embrace. And after a while, mother and daughter let go and laugh together while wiping their tears.

On their drive, Mag proceeds to tell Lucy stories for several more hours as the two drive west to Carmel, California, back home to their first state. The stop in Indiana to visit Jenny, a real Jenny, is surprising and fabulous. Lucy and Jenny exchange Snap accounts.

In Chicago, Lucy asks to be left alone on a bench at the base of the downtown FBI office. The day is cool, and calmness slows the world around her. Cold, frozen clouds blur into a smudged, gray midwestern sky. Sparse pedestrians scatter far off around her; no people seem to talk in the world. Mag waits and watches from the stone steps of a restaurant across the way.

*Dearest Lucy,*

*Now you know I am not your birth mother. But I've never thought of myself as anything but your mom. I was often terrible to you. Harsh and unrelenting, and the biggest evil in* that is that I knew it and couldn't stop it. But I tried, I did. Maybe I could blame my disposition on my own mother, sure, part of that is true. Maybe my disposition is in part due to some other abuse I had as a child, at the hand of a man. But that's my burden. I'm an adult and that is my problem, and I should have been better for you as your mom. I'm skipping the obvious here, that I am not your mother and I stole you. I say that cold and bare, because it is the truth, and you, as strong as you are, I know you will accept the truth.

There are two delusions I cannot bear for you to have in this life. The first is that you do not accept that I kidnapped you. I did. That's true. Accept it.

The second is that you believe I didn't love you and I abandoned you. That is false. I love you more than life itself. I love you more than anything you could ever imagine. It hurts to look at you. I wince sometimes, because to see you is a heartbreak of knowing the future, of watching you grow and knowing you will leave me. It physically hurts, a heartbreak so deep, to love you this much. This last year has been a torturous tug-of-war with myself, the pull of me knowing I need to let you go and allow you to grow, and the pull to keep and hold you tight. Did you notice the purposeful distance I've been building between us since I stopped homeschooling? Hoping to make it easy for you to transition to a life without me.

I did not, because I cannot, could not, never, ever would I ever voluntarily abandon you. Whatever reason we are separated, know that it is not my choice. Either the law or some other intervener, maybe I got ill, maybe I had an accident, something, but something other than my choice has *separated us. Perhaps it's scary to you for me to expose such deep, obsessive love for you, love I do not deserve and that is not mine. But, again, I speak the bare truth to you, Lucy. And my truth is that you are my child through and through, and I love you for who you are: Gretchen Bianchi's daughter. She is a gem, I can admit that on paper to you, because I tell you, even if I don't tell myself, the full truth now. I shouldn't have taken you from her. I just wanted to save you from your father, that part is true. But I was misguided, because I turned it into a lesson for her. And I fell in love with you.*

*I should apologize. I should repent for my evil act, beg forgiveness for being a taker. But I won't burden you with any of that. Do not forgive me for me. You go live your beautiful life. You are the courageous, brilliant, bright-smart, brave girl I always wished I could be, but failed.*

*Love,*
*Laura Ingrace*

Mag, watching from afar, sees Lucy sigh, close her eyes, drop her hands with the note between her legs, and breathe a few beats in such a deep, soulful manner, it seems as though her girl is swallowing words, forgiving and accepting sadness, shielding herself and also steeling herself for what her past had made of her—and how this is a truth both dangerous and beautiful. To her mother's eyes, she couldn't be more proud of the girl who then looks up to the cold clouds and nods, as if saying, *Okay, okay, I understand,* and then looks down and across the outdoor courtyard to Mag as if to say, *Thank you for being here with me.*

In Mag's mind, she says back, *I am always going to be here—a shield, a knight, a soldier, a shoulder. Unwavering love. A place you always have. Your home, my home, wherever we are.*

Meandering along thereafter in the journey, they stop in Riverside, Illinois, for a big family reunion thrown by Squawk, for which all of Mag's sisters fly or drive to attend—including Carly, Jim, and their two daughters from Costa Rica. Lucy is covered in hugs and pecking kisses and gentle questions by scores of aunts and uncles and cousins, as if she's a toddler in a mosh pit of Labrador puppies. Sister Squawk goes all out like the mother hen she plays, worrying and fretting over catering details and making sure the uncles grill everything to each guest's specifications. Even though it's November, the fickle Midwest weather shifts unnaturally warm, so Squawk rented a bouncy house and a cotton-candy machine. Her indoor pool is perfect.

The drive from Illinois to Carmel is raucous, given that Carly and her daughters join in on this leg—the five-woman tribe, plus fur-love Allen, opting to stay in pet-friendly hotels whenever they're tired of driving. Carly's husband, Jim, returns to Costa Rica to "ready some things." Because at the end of this drive, it's been decided and reaffirmed: Lucy and Mag will gift the beast camper to old D at the Triple C and fly out to start their new life, in their second country, Costa Rica, and live in an enclave by Carly, Jim, and their two daughters.

Mag and Lucy also agree to spend next summer with Cord in Italy, working as part of his games-and-ground crew. Nathan and Thomas will come in two months from now to Costa Rica to celebrate New Year's, and who knows? Who knows what comes from that?

Life is good.

And they will live happily ever after in a tropical location part of the year and in Italy for another part of the year and traveling around wherever they want, whenever they want.

*Supplemental reading about the Death March cult, whatever happened to Paul Trapmore, and more at www.shannonkirkbooks.com.*

# ACKNOWLEDGMENTS

This is obviously a work of fiction. But I did get some tremendous help and guidance on topics I know nothing about. Apologies to the professionals and scientists with whom I consulted if I got anything mixed too far afield from reality.

One such amazing resource was the renowned puzzle expert Anne D. Williams, who is the leading American authority on jigsaw puzzles. She's written several books and dozens of articles on the topic. I read her fascinating book *The Jigsaw Puzzle* (Berkley Books). Anne was a gracious professor to me, allowing me into her Maine home to ask her questions and, *BONUS,* showing me her amazing puzzle collection, one of the largest in the world. But her greatest gift was teaching me all about how to use her vintage Rockwell scroll saw. I still have the puzzle piece she taught me to cut, with my own custom "loops and voids" (thanks, Anne, for the correct terminology!), and I'll treasure that for the rest of my life. Honestly, that visit to Anne, who didn't know me from anyone, was the highlight of my whole summer. Thank you, Anne! Shout-out to all the puzzlers in the world. I truly find puzzling fascinating and absorbing, and I'm getting the bug.

Also a tremendous help was my interview with Dr. Alexandra Jane Lewis-Lorentz, a connection made for me by my awesome uncle, John Overlan (whom I call Uncle Buck). Dr. Lewis-Lorentz (thankfully) guided me away from how I was originally going to deal with the bones

(I'll keep this vague for readers who read the acknowledgments first). She taught me what to consider and to read more about, with respect to the preservation of bones in different environments. To whatever extent I took wild liberties with the science of bones, please forgive my untethered pen in messing up her sound science.

I also found the following resources tremendously helpful: *The Genius of Birds* by Jennifer Ackerman (simply a fantastic book), www.massaudubon.org, and www.nhaudubon.org.

Thanks to my beta readers. As they have on all my books, my ever-faithful cousin Beth Hoang and my mom, Kathy Capone, gave really great directions on how to improve the *first* first draft. If a manuscript doesn't pass their tough-love tests, then it doesn't go anywhere. I honestly can't thank them enough for their time and support.

Thanks to my dad, Richard Capone, who told me a crazy story about an eagle and a loon while we were presiding like royalty over Suncook Lake. My dad has always told the best stories, and I hope he finds my rendition of them as a show of honor.

My glorious agent, Kimberley Cameron, is the biggest champion for me. I can't get my brain around how it's been about six years since she plucked me out of the slush pile and changed my life. Remember me screaming for joy when you called? I'll never forget. Thanks for supporting me every step of the way and in all my crazy ideas. Simply, you're my guardian angel. Also, thanks to Mary Alice Kier and Anna Cottle of the Cine/Lit agency, and Whitney Lee of The Fielding Agency (foreign rights), for their representation and unwavering support.

Thanks to Jessica Tribble at Thomas & Mercer for signing me on as an author. What I love about Jessica as my editor is that . . . she gets me. I get her. We get each other. She lets me be weird and try these crazy ideas; and I really, really, really love her for that. She was REALLY right about a huge change in this book from its first draft, and damn, did she earn my forever love for that.

Thanks to my dev editor, Andrea Hurst, who once again helped me see serious flaws I was (admittedly) refusing to see. Clear guidance with such awesome encouragement. Really love working with you, Andrea.

And thanks to the entire Thomas & Mercer team, a band of professionals. The copyeditor, Sara Brady, who saved me from serious flaws; proofreader Jill Kramer; production editors Lauren Bailey and Carissa Bluestone; the PR team, notably Ashley Vanicek, who is simply the best; and the amazing jacket designers, who once again gave me a cover I am just obsessed with.

Last but not least, I can't live the life I do, in such satisfaction and happiness, without the incredible support of my son, Max Kirk, and husband, Mike Kirk. I am a lucky woman, and I'm thankful every day for our pack. I want to thank Max especially for drawing me the Sabin grounds after he listened to me explain the outline and setting of this story. It's hanging framed on my wall and has encouraged me all along the way in writing this book. Max is the center of my world. I love you.

# ABOUT THE AUTHOR

Shannon Kirk is the international bestselling and award-winning author of *In the Vines, The Extraordinary Journey of Vivienne Marshall*, and *Method 15/33*. Growing up in New Hampshire, Shannon and her brothers were encouraged by their parents to pursue the arts, which instilled in her a love for writing at a young age. A graduate of Suffolk Law School in Massachusetts, Shannon is a practicing litigation attorney and former adjunct law professor, specializing in electronic-evidence law. When she isn't writing or practicing law, Shannon spends time with her husband, son, and two cats. To learn more about her, visit www.shannonkirkbooks.com.